THE WITCH WATCH

Illustrated by

HEATHER YOUNG

Published by Twenty Sided Books 2012

http://shamusyoung.com

Book design and illustrations by Heather Young

Summary: A young lady with a head for invention, a boy with a gift for sorcery, and a rotting corpse with a dry sense of humor all find themselves fighting against a strange new threat in Victorian-era London.

ISBN-13: 978-1470105815

ISBN-10: 1470105810

With thanks to Clint Olson, Mari Menix, and C.L. Dyck, who uncovered and compiled my many mistakes so that you won't have to. ~Shamus Young

For Rachel, Esther, and Issac who are awesome and inspiring and were sure we could do it and cheered us on. ~Heather Young

Table of Contents

Ravenstead 1

I 3

II 31

Grayhouse 59

III 61

IV 99

Callisto 153

V 155

VI 181

Woodbridge 227

VII 229

VIII 245

London 263

IX 265

X 279

Buckingham 335

XI 337

XII 345

RAVENSTEAD

I

Gilbert felt suddenly compelled to wake up. At the same time, he felt that waking up would be wrong, perhaps even rude and offensive. He didn't particularly *want* to wake up. Quite aside from the proddings of his conscience, he just wanted to keep doing what was already working for him, but he was finding it increasingly difficult to resist. In the military he'd learned that when you're called, you're expected to get out of bed first *and then* wake up. This habit was deeply ingrained.

The room faded into view around him. Overhead were solemn stone walls, illuminated by a flickering light somewhere off to one side. The walls had alcoves with coffins in them. He was in a crypt, like the kind used by the wealthy to bury their beloved, deceased, and exceedingly well-off relations. It was clean and well-kept, and the only thing remarkable about the crypt was that he was in it.

Gilbert sat up, and he heard someone gasp. His limbs felt numb and heavy. His mind was in much the same condition.

"M-master! Welcome back. Everything has been done according to your wishes," the voice said nervously.

Gilbert turned and saw a young man kneeling on the cold marble floor. His spectacles glinted in the darkness, reflecting the light of the lantern held in his trembling hand. There was a thin mist on the floor around him.

Gilbert waited for things to settle down inside his head. When he was younger, he'd had a few episodes where he had gone drinking with his fellows and awoken later to find he'd misplaced himself. He found that sitting for a few minutes would do wonders in these cases, and eventually the details would come to him. Usually he just needed one memory to get the process started. Maybe he'd recall what he'd had to drink, or the girls he'd met and what he'd said to them. Or perhaps memories of a fight would surface and explain fresh bruises. Once a piece of the previous evening was in hand, the rest would fall into place and he would be able to remember where he was and how he'd gotten there.

Except, this wasn't happening. His memory was obstinately blank.

The kneeling fellow rose slightly and stopped, seeming to test to see if it was acceptable to stand up all the way. When all seemed well, he stood and relaxed slightly. He looked at Gilbert expectantly.

"Where am I?" Gilbert asked at last. The echo of the stone chamber made his own voice sound odd and unfamiliar to him.

"Your Lordship," the young man said with a bow, "You are in the family mausoleum." He consulted a pocketwatch. "It's midnight, or rather recently passed. October first. As I said, everything according to your instructions."

Gilbert looked down to see that he'd been sleeping on a stone slab, although he felt no worse for it. He suspected the pain would set in once the drink had left his system. "What in the name of the Queen's dainties am I doing in a tomb?"

"Ah yes. You did mention that your memories might be a bit... reluctant. That should pass in a few minutes."

Gilbert looked down. He was wearing a white robe. A long staff had been laid on his chest, and was now sitting in his lap. He grasped this curious object and caught sight of his hands. They were yellow, dry and somewhat withered. There were cracks in the surface, like parched earth. "My hands!" he cried, letting the staff clatter to the floor.

"I think you were preserved very well in here. I imagine your remaining flesh should last you quite a while."

"Preserved?" Gilbert asked, suddenly suspecting he'd gotten himself into more trouble than usual this time.

"Your Lordship, do you not remember your plan?" The young man spoke with his head lowered slightly, and with an obsequious attitude, as if he expected Gilbert was going to beat him at any moment. Gilbert could think of no reason to beat the man, other than the fact that he kept talking to him in this infuriating way.

"No. And stop calling me 'Lordship'."

"We managed to obtain the... items required for your revivification, and the spells you devised have worked as planned." The young man held up an unremarkable crystal necklace as evidence.

"Magic? Now you're campaigning for a punch in the nose. I might have done a few things that I'm ashamed of, and a whole lot more that I should be ashamed of, but I've never gone in for the dark arts. The last fellow who accused me of witchcraft got himself dragged out of the pub and kissed the cobblestones until he begged my pardon."

The young man bowed, "Master, this is most unexpected. Is this some sort of test? I don't know what I should do."

"You could stop calling me 'master'. That would be a good start."

"But... you are my master," he protested. At this he pointed to the wall, where the following words had been engraved:

Barrington Oswald Mordaunt

Viscount of Ravenstead

1818-1882

Gilbert looked at the stone. "That name is familiar," he said slowly.

"Yes!" the young man said eagerly. "That's your name. And I'm Simon, one of your inner circle servants. We help you in your studies. Perhaps you remember me? I've been in your service for years."

Gilbert rose and pointed the staff at the engraving. "That's not my name," he said firmly. "I'm Gilbert Hiltman."

Simon had already seemed nervous and anxious, but now he had the appearance of a man caught in the throes of primal terror. "No!" He squeaked as he placed his hand on his heart. His face had gone white and he seemed to be breathing quickly. "But... how did you come to rest in the Master's chamber?"

Gilbert stared at him. After a few moments Simon blushed. "I guess you wouldn't know that yourself." Simon looked around the chamber, as if he expected to see another body at hand. "I don't know what I did wrong. I really don't. Where is the Master?"

Gilbert guessed that Simon was not yet twenty. It was hard to judge. He seemed thin and malnourished, and might look older if he was properly fed. He was dressed in a rumpled shirt which might only be called white by the most generous observers. It was marked with fingerprints of black grime. Over that he wore a brown waistcoat. There was a bowler hat atop his head, under which his hair had been allowed to grow wild. His trousers looked as though they were expertly tailored ten years ago, and thoroughly mistreated since then. The knees were torn and threadbare. He was standing at the center of an elaborate circle of symbols that had been drawn onto the stone floor in charcoal. Along the edge of this was a ring of dwindling candles. Nearby was a large, ragged book, hanging open and revealing unwholesome truths.

"I'd apologize for all the time and effort you wasted in bringing back the wrong fellow," Gilbert said. "It's a shame to see young people dabble in evil business. But I'm rather more upset at the prospect of being dead myself."

"You don't understand!" Simon cried. "We are in a great deal of danger. The others are waiting outside. This is... our group has worked for years to achieve this. When they discover I've brought back the wrong man..." His voice trailed off as he stared out into the darkness beyond the chamber.

"Yes?" Gilbert said impatiently. "What will they do? Notify the police and complain that their illegal magics have been misappropriated? Write a scathing editorial? Sue me? Kill me?"

"Well, yes. Or rather, they will undo the magic binding you to this world, returning you to death. After which they will torture me to death for my failure."

Gilbert sighed, which made a deep, hollow hiss that seemed to echo all around him. "Maybe this is why people don't join cults and practice necromancy. I suppose we must both blame your mother, for raising an imbecile."

A voice called from outside, "Simon! What news?"

Simon put his hand over his mouth. He looked very close to tears.

Gilbert did not particularly like Simon. Quite aside from his necromancy, he seemed to be a coward, and Gilbert could not abide cowards. But he didn't like the idea of the lad being tortured to death, either.

The voice continued to call Simon. It was demanding, and grew steadily more impatient.

Simon paced furiously, casting his eyes around as if he expected to find a means of escape in the dusty corners of the room. At once he stopped pacing and turned to Gilbert. He spoke with a trembling voice, "Perhaps we can pass you off as the Viscount. We could return to the estate, and then I could look in his Lordship's library to see if I can find a way to sort this out."

"We'll see," Gilbert said. He slid himself off the stone slab and stood up. His body still felt a bit numb but his legs were able to hold his weight and he seemed to be as strong as ever.

Simon blinked in surprise as he looked up at Gilbert. "You are very tall!"

Gilbert sighed again, "You know, people have been telling me so since I was fourteen. Constantly. Yes. I am tall. Thank you. I had noticed before, actually."

"Sorry," Simon stammered. "But this might impede our deception. His Lordship is of normal stature, at best. Or was, before his death."

"You think they'll notice? You didn't."

"You were lying down!" Simon said defensively. "And these men have known the Viscount since before I was born. You have to understand, these men are deadly serious. We call them the 'Four

Horsemen'. Not to their face, mind you, but the name suits them. They are the elders of the Order of the Eternal King."

Gilbert laughed. "Was that name not already taken by some other cult?"

"You jest, but these men have done horrible things to attain the power they have. They're all Dukes or Barons or that sort of thing. Some of the other acolytes told me that one of them is even a Member of Parliament."

"If this lot is so bad, why don't you just leave? It's not right getting mixed up in business like this."

Simon shook his head. "I can't. I just... you can't get away from the Lord Mordaunt, even in death."

"Fine," Gilbert said, "Lead on."

Simon stepped out of the circle of writing, being careful not to smudge his work. He snuffed out the candles, leaving them with just the meager light of his lantern. He retrieved a dark robe from the corner of the room.

"You wear black robes in your cult," Gilbert observed. "Why don't cults ever wear yellow robes? It would catch people off guard."

Simon unfolded the robe. "I took it off because I didn't want it dragging all over my writing while I worked, and I was worried that I'd set myself on fire with all these candles about."

"Let me wear it," Gilbert said. "I don't like parading around dressed like this. How short *was* your master? His burial gown looks like a tunic."

They left the chamber and Simon led them up a long set of narrow stone steps. He walked holding his lantern out in front of him, while Gilbert trudged behind in his new black cloak. He'd pulled the hood up, and his face was in deep shadow. He walked with the ornamental staff, using it like a walking stick.

At last they came out into the brisk night air. The stars were out and the moon was nearly full. They were in a small graveyard. In front of them was a low hill, leading up to a darkened manor. To the left the land sloped away down to the road. To the right were open fields, hedged in by dense trees. The place struck Gilbert as familiar, but his memories were slippery.

Four men awaited them, dressed in similar black cloaks. As they exited, the Four Horsemen drew back their hoods and knelt down. All of them were gray-haired men with grim faces.

"Welcome back, your Lordship," the oldest said. He had a gravelly voice with an aristocratic accent. "All is in readiness. What is your command?"

Simon had walked around behind the men and was now grinning nervously and motioning silent applause. *It's working!*

"Stand up!" Gilbert commanded.

Simon grew wide-eyed and glared at Gilbert. He held out his hands in dismay. *What are you doing?*

The Horsemen also seemed curious at this. Perhaps it was his voice. Or his accent. Or his height. They rose, but they did so looking at one another in confusion.

"Gentlemen!" Gilbert boomed, "You stand before the mighty Viscount of Pugilism!" He grabbed the heads of two of the men in front of him and cracked them together. The men went limp and collapsed into a heap of wrinkles and black wool.

"That's not the Viscount!" cried one of them. "What have you done, foolish boy?"

Gilbert socked the man in the bridge of the nose before anyone could fashion an answer for him.

"Treason!" screamed the last horseman, and he reached beneath his robes to draw a sword. Gilbert caught his hand and pushed the sword down before it left the scabbard. The man put his other hand on the hilt, and the two strove like this.

"Gilbert!" Simon cried.

The horseman found he could not overpower Gilbert's grasp, but he continued to try and free his sword. Since he couldn't bring the sword up, he tried holding it in place and pulling the scabbard away by moving and twisting his hips.

“Gilbert, look!” Simon said, his voice rising in escalating panic.

Gilbert allowed the horseman to twist around, struggling comically against his iron grip. Once the man had bent himself into a truly absurd and untenable position, Gilbert yanked sideways and sent him to the ground. A firm kick to the head quieted the old man. “There,” he said to Simon, “Now you’re free to leave these nasty fellows.”

“Gilbert!” Simon shrieked, “The road!”

A party of some half-dozen men had arrived, riding on carts. Some bore lanterns and swords. Others bore rifles.

“I thought you said there were only four!” Gilbert snapped.

“These fellows are not from our order,” Simon hissed in a stage whisper.

“Halt!” One of the newcomers shouted, “In the name of the Ministry of Ethereal Affairs and Her Majesty the Queen, you are ordered to stand and declare yourselves!” They hurried up the hill, their gear clanking as they moved.

“Bloody hell. It’s the Witch Watch! We’ll hang for sure,” Simon said with despair.

“Don’t worry. We’re not with this lot,” Gilbert said as he prodded one of the horsemen with his foot, “Just be polite and explain that you were only working with them out of fear.” Gilbert threw back his hood and walked down to meet the Witch Watch.

“No, don’t!” Simon shouted.

Several things came to Gilbert’s mind in this moment. One was noting that his strange echoing voice - which he had attributed to being inside the tomb - was still strange and echoing, even outside. The second was remembering what his hands looked like, and how the rest of him was likely in similar condition. The third was that he was currently dressed in the black robes of this cult and carrying some sort of ornamental scepter, which would not only make him look like a member but might go so far as to suggest that he was the ringleader. The Witch Watch had found them in the countryside at night, and likely had news of what was supposed to be happening here. They would be expecting trouble, and everything about this scene would tell them that they had found it.

The lamp light fell on Gilbert and the captain of the group went wide-eyed. "ABOMINATION!" he screamed.

Gilbert wasn't sure if he should hold onto the staff to defend himself, or surrender. In a panic, he tried to do both and raised the staff over his head.

"Spellcraft!" screamed the captain.

The men fell to the ground. At first Gilbert thought they were all cowering, but then the rifle shots came and he realized there would be no sorting this out tonight. He spun around and fled.

As he turned, he caught sight of the person at the rear of the Witch Watch. It was a woman. She looked thin, almost waif-like. She had stood at the back with a pistol in her hand, and now that the men had taken cover she was walking up the hill, heedless of the shooting and supposed danger of spellcraft. Shockingly, she seemed to be wearing trousers.

Gilbert saw no more of her. As curious as it was, he was more concerned with not being shot or (worse) captured. Great Britain prided herself on even justice and humane executions, but the Witch Watch was one of the last institutions that - if popular gossip was to be trusted - still wielded the older, harsher style of law enforcement.

Gilbert sprinted away from the watchmen, casting aside his staff as he did so. Simon had wisely begun running several seconds sooner, and thus had a good head start. Nevertheless, Gilbert's great strides allowed him to catch up quickly. He was glad to discover that whatever strange things had befallen him, he was still as able-bodied as ever. He wanted to look back and see what his pursuers were doing. Gilbert wondered if the riflemen were giving chase or sharpshooting. He was also anxious to get another look at the woman, just because. But he didn't dare take his eyes off the ground in front of him. They were running through a graveyard at night while being shot at. Tripping could be fatal.

The gunshots rang out surprisingly quickly, and at an even rate.

"They have very good rifles," Gilbert commented as they ran.

"What?" Simon gasped. His steps were already faltering.

Gilbert grabbed him by the shoulder and hauled him sideways, "This way. Into the trees."

The shots fell silent as Gilbert and Simon dove into the shroud of the forest. The men shouted to each other, but Gilbert could not catch the words.

"We'll never escape them all," Simon gasped. He stopped and conscripted a tree to keep him from falling over.

"We don't need to escape them all," Gilbert pointed out. "They won't all follow and leave the Four Horsemen unattended. I suspect no more than half of them will give chase. Come on. Walk if you can. The woods are big and lanterns can't see far. We should be fine as long as we can get some distance before daybreak."

It was dark here under the trees, and Gilbert could only barely make out Simon's outline as he pulled himself upright. The bright moon was fortunate. There was just enough light for them to move without running face-first into a tree. Simon stumbled now and again on tree roots, but the shouts of their pursuers became increasingly distant.

"How many are there, do you think?" Simon asked as he struggled for breath. "I didn't think to count them." They had been fleeing for perhaps a quarter hour and had now stopped for another rest.

"There were six men," Gilbert replied, "Four rifles. Two swords with lanterns, one of which was their captain. Plus the woman. They won't send both lanterns away, which means we only have one lantern chasing us. Most likely not the leader. He'll want to investigate the goings-on at the tomb, and leave the chase to his men."

"You know a great deal about the Witch Watchers," Simon marveled.

"No. I know a great deal about being a soldier. And the task of running around in the woods looking for a deadly wizard, at night, with one lantern, is *exactly* the sort of job that an officer would delegate."

Simon slumped down against an old tree-trunk and hung his head between his knees. "I see. You're right. They must be assuming you're a wizard. Who ever heard of performing a revivification on a common soldier?"

"Who ever heard of reviving the wrong person?" Gilbert shot back.

Simon was quiet for some time. Gilbert waited patiently as the boy recovered his breath with much coughing and sighing. For his own part, Gilbert didn't feel short of breath or even tired.

When Simon's breathing had settled, he pushed himself upright. "You said there was a woman there. I hadn't noticed her. I do wonder what that was all about. They're wizard hunters. Well, wizard killers, really. I wonder why they would bring along a woman for grim work like that."

"Let us make every effort to not find out," Gilbert suggested.

"We need to find out where they ran off to. That was an abomination, for sure," Alice insisted. She was standing with Captain Turpin in front of the tomb, looking off into the distance where the fugitives had vanished into the trees.

The captain nodded. "I've sent Lieutenant Stanway after it with the rifles."

"Not all of them," objected Private Archer, holding up his own rifle.

"All of the other rifles, then," the captain said with irritation, obviously not appreciating the correction from a subordinate. Turning back to Alice he said, "Jack won't give up the chase easily. You know how he is about the undead. You and I need to sort out things with these four." He pointed at the old men gathered in a heap at the door of the tomb, "No good all of us running off and leaving them loose to make more trouble."

Alice relented with a nod. Of course the captain was right. She wanted to chase after the abomination because it was the most interesting of the problems at hand, but interesting threats weren't always the most dangerous.

She and the captain stooped down and searched the robed men while Private Archer stood with his rifle ready in case any of the men proved more dangerous than they seemed. The captain seized the swords and daggers the men had been carrying. All of the prisoners were alive. Two were conscious, although stunned and muttering incoherently. One of these had a broken nose.

"I wonder why the abomination attacked them?" the captain muttered.

"Perhaps it's a feral. They might have botched the revivification," Alice said, chewing on her lip thoughtfully. The question had been loitering in her mind as well.

"It didn't look feral to me."

"No, it didn't," she admitted. "It ran away, and not towards us when we started shooting. I suppose it could have been a betrayal. These foul sorts are always plotting, even against each other."

The captain examined the tomb entrance. A door of iron bars hung open, and a broken chain was piled nearby. He lifted a padlock and held it up to the light for Alice to see. It had been covered with a wax seal. "Looks like the church sealed this place up, and this lot opened it again."

"They didn't have a key, or they would have used it instead of cutting the chain. And they were up to no good, or they would have called a locksmith. Let's see what we can learn inside."

"Archer, watch these men," said the captain. "Keep them here. Shoot them if they give you any trouble. And watch out for spellcraft. They're dazed now, but we don't know how they'll behave once they recover their senses."

Private Archer sighed and assumed his post guarding four helpless old men.

Alice took the lantern and led the way in. She was very relieved that their working relationship had advanced to the point where the captain no longer insisted on marching out in front. She didn't need to look over her shoulder to know that he would follow her down the steps.

She was glad she'd chosen to wear trousers. She disliked showing off her legs like this, but practicality should always come before propriety. She was wearing a man's trousers and jacket that had been tailored to her unusually narrow frame. She was wearing sturdy riding boots, which came up almost to her knees. She tried to offset the masculinity of her outfit by growing her hair long, and tying it up in many colorful ribbons.

"What does your device say, Miss White?" The captain asked.

Alice consulted her ethergram, which was mounted on her arm with rough leather straps. She flicked one of the dials a few times and watched the needle in silence. "Nothing. No spellcraft, at least. There's a bit of activity, but I'd say that's residual from the revivification."

"That's good. I'd hate to face a wizard in a tight place like this." He looked back at the narrow passage behind them.

They examined several chambers and found nothing amiss. At the end of the hall they found the chamber of Lord Mordaunt.

"Bloody hell. They brought back the viscount, didn't they?" Turpin grumbled as the light fell on the circle of charcoal in the middle of the room.

"Stop here," she told the captain, "Don't follow me into the room." She walked carefully around the sorcery circle, examining it from every angle. Finally her light fell on the bare stone where one would normally expect to find a body.

"Yes," she said bitterly, "His Lordship is up again."

"Bloody hell," the captain repeated.

She crouched and examined the sorcery on the floor. It was the span of a man's arms, and nearly a perfect circle. "Such beautiful handwriting. Note how the lettering retains a constant size around the entire perimeter, and yet each stanza exactly fills the circumference without gaps. No sign of erasing, either. That takes practice." She brushed her fingertips against the floor and quickly withdrew them. "It's still quite cold to the touch. The revivification was done very recently."

"So one of the gentlemen upstairs is the sorcerer," Turpin said with a self-satisfied nod.

"Perhaps. But none of them made this. Their hands were clean." She held up a wedge of charcoal that had been left beside the circle.

"Blast. So that must have been the sorcerer we saw running off with the abomination. Now we have an abomination and a sorcerer on the loose."

"They left us a book to read!" Alice said with mock cheerfulness. She gently lifted the leather-bound volume and cradled it in one arm, and then pulled a ribbon out of her hair to mark the current page. She spent a minute or two leafing through it. "Looks like... another copy of the 1627 Werner Krauss book."

"Looks bigger than the other 1627's I've seen."

"Yes. Some material has been added. And a good deal of it has been translated into English. At least, the German parts have. Lots of annotations. Looks like this began as a direct copy and evolved into a work of its own over the years. I can't imagine why they would leave a treasure like this behind."

Unable to contain his curiosity, the captain stepped into the room and peered over her shoulder. "Can you tell anything else about its lineage?" he asked.

"No, except that it looks like it was all written by one hand."

"Well, those four upstairs will swing for their part in all this. So we have something to show for our efforts here."

"Yes," Alice said without looking up from the book. "Now we just need to track down that abomination."

Gilbert stepped off the carriage and smoothed out his uniform. While he enjoyed London immensely, he was always glad to return to Rothersby. As the carriage pulled away, he looked up the hill towards the house and was surprised to see a plump young man trying to push a trunk up the path with limited success.

"Gilbert dear!" Mother called. She was standing a few steps ahead of the young man. "You came home just in time! Do help poor Leland." She was wearing a broad white hat to protect her from the sun and securing it in place with one hand to protect it from the vigorous spring wind.

Gilbert strode up the path to where Leland had given up on pushing the trunk and taken to sitting on it. Gilbert vaguely recognized him as a neighbor, although he couldn't recall the family name. He was short (although everyone seemed at least a little short to Gilbert) and was wearing an ill-fitting brown tweed suit. Around his neck was a red bow tie, which rose and fell as he heaved for air.

"Mother, I have some good news for you," Gilbert said cheerfully.

"And I have news for you, but it can wait. Help Leland with my new chest before it kills him."

"I'll take one side, you take the other," Leland said as he moved himself into place.

Gilbert frowned. He would rather do this job alone. Not wanting to be rude (Mother would make a fuss if he was rude to a neighbor) he moved into position and lifted up his side. It was challenging to keep it steady, mostly due to the fact that Leland was ready to buckle under the weight. Gilbert was willing to take more of the weight for himself, but their stark height differential made this difficult. Eventually they took slow, faltering steps towards the house.

"Gilbert, I received a letter from your sister in America. It seems they're expecting their first child this fall." She hovered nearby, supervising their work as if she expected they would dash her treasure to the ground at the earliest opportunity.

"Ruby and what's-his-name are starting a family?" Gilbert remarked in wonder.

“Yes. Your sister, *eight years* your junior, is now married, settled, and having children. And she’s very curious as to whether you’ve met anyone or are moving in the direction of marriage yourself.”

“I’m sure her curiosity is minuscule compared to yours, mother. But no, I did not miraculously court, wed, and impregnate a girl while I was in London this weekend.”

“Don’t be vulgar!” She lightly swatted him on the shoulder. Gilbert suspected her lenience was for the benefit of her trunk, and not his arm.

There was some confusion as they reached the steps. Gilbert and Leland both tried to go first, then they both tried to steer the other up first, and then they sort of staggered around in a circle. It was really hurting Gilbert’s back to carry the trunk while bending down to Leland’s height and while trying to correct for the boy’s hopeless vacillating.

Finally Gilbert was done being polite.

“Here.” He hoisted the burden away from Leland and placed the weight against his own chest.

Leland stood there dumbly, lost for what to do next.

“The *door,* if you please!” Gilbert growled.

Leland hurried up the steps and hauled the door open, then stood in the way, then figured out where to place himself so that Gilbert could enter.

“This means you’re going to be an uncle!” Mother called after him as he went inside. “At last,” she muttered a few moments later.

“Please tell me this isn’t destined for the upstairs,” he said.

“Sitting room,” she instructed as she followed them in. “And do be careful with it.”

The trunk landed in the proper room with a thud. “So what’s the good news?” Gilbert asked innocently.

“You know very well I just told you the good news!” she scolded.

“That strikes me as terrible news,” he said, maintaining the pretense.

"Now you will redouble your efforts to marry me off."

"I just want to see that you manage to produce grandchildren before I leave this world."

"Stop being silly, Mother. You aren't leaving this world anytime soon."

"You're thirty now, which means I can no longer go around pretending to be so myself."

"I don't see why not," Gilbert smiled. "I'll tell people you're my sister." Mother was still young and vigorous, and the only damage she had suffered from age was that her smile was more deeply ingrained on her face.

"Save your flattery for the unmarried girls you meet. Their youth will make them susceptible to your nonsense."

Leland tried again to sit on the trunk. Gilbert shoved him off and swung it open.

"Now, don't open-" Mother said, several seconds too late.

"Ugh!" Gilbert winced as he was met with the smell of must and mildew. "It's filled with moth-eaten blankets!"

"I didn't buy it for the blankets. I bought it for what you'll have once you take them out."

"What's that?" asked Leland. He rummaged through the pile, looking for the treasure. Puffs of dust rose to meet him, and he began sneezing.

"An empty chest, of course!" Mother said. Turning her back on Leland she explained to Gilbert, "I bought it from the Brewers. Maybell was good enough to lend me Leland here to help bring it home."

"If you didn't want the blankets, then why were we made to carry them?" Leland demanded between sneezes.

Mother raised her eyebrows. "I suppose we could have left them on your doorstep, but then you would have missed out on the exercise of pushing them here. And you are positively starved for exercise,

Leland. How will you get a wife with your looks in such a sad condition?"

"Looks are hardly important to a woman in search of a husband!" he protested. "Your son is built like a dock-worker and it's done him no service as a suitor."

"That's more to the discredit of the women in this country," Mother insisted.

"But why did you buy a trunk?" Gilbert asked, noting that it was rough and didn't really match anything else in the house, much less the room.

"I need something to hold my belongings when I go back to America," she said casually, as if this was a perfectly ordinary thing for her to do.

"You're visiting Ruby?" Gilbert asked with incredulity.

"No. I'm *moving in* with Ruby and Walter. And you should come along. There's another nation full of women over there. Maybe one of them will have you, since you seem to do so poorly with the ones in this country."

Gilbert was stricken. "But... you can't just *move*. I mean..." He trailed off, confused.

"And why not? We don't have any connection to this country now that your father is passed on. You spent the first fifteen years of your life over there, and it suited you well enough."

"But I've spent the last fifteen years *here*," he protested. "I don't want to just pick up and leave."

Mother took off her hat and headed out of the room, still talking to him. "You act as though you have some sort of life going on here, but you're a piece of driftwood, dear Gilbert. Look at Leland. Ten years your junior and he's begun his career. He's going to work for the church."

"I'm going to help track down magical deviants," Leland proclaimed.

"You've been accepted to the Witch Watch?" Gilbert asked

doubtfully.

Leland bristled at this. “It’s called the Ministry of Ethereal Affairs, and no, I’m not working for them. I’m working for the church.”

“I didn’t know there was a difference,” Gilbert shrugged.

Leland gave an impatient snort. “*The Ministry* is a government institution and really only concerns itself with big public cases. Wizards, mind-controlled Members of Parliament, magical attacks on the royal family, that sort of thing. The church is less interested in headlines and more concerned with weeding out dangerous sorcery at *all* levels of society.” He stood up straight at this, like a soldier reporting for duty.

“You see?” Mother said with pride. She patted Leland on the back like a child who had just cleaned up after himself. “He’s going to be doing important work.”

“But that’s what I wanted to tell you,” Gilbert said. “I *have* found work.”

“As a dock-worker,” Leland quipped, to his own amusement, and the indifference of everyone else.

“I’ve been accepted to act as the personal guard of Viscount Mordaunt of Ravenstead."

Gilbert led Simon as best he could through the unfamiliar woods. They left the pursuing lantern behind and allowed themselves a short rest. Thinking the chase was over, they began discussing where they might stop and rest for the night.

Before Simon could close his eyes, the lantern returned and began tracking them again. They saw the light bobbing through the trees in the distancc, and when the wind was right they could hear the clamor of men carrying their fighting gear.

This time Gilbert could not shake them. He led them through streams, he doubled back, and he climbed over rocky places. Their tracker would move some distance, then stop for a minute, and then begin moving again, never falling for any of Gilbert's tricks.

Eventually Gilbert abandoned subterfuge and opted for speed, pushing through the darkness as fast as Simon's weary legs would allow. Gilbert never heard any sound of barking, even though a bloodhound was the only thing he could think of that might explain this uncanny pursuit.

Towards morning they were finally able to leave the lantern light behind, although it was more likely exhaustion than lack of direction that ended the chase. Simon was nearly spent as well, and Gilbert knew he couldn't push the boy much further.

They struck a road and followed it, not having any idea where it went or even what direction they might be heading. It brought them to a small village which neither of them knew. Before sunrise they found a humble church crouched on the edge of town, dark and quiet. They slipped in and hid in the tall space beneath the church bell. (This space was really too small to be called a "bell tower" by a serious person.) It wasn't much in the way of a hiding place, but it was the best they could manage in such hasty circumstances.

They sat on either side of the bell rope. Simon wrapped himself in Gilbert's cloak and dropped off to sleep almost immediately. The terror had left the boy as fatigue set in, and by the end he was ragged and speechless.

Gilbert found he wasn't tired at all, even after their long run.

Gilbert sat motionless and quiet, watching over the sleeping Simon as the boy tossed and shivered in the damp October air.

Daylight found its way into the church. This was a quiet town, and even at the height of the day few sounds reached his ears. If not for the sound of the odd horse, Gilbert might have suspected this place was uninhabited.

As daylight began to fade, Simon stirred. "What hour is it?" he asked sleepily.

"You're the one with the timepiece," Gilbert whispered. There was no real reason to whisper. They were alone and the church had been quiet all day, but the setting seemed to demand it.

“Of course,” Simon consulted his pocket watch. “Half five,” he remarked. “Did I miss anything?”

“Around midday I heard horses enter town. Lots of conversation outside. Could have been the Witch Watch tracking us. Could have been gossiping travelers.”

“What will we do now, I wonder?” Simon asked. He wore an anxious expression on his face, and his hands seemed to be trembling slightly. The night before, Simon had finally reached the point where he was simply too tired to be afraid. Now that he was somewhat rested, he seemed to be finding the energy to worry about things again. “I haven’t ever exercised myself like I did last night. I am still dreadfully thirsty.”

“You could slip out and drink a bit more of the holy water.”

“Perhaps,” Simon said. “But I don’t like doing that.”

“As for what we will do next, I’d like some questions answered first. I’ve done nothing but sit here all day, and I’ve had a lot of time to think about what’s going on.”

“I doubt I know more than you, but I’ll hear the questions,” Simon stretched and rubbed his bruised eyes.

“You seem like a surprisingly nice fellow for a witch. How did you come to be mixed up with this cult?”

“The Viscount has another place here in the countryside, the Ravenstead Academy, which he calls a ‘boy’s school’. But it is actually a prison where he keeps and trains servants. He takes orphans or other unwanted boys and teaches them to fear him. It is a cruel place. Many beatings. Little light. Less food. Dreadful cold in the winter. A lot of them don’t make it. Generally only the strongest and most loyal manage to ‘graduate’ and serve the Master directly. I’ve been with him since I was a very small child, and I’ve never had any say in the matter.”

Gilbert liked Simon a bit more after hearing this. The lack of food and harsh treatment had reduced many stern soldiers to apprehension and weakness. Perhaps the boy might perk up with a hot meal? As for the academy, Gilbert wondered how such a thing could exist without being discovered by the outside world.

"None of the boys ever escape to get help?"

"Sometimes, but we were far from any city. The boys usually end up crawling back once their empty belly gets the best of them. This happens sooner rather than later, since you have to fight for every mouthful in that place."

Gilbert grunted. "What about you? You don't seem like the strong type. How did you make it?"

Simon found his bowler hat and returned it to his head. "I might not be strong like you, but I have strength of my own. The strength to *endure*, if you like. And I always did as I was told. The other boys tried to get away with things when the Master wasn't looking. But I knew. He was *always* watching."

Gilbert had spent all day playing the scene over in his mind. When he emerged from the tomb with Simon there had been four men. Were any of them witches? "So you were obedient. Is that why you were chosen to do the ceremony, or spell, or whatever you call it? Why didn't one of the Four Horsemen do it?"

"You're asking why I was the one to go into the tomb to revive his Lordship? Well, it wasn't an honor, if that's what you're thinking. The process takes a long time, most of which is spent kneeling on the stone floor. You can see why the old men would rather I did that." Simon swallowed hard as he said this, his eyes darting around as if he expected his old masters to be hiding in the shadows.

Simon abruptly left their hiding spot and went out to the sanctuary. He returned a minute later, wiping his mouth. He'd evidently helped himself to more holy water. He seemed to have recovered his nerve enough to continue his story.

"Kneeling on the stone floor aside, the main reason they sent me to revive the master is that revivification is tricky business. There are stories that sometimes the dead return mindless and enraged. Feral. I don't know if it's true, and neither did the elders. So they sent me in alone. If you had killed me, they would have simply sealed the place and walked away."

This unraveled a great many mysterious details for Gilbert. He now was convinced that the boy was reliable. Whatever crimes he might be guilty of, lying was probably not among them. An accomplished liar would have crafted a better story, and an amateur liar would have given himself away by now.

Gilbert felt the need to take action soon, but he had one question left. "And now the thing that's been gnawing on me all day... If you were so loyal to the master, how could you possibly have failed to notice you were reviving the wrong man?"

"You really don't know?" Simon asked slowly.

"No."

Simon drew out his pocket watch and handed it over. "Look," he said.

Gilbert took the watch. A name was engraved on it. "Who is Donovan White, and why do you have his watch?"

"I have no idea who he is. Probably some poor sod the Master killed or turned into a frog or foreclosed on or something. It was a graduation gift to me from his Lordship. Flip it over. Look at your reflection."

Gilbert saw that his once ruddy skin was now the color and texture of dried leaves. His lips were pulled back into the horrifying grin of a skull. His nose was gone, replaced with an empty hole. His eye sockets were dark save for two dim, remote lights that flickered like candles in a distant window.

"I really am dead," he said.

Simon nodded. "You can see how it would be hard to recognize someone when their face looks like that. To be honest, I was horrified at the prospect of what I was doing and I tried not to look at the body. At you, I mean. I saw the name on the wall and that was enough for me."

They were quiet for a long time. Night settled in around them and the sunlight vanished from their hiding space below the church bell. Gilbert wanted nothing to do with this business and thought it would be much better for everyone if they could just put him back where they found him. He tried not to think of his family.

"Is there any way to undo this?" he asked at last. "Can you make me look normal again? Or return me to death?"

Simon pulled out a necklace, although it was now too dim for Gilbert to see it in any sort of detail. "Last night, I was given this necklace to use in the revivification spell. It glowed, filled with the vigor of another human being."

"Vigor."

Simon put the necklace away and clasped his hands together, perhaps to keep them from fidgeting. He seemed very uncomfortable with this line of questioning. "That's what the book called it. Their life, basically. When your body is ruined by injury or disease or age, it loses its grip on your soul, and you die. But you can re-attach the soul as long as you can find another source of vigor."

"I imagine this involves killing someone."

"I think so. Remember I'm just going by what the book said. I haven't studied this personally. Apparently it takes a lot of vigor to make the spell work, so you need someone who is old enough to have the strength of adulthood, but not elderly."

"You're saying someone had to kill a young, healthy person in order to bring me back?" Gilbert stood up, suddenly feeling like a party to a murder.

Simon flinched when Gilbert stood. He spoke without making eye contact. "Not just any youth. The book says they need to have royal blood in them."

"So someone killed a prince to revive me?"

"Princess. Princess Sophie, who turned sixteen just last month. I don't know how they acquired her, but their talk revealed that they performed the extraction a few nights ago."

"Murder! Your master is a thrice-cursed villain," Gilbert fumed. He clenched his hands into fists, and tried to figure out who he should be hitting with them. "I hope they didn't... I mean, she didn't have to suffer anything unnatural, did she?"

"No. In fact, to my understanding she had to remain unharmed. This was their chief concern. She was feisty, and they worried that she would harm herself in her struggles. The extraction had to take place on a healthy, living individual, and afterward they wanted the body to remain safe and undisturbed."

"So perhaps her life could be restored?" Gilbert asked with sudden excitement.

"The Horsemen speculated on that topic themselves. If the revivification failed, they thought to return the princess to her family, either through ransom or through a feigned rescue. They were always working on such schemes."

"Well then, we now have purpose. We are going to save the princess," Gilbert said as he pulled Simon to his feet.

"How?" Simon seemed put out and confused at this sudden course of action.

"We'll go and give her back the vigor."

"I don't even know where she is," Simon said.

"Oh." Gilbert sat down, feeling dejected again. "Do you know where we might look?"

Simon thought for a minute. "She certainly wouldn't be at the academy. But she wasn't distant, based on what the elders have said. I suppose she could be in the manor."

"Perhaps we could go there, find her, and give her back her vigor."

"Do you realize that this would kill you? Or un-revive you." Simon said this nervously, backing away from Gilbert as if he expected a blow.

"It burns my heart to think I'm robbing a young girl simply by not staying dead."

"Well, it's no good anyway. I have no idea how to do it. I was trained in sorcery, but they never taught me more than I needed to know. I was never involved in their plans."

“Well, maybe this is your chance to revenge yourself on your master. Freeing Princess Sophie and exposing this conspiracy should ruin his work. Certainly there must be some book in the place that can instruct you on how to restore her.”

“I’m sure there is. Sadly, I think I left it on the floor of his Lordship’s tomb last night.” Simon did not look particularly sad about this detail.

Gilbert stood again, feeling he was at last coming close to having some sort of plan. “So we go in, fetch the book, and make things right.”

“I don’t know,” Simon said. “We don't know where she is. She will be guarded. It's just... hopeless.”

Gilbert saw this as a simple morale problem. He’d never been one for inspiring men with words, but he decided to try his hand at it now. “Think about the situation you’re in. You’re chased by the Witch Watch and by your former masters, either of which will most likely kill you if they catch you.”

“Only if I’m very fortunate,” Simon lamented.

“But here is your chance to make your own fortune. Ruin the house of Mordaunt, save the princess, and become a hero. I’ll be dead... again. So the credit can all go to you. The Witch Watch probably won’t hang you if you explain that you were a slave and worked against your master as soon as your bonds were broken.”

“This is absurd. We can’t possibly best the Viscount.”

“We do have the strategic advantage of him being dead.”

“You don’t understand. He still commands his servants from beyond the grave. He is terrible!”

“All the more reason to ruin his schemes.” Gilbert found this business of persuasion was becoming tiresome. Of all the emotions a man might experience, it seemed that cowardice was the most obstinately unreasonable.

Simon was silent and stared at his feet. Gilbert waited to see if the boy would refuse, or if he would find some courage. The boy didn’t seem inclined to do either.

“Very well,” Gilbert said after a long silence. “I am going back to the manor and will attempt the deed alone. I place no value on this second life I’ve been given, and I’d rather expend it in the service of something worthwhile than skulk about hiding and fleeing. You can go your own way, and I hope it does not end at the end of a rope in Tyburn.”

Simon swallowed. “I will go with you,” he said without looking up from his shoes.

“That’s a good lad,” Gilbert said as he clapped Simon on the shoulder. “I think you’ll find courage suits you once you taste a bit of it.”

The two of them slipped out of the tower and passed through some back rooms. They were reluctant to enter the main sanctuary. They did not want to compound the sacrilege of bringing the unliving into the church by parading him around before the holy symbols. Simon helped himself to another draught of the holy water, begging pardons in the general direction of the ceiling as he did so.

Gilbert wrapped himself in the black cloak again, if only to cover the white garment he was wearing. He meant to slip quietly out of the side entrance and simply follow the road out of town.

Gilbert opened the door, took a step, stopped, and jerked back inside, nearly knocking Simon over in the process.

Outside the door was a young woman, inexplicably wearing trousers. Her hair was done up in ribbons and she was standing just ten paces from the door, looking at her wrist.

“What’s wrong?” Simon whispered.

“It’s the Witch Watch. The woman from last night. She’s right outside.”

“Did she see you?” Simon hissed.

“Assuming she’s hasn’t been struck blind. She looked right at me.”

“Now what should we do?” Simon demanded.

"Now we will find out if you're capable of courage," Gilbert said.

II

"Do try to have some courage about this, Gilbert dear," Mother chided as she opened the door for him.

"It's not about courage at all. I'm quite capable of living on my own here," Gilbert protested. He pushed through, trying to keep the load of clothing steady as he headed down the stairs to the parlor. It was a bright day in April. Sunlight flowed through the windows and revealed the dancing motes of dust that their work had set in motion.

"That claim is yours to prove," she retorted.

"It's about common sense. I see no reason to pack up our whole life and go running off to America like this." Gilbert set the load down on the floor beside the trunk.

"Perhaps you don't. But I see no reason to stay here where we have no relations and so few friends." She began to sort through the pile, putting wanted items into the trunk and setting the rest aside.

Gilbert looked at the trunk and at the pile of clothing. The two were of similar size. "I don't see how you can hope to fit everything inside this trunk."

"Then it's fortunate I don't plan on taking 'everything'. I plan on taking just the personal items and valuables. The rest of it can all burn. No, not truly, but you know what I mean. You remember your father's friend Mr. Hughes?"

"The barrister with the enormous nose and no hair?"

"Solicitor, not barrister. He has kindly offered to sell off the unwanted items and send me the proceeds."

"What unwanted items?"

"I don't think the furniture will fit in my trunk, for starters."

"*Furniture!*" Gilbert said indignantly. "You mean to leave me without furnishings?"

"Very well. I'll leave the furniture. I think you'll find them less useful without a house to put them in, but you're welcome to drag the tables and chairs through the streets of London if you think they will be useful."

"You're selling the *house*?" Gilbert boomed.

"Did you think I was going to just leave you the family fortune and crawl back to your sister a vagabond?"

"No," Gilbert said after a pause that indicated the opposite. "But see, what you're doing is going to make *me* a vagabond."

"Well if you had a family I might consider giving you your share of the fortune now. But you're strong, you're young, you're *single,* and you're more than capable of seeing to your own needs. And if not, you can always come back to America with me. It would save me the trouble of finding someone to carry this trunk." She held up one of his father's suits to him and frowned. "Curse your unnatural size," she said.

"It's not *unnatural*. Father was tall as well."

"Your father was tall, but you are a titan. Look at your shoulders. What a shame. Such a fine suit." She dropped the suit into the pile of unwanted items.

"You're getting rid of father's suit?" This was absurd. Did Mother really want some stranger parading around in Father's favorite suit? This almost felt like grave-robbing.

"I doubt very much he should need it again. The one we buried him in was quite lovely and he won't need another."

Gilbert frowned. "This whole business is very sudden."

"Not as sudden as it seems," she said. "I don't plan on leaving until near the end of the year. I should like to spend Christmas with my new granddaughter. Or grandson, if it comes to that."

"Then why are we packing now?"

"Because you're leaving for your new job soon, and I want your help in moving heavy things about the house. You're like a horse that can work indoors." She smiled and patted him on the head like a beloved animal.

"Won't you miss it here?" Gilbert asked, not rising to the bait.

"Miss? Well, I'll miss you of course, but if you're set on breaking my heart then there's little I can do to stop you. But if you must know the only thing I'll miss is Victoria herself."

Gilbert sighed. "You know, you might have an easier time making friends here if you didn't insist on referring to Her Majesty the Queen by her first name as if she came over for tea. It really does offend people."

"Well, I see it as a sign of affection. It's their business if other people want to keep her at such arm's length. I must admit I feel a certain sisterhood with her."

"Is that because you share the same first name?"

"Don't be silly. It's because she's the finest monarch in a thousand years, and has been good for the national character. Maybe people will get it into their heads that more women should be in places of importance. We certainly couldn't do far worse than the men, no matter how hard we tried." Mother held up another of his father's suits, then disassembled it and held each piece up in turn. She dropped it all onto the unwanted pile with a sigh.

"I can see you're trying to scandalize me for your own amusement," Gilbert grumbled, "but I'm just not interested. Politics bore me." He'd heard this sermon from her before, and he wanted to avoid the long version.

"For example, that fool husband of hers," Mother continued, ignoring Gilbert. "He's a lovely man, but is impoverished of common sense."

"What's wrong with Prince Albert?" He regretted asking the question before she answered it. Gilbert realized too late that he was bringing this on himself.

"This idea of his that we should have leniency towards 'benign sorcery'. It's quite dangerous and barbaric, and I wish Victoria would set him right."

"He's only suggesting that we shouldn't go around killing people who use magic for medicinal purposes. I hardly see that as a call to barbarism."

"Oh? Did you hear what happened last month? The assassination attempt?"

"No?"

"You really should pay more attention. Some fool hedge wizard tried to kill Victoria and Prince Albert. Some mad Irishman named McLean. He tried to roast them alive. Ended up setting their coach on fire."

"If he was named McLean, wouldn't that make him a Scotsman?"

"Oh, whichever," she said impatiently. "The point is that lenience only encourages more people to dabble in it."

"I don't see the harm in healing people," Gilbert said.

She gathered up the unwanted clothes and put them back in his arms, then gave him a gentle shove in the direction of the stairs. Gilbert obediently took his burden up while she followed after him with a few of the nicer items that she probably didn't trust to his brutish embrace. "You're too young to remember the forties," she said as she followed him up the steps. "The Potato Famine brought in waves of tricksters and magicians of all kinds. Men that commanded animals. Women that could move unseen. It was chaos and crime for years after."

Gilbert allowed himself an eye-roll while she was behind him. "You were still a young girl and living in America when that happened. So you don't remember it any better than I do."

"But I'm old enough to remember the gossip about it. And I

remember well enough the trouble that comes from those who dabble in magic."

"Are you sure the cause wasn't poverty, homelessness, and starvation that came from hundreds of thousands of people fleeing the famine?"

"Which itself was the work of witchcraft!"

Gilbert sighed. "You don't know that. Nobody knows that."

"I can't imagine any *natural* blight that could cause destruction on such a terrible scale. Use your head, Gilbert. The potato blight had to be the work of magic."

"Perhaps. But if I was sick and a wizard offered me a cure, I might take it."

"That would be most unwise. You could end up ejected from the church."

"We've got to get out of this church," Gilbert said as he paced in the aisle.

"I wonder why they haven't attacked us," Simon said. He was looking out through the stained glass windows, trying to catch some glimpse of their adversaries despite the distortion and pervasive darkness.

"I've been asking myself the same question. They know we're in here and they know where the exits are. They have us cornered. Perhaps they're waiting for reinforcements. Perhaps they're reluctant to engage in violence in a holy place. If it's the latter, we might be able to use it to our advantage."

The sun had faded, and their only light came from the torches and lanterns gathered outside of the church. There was just enough light that they could move about without crashing into things. This was not a large church. It would take less than fifty people to fill it to capacity.

Simon threw himself down in one of the pews. The impact was very loud in the empty space. “This is terrible. We can’t stay in here forever. I’m already so hungry. I was given a meal before I entered the tomb last night, but I haven’t had a bite since then.”

“I don’t suppose you know any spells that might aid us?”

“You’re suggesting we use magic in *here*?” Simon gestured at the holy symbols at the front of the room. “I’m not even sure His Lordship would have done such a thing. At any rate, no. I don’t know any spells that would be of use to us.”

“We don’t need much. A cloud of smoke, bright lights, some noise in the distance? Something along those lines?”

Simon drew in a deep breath and began ticking off possibilities on his fingers. “If we had a dead dog, I could bring it back to life mindless and feral.”

“I suppose that’s not terribly useful,” Gilbert admitted.

“I could make a goblet of blood boil. I can ward off certain kinds of animated dead.”

“Forget the matter. I’m sorry I brought it up.”

“And as I learned last night, I can raise a dead viscount if supplied with a princess first.”

“Please stop telling me these unwholesome things.” Gilbert waved his arms to signal his surrender.

Gilbert went to the window and did his best to count their foes. He found it likely they were facing the same six men as the previous night. He knew the number of their enemy, but not where they were positioned. They would need to cover all possible exits, of which there were two. The Witch Watch believed they were going to face a powerful wizard, so they were bracing themselves for an attack that could fall at any moment. This would fill them with nervous energy and make the men prone to fidgeting. Gilbert hoped this would make it possible to see them. After ten minutes of silent observation, he perceived a few points of subtle movement in the shadows outside.

“I’m not going to lie to you,” he told Simon. “This is bad. It looks like they have three men out front. I’m betting the other three will be guarding the side door, with the mystery woman. They have good rifles and they know we're in here. We have no weapons, we're outnumbered, and they know we're coming."

Simon nodded. He seemed to be choking back tears.

Gilbert regarded him and thought about the long years of torment the boy had suffered. Gilbert had faced the threat of death, and his nerves had been tempered by it. His fellow soldiers had been mocking towards civilians and their assumed cowardice, and had thought it odd that folks with so little honor would value their lives so highly. Gilbert had always thought this was a backward way of thinking. Their purpose was to safeguard the lives of the innocent. Soldiers faced the terrors of the world so that commoners didn't have to, and if commoners lacked courage then it was a sign that the fighting men were doing their job.

Gilbert thought they could simply surrender, but he wasn't sure what the Witch Watch would do. Certainly he and Simon would hang. Or burn. Or whatever was in fashion for condemned sorcerers these days. But even if they told all they knew before they died, he doubted the Witch Watch would act on it. If restoring the life of the princess required additional sorcery, then they might prefer to leave her dead.

All Gilbert wanted was a course of action that would allow him to save someone. If he couldn't save the princess, then perhaps he could save the boy.

"Look Simon," Gilbert said. "I would rather you escaped from this unharmed. They were mostly concerned with me last night. It's even possible - though not likely - that they overlooked you altogether. If they kill me, I'll be no worse off than I was this time yesterday. I propose that I make a commotion and attempt to lead these bloodhounds away. You'll be free to escape."

Simon opened his mouth and closed it again, apparently stunned by the offer. "But surely they'll run you down?"

"Probably. But I don't imagine you'll be of much help to me if it comes to that. Better that one of us should escape, and you're the one with the knowledge to help poor Sophie."

Simon seemed encouraged by this line of thought. He straightened himself up. "I don't see how you can hope to lead them away. Surely you'll be cut down the moment you set foot outside the church."

"Yes. I'll need to find some other way of leaving this place." Gilbert explored the building once again, hoping to find some detail he'd overlooked before. The windows were another possible exit, but then he considered the time it would take to smash one open. (Which was something he was reluctant to do; quite aside from the sacrilege, he adored stained glass windows.) By the time he broke it open and hoisted himself out, the enemy would be onto him. Likely as not he'd just end up shot while hanging halfway out of the window.

It was a very small church, and his search did not take long. It ended in the belfry, with him looking up at the pinch of starry sky that was visible at the top. "I'm going to leave this way," he said to Simon. He began climbing.

The belfry was narrow, and he was able to climb it by bracing himself against opposing walls. He was careful to avoid getting caught on the rope, as he didn't want to give away his plan by simply ringing the bell. The bell itself was quite small, perhaps only half again the size of a family cooking pot. Simon stood beneath him and watched his progress until the rain of dust and splinters drove him off.

Gilbert reached the top. Since he was looking down to watch his footing, he cracked his head against the bell. The note rang clearly in the night air, rolling out far beyond the borders of the town. He cursed loudly. Now that he was at the top, he could see that the openings were not as large as he had assumed. They were quite narrow, only just barely large enough to allow him passage.

He hoisted himself up and looked out through the bell windows. Directly below was the church roof. It was a short enough drop, although if he tumbled off he would fall into the street where he would then be smashed against the stony ground and (probably) shot. However, if he could keep his footing he could cross the roof and perhaps leap to the adjacent building, which looked like it might be stables. Although, it was difficult to be sure in the dark. From there he might gain a horse (assuming this was the stables and also assuming horses were kept there at the moment and that there would be a saddle handy) and ride out of town. The Witch Watch would ride after him. Perhaps he could abandon his horse after a mile or so and double back, leaving his pursuers in confusion.

It was a ridiculous plan, filled with holes, and most likely doomed to fail. The alternative was climbing back down and waiting for his foes to attack on their own terms.

He pulled himself up and out of the not-quite-Gilbert-sized opening, and became stuck. He flailed his feet, struck the bell again with his heel, and tumbled out headfirst. There was a great impact. He landed on his back, more or less. This was followed by a short drop and a rain of debris. Gilbert found himself suddenly back inside the church, looking up at the sky through a fresh hole in the roof.

"Are you all right, Gilbert?" Simon rushed to his side.

"At least I didn't break any of the windows."

Alice stood behind the church with Captain Turpin. She was looking up at the bell and trying to make sense of the events so far.

Last night they had tracked the abomination to this town. Her ethergram pointed unmistakably at the church, meaning it was hiding somewhere inside. When morning came the captain had advised the locals to stay away, and they were more than happy to hide indoors and leave the problem for the Witch Watch to handle.

The church had been silent until a quarter of an hour ago, when they heard some sort of scuffling inside. Then the bell was rung once, followed by profanity, a second ring, and a loud boom. They had hurried around the church, expecting some sort of ambush or wizardry, only to find it quiet again.

"If he's trying to get away, he's taking an odd way around," Captain Turpin said.

Jack, the Captain's second, joined them. He had been left to watch the side door but curiosity over the ringing bell had evidently drawn him here. "Is that something on the roof?" he asked, pointing to a spot beside the belfry.

Alice squinted, and made out a dark spot there. She drew close to the church and discovered a shingle. She held it up for the others to see in the lantern light. "It's not something on the roof. It's a hole."

"What do you make of that?" asked Turpin. "Can't fathom the use of blowing holes in the roof of the church. The walls, maybe. But not the roof."

"We should go in," Alice said firmly. "Unless we mean to stand out here while he tears the building down a beam at a time."

"These folk are scared enough already," said Turpin, meaning the townsfolk that were peering out the windows at them. "They don't want any bloodshed in the church and I have to say I agree with them."

"We're destroying an abomination. There won't *be* blood," she said patiently.

The captain lowered his voice. "I know the men used to give you difficulty on account of you being a woman. But those days are long past. You've proven your worth and sundry, and nobody questions your dedication. You're like a brother to them, if you take my meaning."

"I don't think I do," she whispered back, slightly irritated.

Archer - the other member of their foursome - walked into view, leading their horses. He had been out front, where the captain had ordered him to stay with the horses. This was apparently his way of obediently abandoning his post so he could see what everyone else was doing.

The Captain gave a sidelong glance in Archer's direction. "I'm saying you don't need to demonstrate your courage by advising rashness. The men would lay down their lives for you, but there's no reason to make them do so tonight. Mordaunt will come out sooner or later. Better we keep him bottled up and make him fight his way out than the other way around."

"It's not rashness," she hissed back. "I just don't see the sense in allowing him time to prepare some devilry for us."

"Look!" Jack shouted.

Alice looked up and saw a black-cloaked figure fleeing from the church, where the side-door was left hanging open.

"Did nobody hold their post at the doors?" Turpin boomed. He shouted for everyone to rally, but there was little need. All of them were standing together, having come to see the business with the roof.

The abomination rushed through the pasture, heading for the trees on the far side. Archer took a shot - an act of absurd optimism given the distance and darkness. The captain and Jack mounted their horses, and the chase was on.

"That way," Alice said to Archer. "The captain will try to drive him back here so we can close in around him. Let's just hope we can fight him in the pasture and that he doesn't make for the village."

Even as she spoke, the abomination began doing exactly that. When it saw it was going to be overtaken, it turned sharply and made for the relative shelter of the nearby houses.

"Why doesn't it use magic?" Alice wondered aloud as she ran.

"I think it is. Look at how fast it's running!" answered Archer.

They were fortunate to have the moon on their side tonight. It shone on the fields and village with enough strength to cast shadows. The abomination could not hide easily, despite its dark cloak. It ran through an orchard, staying close to the trees to prevent the horses from drawing too near. Then it climbed over a fence that the captain did not dare on horseback, and so broke away just before they ran him down.

The Witch Watch scattered and combed through the town while the inhabitants cowered inside. Alice heard a woman scream. Thinking the abomination had been found, she hurried towards the sound only to discover that the woman had simply been startled by Archer moving past her window.

Alice consulted the ethergram. As before, the needle was still slightly inclined to point towards the abomination. It was not strong, and she had to hold very still to see the movement. This was difficult because she was winded. When the needle settled down, it seemed to be pointing away from the area where the men were hunting. Had the abomination doubled back? She turned and went around the nearby house. Now the needle was moving quickly. She thought this might be a malfunction, but this might also happen if it was extremely close.

A black shape rushed in front of her and she cried out. It wheeled to face her. She had no time to draw a weapon, and so in a panic she simply held out her hand and unleashed fire. The abomination spun again, shielding itself from the flame with its cloak. Then it fled, still burning, towards the road.

Her cry drew the attention of the others, and soon they were closing in around it, a specter of flame and smoke rushing through the night.

The abomination threw itself down in the dust and beat out the flames. By the time it rose again, the horses had caught up with it. Alice watched as the captain tried to hew it with his sword, but their foe was unexpectedly crafty. It stayed in front of the captain, using the horse's head as a shield. Turpin turned quickly and swung, but the abomination ducked the blow and slapped the horse's hindquarters, sending it galloping forward. Turpin cursed as his mount carried him away from the battle.

Jack rode forward and struck true. His sword landed between its shoulder blades, and the abomination fell on all fours.

Alice threw up her arms in frustration. "The head! What are you doing? You ass! Take off the head!" She was shouting at Jack with the tone of a governess scolding foolish children.

The abomination stood up, still with Jack's sword driven into its back and protruding from its chest. It looked down at the blade curiously. The sword had been thrust in from above, so the hilt hovered over its head like a flagpole.

“Extraordinary,” it said. “I’m still alive.” There was a pause while it tried to expel the blade by pushing on the tip. “Well, you know what I mean,” it added.

Archer ran up beside Alice, panting and coughing. He bent forward with his hands on his knees, trying to ask what was going on between gasps.

The Witch Watch looked on, dumbfounded, as the abomination lurched around, trying to pull the sword free. It reached up and gripped the hilt, awkwardly pushing and pulling, wiggling the blade back and forth. After much muttering and staggering about, it withdrew the blade.

Turpin, having recovered control of his horse and dismounted, approached with his own sword in his hand.

The abomination drew back its hood, revealing a grim, yet smiling skull. Only a few ragged strands of hair remained. It looked at Captain Turpin. “I see you mean to put me to the sword. Before you do, might I ask you what crime I’ve committed?”

“You’re an abomination!” the captain spat.

“Abomination is such a harsh term. I prefer to think of myself as an affront,” it replied.

“Mock all you like, Your Lordship,” Captain Turpin said coldly, “We’ll soon have you back in your proper grave.”

“Very good. I was in the wrong grave the last time I was dead. I’m not the Lord Mordaunt.”

“You can claim to be whoever you like. You’re still going back to the grave.”

The abomination then turned his sword around and offered it back to Jack. “Very well,” it said, “I surrender. But before you further dull your sword on my ribs, perhaps I can give you news that will be to your advantage.”

This struck Alice as exceptionally strange. In all her years with the Witch Watch, there had never been an abomination that behaved this way. Some were murderous beasts. Some were mindless and wandering, and still others might be cunning but mad. But the idea that one would surrender to them was preposterous.

"You'll find your lies in small demand here, your Lordship. Or whoever you claim to be."

"He's telling the truth," said Alice. "At least, he's not Lord Mordaunt."

"You saw the empty tomb yourself, Miss," the captain reminded her.

She approached their foe. In earlier days they would have forbidden her, or told her to shut up, or insisted that this was too dangerous. But they now trusted her to know her business. "I've heard that the Viscount was a short, bald man, thin and fragile. And yet this one is absurdly tall, broad even in death, and still has remnants of a young head of hair. And if that is not enough to persuade you, have any of you heard of an English Gentleman talking with such a coarse accent. I can't place it. It almost sounds American."

"My mother is American," the abomination offered helpfully.

"No Mother, I can't throw away this job and go to America with you," Gilbert said. He smoothed out his uniform and regarded himself in the mirror one last time to make sure he hadn't forgotten anything. He didn't want to make a bad first impression.

They were in father's old study. After his passing, this room became a place to keep all of his things, and a neutral ground for arguments. Morning light poured in through the windows.

Mother was standing in the doorway wringing her hands. "All these years you've spent dithering, and suddenly you've found a job. I arranged so many opportunities for you and you never took any of them. Why start now?"

"This is the sort of job I've been looking for since I left the military. I don't want to spend the day sitting around." Gilbert struggled to fasten the topmost button in his uniform. Tailors seemed unable to believe their own measurements of his neck, and too often tried to make his clothes in more conventional proportions.

"Then why did you remain unemployed?" she said with exasperation.

"You know what I mean. I don't want to go around, poking my nose in where it doesn't belong or putting ink to paper all day. I want a job that matters. I want a job keeping people *safe*. I never felt so happy as when I was guarding and protecting. Other men have such contempt for guard duty but I see it as a great honor. Perhaps even sacred. Boring, yes, usually. But I was satisfied knowing that if trouble came, I would be the first to act against it. The robber, the vandal, the assassin. When I stood guard, I was their chief fear. My watching made it so that others could sleep more easily."

His top button was now secure. Gilbert tugged on the collar in an attempt to gain some breathing room. Mother folded her arms and frowned at him without comment.

"You always say I'm too big, and it's true. But my size is a lot of use in that line of work." Gilbert looked out the window in the direction of London, muttering, "I'd have worked at Scotland Yard, but they wouldn't have me."

"If you liked guarding things all day, then why did you even leave the military in the first place?"

"You know why, and you know I don't like to discuss it," he said bitterly.

"I think you've been very silly. You've passed up many good jobs just because they weren't enough like the job you gave up."

"Well I've finally found a job where I'll be doing what I love," he said with a satisfied nod. "The Viscount is apparently a man of great importance to need a personal guard. I'll see to the protection of his family, or estate, or privacy, or whatever is in need of safekeeping."

"I'm sure there are things in America that need uniformed men with polished boots to stand around them. You're being quite cruel by leaving me like this."

"You are the one who is leaving, not me," he reminded her. "And besides, you make it sound like this horrible thing. You're making a fuss over nothing,"

"And how would you know?" she demanded. "You don't have children. You don't know what it's like being forced to choose between your offspring."

"Forced? Now you're being silly. Nobody is forcing you to choose anything," he said with irritation.

"Of course I am. Every day, since your sister moved away."

"Well the blame is on her then, not me." Gilbert took Mother by the shoulders and gently steered her out of the way so that he could go downstairs. When he reached the front door he turned to find Mother was still at the top of the steps, looking down on him.

"Oh Gilbert. I know I fuss at you but I'm so very fond of you both. I only wish to have all of my chicks under my wings."

"Grand-chicks, you mean."

"If you like. Maybe it's too much to ask for, but I don't think it's too much to hope for. How far away is this job?"

"Not far. Closer than America, at any rate. It's just on the other side of London. It's a day's journey at most. Probably half a day, if I was in the mood to hurry."

"And this Ravenstead fellow..."

"Mordaunt," Gilbert corrected her.

"Well, whoever he is, I've never heard of him."

"He is a Viscount, Mother. And his representatives were very particular. Asked a great many questions about my career, such as it is, and about my lifestyle, and family."

"Sounds like a busybody."

"I admire his thoroughness. Very professional. It shows he isn't content to hire any vagabond that claims he can hold a gun."

"And you're sure you won't reconsider? Don't you want to meet your niece?"

Gilbert sighed. "Or nephew. And yes, I would like to meet him. But

I've only just now, finally, acquired a job. A job that promises a great deal of money I might add. I can't bear the thought of walking away now."

It was high August, and even though it was only mid-morning Gilbert was already red-faced from the heat. He thought perhaps it might have been wise to trim back his muttonchops and let the skin breathe a bit more. Perhaps he would have it done when he reached London.

"You wouldn't have encountered so much trouble finding work in America. Our lack of connections here has held you back." She said this almost as if it was an apology. "And is probably still hindering your hunt for a wife, although the chief blame for that should go to your lack of effort."

Gilbert picked up his bag.

Mother came downstairs and fussed over his uniform. "You will come and visit me again before I leave?"

"I'll make every effort to do so, but I can't make any promises." This was actually very unlikely, and Gilbert knew that this would be the last time he saw Mother for quite some time. He had a sudden urge to abandon the job and sail off with her to America. Then he got hold of himself and put the idea out of his mind. He had found work, *real* work this time, for proper pay, and now he intended to pour himself into it.

They embraced.

"I love you Gilbert, do be careful," she said quietly.

"Not to worry." He smiled. "I can take care of myself."

"I still say we should take care of him right now," one of the men said.

Gilbert lay dejectedly in the back of the cart. He had explained what he knew. He told them about Simon, Princess Sophie, and had related the strange events that had taken place in the tomb the night before. They asked him a great deal about the book Simon had used and about the sorcery he employed, and were very annoyed when Gilbert insisted that he knew nothing other than what he saw. They had then loaded him onto their cart and withdrew to discuss his fate among themselves. Two of the men had bound him with rope, just in case he changed his mind about surrendering.

Gilbert found he didn't mind the ropes. They were very tight, but they didn't seem to hurt. Nothing did. Even the sword - which would have pierced the heart of a living man - had created little more than a fleeting sting, like the memory of an old injury. The only thing that bothered him was that they had hauled him into the cart face-down, leaving him to stare at the floor.

"I don't want to be rude, but are we going to sit here much longer? Or perhaps you could roll me over? I think I've witnessed everything these boards have to offer in the way of entertainment."

"Quiet you," said one of the men guarding him. This was followed by a knock from the butt of the man's rifle. "I don't like hearing your voice. It's unnatural. Goes right to my spine."

"Sorry," Gilbert replied, which was answered with another knock.

The Witch Watch was down to four. There was the captain, the woman, the rifleman, and the angry fellow who had been occasionally kicking him for the last half hour. He heard them mention that the other three were transporting the 'other prisoners', and feared that they had managed to capture Simon during the chase. But then he realized they were most likely talking about the Four Horsemen.

The captain was like many captains Gilbert had known during his time in the service. He was a man of about forty, serious, determined, and not prone to showing emotion. He was regarded as more knowledgeable than brilliant. He had a weathered face with a handlebar mustache.

The woman fascinated him most of all. She appeared to be in the midst of her twenties. Her face was beautiful in a way that reminded him painfully of his lost life, although she was much too thin for his tastes. She seemed to be an adviser of some sort. The captain ran the men, but he deferred to the lady on all subjects relating to magic.

These two were at an impasse now because they had contradictory goals. They needed to destroy the 'abomination' as they called him, but now it seemed like destroying Gilbert could aid the cause of whoever revived him. He seemed to be very helpful and forthcoming, and they were reluctant to get rid of him while he might still possess useful information. In addition, the news of the princess was new to them, and they were undecided on whether they should believe him or what should be done about it.

The cart jostled as it was boarded. A foot prodded him. "You. Corpse. We have more questions for you." It was the captain's voice.

Gilbert sighed. He had hoped the discussion was over and that his captors had come to some conclusion regarding his fate. He was disappointed to find they had simply moved to another round of debate. "I have very little else to keep me occupied, so I shall be happy to answer them," Gilbert said.

"Regarding this associate of yours..." the captain began before trailing off again.

"Yes?" Gilbert said patiently to the floorboards.

"Here now, this won't do. I can't interrogate a sack at the bottom of a cart. Flip him over at least, Jack."

Many hands grabbed him and Gilbert was rolled over onto his back. He looked up to see a circle of faces examining him, shining brightly in the lantern light against the starry sky. "Thank you," he said cheerfully, mostly because he sensed that his manners annoyed them.

"You can keep your thanks. It wasn't done for your benefit," said the captain. "Now, this associate of yours. You said he ran off, but not where he was going."

"I don't know where he was going. My concern was saving him from your noose. I felt pity for the boy. He apparently suffered much at the hands of the Viscount."

"So you said," replied the captain doubtfully. "But all the same we'd like to interview him and see if he corroborates your story."

"Since the interview would likely end with his hanging, I am content to be called a liar if you won't take me at my word."

"What preparations were done to your body before you died?" asked the woman.

"I don't know. I don't remember how I died. Or even where or when. My memories are taking shape, but slowly. The last memory I have is of riding a coach to Ravenstead to work for Lord Mordaunt. As a guard, mind you. I went into the job expecting no more or less than standing about and polishing boots. I certainly wasn't expecting sorcery, or I wouldn't have taken the position."

"And this business about the princess," the captain said accusingly, "Do you have anything that might support your claim that there's a member of the royal family being held hostage and being subjected to magic in Ravenstead?"

"Nothing," Gilbert said sadly, "And I'm only going by what Simon told me. For my part, I believe him. But he may have misunderstood, or have been deceived. Even his account was based on hearsay; he never saw the princess and had no idea where she might have been hidden."

"Seems odd that a member of the royal family could go missing without us hearing about it," the captain said accusingly.

"Perhaps odd, but not impossible," the woman replied. "And the book corroborates his story in a way."

"You have Simon's book!" Gilbert said in surprise at seeing the evil thing in her hands. Although, it looked much less menacing now. A number of bright hair ribbons hung from between its pages, waving slightly in the wind.

"Werner Krauss was a strong believer in the power of royal blood. He was physician to... Ferdinand II, I think?" She seemed to be asking herself this question. "He did a great many experiments on royal blood and was convinced that it had unique magical properties. For my part, I don't believe it. I don't see why sitting on any throne, no matter how well adorned, should impart any special magics to the blood. If his studies were based in any way on observation, then he was probably simply seeing the effects of comfort, cleanliness, and having a good diet. I suspect that anything he wrote about royal blood could apply just as well to anyone well-fed and well-rested."

"Would you mind not teaching sorcery to the abomination?" the captain snapped.

"The abomination has a name," Gilbert offered. "My surname is Hiltman."

"So you said," muttered the captain.

"You can also call me Gilbert, if we're going to be friends," he added. Gilbert could no longer smile, so he did his best to convey one with his tone as he said this. It earned him another kick from one of the men. It reminded him of being in a fight while drunk; he could feel the blows, but the pain was subdued and distant.

"Please stop that, Jack," the woman said, slightly irritated. "Call him whatever you like, but there's no sense in beating on him. It's obvious he doesn't care or he would have stopped antagonizing you several blows ago." She turned to the captain and held up the book, "At any rate, I wasn't teaching him sorcery, but history, which is harmless enough. The point is that Krauss would have called for royal blood in a revivification like this. Since this cult was working from this book, it stands to reason that they would follow his methods."

"So let's assume he is telling us the truth," the captain said. "Would it hurt the princess if we were to take his head off?"

"Possibly," she said, looking down at the book again. "The cleanest, safest way of resolving this would be to recover the vigor from this one and restore it to her. Then we could be sure that he would stay dead and that she would recover fully."

"That means doing sorcery, doesn't it?" the captain said warily.

"Yes."

The captain let out a long, uneasy breath. They were obviously on shaky ground here. He seemed to let this idea settle before he spoke again, "Do you know how to do it?"

"No. Research will be required. And I'll need the specimen." There was murmuring from the men at this.

"Are you talking about bringing this... thing back to Grayhouse?" This came from Jack, the fellow who had been cursing and stomping on Gilbert.

"Do you have better lodgings?" the woman asked. "I shall need use of my library and tools, and would prefer to have a roof over my head while I employ them."

"We are charged with exterminating these monsters, not making them our pets!" Jack fumed.

"We are charged with protecting the people - and Her Majesty in particular - from supernatural threats," she reminded Jack. "Killing the unliving is one means to that end. This is another, however unsavory you may find it."

"We are not bringing a God-damned abomination back to the lodgings given to us by Her Majesty," Jack shouted.

The captain raised his voice to match Jack's, "Kicking this slab of dead flesh did not earn you a sudden promotion, Mister Stanway, and so I remain in charge. If your concern is for holiness, then perhaps you ought to see to your own blasphemy. And if your concern is for Her Majesty, then ask yourself which is more precious to her? I imagine she would gladly trade our home and everything in it to have her daughter returned."

Jack stood, which caused the cart to wobble slightly, "We don't even know that she's in any danger at all. This creature is certainly filled with lies, and I can scarcely believe you're entertaining them. I should almost think you were bewitched."

The captain stood also, but he was suddenly quiet. "Are you charging me with bewitchment, Mister Stanway?"

A long silence hung over the cart. The two men met each other's gaze and held their stalemate for several moments. "No," Jack said at last, retreating slightly. "I'm only saying it is unlike your custom to show deference to the unliving."

"Not to the unliving, but to Her Majesty."

Jack looked around. "Does no one else stand with me?"

The reply was silence. Jack sat down. "Very well, I have nothing more to say on the matter." His tone seemed to indicate otherwise.

"Good. Go around and knock on a few doors. Let folks know the abomination is dealt with, and don't say more beyond that. They're spooked enough and are probably expecting the end of the world, so be gentle with them. Speak to the priest and tell him he can have his church back. He'll be glad for that."

The mood cooled once Jack left with the other member of the Watch. This left only the captain and the woman.

"So how do we get it inside of Grayhouse?" the captain asked.

"I can walk when not bound," Gilbert offered.

The captain looked down at him, "You'll be quiet if you know what's good for you. I'm not so delighted with this plan that I won't just take your head off if I find half a reason, and I'm inclined to go against your requests, so perhaps you'd best keep them to yourself."

The woman peered down at Gilbert. "You should not antagonize the captain. If you knew anything at all about necromancy you would realize your peril. If the captain takes your head, you won't return to death. Your spirit will remain bound to that dried skull on your shoulders, helpless and without the use of your body. Many necromancers have been buried so, trapped in darkness without hope. The illegitimate Pope Adrian II was buried this way a thousand years ago, and we could dig his head up today and find him still screaming for release."

Gilbert nodded and kept quiet.

She turned back to the captain. "So, to simplify the problem down to its essentials: He can walk in, or we can carry him."

"Allowing him to walk unbound is out of the question," the captain said firmly. "However polite he is now, we can't be sure this isn't some ruse. Or he could turn feral. We might put him in chains, but then we'll be leading a man in chains, and anyone that sees us entering Grayhouse will want to know why we're keeping a prisoner there instead of putting him in a proper cell. "

"So we have to carry him," the woman said. "I don't know that carrying a body around will look any better than leading about a man in chains. I wonder if we would get a casket here in town?"

The captain leaned back and considered this, "A casket? I suppose that would be preferable to hauling the body around like a sack of potatoes. Would still set jaws in motion, if it were seen."

"We could make sure to bring him in during the night."

"That would make us look even more suspicious, but less likely to be seen."

Gilbert did not like the sound of this plan at all. He thought about what would happen if they changed their mind and simply decided to bury him.

It turned out that there was a coffin available. Several, in fact. An enterprising carpenter had heard all the gossip concerning the Witch Watch and the church being closed, and had anticipated that there would be a demand for them before the week was out. He'd built three of them during the day, with more planned, and was slightly put out when he discovered that only one of them would be needed.

The Witch Watch made every effort to support their deception. They placed Gilbert in the coffin (which was a tight fit) and nailed it shut, and then sent for the priest to have him perform the long-form Final Rites of Resting on the 'body'. These unnerved Gilbert even more than being sealed in the coffin, and he counted it the worst part of the ordeal. Gilbert had never noticed before how much of the rite was dedicated to commanding the deceased (in the name of God) to stay so, and calling down penalties (also in the name of God) on them if they failed to comply. He thought it curious that the church put so much of the blame and punishment on the departed, and never stopped to address the question of what other people might do with your body once you had left it. This struck him as being like arresting a man for burglary because his house had been robbed. Was he responsible for his return to this world? Could he have refused? He wondered.

Once that unpleasantness was over, Gilbert felt himself being loaded onto the cart, and they began the bumpy journey to London.

Mr. Brooks,

I apologize for the delay in sending this letter. My duties with The Ministry of Ethereal Affairs are consuming a considerable portion of my waking hours. The remainder of those hours is spent attempting to raise a young girl. This has left little time for the conducting of correspondence, even with dear friends.

Alice is thriving, looking less like a child and more like her mother each day. She begs you for more watches, or watch parts, or tools, or any other items you may not want. Quite to the contrary of your purposes, giving her a few trinkets to play with did not satisfy her curiosity, but intensified it. She took the broken items you provided and combined the parts to form a single working whole. She now wears this watch constantly, much to my pride and to the frustration of everyone else. She has been reminded many times that a pocketwatch is not a proper adornment for a lady, but I would rather have my daughter demonstrate mechanical genius than fashion sense.

Before I address your question, allow me to correct some of the sloppy language you used in your letter. Specifically, the usage of the various words we have for people who use magic.

A WIZARD is someone who can invoke or command some of the primal forces of nature. They can, with no special equipment or training, cause supernatural physical activity around them. Fire is by far the most common, and in the last few years we have encountered perhaps a half dozen such wizards. Others can cause moisture to form in the air around them, which appears like momentary rain. I have also read about (but have not personally witnessed) individuals who can cause wind to blow or hurl small objects about. Less reliable texts mention wizards who could command arcs of lightning to strike. Regardless of the form it takes, this activity is physically exhausting for the wizard.

When I took this position, it was thought that less than one in a million people possessed the power of wizardry. As our work at the Ministry of Ethereal Affairs (PLEASE do not refer to us as 'The Witch Watch' again, I beg you) progressed, we revised that to one in a half million. I suspect that we are still under-estimating their numbers. I do not mean to suggest the number of wizards is increasing, only that they are more common and well-hidden than anyone dared guess.

By contrast, a SORCERER is someone who can create supernatural events through the use of sorcery circles. They write commands in circular patterns on the ground in order to bring about this magic. The commands must adhere to a rigid system of rules in order to have any effect.

The word WITCH applies equally to both kinds of magic users, and I must say I do not like the term at all. It was created in a time where people did not know or understand the difference between wizards and sorcerers, or even that there WAS a difference. Indeed, both the courts and the church still charge people with witchcraft, without bothering to designate which sort.

As I've gone through old records, I've often been saddened and frustrated by this imprecision. Over the last hundred years, almost a thousand people have been executed at Tyburn for capital witchcraft. Not once did anyone bother remarking whether the condemned was a wizard or a sorcerer. If they had only noted these very simple details, we would now be able to answer many important questions: How common are wizards? Is our confiscation of materials keeping up with the execution of sorcerers, or are there unknown books still in circulation? How many wizards are also sorcerers?

I suspect there is nothing that can be done to correct the use of "witch" in the papers, but I urge you as a man of education to be less reckless with your words.

Which brings me to your question. What is done with confiscated books? We keep them in a residence that has been provided to us. They are labeled and sorted, so that we know where each book was found and under what circumstances. I'm well aware that The Church would be enraged if they knew we were keeping these. In addition, I'm sure a great many aspiring sorcerers would delight to obtain them. I have often thought that it would be wise to find a more secure location for the books, but I can't request for more secure facilities without explaining why. Right now the only thing keeping people away from them is that nobody knows they exist. Perhaps this is the most secure lock of all.

In friendship,

Sir Donovan White

Director, Ministry of Ethereal Affairs

June 2, 1875

GRAYHOUSE

III

Grayhouse was a sprawling construction of red brick, adorned with many tall windows and almost as many chimneys. It sat in London, sleeping in a neighborhood otherwise filled with busy upheaval. All around, small houses and open lots were gradually being cleared to make way for manufacturing buildings. The neighborhood was dirty and noisy, even at night.

The members of the Ministry of Ethereal Affairs often said that the building was “a gift from the Queen”, but this was somewhere between hyperbole and jest. In truth, it came into the hands of the ministry from Prince Albert, and it came into his hands through a convoluted series of transactions involving nobles and politics, most of which were quite beyond a person of Alice’s station. At some point the place had been in the hands of someone named Gray, and their name clung to the address even after ownership passed on. Many people mistook the name of the house for a description of it, and would either show up looking for a grey house or attempt to correct Alice on her spelling in their correspondence.

Since middle age, Prince Albert had campaigned to extend leniency to “medicinal sorcery”. A side-effect of this initially unpopular move was that he needed to show people (and the church, in particular) that he wasn’t an apologist for sorcery in general, and that his aim wasn’t to legitimize and evangelize the dark arts to England’s impressionable, God-fearing youth. So the Ministry of Ethereal Affairs was created. An amusing novelty at first, they gradually captured the public attention through the papers. People were more inclined to like and trust the Witch Watch (as the papers came to call it) because their methods more closely resembled the system of due process given to other sorts of criminals. By contrast, the church had a reputation for poking swords into anyone found too close to a forbidden book then praying that God would forgive them if any of the slain had been innocent of reading it.

This fame worked against the members of Ethereal Affairs. Their exploits were usually greatly exaggerated, even before publication. From there common folk would assume they were missing out on the most thrilling parts, and made sure to add those themselves if they repeated the tale later. This meant that the members of the ministry were watched closely by their neighbors, and the newspapers seemed to employ people with no other purpose than to loiter around Grayhouse and look for news that could be spun into gossip. This fact was foremost in the minds of Captain Turpin and Alice White when they arrived home to find an electric streetlamp had been constructed in front of Grayhouse.

"Someone has stolen all of the darkness from in front of our house," the captain said.

"What's that doing there?" asked Private Archer indignantly.

"They've been building these all over the city for years. It was bound to happen on our street sooner or later," Alice said.

"Just our luck they did it now," Archer muttered.

There was nothing to be done about it. Perhaps if they had more time they might have concocted some other disguise for their cargo, but they were all too tired for creative subterfuge. All four of them carried the coffin into the house, right under the light.

"Where now?" asked Archer, once the coffin had been set in the entryway and the door closed.

Alice thought for a moment, "The library. It's above the street so we won't have to worry about folks looking in. It will be near my books and tools, and there's plenty of room. And there's only one way in, which makes it easier to guard."

"Wouldn't it be safer to chain it up in the basement?" Turpin suggested.

"We can chain it up anywhere we like, but I don't know that the basement is a superior place to be assaulted than the library. And I'd rather not have to work down there."

The library was very much Alice's domain, as there was rarely any occasion for the others to visit. It was a large room with a high ceiling. The tall windows faced the disheveled, overgrown garden behind the house. Bookshelves lined the walls, and a great many unshelved books were piled in front of those, forming a miniature city. On the wall opposite the door was Alice's workbench, which no one else dared touch. It was covered in fine tools like those used by a watchmaker, and had many open books and scrawled notes piled high. In the center of the room was a large table that was seldom used, except as a temporary holding spot for unsorted books.

They moved the table off to one side and set the coffin in the middle of the room.

"Now, one of us needs to stay here and protect you," Turpin said to Alice once they had put the burden down.

"Protect me?" she asked incredulously.

The captain nodded at the coffin in reply.

Alice rolled her eyes. "Don't be silly. It's still in its box. Go home and sleep. All of you."

The captain shook his head. "I won't hear of it. As long as the abomination is here, you should have a man guarding it. Who is going to take first watch?"

Out of habit, they all looked towards Jack. He was the most stalwart of the men, and made light of hardship. But he said nothing. He had spoken very little since the decision to bring the abomination home.

"Right," said the captain. "Private Archer it is." Archer opened his mouth to protest, stopped himself, and shut it again.

"Good lad," said the captain, clapping him on the shoulder. The other boys should have dropped our four guests off at the lockhouse. They'll probably be asleep by now. I'll send one of them along soon so you can get some rest."

The captain bid them good night and left. Jack had already walked out of the room without saying a word.

"Well," Alice said, turning to Archer, "if you must stay then you can help me get this thing open."

"Now?" Archer asked, eyeing the box nervously. "Shouldn't we wait until we have more fellows on hand? In case something goes wrong, I mean."

"Nonsense."

Suddenly they heard someone on the stairs. A moment later the captain poked his head into the room, "Alice! Under no circumstances are you to open that box!"

Her arms fell to her sides. She had already fetched her crowbar. "I see no reason to wait."

"Perhaps you don't, but there are many good reasons nevertheless. But I am too tired to teach you wisdom tonight."

"It's morning, really," she said. The sky was already beginning to brighten slightly.

"All the more reason for you to seek sleep. I will see you this evening, and then we can set you to work on this project. In the meantime, if you really can't sleep you should call on Mr. Moxley and see if there is any truth in these rumors about the princess."

Alice sighed as the captain left again.

Resigned, Archer took a chair facing the coffin and began his frequent ritual. He drew out his well-worn straight-stemmed Peterson Pipe and set to cleaning it. He spent a great deal of time on this, far more than most smokers might consider reasonable or productive. Once it was cleaned to his satisfaction, he loaded it and lit it, then set to work cleaning his rifle with the same level of care and attention. He puffed away on his pipe as he did this. The curious thing about Archer was that he never seemed to extend the same passion and diligence to the rest of his work. His uniform was never as neat as those of the other men and his boots were never as shiny. He lacked punctuality and was prone to slouching.

Alice sat down beside the casket. "Are you there, fiend?" She said this in a friendly tone.

"I have no idea where 'here' is, but yes," the box replied. The abomination's strange, otherworldly voice was muffled somewhat. "Although I would be grateful if you would call me Gilbert. Mr. Hiltman would work as well, if you're wary of sounding too familiar."

"As you like, Gilbert," she said as she leaned against his box, propping herself up on one elbow. "I am Miss White. Or Alice, if you're wary of sounding too formal. I'm afraid you're going to be sealed in there for a while longer."

"So I heard," Gilbert lamented. "Although I'd find the wait more comfortable if I had fewer questions needling me."

"If I can ease the discomfort of being bound in a box for a day by simply answering questions, I'll be happy to do so."

"Splendid," said Gilbert, sounding surprisingly cheerful. "Being bound in a box isn't nearly as painful as you'd expect. I likely would have suffocated by now if I was properly alive, but in this state I think my chief foe is boredom. At any rate, I'm very curious about what you plan to do to me."

"I'm afraid I don't quite know yet myself," Alice said, scanning the piles of books and wondering where she would begin. "There are many types of necromancy and several different ways of animating the dead, none of which are well understood. I'll need to figure out how you were revived before I can consider what might be done to reverse this. The story you tell about your companion's necklace is strange to me. I have not read anything before about vigor being held in a container. Perhaps this is new knowledge."

"I don't suppose there are scholars you might consult?" Gilbert asked hopefully.

"I must regretfully report that I am our scholar. Ethereal Affairs is the only place in Great Britain - or indeed, most of the world - where people are permitted to study sorcery. Of course, we only do this to catch sorcerers. My father was the first man to legally study the subject, and a great deal of our understanding was lost when he passed. I have been a poor substitute."

"How is it that nobody knows about how magic works?" Gilbert asked.

"For centuries the dark arts have been wholly mysterious to those that do not practice them. We have mostly the church to thank for this. Their habit of burning books along with their owners has kept us in perpetual ignorance. It wasn't until this ministry was founded that we even began to study what we were fighting. You can't see it, but this room is filled with forbidden books. Well, the left half of the room, anyway. On the right the books are more scientific in nature, and much more to my liking. I don't really enjoy magic except where it can be illuminated by science."

"Magic and science are related?" Gilbert asked dubiously.

Alice sighed. "That's much too large a subject for now. The point I was making, is that the church would slay a commoner for possessing most of the books on the left side of the room, whether they were capable of reading the work or not. Some we imported from places where laws are less strict. Others we have acquired in the course of our work. It's a daunting mountain of learning, and despite my vigorous study I've barely taken in a tithe of it. And even if I were to suddenly know all of these books, it would still be but a sip of the whole cup of forbidden knowledge."

"Another question, if you'll indulge me. You talk about this place like it was a house. Is that the case? If so, why does everyone sleep elsewhere?"

"Grayhouse used to be a proper house. Then it was given to Ethereal Affairs as a sort of headquarters, and all the rooms were converted for that purpose. The men are all on loan from Her Majesty's Service, and so they sleep at the barracks, which is a short walk from here. When I joined it was decided that I couldn't sleep at the barracks, and so a bit of the upstairs was given over for my use."

"So you live here?" the box asked curiously.

"When I'm not being dragged through graveyards and sleeping in ditches, yes. I am sorry for the lack of hospitality you've been shown."

There was a thoughtful silence. "It doesn't bother me as much as you might imagine, and I don't think you have much that could make me more comfortable than I am now. Since I was... awakened, I haven't felt the need for sleep or food, or even drink. And as I discovered last night, I don't need to breathe."

"Yes!" she said with enthusiasm. "Ever since we boxed you up I've been eager to find out what it's like to exist as an abomination. The specimens we've encountered before have been more interested in murder than science. We knew that they could not be starved, or suffocated, or throttled, or drowned, or killed with thirst. This much has been known since at least the thirteenth century, and probably long before that. But what does it feel like?"

"I'm afraid the answer is very boring," answered Gilbert. "It doesn't feel like anything at all."

"That won't do!" she scolded. "I'm sure there are lots of things to discover about you. We shall have to do some proper tests once you're out of that box. Do you remember what it was like being dead?"

There was a long silence, "You know, I hadn't realized it before, but now that you've put the question to me I do seem to have a memory. I remember a girl."

"Someone you knew in life?"

"No. I've never seen her before. Now that I think of it, the memory feels more like a dream than a recollection. I don't know. But there was a young girl. It was very vivid. Dark braided hair. Her mouth was moving, as if speaking, although I couldn't hear what she was saying. I could tell she was upset. Angry. I remember feeling afraid of her. Maybe she was scolding me? After that, I awoke in the crypt with Simon."

"Strange. I've never heard such a thing. Do you remember anything else?"

"Nothing."

She sighed, “Well, I suppose I should either go to bed or prepare for my day. I am too excited to sleep and too exhausted to stay awake.”

“You’re meeting with that Moxley fellow?” Gilbert asked.

“You are a careful listener, aren’t you?”

“Not particularly. But there’s not much else to do in here.”

“Well, Mr. Moxley is our director. The captain answers to him. He seldom takes a close interest in what we’re doing. If you meet him, do not think him to be a self-interested dandy. His demeanor is rather disarming and you might foolishly reckon him a simpleton, but he is a genius in court politics. He’s also a bloodhound for news. He has spoken for us many times among the Lords, saved us from scandal in the papers, and has often obtained the exotic supplies we needed whether we had funding for them or not.”

“I don’t expect him to visit me in here but I will be careful not to underestimate the man if he does,” Gilbert promised.

“Good. Now I hope your curiosity is satisfied, because the day calls and I must answer or retreat to bed.”

Alice ate, and brought poor Archer a bite and a bit of tea to help keep his eyes open. Then she bathed and put on proper clothes. She was anxious to escape her trousers and she needed to look like a lady if she was to meet with Mr. Moxley.

No sooner had she picked out a hat then there was a knock at the door.

“Mr. Moxley, I was coming to see you just this morning! So rarely do you visit us here in Grayhouse,” she said as she showed him in. “And for you to visit us on such a menacing day. It looks like the clouds will fall on us at any moment.” The sun had risen to little effect, and the sky was the color of charcoal.

“I do not permit it to rain while I am out,” he declared proudly. “I would not suffer to have my ruffles spoiled by something as common as the weather. And moreover, I suspect those rain-clouds are more than half smoke. If this unseemly industrialization continues the smokestacks shall blot out the sun.” He dusted his coat as he said this, but it seemed to beat the soot into the fabric rather than dislodge it.

Mr. Moxley was dressed flawlessly, and with far more care than Alice had given herself. As always, his coat had many buttons, his shoes were small and well-polished, and he carried a black cane. He was adorned with a great degree of finery, stopping perilously short of bad taste. Despite his age of fifty, he had round, boyish cheeks and long dark locks of hair resting on his head.

"Miss Alice White, you look delightful!" he bubbled. "Is that dress new?"

"A gift from my mother, for my birthday," she nodded.

Alice attempted to offer him tea, but he refused all forms of refreshment and seemed eager to chat.

They sat in the front room. Originally the sitting room, it had been converted into a storage area for unused military gear by the early members of Ethereal Affairs. Since moving in, Alice had hung or placed as many items as possible in order to create the illusion that these items were on display. This, combined with a few hunting trophies left by previous owners, gave the impression that this was the home of an extraordinarily aggressive and well-armed huntsman.

"You should more often come and visit me at court", Mr. Moxley declared, "The handsome young men would slay one another for the opportunity to speak with you."

"Then I think I should stay here, if only to preserve England's stock of handsome young men."

"Having you live in this blackened fortress is like growing a lily in a coal cellar. Certainly the young men are mistreated at being denied your face."

"Perhaps so," she said carefully, "But through my efforts they are kept safe from greater dangers than my absence."

"Quite right!" he replied, suddenly brightening. Mr. Moxley often began their talks this way, disparaging her situation until she reasserted her desire for it, at which point he would cheer up and change the subject. She never understood his purpose in this, but was always happy to play along.

"Now, it is about that very business that I called this morning," he began. "I read the most extraordinary claim in the paper recently. It made the most assuredly slanderous assertion that you had been spotted carrying a coffin into this very house."

This was how Mr. Moxley referred to gossip. He never called it rumors, but always spoke of it as if it was something he'd read recently. He even did this when the claim of having read it was patently absurd, such as now, when the rumored event was no more than a few hours old. Alice never understood this, but also never questioned the habit. It suddenly occurred to her now that acting as if the news had appeared in the paper removed the question of who had given him the news.

"Do you think many others will read that story?" she asked timidly. She was no good at politics and the art of communicating things without saying them. She wished that her father was still here, so that he could handle this sort of business and leave her to her science.

"Not yet, but soon I expect it will be read by everyone. This will lead people to begin theorizing about who was in the casket and why they hadn't been buried as is customary. Others might wonder why the body was brought indoors."

"The... body is needed for study. But not for long," she added quickly. "Just a few days."

"I see," Mr. Moxley said. He had suddenly become very hard to read. "People will be alarmed at this news." He looked at her for a few more moments and then brightened again. "But I'm sure it will be fine."

"Good."

"Provided it really is only a few days," he added. "Public curiosity is a dangerous beast to leave in the dark, and unfed."

The subject changed again, and they spoke about the other members of Ethereal Affairs, men's fashions, the unappealing thought of the oncoming winter, and the effects of industrialization. Eventually Mr. Moxley drove the conversation, as he always did, to the subject of the royal family.

"Actually," Alice said, interrupting him mid-thought, "I had a question about the royal family. About Princess Sophie in particular." For the first time in her life, she had managed to surprise Mr. Moxley. Suddenly the preening man with the vacant smile slipped away, and she caught a glimpse of the shrewd planner who had survived for decades in the gossip and intrigue of the royal court.

"Why do you ask about that?" he asked quietly.

"It relates to the case we're working on now."

"That story," Mr. Moxley said seriously, "Has not yet appeared in the papers. It's a story I'm still trying to puzzle together for myself. I should very much like to know if you have anything to contribute."

Alice sighed. "I'm not sure how to say this. I know in the past you've expressed a preference for remaining ignorant of our more unsavory work, so I don't know if you'll want me to tell you about this or not. Only that it might be connected to the princess."

"Very well," he said decisively, "I will tell you what I know - a rare privilege which I hope you do not abuse - and you can decide if your contribution is worth adding. Three days ago I became aware that something was wrong in the palace. There were no rumors, but a few people seemed more worried and tight-lipped than usual. Naturally I set to work on this at once, fearing it was some matter of politics or scandal, and I wanted to know where to position myself when the storm fell. I extended all of my ability, and came back empty. The next day I had more luck. There were rumors that Princess Sophie was late. She had been on some sort of excursion - a simple holiday no doubt - to the Isle of Wight. But she did not return on the expected date. At first this looked to be a scandal in the making. She and a boy - forgive me, his name escapes me this morning - had a mutual romantic interest, which the Queen strongly opposed. It was feared that the two had run off. A search was performed, quietly.

"The next day it was revealed that the boy was found, and not with Sophie. His alibi was beyond doubt. He had not been with her or seen her in some weeks. This is when worry of scandal transformed into worry of a more serious sort, and this is where I finally caught up with the story. It is very hard for the royal family to panic in secret. Since then there has been no news. I know that a search was performed between Buckingham and Wight, but no news has come. Indeed, another, more thorough search has been sent out, so we can conclude that nothing was found by the first one.

"This is dangerous business, Miss White. Members of the royal family don't just vanish. And now you come along, asking about young Sophie. So what of it? Are our tales related?"

"I fear they might be. Two nights ago we found an abomination in Ravenstead. Shockingly, it surrendered to us, and told us that a sorcerer had raised it, and that Sophie was involved."

"Involved?" Mr. Moxley could not hide his unease at this idea.

"Not as a perpetrator, but as a victim. A necromancer needs one life to restore another. The style and mechanics of the magic change from time to time, but the need for a living victim remains. The life of one is given to the dead."

Mr. Moxley looked down at the floor, shaking his head, "This is far worse than I might have guessed."

"But it's not as final as you might imagine. If we can recover Sophie, it may be possible to restore her to life."

"I see now. So you don't know where she is?"

"Correct. We guess that she's at the Viscount's estate in Ravenstead, but we can't be sure. And so now we're studying the magic and looking for how it might be undone."

A look of surprise suddenly flashed on Mr. Moxley's face, "Wait! You said the abomination surrendered. Are you telling me that the casket you brought-"

Alice nodded.

"And is it still... animated?"

She nodded again.

"Alice, you must understand, what you are doing is far more dangerous than chasing hedge wizards through the streets of London. If word of this gets to the church, they will want to hang you. All of you. They've never liked the idea of us fighting against magic. They saw that as their exclusive domain, and warned against it when the Ministry of Ethereal Affairs was formed. And they have greatly resented the success we've had over the years, both in fighting malignant magic and in capturing the hearts of the public. They hated your father most of all, and I'm sure you inherited that hate when he died."

"I know," she said.

"Alice, I know you imagine that I wield the power of Her Majesty the Queen, but it is not so. If the church moves against you and discovers you're housing an abomination - regardless of your intentions and the peril of young Sophie - they will hang you all, and there will be nothing I can do to stop them."

Alice nodded slowly. "It would be easy enough to destroy this abomination. It could be done this hour if we decided. It's upstairs, sealed in a casket and bound tightly. We could burn it, or even have its head if we wanted to be sure it was ruined. That would end the abomination, but it would doom Sophie as well."

Mr. Moxley let out a long, slow breath. "I don't know, Miss White. I cannot advise you. Will you risk the lives of yourself and all your fellows to save the princess? It is a terrible gamble. Just remember that for every person who knows your secret, your danger is increased tenfold."

Mr. Moxley stood. "I sense I must leave now. I must leave and not return until this dangerous business is over with. If I had known, I would not have called on you. Perhaps you will think me heartless, but I am not willing to risk my own neck in this venture. I intend to place myself far away from you, so that I can claim ignorance if the worst comes to pass. I might lose my position, but I shall be spared the sword."

"You are right, of course," Alice said, "You should not get mixed up in this. And I doubt your skills could aid us in any event. The only thing I ask is that you send word if you hear rumor of our discovery."

"That I will gladly do," he said, lightly. He was slowly restoring his mask of amusement and indifference. "If you have any other gossip for me, do remember to save it for my next visit. I can tell by your yawning that you are, regardless of your outward beauty, haggard and in need of sleep. I shall leave you to it, and see myself out. Good morning!"

Mr. Moxley strode from the room, head high. A moment later the front door opened and he cried out, "Blast it!"

"What?" Alice ran after him, wondering if danger was already come.

"It has begun raining."

Gilbert was drenched.

He'd had the coach drop him off at the edge of the estate, wanting to get to know the grounds for the first time on foot. The August sun had roasted him for this eagerness.

He mopped his forehead with his handkerchief as he lumbered up the lane with his bag slung over one shoulder. He suddenly realized that in a few months Mother would move, and the items in this bag would be the entirety of his share in the world.

To the right was a shady graveyard with a slumbering tomb at its center. Above that, at the top of the hill, was Mordaunt Manor. The manor was a dreary, darkened place, insistent on appearing gloomy even at midday. Drab trees crowded around its feet, strangling out the plants below and the sunlight above. The grounds were shabby. Long grass spilled over onto the path, and pale weeds had wormed their way into the gaps of the stonework. The hazy air had the smell of wet earth and rotting vegetation.

The path took him through a circle of four statues, which stood perhaps twenty paces from the house. Lifeless grey figures in the shape of military men huddled around the shaded walkway, looking inward.

Gilbert heard a sound behind him and turned. One of the statues was fidgeting. They were actually men, and didn't look much like statues at all. Their uniforms were dingy and colorless, but they hardly looked like stone. How could he have mistaken them like that?

He turned away from the oddity, back towards the house, and discovered a long, narrow face looking at him. The man had hollow cheeks, with dark circles under his eyes. He wore a tattered top hat. The rest of his clothes were a similar mockery of gentleman's attire, with a fine suit nearly reduced to yellow rags. His eyelids were low and squinting.

"Good morning?" Gilbert said with a slight bow. "I am Gilbert Hiltman, offering my services as agreed-"

"The Viscount Mordaunt of Ravenstead is a busy man," he said. He smiled as he said this, revealing rows of crooked, blackened teeth. "He will not be receiving you in person. You are to report to the guard house behind the manor. From there you will be directed further."

"A pleasure to meet you," Gilbert stammered untruthfully, but the man had already turned away and was returning to the house. "I'm sorry, I don't know your name, sir? What should I call you?" Gilbert called after him.

"Headmaster Graves", he said over his shoulder. The door shut with firm slam, leaving Gilbert alone.

The front door opened and shut many times. Voices gathered downstairs, although Gilbert couldn't catch what they were saying. There seemed to be some sort of argument. For a long time he worried that they had changed their minds and were simply going to have his head.

At length there were footsteps on the stairs, and then the voices seemed to gather around his coffin.

"So which will it be?" a man asked. "If it's to be fire, then we'll need to carry it outside first."

"It is not to be fire," came Alice's voice. "I merely said it was an option if things take a bad turn. It would be the safest way to resolve this without being revealed, but it should only be used as a last resort. And at any rate, mind your words. It does not sleep and can hear what we say."

There was an awkward silence. Finally the captain's voice emerged, "Your safety from that beast is my primary concern, whatever you may say about its manners. I should like some reassurance that it won't tear you to pieces as soon as my back is turned."

"Fine," said Alice with exasperation, "Here is what we will do." Her footsteps crossed the room and there was the sound of her sifting through tools or supplies of some sort. Then she crossed the room again, pausing beside his coffin. Gilbert very much wanted to simply ask what was going on, but he did not want to disturb the seemingly fragile agreement that was sparing him from fire. He hadn't even considered fire until now. Would it hurt? He suddenly felt a strong urge to escape the coffin as soon as possible.

There was the sound of scratching on the floor nearby. Irritated mutterings were heard from some of the men.

"What sort of work is this, Miss White?" This was the captain's voice. There was no answer.

The scratching sound continued, eventually migrating to the other side of the coffin.

"There," said Alice at last. "Better than chains, and less cumbersome."

"I hate this business," a voice muttered.

A moment later there were footsteps everywhere. Gilbert expected to be hoisted into the air and carried off to a fire, but instead hands began working at the seams of his prison. Light appeared through the cracks and soon the lid was pulled from his coffin.

Miss White was the first person he saw. She was standing at the foot of his coffin, arms folded, regarding him with a curious expression. This time she was dressed in what was probably fashionable lady's clothing. He might not have recognized her if not for the distinctive colorful ribbons that bound her hair.

"Abomination," she said firmly and threateningly, "I have placed magic around this coffin."

Gilbert sat up, still bound in rope, and examined the floor around him. A sorcery circle had been drawn. It was very different from the circle Simon had drawn days earlier, and much less elaborate. But it was still a work of sorcery and it made his dried skin crawl.

"This circle is a prison for you. If you set even the least of your parts outside of this circle, it will sever your connection to this world. Your spirit will flee and you will return to death, dooming young Sophie to a similar fate. Do you understand?"

"Clearly. I'm quite content in my circle, although I hope it doesn't seem ungrateful if I ask: Do I still need to be bound?"

There was more grumbling and arguing, but eventually the ropes were removed and the coffin taken away. Gilbert found himself standing adrift in the middle of the room.

It was night, and the room was alive with flickering candles. The curtains had been drawn. The door was blocked by the men, who all had weapons in their hands. On the other side of the room, looking very small and quite pleased with herself, sat Alice. She had an open book on the table in front of her, none other than Simon's book. She had another book, mostly blank, where she was making notes. It was very strange to Gilbert to see the young girl (she looked more like a young girl now that she was in proper clothes) writing about such profane business, like seeing a child readying to perform an autopsy.

As Alice had promised, there were many books about, and few of them seemed to be in English. Many looked to be linguistic crossbreeds, to the point where the author could not constrain themselves to a single tongue, even when composing the spine. They were dusty and worn, as anyone expects of piles of old books, but there was something genuinely unsettling about seeing the work of so many deviants and murderers piled up, sorted, and catalogued. Some hung open, and Gilbert was torn between the desire to shut them and revulsion at the thought of touching them at all.

The interview dragged on into the night. After some hours it became clear to the men that Gilbert was not going to pounce on Alice and devour her. They became restless and wearied of the uncanny talk. Eventually most of them retired back to the barracks. The sorcery circle, at any rate, seemed to be enough of a cage that they could leave the room without worry.

Gilbert had expected that the process would begin with strange symbols and signs and horrifying magics, but it turned out that her investigation was every bit as mind-numbing as his morbid imprisonment. She asked him many questions about what his health was likc before he died, how old he was, and if he had ever dabbled in any sort of witchcraft. The conversation impressed upon him what a completely mundane and uninteresting fellow he was, aside from his being unusually tall and deceased.

At length she left him alone and turned her attention to the book. She busied herself making tracings and copies of certain material that she found interesting. Once in a long while she would consult one of the other books in the room to find the meaning of obscure words or ideas. Gilbert had nothing to do during this time. He eventually requested a chair be brought into his circle so that he wouldn't feel so much like he was loitering. He felt like a man whose physician had abandoned him in the middle of the examination in order to finish medical school.

"So what have we learned?" Gilbert asked after an hour of listening to rain splatter against the windows and Alice's pen scratch against the paper.

She stretched and rubbed her neck, "Little. The bulk of this book - the book we found in your tomb - is a simple translation of an already-familiar book. I have another copy on the shelf behind you, although the handwriting in this one is superior and the diagrams are more carefully reproduced. Then here," she put a finger in the book, indicating a spot slightly past the halfway point, “it stops being a reproduction and matures into a work of its own. The author - who is likely Lord Mordaunt, but not for certain - has begun exploring different ways to use, extract, and store vigor. You said that your friend admitted to being capable of performing a revivification on a dog. That’s this page.” She held up the book and showed him a wheel of symbols drawn around a skull, which he assumed belonged to a dog. “Your friend’s perception of it was incomplete. The full experiment is to slay a dog, capture the vigor, and then use the vigor to revive the dog as an abomination. It’s an exercise, to test the magic before trying it on more costly subjects.”

“But to what end? What’s all this nasty business for?” Gilbert asked.

“The aim of Lord Mordaunt was, I’m sure, to become a lich, an unliving wizard. I’m sure you’ve noticed the advantage of being dead?”

“I don’t know that I would call anything I’ve experienced an advantage.”

“Well, you’ve been stabbed several times without harm. Getting stabbed with swords is a wizard’s chief fear. Particularly swords owned by the church.”

He thought back to the night he was captured, and how she had thrown fire at him. “That reminds me. How is it that a member of the Witch Watch is both a sorceress *and* a wizard?”

“Do not jostle my line of thought, it is already precariously balanced,” she said, “I will come back to that question. As I said, an unliving wizard is a lich. There have been three documented cases in history, as well as many others which may be fiction or embellished. A lich is frightfully difficult to destroy, generally requiring small armies. Many malignant wizards aspire to lichdom. Perhaps they all do. The only thing saving us from being overrun with them is that a wizard must die and trust in compatriots to revive him. Their own cowardice, isolation, and mutual treachery keeps them from attaining it. That, and it’s frightfully complicated business. I often wonder how many wizards simply off themselves and accidentally stay dead without us ever having to deal with them.”

Gilbert had heard of liches, but the stories about them were generally confused and contradictory. He had assumed they were just fictional creatures, like dragons. "So, if I had been a wizard in life, I would now be a lich?"

"Yes. It was very close. It was only their blunder of bringing back the wrong corpse that saved us from that terror."

"But what's to stop them from collecting more vigor and trying again to raise him? Assuming they find his body, I mean," Gilbert asked.

"Because they believe - incorrectly, I think - that they can only do so with royal blood. You have Sophie's vigor, and members of the royal family are generally not available for kidnapping. Now, you are determined to steer my line of thought aground. Please stop interrupting. Where was I? Yes. Not all of the Viscount's work was based on attaining lichdom. A great deal of this book is still mysterious to me. It also seems like he was being scientific about his learning."

"This is surprising?" asked Gilbert.

"Shocking, in fact. Most wizards are in a great hurry to unleash their schemes. I study magic out of curiosity, but they study it simply as a means to an end. They don't care how it works, as long as it does."

"I am sympathetic to this point of view," admitted Gilbert.

"You told me you were a soldier, so I am not surprised. How can I explain this to you? A rifle is a useful object, is it not?"

"When the alternative is waving a sword as I charge into a line of muskets, I must say I am very fond of my rifle."

"Imagine they were unknown in warfare, and you obtained one. A soldier will see it as a means to an end. He will investigate only as much as is needed to discover how to use it. When it runs out of ammunition, he will conclude that his treasure is 'broken'. Confused, he will return to his sword. But a *scientist* will study the rifle and determine how it works, and why. A scientist would rather learn how to make her own rifle, and her own ammunition. In time, she will improve upon it."

"That makes wizards sound sort of brutish and simple. I'd always imagined them as intellectuals."

"I suppose they are intellectual when compared to other sorts of villains. But Lord Mordaunt is not 'brutish', as you put it. His book is old. This was not an abrupt or hasty undertaking. No fit of passion led him to these things. I imagine he's been working on this since before I was born. His studies have been careful and thorough, and his writings contain much that is new and original. Or at least, much that does not appear in any other of our many confiscated books. His aim was clearly to become a lich, but there are many pages here that do not contribute to that purpose at all, but are simply essays in grotesque knowledge and a salve for profane curiosity."

"What about Sophie? Have you discovered a cure for her?"

She yawned. "No, I have not unwound that secret yet. And if I spend all of our time answering your questions I will never see to my own."

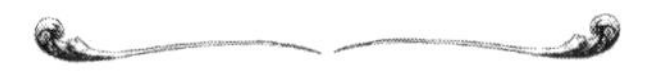

Alice sat upright with a jolt. A furious banging had awoken her, and now her mind was groping for purchase. She had apparently fallen asleep in the library, again. The candles had all expended themselves. The curtains were drawn, and fingers of daylight reached between through the gaps. Her fingers were blackened with ink.

The abomination - *Gilbert,* she reminded herself - was sitting in the middle of the room. The men had left, save for poor Archer, who had once again been chosen to guard her in the last hours of the night. But he had inadvertently abandoned his duty by falling asleep in his chair.

Another series of pounding blows came, followed by a bell. The door! Archer was startled from sleep by the sound, and military reflex compelled him to leap to attention. His rifle, which had been reclining in his lap, now clattered to the floor. He wobbled slightly and rubbed his eyes. "I'll answer it," he said blearily.

What time was it? Alice often thought she should add a clock to the room. It would make her more able to see when it was time to go to bed, and make it less confusing the next morning after she had failed to do so. But she only ever thought of it in moments like this, and forgot about it once she was fully awake.

She heard the door open downstairs, followed by the sound of something heavy being dropped. There was the sound of raised voices, which did not belong to anyone she knew.

She motioned to Gilbert to keep quiet and hurried downstairs.

"Get off!" shouted Archer as Alice reached the entryway. Two young men in shabby clothes were sitting on him. A few more were standing by, rummaging through her things. All of them wore red sashes about their waist. Those that did not bear swords were carrying rope. An old man, whose face was stern and encumbered by great hanging jowls, stood in the center of the room holding a high scepter. The scepter matched his height, and at the top was a great bronze circle with a star affixed in the center. The Church had come to visit.

"What is this?" Alice demanded. "You are all trespassing on the property of *His Royal Highness* Prince Albert, Duke of Saxony. Furthermore, this organization is under the leadership of Ethereal Affairs Minister Sir Robin Moxley, and you have no authority or right of arrest over us."

The man looked at her disdainfully and snorted, as if he believed these were the most blatant and offensive lies she could possibly have contrived. "You have named many honorable titles, but none of them are yours. I take it you are Alice White?"

"I am," she said defiantly.

"I am Hierarch Prothero. We are here seeking the unholy abomination you and your associates willfully brought into this house only yesterday. It must be destroyed."

"You have no authority," she repeated, but her voice faltered. She knew her words could not turn away this many armed and determined men.

"The church has tolerated your blasphemous collection of unholy knowledge, but you have tested God's patience one time too many, Miss White. You are a witch and a transvestite. Give over your contraband and you will be shown mercy."

Alice struggled to master her fear and anger. She saw her situation was hopeless. Archer was overpowered, she was unarmed, and their adversaries had come with tools of violence. Her only thought was that she could perhaps delay the Hierarch until other members of the watch happened to arrive, or until she could contrive an escape. "God has not expressed any impatience to me," she told him. "Perhaps you are mistaken. Perhaps you should ask again. And while you are at it, you could find someone to teach you the proper meaning of the word 'witch'."

"You are perverse," he said hotly. "And your words will be added to the charges against you."

"Perverse? I would say that an organization that murders suspects and burns evidence in the course of conducting an 'investigation' is perverse. And again, you have no right over us."

"We have the right to seek out and execute witches throughout the British Empire, which includes your *borrowed* house. A house which you have defiled by making it into a den of sorcery."

There was a great deal of noise and activity in the room. The men were treating the place roughly, searching where they pleased.

"You presume much, and with no evidence, as is your custom," Alice said. "But evidence is in small demand when the suspects are executed before they can speak for themselves. Do you intend to furnish proofs, or are your swords your only arguments?"

"The trial does not take place during the arrest, Miss White."

"Or at all, when your kind is involved," she retorted.

"You want to see the evidence? So do I." With that, Hierarch Prothero marched upstairs. "Bring her," he commanded his men.

The men grasped her and dragged her upstairs to the library, where she was deposited on the floor. She was hedged in by men with red sashes. She heard the sound of a sword being drawn.

Alice looked up, and found thc room different from how she had left it. Gilbert was not in the center of the room. Instead, one of the rugs had been taken from its proper place and placed over the sorcery circle that she had drawn. The open books had been shut. For a moment she thought he had vanished through some act of sorcery, but then she saw the coffin was once again occupied. His hands were posed on his breast.

Alice stood. She tried to move to see him more closely, but the men shoved her back. Curiously, several of her tools were around the coffin, and a small vice was clamped to Gilbert's jaw.

The red sash that had drawn his blade was standing over Gilbert. With a nod from the Hierarch, he began stabbing Gilbert in the chest. The first stroke was bold and triumphant, but when it did not provoke a response he stabbed again and again. He became frustrated and angry, finally hewing at the coffin itself in humiliation and rage. Finally he looked back to the Hierarch and shrugged.

"Is this what you came here to do, you holiness? Break into my home and defile a corpse?"

"It is wickedness to keep a body indoors like this."

"Then you should correct your wayward religion for its evil practice of holding funerals."

"A funeral is for showing reverence for the departed."

"A more obvious way of showing reverence would be to avoid mincing them with swords," she retorted, gesturing to the man standing over Gilbert's coffin and panting.

"I should very much like to know what you are doing with a corpse," Hierarch Prothero said. His arrogance had faded, and he sounded defensive now.

"Investigating, gathering evidence. I am not surprised the process looks unfamiliar to you. We do this so that we don't inflict punishment on the innocent."

"We are guided by the hand of God, who protects the innocent," he said.

“Was your corpse abuse done at His direction?”

Hierarch Prothero struck his scepter against the floor, and his men filed out. A moment later the front door slammed, and they were gone.

Alice sat on the steps and wept for several minutes as her anger and nervous energy worked their way out of her system. Downstairs, Archer picked himself up and washed his face; they had slammed him against the floor for resisting, and he had a bloody nose.

“It’s safe,” Alice said. “They’re gone now.”

As morning ran out, the captain arrived at Grayhouse with a few of the other men. They came to relieve Archer and find out how the research had progressed overnight. They were enraged when Alice explained what had happened with the church. They gathered in the library to discuss matters.

Turpin paced the room, shaking his head. “What would possess them to behave this way?”

“I’m sure they were after Gilbert,” she said. “They had news of him. The Hierarch knew exactly where to go to find him. They came directly to the library.”

“Who could have told them? Perhaps Moxley was afraid of discovery, and so gave us over?”

“Captain, they knew when to strike. They came in the morning when Archer was my only guard.” Alice did not mention that Archer had been sleeping. She was actually grateful. If he had been more awake (and if he hadn’t left his rifle upstairs) he might have tried to defend the house alone. There would have been bloodshed, and he would certainly have been killed.

“Perhaps they were watching the house?” the captain thought aloud. “But that doesn’t explain how they knew about the library.”

“Captain, when was the last time anyone saw Lieutenant Stanway?”

The captain nodded, but said nothing more. Jack hadn’t been with them since they arrived home the previous morning.

"We are lucky the church holds ignorance in such high esteem," Alice said. "If the Hierarch knew anything about the unliving, they would have taken Gilbert's head and not simply hacked away at his bones."

"Their stupidity has always been our greatest asset, even from our founding. What I don't understand was how you got out of your circle and back into your coffin." The captain said this to Gilbert.

"I walked out," Gilbert said with a shrug.

"I have a confession," said Alice timidly. "The circle I put around Gilbert was just for show. There is no such spell. Not that I know of, at any rate. But I knew everyone was terrified that he was going to run off and do some horrible thing, and this seemed like the best way to put the popular fears to rest."

"I am not pleased to find I have been the victim of deception," the captain said. "And it makes me wonder what other lies you may have built that have not been exposed."

"None that we should inventory now, I think."

"Well, your deception probably saved your life. I suppose I would rather have you breathing than sinless. But how did *he* know the circle was harmless?" At this the captain gestured towards Gilbert.

Gilbert spoke for himself, "I didn't. At least, I wasn't sure. I thought her spell seemed a bit convenient, and it also occurred to me that if such a thing existed that it would make dealing with feral unliving very easy. When the church arrived, I heard the talk downstairs, and realized things would go very badly for Alice if I was discovered. I figured that if the spell was real, the circle would kill me and they would find nothing more incriminating than a corpse. If it wasn't real, I might be able to hide her work some other way."

Alice saw that this made an impression on the men. To their shame, they had been in bed when danger struck. One of their own had betrayed them. And yet the abomination had risked its own neck to set things right and protect her. From that point on, they took Gilbert at his word and allowed him to move unhindered.

"What I don't understand," said Alice with amusement, "Is why you screwed my vice to your jaw."

"I thought there needed to be some explanation for why you had a corpse, and that the vice would make it look as if you were somehow working on me. Perhaps looking at my teeth? I don't know. I've never studied a corpse. It was at hand, and I trusted you would find an excuse if you needed one."

"Thank you, Gilbert. You are as decent and honorable a corpse as I've met."

Gilbert bowed.

"But you must let me do something about your outfit," she said, "What that man did to you is simply ghastly." Gilbert's white gown had been slashed to pieces, and the bits of him that showed through were not attractive.

One of the storage rooms upstairs held unwanted clothes. Most of it had belonged to her father, but bits of it were from other men who had been a part of Ethereal Affairs and had left things behind when they died or found other work. With great relish Alice mined these heaps, looking for items that might fit Gilbert.

The bell rang before she could lose herself in the task. Fearing the church had returned with more arguments, everyone (except for Gilbert) went downstairs when Alice answered the door.

"Mr. Moxley! I am very surprised to see you!" she cried.

"I imagine you are. I imagine most assassins are shocked when they discover their victims are still alive." Mr. Moxley had a strange, animated irritation about him this morning. He seemed to be outraged and jesting at the same time.

"Assassin? What is this silly business?" Alice demanded.

"Yes!" he replied, pointing an accusing finger at her, "An assassin. You, all of you, have waylaid me with your absurd foolishness, and if it does not lead to my death then it will be miraculous."

"Is this about the church?" Alice asked.

"The church! No. Thank God no, and may He forgive me for saying that I hope to have nothing whatsoever to do with them again. I have never met anything so bad for religion as the church."

Alice considered telling him about the altercation this morning, but thought better of it and let Mr. Moxley continue.

"Last evening! Imagine the heart-stopping shock I experienced last evening when a Member of Parliament called on me and informed me that I had thrown Sir Edward James Brooks into prison. I insisted that I had done no such thing, and would certainly remember it if I had thrown Edward into the lockhouse. This person suggested that perhaps it was done by one of my subordinates. 'No!' I insisted. I had just visited that morning and spoken with the lovely and altogether brilliant Alice White, and she had never breathed any mention of any arrest into my ear. And certainly she would not have sat with me for an entire morning without bothering to inform me that she had locked away a very powerful and influential member of parliament, tossing him into the cage with all sorts of cutthroats and lunatics. Imagine my utter, nearly fatal shock when I learned that you had done precisely that."

"Oh Mr. Moxley, I am so-"

"But!" he shouted before she could begin to devise an apology, "I learned later that this report was not accurate. It was, in fact, foolishly, madly optimistic. The truth, the real truth, which I only discovered when I arrived to release Edward, was that you had, in fact, locked him up along with a powerful industrialist, a famous general, and a well-liked judge."

Alice didn't dare say anything, but could only stand with her mouth open.

Captain Turpin came to her rescue. "See here. If you've objecting to the imprisonment, then take it up with me. It was done under my orders and I don't apologize for it."

"Then Captain," replied Moxley, "I do not pretend to know all the pressures your job might entail, but I'm afraid I must give you this order: Should the occasion ever come where you want to imprison four incredibly wealthy, powerful, and beloved men and charge them with capital witchcraft, then you should also bring with you some shred of proof, some fragment of evidence to which you might attach your outlandish and controversial charges. Barring that, I should hope you would have the decency to send one of your men to come round and shoot me, so as to spare me dealing with the aftermath."

"I can assure you, we had a bounty of reasons to arrest those men, whoever they may have been," Turpin said stoically.

"Indeed. Well I have heard their case - or as much of it as I could make out over my own terrified groveling - and I think I know enough to argue it for them. Would you like to try and convict them in my eyes before you attempt it in a court of their dear friends who all owe them favors? Go ahead. Make your case, and I will be an advocate for the accused." Mr. Moxley led them into the sitting room and placed Alice behind a small table. "You shall be our judge," he said with a bow. "You don't need to say anything at all. Just listen to our arguments with minimal interest and worry about your future career prospects should your Ladyship rule incorrectly in this case."

"Mr. Moxley," Alice said patiently, "This is absurd. I know almost nothing at all of being a justice."

"How fortunate. This will add an unexpected element of authenticity to the proceedings. Now Captain Turpin, come over here and stand opposite me. Yes. Now simply explain the arrest of these four men." Mr. Moxley made a grand gesture towards the empty couch.

Captain Turpin foundered and looked around the room in dismay.

"Come now, Captain," Mr. Moxley coached, "This will be far more difficult in a court packed with outraged friends of the accused.

"They conspired to raise a body from the dead," said the captain, gradually getting into the spirit of the thing. "The tomb of Lord Mordaunt had been sealed, and the tools to break the chains were found nearby."

"Did they? What was their role in this necromancy? Did any of them perform the magic themselves?"

"No. That was done by another, who they employed, and who is still at large."

Moxley nodded. "When I released the accused from prison, I found they had been beaten. Was that your doing?"

"Certainly not," the Turpin bristled. "That was done by the fellow who got away. Or by the abomination."

"But a moment ago you said the man was their employee, and you're claiming the abomination was created at their behest. Why is it that this supposed servant assaulted them? Doesn't it seem more likely that my clients were visiting the resting place of a dear friend on the anniversary of his death, and were set upon by grave robbers?"

Turpin was becoming visibly frustrated now. "They were on the land of the late Viscount Mordaunt. Very suspicious!"

"When Viscount Barrington Oswald Mordaunt died, his property passed to Sir Edward James Brooks, one of the accused."

"They were in league together. They were all wearing black robes!" Turpin said hotly.

Mr. Moxley sighed. "Mr. Turpin, have you ever been inside of a criminal court? A real one, I mean, and not one held in your sitting room and presided over by a girl of twenty-four."

"The court asserts, for the record, that Her Ladyship is no less than twenty-five," Alice said grandly.

"I have been to court on occasion," said the captain. "More so in your predecessor's day, when I was needed to be a witness against men accused of witchcraft."

"Do you recall how the men, particularly the judge, dressed on those occasions?" Mr. Moxley asked smugly.

"They wore... dark robes," Turpin muttered in frustration. "But see here, these robes were different! They had hoods! And it was well after midnight, so their claim of simply visiting the grave of a friend is preposterous."

"So the core of your arguments, as I understand them, is that these four powerful men should be charged with the capital offenses of trespassing on their own property, wearing the wrong robes, and staying up late?"

Turpin bowed his head in defeat before sitting down on the couch with the accused. "So what is to be done now?"

Alice wished she had a gavel so that she could end the proceedings properly. Instead she relinquished her post and sat beside the captain.

Mr. Moxley faced the large front window and watched the busy street traffic. Sooty rain fell down in icy curtains, robbing the outside world of color. It was nothing so exciting as a storm, but only a long, dull complaint of grey water that washed over all things without making anything clean. The street was overrun with laden carts driven by dirty workmen. The air was filled with the clatter of their passing over the soaked cobblestones.

"It has already been done," Moxley replied. "The men are all released, their names are cleared, and I have begged them for mercy on your behalf."

"I suppose I should thank you," the captain said bitterly.

"I suppose you should," said Moxley. "If it is of any comfort, I believe you. I'm sure the men are as guilty as you say. And I'm sure many others will come to the same conclusion when they hear the story. But since we lack the evidence to convict, all we have done is kindled their anger and rallied allies to their side."

"Allies?" asked Alice nervously.

"It is to the advantage of a Nobleman to not have friends convicted of witchcraft. Guilt tends to spill over in these sorts of cases. People will ask a man, 'How is it that you were such close friends with Sir Edward James Brooks for all these years and never knew about his sorcery? Perhaps you are one of his conspirators!' You can see how they would want to avoid that, particularly if the church gets involved. No, your charges are politically dangerous to many people, and they will treat your accusations as slanderous. Even if they secretly believe you!"

"There is one more thing," Alice said cautiously.

"Your tone of voice tells me that you are about to assail me with more bad news. I wish you wouldn't. No, that's not quite true. I would rather suffer the news than endure the agony of curiosity unquenched."

"We have betrayal within our group. In the Ministry, I mean. The church was here this morning…"

Mr. Moxley cried out at the mention of the church, "The church! Our foes are now beyond counting."

"They were here, and they knew about our prisoner. They knew exactly where to find him. They even knew what hour to strike so that they would find the house under minimal guard. It was just myself and one man. We were overpowered and the house searched."

Mr. Moxley bowed his head, "That does explain why the place is so suddenly disheveled. When I arrived, I joked that you were trying to kill me. But it seems you were courted by death yourself. I wonder how you survived."

"Through wits," she said. "There was an unexpected bounty of them on our side, and a predictable famine of them from the church. But nevertheless, one of our number told them when and where to strike."

"And I assume this Judas is still at large?"

"He is," said the captain. "Jack. Lieutenant Stanway. He has been missing since yesterday morning."

Moxley looked up at the ceiling, searching his memory. "Stanway? Is that the fellow I appointed to the group last year?"

Captain Turpin nodded. "You sent him along when Lieutenant Fisk was stabbed while chasing after those bone collectors. Nasty business."

"Yes, I remember the man. Stanway, I mean. Intense. Eager. Bit of a crusader. I thought he would make a nice counter-balance to your pragmatism. Well, it seems that this morning none of us is innocent of self-sabotage."

"I certainly don't hold you responsible for his treason," the captain said. "Jack has been loyal and eager enough since then. A bit overzealous, maybe, but I always assumed he would cool with age. I expected him to make a fine successor when I retired."

"Still, he had to understand that by sending the church to our door he was killing Miss White," Mr. Moxley said grimly.

"I suppose that's true," said Alice slowly. "I had not thought of it that way."

"Well, if he's decided to attack with gossip and secrets then he has entered my domain. I can disarm him, but not instantly. In the meantime your enemies will multiply whenever he exposes your secret. You should move your prisoner, or finish your business with it, and you should do so as soon as possible. Now that his bid with the church has gone awry, Jack will look elsewhere for allies. I will need to anticipate these and head him off, and to do that I will need to see what the papers have to say." With this he stood up and made for the door without any of his usual pleasantries. "Curse that I must endure the rain twice in as many days. I will intensify my revenge for this cruelty."

When he had gone, they retreated upstairs to find that Gilbert had seen to his own fitting. He'd managed to find clothes that were large enough to be put on. He was perhaps overdressed for their purposes, and looked like he had just arrived from a ball and not the grave. He wore a dark suit, and had found some gloves to cover his ragged hands.

Alice applauded. "Splendid! But I don't think the black robe is a good match for the rest of it."

"They are of similar color," Gilbert pointed out.

"My father was famous for such errors of fashion. I don't know why men assume that dressing one's self is simply a matter of matching hues. Items should also match in their purpose, and degrees of formality. The suit is very fine, but the cloak is tattered and singed."

Gilbert raised the hood. "Well, Lord Mordaunt has not invited us to a dinner-party. The hood will shadow my face so that I can walk about on my own."

"You look rather severe. You have an excess of black, even without the cloak," said the captain. "Too much like funeral attire."

"This seems appropriate, given my condition," said Gilbert. "Wherever I go, it's always to a funeral."

The captain frowned behind his whiskers. "This makes it safe for you to move about, I suppose. You can walk out on your own when the time comes."

"I'm glad of that. Although I have no idea where I would go," Gilbert said.

Alice sighed, "I still don't see the entire picture, but I can tell that to restore Sophie we'll need to have the two of you in the same room. Perhaps we could bring her here, but it might be better to take you to her. Provided we can find her at all, of course. She will be in some sort of state between life and death. It might not be safe to move her in that condition. Even if it is, I think that walking with you in your disguise is less likely to draw attention than hauling around an apparently lifeless girl. And I don't think we should attempt the coffin disguise again."

"I wouldn't dream of nailing her highness in a coffin," said the captain. "But I think you're right. Once you think you can reverse the spell - or whatever it is - then we should take this one to Ravenstead to try to secure the girl. Hopefully, that's where she's being kept. Normally I'd request reinforcements with a job of this importance, but I don't dare bring more soldiers along with all the sorcery that will be going on. We'd have mutiny or scandal before we managed to set things right."

"At least one more night of study, I beg you," Alice said. "I know time is pressing, but I simply don't know enough yet. If I was standing over Sophie this moment I could do nothing to save her from her predicament."

"In the meantime, we need to do something about these rumors," said the captain. "Yesterday morning the busybodies saw us bring a coffin in here, and that picture is likely pressing on their minds. We should take the coffin out."

"Not occupied, I hope?" Gilbert asked with obvious unease.

"No, we'll fill the box with something unwanted. We were given a plot of land near Tyburn for burying troublesome dead. It's fenced in and locked, so if anything did come back up it would still be caged. Seeing us bury the box will put minds to ease, and the gate will keep anyone else from investigating. Archer!"

"Sir!" yelped Archer, who hadn't really been paying attention.

"How do you feel about hauling a heavy coffin and digging a grave in the rain?" the captain demanded.

"Mercy no sir!" he whined.

"Fair enough. Guard duty for you then. Watch Miss Alice."

The captain took the other three men with him. "Curse Jack and his betrayal. Apart from all this trouble he's caused, I could use another set of hands. Archer, keep watch. And no sleeping."

Your Lordship,

I must thank you for your encouraging letter. I am always grateful to see our efforts are admired outside of the newspapers. Additionally, I must express my extreme appreciation for your constant support in Parliament these last two years. However, I must admit I find your question to be more than a little vexing. There is, in fact, no "secret" as to why Ethereal Affairs has been so successful. I have always been happy to share our knowledge in as much detail as any can stand, and yet the accusations of us having secret techniques persist. If our methods are secret, then a man shouting news from the rooftops to the indifference of everyone might be called discreet.

No doubt you are aware that before I was appointed as the director of Ethereal Affairs, I served the church. First as a lowly Red Sash, and later as a Purifier. I spent nearly a decade there, hunting down necromancers, wizards, and other practitioners of evil magics. During my tenure I advocated many reforms. I did so frequently and loudly, and eventually these debates were the cause of my departure from the order. When I came here I adopted my policies, and I believe that the success of Ethereal Affairs has vindicated my position.

Our success is due largely to two important factors:

The first is that we employ tools other than death. The church maintains that practitioners of evil should be put to death, and in this much I agree with them. Quite aside from the issue of blasphemy which so preoccupies the church, these individuals are simply too dangerous to be chained. The powers they wield make them a threat to the great and the small, the living and the dead. You may recall that I have seen to the executions of no less than a dozen of these sorts since my appointment. Please do not mistake that I am advocating leniency or clemency for dangerous sorcerers and wizards.

But not everyone arrested for crimes of magic falls into this category. In fact, many arrests are of much less threatening people. For the necromancer and for the woman caught with a forbidden book (even if she is herself illiterate and ignorant of its contents) the church has but one solution: death. In the lesser cases, death is not only unwarranted, but also counter-productive. In Ethereal Affairs, we send some to death, but others are sentenced to transportation or prison. Still others might go free. In this way we find the tongues of the arrested to be greatly loosened, as they are eager to play for one of the lesser penalties. The corpses that decorate the gates of Tyburn tell us no secrets. Our goal is to keep Her Royal Majesty and Great Britain safe, not to keep the hangman employed.

I have found that in most cases, the captured are members of some conspiracy. The collection of books and reagents is usually too large an undertaking for a single person. The most common cult is led by one or more nobles who will enlist the foolish, the ignorant, and the desperate to their cause. Only the nobility have the means and the leisure time to pursue such demanding work, but they generally do not like to risk their own necks transporting contraband and searching for illegal books.

You may notice that the church hasn't arrested or tried a noble in half a century, even though they have hung or burned more than a hundred commoners in that same time. They are ever hacking at the leaves, but rarely do they strike the branches, and never at the root.

The second "secret" of our success is that we do not burn evidence the moment it falls into our hands. By contrast, the church seems to be eager to burn their evidence in direct proportion to its usefulness to their cause.

I have in front of me four books. All of them are copies of a work written in the fifteenth century. The original author is unknown, but the book has come to be called Kutná Hora, after the city in which it was supposedly written. The original manuscript has never been found, but many copies have been made over the centuries. By comparing different versions we can see similarities and differences that tell us about where and when these copies were made. Three of the books in front of me form a clear line of succession, where changes (whether deliberate or erroneous) are propagated to later works. The fourth book is clearly of an entirely separate lineage, and we can tell that the person who produced it was fluent in Czech and barely capable of comprehending English. The translator was also fluent in Black Latin, as they made no effort to annotate any of the sorcery, which is unusual in works of this sort.

These facts give us a picture of how these books have spread over the years, a process which is still wholly mysterious to the church. Of more immediate use, these clues, along with the testimony of several captured parties, very clearly point to the presence of an additional cult somewhere in Wales, run by at least one noble who is fluent in Czech. In addition, we know that this man is either himself left-handed, or he employs a left-handed scribe. I anticipate that we will find this man before the end of the year. If we simply burned books as we found them, we would know none of these things. Not only would we not stop this man, but we would not know that he exists at all! We wouldn't know about him until his plans were ripe, at which point many might come to harm, and he might himself be a more dangerous adversary.

Again, I am not ungrateful for your advice and support. I am hopeful that someday people will stop referring to our methods as "secrets" and instead call them "ignored advice".

Sir Donovan White

Director, Ministry of Ethereal Affairs

August 11, 1876

IV

Gilbert paced around the library restlessly. It was early evening. He had been stuck in the room for over a day now, and had begun to feel the urge to move about. Alice was fully engrossed in her work, and he didn't want to speak for fear of delaying her search for answers.

The library bored him, but he did enjoy the view of the garden outside, which was both captivating and haunting. A large stone pool was filled with mossy green water. Tattered grass spilled from between every crack in the vine-wrapped stonework. Statues of angels stood guard on either side of the pool. Their arms and faces were intended to show them looking joyfully to the heavens, arms outstretched, but weather and decay had taken their toll. Their faces looked terrified and they seemed to be reaching up, begging for rescue from the vines that clutched at their heels. Gilbert thought it was a thoroughly beautiful ruin.

"Ethereal Affairs does not employ a gardener," Alice said without looking up from her work.

"It's too late for a gardener," Gilbert said, still looking out the window. "It would be more practical to hire a forester at this point."

Alice laughed. She had a playful, young laugh although she rarely allowed it to escape her lips.

"Mr. Moxley is always trying to get us to hire servants to look after the house, especially since I came to live here. But we're fearful of hiring spies from the church, or people who might be terrified of my work, or thieves. And looking for candidates is such a bother. So the positions are never filled."

"So you're not looking to hire a gardener now?"

"Are you applying for the position yourself? I shall need references," she said dryly.

"No. But I am wondering why this fellow is sneaking around in your garden," Gilbert said, nodding towards the window.

"Are you in earnest?" Alice asked, suddenly worried.

"He's hiding behind the bushes now, but I saw him slip in a moment ago. Crafty fellow. If I could blink, I might have missed him."

Archer and Alice joined him at the window. For a while they saw nothing. Then a slight movement gave the visitor away. He turned his head, clearly examining the house. He was still again for a long time, and then he suddenly darted to other bushes, closer to the house.

"I should think that white would be a bad color for an assassin to wear, but in this rain he looks like a spot of mist," Alice said.

"I saw his sword clearly enough," said Gilbert.

Archer cleared his throat nervously, "Do you think I should...?"

Alice was quiet.

"I think you should stay here," said Gilbert. "You could go out into the garden and shoot him, but the sound would bring unwanted attention. Especially if you had to shoot more than once."

"I would *not* need to shoot more than once," Archer insisted with uncharacteristic confidence.

Gilbert continued, "You could face him with a sword if you have one available, but you could end up not winning the exchange and leave Alice without a proper guard. I should go." Gilbert turned from the window and headed for the stairs.

"Don't be absurd!" Alice scolded. "You should stay in the house. You don't want to be seen!"

"I don't care if an assassin sees me. What will he do? Run away and tell the police he saw an abomination while he was trying to break into a house? Besides, if he was sent by this Jack fellow then he probably already knows about me."

"Foolishness!" she shouted down the stairs after him.

Gilbert aimed to go out and give the man a beating until he told them who he was and who sent him. Gilbert didn't fear the sword, but he did hope to find some metal object to ward off blows until he could get within punching distance. He did not want to see his new suit slashed apart. He looked around, hoping to find a fire poker or a cane. He came to the sitting room, and found it bristling with blades and guns.

He picked through the selection in amused awe. He didn't want to take anything too nice. He was going to be brawling in the rain, and didn't want to dirty a well-kept blade in the process. He found a plain sword and took it with him. He exited the house through the rear door, stepping into the rain-soaked garden.

Gilbert held the blade out as he moved cautiously. The overgrowth afforded many hiding places for the intruder. He crept from one likely spot to the next, occasionally swatting at the bushes with his sword. Finally he completed his circuit around the stone pool without finding anything. Had the intruder slipped away? Perhaps he went around the house?

Gilbert turned back to the house and saw movement above. The man had climbed the wall (Gilbert had no idea how he'd accomplished this in the cold rain) and was studying one of the library windows.

"The front door is not locked," Gilbert called up. "Perhaps if you knock you might-"

Gilbert's taunt was cut off in a flash of white clothing and silver steel. The man had jumped down, drawing his sword in mid-air. Gilbert was just fast enough to deflect the stroke before it struck his head. The attacker landed on the mossy ground behind him and lunged towards Gilbert in a storm of blows.

Gilbert had always prided himself on his sword-work. During his time in the military, he found rifles to be untrustworthy, and so invested his extra time in fencing. He was fast for a man his size and his long reach and strength gave him an amusingly unfair advantage.

But here both his skill and his reach were failing him. This fellow was furious and flawless in his swordplay. His blade carved through the air, sending arcs of raindrops outward as he darted past Gilbert's defenses.

Gilbert gave way, stumbling backward under the relentless strikes. He kept trying to establish his footing, to get himself standing upright, but every time he had nearly gained his composure the man made another play for his neck. Gilbert didn't like retreating amongst the overgrown bushes, and so he tried to move into the open. The man in white always seemed to know which way he wanted to go, and would circle around him to frustrate his movement. Gilbert felt himself being steered away from where he wanted to be. He began to get angry.

He hadn't wanted to hurt the man when this began. He just wanted some questions answered. But now he was enraged and confused. Finally he cried out and slammed his sword forward, hoping the sheer weight of the attack would knock his foe backwards. Instead, he carved at the air and stumbled forward. There was a blow at the back of his head as he tumbled face-first into the mud. He rolled over, reflexively throwing his arm in front of his face. There was a jolt, and his opponent's sword was embedded deep into the bone of his arm. The blow had been aimed at his neck.

Gilbert's hood had been thrown off, but the man didn't seem surprised to find he was fighting an abomination. Gilbert had many small cuts on his arms and thighs. If he were mortal, he would be losing a great deal of blood.

They were at a bit of an impasse. Clearly, the man somehow knew that he needed Gilbert's head to win the fight, but Gilbert was on his back. Gilbert could just curl up and deny him the target. The man certainly wouldn't come closer, or else Gilbert would be able to change this contest from fencing to wrestling. Gilbert remained on his back, holding his sword up in a futile gesture of self-defense.

Finally the man stepped back. He flicked the water from his blade and nodded for Gilbert to stand.

The man was about thirty. He had narrow, angular features. He was built like an athlete, or a dancer. He had a thin mustache and head of parted brown hair, now slicked back in the rain. He was not dressed in proper fighting clothes, but instead was wearing a fine suit and tie.

"I'm quite happy here, thank you," Gilbert said in response to the man's offer.

"Up, damn you! Beast!" the man spat. Despite their vigorous battle, the man was only slightly winded.

"I'll get up if you tell me why we're quarreling," Gilbert offered.

"I'm here to avenge my sister!" he shouted.

"Do you mean Alice? I haven't harmed her," Gilbert looked sideways and saw Alice standing in the door.

"Is he here to kill you, or me?" she called to Gilbert.

"He's here for me," Gilbert called back.

"I'm here for my sister!" the man roared.

Gilbert stood up, as agreed. "If Alice is not your sister then-" He was again silenced as the man renewed the attack.

Gilbert resumed his retreat. He moved to use one of the statues as a shield, but he was cut off before he could reach it. Then he was again driven back and ended up toppling backwards into the pool. He stood up, covered in moss and leaves.

"Sister!" said Alice suddenly. "You're talking about Sophie, aren't you? That makes you Prince Leopold!"

Archer had appeared in the door behind her, rifle ready. He lowered it as he heard this. "I don't care what he does, I'm not shooting a prince."

Gilbert waded away from the man, trying to wring some of the water out of his cloak as he did so. "Well, Price Leopold! My mother would be giddy if she knew I'd met you. Less so if she knew you were trying to kill me." He sloshed out of the pool opposite Leopold, closer to Alice. Leopold circled around after him.

"Be reasonable, man," Gilbert protested, "I didn't-"

Leopold renewed the contest once again.

Gilbert could see there was no besting the prince. Gilbert had a couple of years of fencing training, but he was facing a man who had been doing it for most of his life. Gilbert remembered his mother explaining once that Prince Albert had been noted as a fine swordsman in his day, and his son reportedly exceeded him in both passion and skill. Eventually his blade might find its mark and Gilbert would lose his head. Now that Gilbert was heavy and waterlogged, this was likely to happen sooner rather than later.

"Stop!" screamed Alice. She had thrust herself between them, arms outstretched. "Stop this foolishness!" she shouted at Gilbert.

"I'll withdraw if he does. I have no quarrel with him," Gilbert said defensively.

The prince spoke with earnest politeness. "Stand aside, Miss. I mean to destroy this abomination."

"Then you are working to ruin Sophie's chance at rescue!" Alice turned to face him. She offered a curtsy. Protocol would normally require much more formality than this when addressing a member of the royal family, but there weren't any rules dictating how one should show respect to a prince when you are against him in a sword fight. "Please, Your Highness," she said softly. "You must know we would never harm the royal family. Quite the contrary, one of our primary purposes is to protect you."

"Isn't it true that Sophie was sacrificed to bring this horror back from the dead?"

"You have been told a half-truth, Majesty. Yes, Sophie's life was used to bring back this man, but simply destroying him will not revive her. This must be done carefully, and not with a sword."

"She can be revived?" he asked skeptically.

"I can make no guarantee. We have only guesses and a warm ember of hope. That is the only reason the abomination is still walking. We would gladly ruin it otherwise."

Gilbert thought this was a rather cold-hearted way to put it, but he guessed - or hoped - that she was only doing so in order to persuade the prince.

The prince lowered his sword and looked at her intently. "I am told your father was a vigorous opponent of witches and necromancers, and loyal to my father. I have also heard that you follow in his footsteps."

"I wholeheartedly agree on all points," she said with a slight bow.

"Then *why...*" the prince asked, gesturing towards Gilbert.

"Majesty, this man is just a bystander caught up in this. He did not ask to be raised and I am sure he's never practiced magic. I'm not even sure he's literate."

"I can read!" Gilbert protested.

"Please stop waylaying my thoughts," she snapped at Gilbert. "Majesty, please understand that this abomination is not your foe."

There was a long moment as the rain washed over them. Alice was quickly becoming as waterlogged as Gilbert. He saw she was outside in her bare feet. Wasn't it a bit cold for that? He couldn't tell. He realized he hadn't found anywhere to be particularly hot or cold since he'd been awakened.

At last the prince nodded, and Alice stepped aside. "So who is our foe, if not the abomination?" he asked.

"That would be the Viscount Mordaunt," Gilbert said.

"Slander!" spat the prince with renewed anger. "Do not speak ill of Oswald!"

"The Prince Leopold, Duke of Albany is *friends* with a necromancer?" Gilbert laughed.

"Gilbert!" Alice scolded him, an instant before the prince launched a fresh offensive.

It took all of his skill just to keep the prince's sword at bay. Several times it fell perilously close to his neck. Alice stepped forward, trying to get between them again, but the prince cut her off.

"Stop this, both of you," she cried. "If either of you is harmed it will be to the ruin of us all!"

The prince was full of fury, and his attacks came more quickly than before. Gilbert told himself that this might tire the prince out more quickly, but that would be of little comfort if he lost his head waiting for it to happen. Sensing that it was time to be reckless, Gilbert deliberately struck heavy and wide while at the same moment lunged forward. Leopold parried the blow effortlessly, and then did exactly what he'd been taught to do, what he'd spent the last twenty years doing when people left themselves open as they advanced. He ran Gilbert through.

Too late he realized his error. Gilbert turned sideways, wrenching the sword out of his hand and walking away with it still buried in his chest.

Leopold stood defiantly, his hands clenched into fists. "You are wrong about the viscount. He was a good man and I will not have you speak about him so ignorantly. Perhaps you are wrong about my sister as well."

Gilbert thought to offer a cutting remark, but Alice jumped in first, "Perhaps we are wrong. I would be happy to learn the truth if you would teach it to us."

"I would gladly clear his name, but it is not permitted to speak of these things far from my family," Leopold said.

Gilbert scoffed, "Your defense of the viscount is, 'he's innocent, but it's a secret'? Only an imbecile would offer such testimony. And it would take a bigger imbecile to accept it."

The prince flared with rage. For a moment Gilbert thought their battle would become a brawl, but Alice rushed in. "Please Highness. I know this is asking a great deal, but the more we know, the better Sophie's chances are. If the viscount is not our foe, then perhaps your knowledge can lead us to him."

The prince cooled and began pacing as he spoke, "It is not widely known, but I was born a hemophiliac. I probably wouldn't have lived to adulthood. But Oswald, then only an acquaintance of the royal family, quietly offered us aid in the form of magic. I was cured within a year. He asked no favors. Refused all attempts at payment. All he wanted was to spare me from a shortened life of enfeeblement."

"Your father's campaign to legitimize benign magic suddenly becomes clear," Alice observed.

"There's more," Leopold said. "When I was a boy, Father became deathly ill. Oswald came to our rescue once again, and brought Father back to health with magic. Mother is certain we would have lost him if not for the viscount."

"Thank you, Your Highness," Alice said softly. "We will keep your secret. It will certainly change our thinking in this investigation."

Leopold nodded in reply.

Gilbert drew the sword from his chest. The sound was almost worse than the sensation. He offered it back to Leopold.

Leopold snatched the sword away. For a moment Gilbert thought he was going to begin fighting again, but he sheathed the blade. Then the prince spun around and marched off into the rain without a word.

"I wonder what he'll do now?" Alice muttered.

"Can we go back inside now?" Archer asked. "I'd like to go back in while parts of me are still dry." He had followed Alice out into the rain, and now seemed to be at a loss for what he should be doing.

"In a moment. I came out here for a reason." She slipped into the bushes near the door and began searching. Gilbert saw she was carrying a canning jar. "Oh, there's one!" she said after a few moments.

"What are you looking for?" Gilbert asked.

She held up the jar triumphantly, "A frog!"

A while later they had reconvened in the library. Alice had lit the fireplace so that they could warm themselves after being in the rain. She instructed Gilbert to stay by the fire until he was completely dry, and warned him to watch out for mold. Archer ignored his wet clothes, preferring instead to dry his rifle and smoke his pipe.

Once she'd had some tea, Alice sketched a sorcery circle onto the table, and beside this she placed her imprisoned frog.

"What's the frog for?" Archer asked.

"For magic," she said cryptically. Turning to Gilbert she explained. "Yesterday you asked about my being a wizard. I know it seems strange, that wizard hunters should employ a wizard of their own."

"Does the church know?" Gilbert asked.

"Do not skip ahead," she scolded. "My father was the leader of Ethereal Affairs at its inception. At the time, he filled the duties of Mr. Moxley, the captain, and myself. He was the director, he led the men in battle, and he was the chief scholar. He was, I must insist, an altogether brilliant man."

"He would only need to be half as clever as you to accomplish that."

"When you died, the world was deprived of a skillful flatterer. A pity your sword was not as deft as your tongue."

"You would have preferred that I run the prince through?"

"No," she admitted thoughtfully, "I suppose in this case your ineptitude worked in our favor. But you have sidetracked me again! Where was I? My father. Yes, when we discovered that I had the 'curse' of wizardry, he moved to make it so that I would be placed in the custody of the ministry. He argued that it would be advantageous to study a wizard that wasn't harmful, and also that it would be good to have me here for observation to make sure I did not become so. In truth, I'm sure he was only trying to save my life. I was never the subject of any strenuous study, at any rate. When he died, I was the only other person who understood anything of the sorcery books and the only one who could read Black Latin. If they got rid of me, well... they would have needed to start over altogether. Since I was not apparently harmful, I remained in the care of the ministry. At first I stayed here and studied, but last year they began taking me along for 'field work'. Now, to answer your question: No, the church does *not* know about my ability. Very few people outside of the ministry know of it. And if it were found out, it would be no less scandalous than discovering we were sheltering an abomination. This house is now *packed* with hazardous secrets."

"And a frog," Gilbert said, nodding towards their new companion.

"Yes, the frog. I think I've unraveled a bit more of Lord Mordaunt's book. A lot of it seems to be related to feeding wizards."

Gilbert looked at her slender frame. If not for her clothes, an observer might assume she was destitute. "So it's a cookbook, then?"

"I'm not talking about food, of course. I'm talking about magic. Wizards are limited in how much magic they can perform. As they use their power, their bodies grow feeble and they become faint. There is a reason wizards are famous for being thin, and it is not because they become so involved with their work that they forget to eat, as some assume. Performing magic drains the body. Observe."

Alice held out her hand and a flash of fire erupted from it. She paused, took a deep breath, and did it again. This time she was blinking and seemed to be breathing heavily. "Quite exhausting," she said, sitting down. She waited a few moments and stood again. "One more," she said. Again the room was lit with a brilliant red light.

She sat down suddenly. Sweat was now rolling down her face, and she was panting. "That's the last one I dare attempt on my own. I would surely faint if I tried another. But give me a moment."

Once she caught her breath she stood again. She took the frog and placed it at the center of the circle she'd drawn earlier. "I've placed our new friend here in a sorcery circle like the one in Lord Mordaunt's book, only I've altered the inscription to replace his name with my own. A 'feeding circle', this is called. Now we will see." She looked towards Archer. "If I should pass out, don't panic. Just bring me some water and wait. I'll wake up again on my own."

Archer nodded and made every effort to conceal his terror at the proceedings.

Again fire appeared, only this time the plume was far larger and brighter. Gilbert could feel the heat of it from across the room. She giggled. "Oh my! This is wonderful!"

"You're not feeling faint?" Gilbert asked.

"No! It's effortless! It's as easy as drawing breath!" She held her hand out and another blossom of flame roared from her palm. The air in the room churned with the heat. A few nearby pages caught fire. Archer ran forward and beat out the flames. She gestured with her hands, and water droplets filled the air, dousing the fire.

"Oh my," she said. "I will have to be more cautious, unless I want to incinerate the library. It's so much stronger now." She followed this with a few small, playful puffs of fire. "Oh! I am feeling tired again." She stumbled back, blinking and breathing heavy.

Alice lifted the jar from the sorcery circle, "Oh, I'm so sorry, frog." She turned the jar over and the frog fell onto the table, lifeless. It was dry and withered, like a November leaf. She looked at the other two, apparently awaiting some response.

"I don't understand," Archer said at last.

She sighed. "Lord Mordaunt seems to have found, or discovered, this feeding circle technique. He can place someone in such a circle and then cast magic without regard to the limits of his own strength. At least, until the victim is used up."

The sun gave up, having never properly risen in the first place, allowing the city to change from grey to black. Eventually the men returned, cold to their bones and with aching backs. They had successfully buried Gilbert's coffin, and were happy to report they had a respectable audience while doing so. Whatever rumors were being said about the events in Grayhouse, this would, it was hoped, throw them into doubt.

Alice reported on what had happened with the prince, and the fruits of her research.

"I don't like this news with the prince," the captain said gravely. "I don't think we can continue to wait for you to discover the secret to rescuing Sophie. Sooner or later, Lieutenant Stanway is going to rouse someone dangerous. We can't just sit here while our enemies multiply."

Alice looked sideways towards Gilbert, and then back to the captain. "Are you suggesting that we give up?"

"No. I am saying that we need proof. It will be much easier for our cause if we can show the princess. Right now we have nothing, and if anyone storms the house we have only our word to explain what we're trying to do. If Sophie were in our custody, our case would be much stronger."

"You're thinking we should assail Ravenstead and look for her?"

"If we don't find her, we should at least find some more books or clues regarding her whereabouts. At the very least, we should find some proofs regarding the Four Horseman. I do feel bad about the mess we created for Mr. Moxley, and I'd like to make things right." He turned to the men, "Get some food and some sleep," he ordered. "Tomorrow we head for Ravenstead."

Ravenstead was a miserable disappointment.

Gilbert had expected to join a proud company of men dedicated to guarding the life and property of an English nobleman. The information and credentials demanded of him suggested that the viscount was highly selective in choosing his personal guards. Gilbert anticipated clean quarters, quality uniforms, rigorous discipline, orderly behavior, and the chance to forgo all of it when on leave. In short, it would be everything he loved about the military without any messy politics.

The men lived in a disused stable. None of them had bothered to properly convert the building for its new purpose, much less paint or repair. The bedding was in tatters. There was a single bathtub available on one side of the room, which was filled with dust. The food was dreadful, even by military standards. About the only acceptable aspect of their provisions were the uniforms they were given. These were plain, but serviceable. They were marked with the crest of their master, but otherwise unadorned and lacking in any form of insignia or rank.

The men themselves were uncouth, unruly, and unkempt. Many were in poor fitness, being either underfed or (more commonly) overweight. One of the men had a prominent "D" tattooed under his left arm, marking him a deserter. Others had brandings or marks that singled them out as criminals of one sort or another.

Gilbert was greeted with lewd comments and wolf whistles when he arrived. The men made sport of his (British Army) uniform and his neat appearance. “The prettiest lady we’ve seen in a month!” shouted one of them. Gilbert was obliged to give the man a beating for this, which ended their taunts without earning him any friends.

The men were led by Graves, who was inexplicably referred to as “Headmaster”. The man clearly had no knowledge of military organization, leadership, or discipline. He was both cruel and disinterested. He rarely corrected the men for their wayward behavior, and when he did his punishments frequently exceeded the crime and usually fell on the least deserving. He never bothered to learn the names of his men, but instead referred to them using names of his own devising. One was called “BC”, after the tattoo on his hand. (Which stood for “bad character”, a tattoo given to the worst sort of malefactors in the military.) Another he called “bald top” and another was named “toothless”. Another was “one-eye”. More than one man answered to “Plump”. Gilbert was named “Maypole”.

Their duties were simple and to Gilbert’s liking. Two men stood watch inside the front doors and another at the back door. Another walked the grounds. Four more stood along the path leading up to the main entrance. Gilbert noticed that his experience on the path was not unique. Everyone who came to the front door ignored these guards as if they did not exist. If one of the men stirred or made a noise it would startle and unsettle the visitor who had mistaken them for statues. Was it their grey uniforms? A trick of the light? Did the foreboding appearance of the house distract them? It was impossible to tell, but it was uncanny how visitors would be confused by the illusion. The men usually made a point to cough or greet a visitor once they passed, just to see them jump.

Headmaster Graves rarely took interest in what went on at the barracks, which everyone still called stables. He was a grotesque man, fond of cruel jokes and cutting remarks. The misery of others was the only thing that could make him reveal his twisted smile of slate-colored teeth. The men called him “tatters” when he wasn’t around, after the condition of his once-fine clothing.

Gilbert briefly considered going back to Rothersby, but he wasn’t fond of giving up and was even less fond of what Mother would say when he explained the ridiculous circumstance of his new job. He couldn’t help but think that this really could be the position he’d dreamed of, if only they had a proper leader to whip the men into shape. They had more than enough manpower to fix everything that was wrong with the place. They just needed leadership.

This planted the seed of an idea in his mind. Perhaps he could be that leader. Headmaster hated dealing with the men and had other, more mysterious concerns that dominated his attention. Perhaps Gilbert could take command of the men? It should be a simple matter to make his case. He only needed to distinguish himself in the eyes of the viscount.

The carts rumbled up the lane towards the Mordaunt estate - or whatever it was called now. A mist hung over the land and their lanterns were barely able to penetrate the darkness around them. All of the members of The Ministry of Ethereal Affairs were here, save for Lord Moxley and Jack. The captain rode in the lead cart, along with Alice and Gilbert. The rest of the men rode in the rear cart.

Gilbert was left unchained when they departed Grayhouse earlier in the day. Gilbert was still their prisoner and proper protocol demanded that he be restrained in transit, no matter how pliant he seemed. At the same time, the captain did not like the idea of leading a chained man out of the house in front of the eyes of the public. It would only renew the speculation they had attempted to bury the day before. After some debate, they decided the danger of scrutiny was greater than the danger of having Gilbert run wild.

Gilbert had kept to himself for the journey. If everything went according to plan, they would recover the missing princess and he would return to the grave so that she could leave it. He should be feeling like a man on the way to his own execution, but he was strangely at peace with the idea. He hadn't felt truly alive since he was awakened so it didn't really feel like he was facing death now. The idea of someone taking off his head and leaving him helpless terrified him far more than thoughts of returning to death.

The captain called the company to a halt.

"Remember our purpose," he said to the group. "First and foremost, we're here looking for signs of Princess Sophie. Barring that, we'd like to collect a few of the malefactors who might know where she is."

The men seemed content with this. A few patted their rifles, eager to put them to use.

"But this house is now owned by a Member of Parliament. We can't simply storm the manor and expect to walk away unscathed. The place might be guarded. In any case, if we do harm to the property or the inhabitants without finding evidence of witchcraft, it will be to our ruin. We need to use our heads. Keep your rifles down and your mouths shut unless I say otherwise."

The men nodded reluctantly at this.

"Miss White, keep an eye on your device."

"I've put both eyes to the task already," she said without looking up.

"Proceed," the captain said. The carts moved forward.

Galloping was heard on the road. The men braced themselves, and would have drawn their weapons if the captain hadn't steadied them. Riders could be seen in the shapeless dark ahead. There was a rush of sound as they passed, and for a moment they were revealed in the lamplight. Gilbert saw three men on horseback. The leader smiled at him, revealing two rows of blackened teeth as he clutched his tattered top hat to his head. They passed in a cloud of dust and vapor, and the road fell quiet again.

The carts turned up the lane and approached the manor.

"Stop!" Alice commanded.

"Spellcraft?" Captain Turpin asked guardedly.

“Perhaps,” she said slowly at she regarded the contraption on her forearm. “It’s difficult to say. The movement is very slight. It’s coming from...” she turned her body, orienting herself according to the gauge on her arm, “...there!” She pointed directly at the tomb where Gilbert had found himself three nights earlier.

“Could this be leftover from the necromancy?” the Captain asked.

“I don’t know,” she admitted. “But I must investigate.” She jumped out of the cart.

“Archer,” the captain said, nodding towards Alice.

“Why me?” he protested. He looked longingly at the house, perhaps thinking of the promise of action. He tried to say more, but his fellows lifted him up and dropped him out of the cart. They watched as Alice and Private Archer crossed the shrouded field to the tomb, and vanished from sight. The group was down to only a few now. The captain rode in the lead cart along with the driver and Gilbert. Two men remained in the rear cart.

“I wish Lieutenant Jack hadn’t turned on us like this,” the Captain muttered to himself.

The carts moved forward more slowly this time. The eyes of the men strained to see the road ahead. It was not a particularly dark night, and the fog was not especially thick, but together these frustrated their vision. Even when they were close enough and there was enough light that they ought to be able to see plainly, objects seemed to refuse to take shape. The men looked at each other nervously, but said nothing.

Figures loomed on either side of the path. Gilbert saw statues flanking them, carved in the shape of military men. Memories stirred in his mind. He struggled with them, as if trying to remember a dream. A sense of unease gripped him. He knew this place. He’d stood here himself, once. Beside these statues? No. Near them? Why couldn’t he make sense of this memory?

Realization gripped him and he sat upright, “Stop!” he screamed. “Don’t go between the statues!”

The men took their eyes off the mists around them and turned towards Gilbert. Suddenly the illusion was shattered. The gray-clad guards had already drawn their rifles and taken aim. The men cried out, confused to find themselves suddenly surrounded. There was a roar of gunfire, and Gilbert found he was the only person in either cart who was still upright.

The captain lay on his back, bleeding from a grievous wound along his collar. Gilbert reached down and grasped the man's sword. The captain clenched the hilt and looked at Gilbert in dismay.

"Betrayal?" he asked.

"Doing my duty," Gilbert replied.

Then the captain understood that Gilbert wasn't turning on him, but defending him. Their eyes met for a moment. The captain nodded, and relinquished the weapon.

Gilbert drew out the sword as another volley of gunfire rang out. The four guards had surrounded the carts, and their rifles were intent on finishing off the members of the Witch Watch. Nobody had taken aim at him. He jumped down, landing on one of the attackers. He swatted the rifle away and gripped the man's neck in his left hand. With his right, he drew back his sword to run him through.

"Gilbert!" a voice cried out.

Gilbert held, and turned to the voice. Simon stood on the front steps of the manor, holding a candle. "Gilbert," he said again. "Don't do it. You'll only make things worse for yourself."

Gilbert stared at Simon in disbelief, unsure of what to do next. He wasn't sure how Simon had come here, or what his purpose was. He wasn't even sure if Simon's statement was a threat or a warning.

The man beneath him was flailing around, trying to free his neck from Gilbert's vice. Gilbert struck him in the forehead to stun him, and then stilled him with a blow to the side of the head. The other guards had gathered around him and were threatening him with their rifles. He ignored them and spoke to the boy. "What are you doing here, Simon?"

Simon's voice shook as he spoke. "Lord Mordaunt, Viscount of

Ravenstead, demands your presence." He opened the door, beckoning Gilbert to come inside.

Gilbert looked in the cart, trying to see if the captain was still breathing. "I'm going to see to my companions," he growled.

A rifle sounded. One of the guards had shot Captain Turpin again as Gilbert approached him. They began snickering.

"Stop that!" Simon said to the guards. "This one isn't under command of the master, and if you provoke it you'll have to deal with the consequences yourself." Their laughter was silenced, but they continued smirking like mischievous schoolboys.

"Please Gilbert," Simon begged, "Your companions are gone, you can't help them. Don't keep the master waiting, and he might be merciful. At least hear what he has to say before you do anything rash."

Gilbert weighed things in his mind. Was the viscount revived? If he took revenge on these guards, the viscount might run off before he could be brought to justice. If these men were foolish enough to let him in to see their master, then Gilbert decided that it would be more sensible to start at the top and work his way down. These guards weren't likely to go anywhere anytime soon. If they did leave, Gilbert thought he could remember where the barracks was. Wasn't it near the stables? No, it *was* the stables! It was coming back to him, slowly.

"Lead on," he said to Simon.

"Leave your sword," one of the guards barked.

"Only if you plan to keep it in your guts," Gilbert said, waving the tip at the man's midsection. They stood aside, and Gilbert followed Simon into the house.

They entered a grand room with an imposing Imperial staircase. Candles flickered in the corners, struggling hopelessly to illuminate the vast space. Gilbert looked up at the balcony overhead and a sudden deluge of recollection washed over him. He saw the room in daylight. He was standing on the second floor, looking down on a commotion of some sort. He was dressed in white. Everything seemed to be moving slowly. Someone was standing at the center of the room below. Who was it?

"Gilbert? This way," Simon said, leading him through a broad archway. They passed through a hall of statues. Gilbert smacked one of them with the side of his blade to make sure they were truly made of stone. It rang with the blow. It was actually bronze.

Simon spun around in terror at the sound, and then laughed nervously when he saw what it was. "You scared me half to death!" he gasped.

"What are you doing here?" Gilbert asked again. "I threw myself into the arms of the Witch Watch to give you the opportunity to escape. Why did you come back here to this evil place?"

Simon's shoulders fell, and he seemed to tremble a bit. "I am so sorry. I didn't want to come back here, but I didn't know what else to do. I've been a prisoner of the viscount for almost as long as I can remember. I don't know my way around the outside world. I was all alone, lost, chased by the Witch Watch, with an empty belly."

"You might have begged for food," Gilbert said.

"And I might have been turned over to the Witch Watch and executed for my trouble. Please understand. I hate this life. And I hate disappointing you, especially after all you tried to do for me. But this is all I know."

"You just need a bit of courage," Gilbert suggested. "Turn on him. He might bite, but you'll see his teeth aren't as sharp as they seem. And if they are? What value is there in a life of jumping at shadows and doing evil for some monster? You don't have much to lose, and everything to gain."

Simon shook his head. "You'll see when you meet the viscount. He is a nightmare, and not to be underestimated."

"Get on with it, then," Gilbert said. "Let's see if his teeth are sharp enough to hurt the dead."

Simon brought him into the drawing room. On the far wall was a great painting, a portrait of Barrington Oswald Mordaunt. Gilbert recognized him when he saw it, although the picture looked perhaps more vigorous and had more hair than the man hiding in Gilbert's memories. Beneath the painting was a roaring fireplace, washing the room in angry orange light. Chalk symbols had been scrawled onto the floor all around this.

The room was nearly empty. There were no couches, no chairs, no rugs, no other art hung on the walls. There was a small pedestal in front of the fire, on top of which had been set a large silver bowl. Beside the pedestal was an old man - another one of Mordaunt's craven servants. He had narrow eyes and a pale, yellowing complexion, like spoiled milk. He had long twisted fingers, and held a knife in one hand. Gilbert could vaguely remember that the man was called "Steward", but he couldn't recall if that was his name, or position.

"You don't offer your guest a chair? Seems rather rude, don't you think?" Gilbert said to the man.

"You are not permitted to sit in the presence of Lord Mordaunt," Steward replied. He spoke in a long, rolling manner that suggested the listener was witless and slow. "You must either stand out of respect... or kneel."

"I will stand in *dis*respect. Let's see if he can tell the difference."

The man stooped and lifted a large pitcher from beside the fireplace. He used this to fill the silver bowl. He took a vial out of his pocket and sprinkled some powder into the water, which began to hiss as he muttered something incomprehensible. Then he lifted his knife. Thinking the man was planning violence, Gilbert lifted his sword. For a moment the two men faced each other - the tall and imposing Gilbert with his sword, the withered Steward with his kitchen knife.

Steward held up his opposing hand, and slashed it across the palm. He clenched the wounded hand into a fist, and squeezed the blood into the bowl. The fire was suddenly invigorated, and the waves of heat rolled outward. The room turned red. The surface of the water bubbled and churned as if it was boiling. Out of the sound came a vibration that became a voice.

"Mister Hiltman," chided the voice. "You have caused me a great deal of trouble." Although he was sure he had only heard it a few times in his life, Gilbert knew that this was unmistakably the voice of the viscount.

"Purely by accident," Gilbert replied. "Although rest assured that any trouble I cause from now on will be deliberate."

"Full of swagger, aren't you? Mister Hiltman, your insolence is childish and counter-productive."

Gilbert addressed the painting. He didn't like looking up at the viscount towering over them, but it felt more natural than conversing with a bowl. "What can I do for your Lordship?" he asked mockingly.

"You have something that belongs to me," Mordaunt replied in a threatening voice.

"The cloak?" Gilbert held up a corner of his ragged, half-burned garb. "I only borrowed it out of necessity. After I put your degenerate guards to the sword and burn down your house, I'll be happy to return it by adding it to the fire."

"The vigor!" Mordaunt said impatiently. "It's *mine.*"

"Actually, if the gossip is true then it belongs to Sophie, and I plan to give it back to her, right after I take revenge on your household."

"Please Gilbert!" Simon pleaded softly. "Do not provoke him."

"I did not give you leave to speak, mouse," the viscount said. "You haven't yet been punished for your part in this foolishness."

Simon bowed his head and kept quiet.

"Mr. Hiltman. I did not bring one of my own employees into my house in order to haggle for my own property. You are interfering with a plan set in motion before you were born. Your obstinacy works to the disadvantage of Great Britain herself."

"Employee? I remember working for you, but I don't remember being paid. In which case I am not your employee, but a man you have robbed."

"Surrender the vigor."

"Shall we fight over it? I see you've forgotten to bring a sword. And arms to hold one." Gilbert assumed a fencing stance, "You may begin when ready."

Mordaunt spoke again, but his voice sounded far weaker and more distant, "Why is the bowl running low? Do I need to send one of the guards to help?"

"No master!" cried Steward fearfully. He slashed himself again, renewing the flow. He squeezed the wound furiously, pouring fresh blood into the bowl.

Mordaunt's voice returned. "Now Mr. Hiltman. Be reasonable. This is not your business. Your life is ended. If you continue to run around in the wide world as an abomination, sooner or later you will be caught and destroyed. Sophie's sacrifice will go to waste. Only I have the knowledge and opportunity to make use of the vigor. Surrender it, and your body will be laid to rest with proper respect, as a man who has been faithful in his duties."

"Your Lordship. The only thing I have for you is the end of my sword," He moved towards Steward.

"Master! Help!" Steward said in fear.

Gilbert felt his body go numb. The room spun, and as he headed for the floor the last thing he saw was the sorcery circle into which he had stepped. There were many strange shapes drawn on the floor, and the circle had been camouflaged amongst the ugly scrawlings. There was a clatter as he landed, although he couldn't feel the impact.

"Turn him over, mouse," said the viscount. "I want him looking up in respect when I pronounce his sentence."

His view shifted, and he found himself looking up at the painting. He felt nothing. He couldn't move, or even speak.

"Did you think I brought you here so that I could beg for my own possessions?" the viscount asked coldly. "Did you think to make me grovel in my own house? I did not pass into death only to be outwitted by a blundering soldier. Did your time in the void blot out how you came into my service? Did you forget how you told my men of your history, and of your family relations? I cared nothing for your credentials and qualifications as a soldier. I only needed to know where to strike if you chose to betray me."

Gilbert felt himself becoming drowsy. The sound of the room seemed to come from a remote distance, and his view of the world was slowly darkening.

"You remember Headmaster Graves? He's on his way to visit Victoria Hiltman as we speak. Perhaps you passed him on your way here. I was going to spare her if you surrendered the vigor willingly. But since you thought you would slaughter my staff and burn down my house, I will repay in kind. Your words have earned her death in agony, after which your house will be reduced to cinders. Normally justice would require that I punish you directly, but that is not possible in your case, so Victoria must suffer in your stead. Now, leave this world knowing what reward your arrogance has brought your mother." The room echoed with the booming of his voice.

Simon entered his view. The boy looked down on him in sadness.

"Now, mouse," the master commanded. "Retrieve the vigor and bring it to my chamber at once. Then all will be forgiven."

Gilbert watched helplessly as Simon removed his crystal necklace. "I'm sorry," he muttered as he wiped his nose on his sleeve. Then he reached out and held the necklace overhead. Light poured from Gilbert's body. Dots of light, no bigger than motes of dust, gathered like a cloud of fireflies. They swirled like a vapor and flowed into the crystal, which began to glow brightly. Gilbert's vision grew dimmer still, and soon the light of the crystal was the only thing he could see, like the flicker of a distant star.

Gilbert walked along the line of trees, past the orchard and the barn, heading for home. Before he could reach the door, he found himself facing a young girl with dark braids. Her back was to him, yet he somehow knew what she would look like, even before she turned around. Her face was innocent, yet serious. He felt a sort of kinship with her.

Her mouth moved quickly and soundlessly, like watching someone pray the rosary. She was disappointed. Somehow he apologized without speaking. She understood. Her mouth continued moving, and for a moment Gilbert almost thought he could hear her, as if they were drawing nearer. He felt like he was immersed in water, and all sounds seemed deep and remote. She smiled. Not happy, but accepting. He wanted to know what had happened, or how he had failed. Her lips stopped moving.

They were pulled away from each other, and she vanished.

"Fool! What have you done! Blood! You will pay in blood! You will never eat again!" Lord Mordaunt's voice boomed through the room, abruptly sounding very near. Everything flashed into view, like a sudden flame in a dark room. Gilbert could feel the cold marble beneath him, and was surprised to find that he was drenched. Simon was standing over him, holding an empty pitcher.

Steward slashed at the boy with his knife. Simon ducked, and the blade knocked the hat off his head. Gilbert struggled to his feet. He grabbed Steward from behind, lifting him into the air and throwing him down again. Steward lashed out with his knife, and Gilbert ran him through.

The fireplace roared and Mordaunt cursed them with threats and evil words.

"Thank you for your hospitality, your lordship," Gilbert said with a bow. "But you should get back to being dead. Take comfort in the fact that I'm about to send some of your servants to keep you company," Gilbert grabbed the silver bowl and tossed it into the fire, which silenced the screams. Looking down, he saw that Simon had dumped the pitcher of water onto the floor, which had erased the chalk lines of sorcery.

Simon was standing nearby, breathing quickly and looking at Gilbert's sword. He swallowed hard and nervously met Gilbert's eyes. Gilbert grabbed the boy and pulled him into a hug. "I told you courage would taste good once you had a drink!"

Gilbert scooped up Simon's hat and planted it on his head.

"Thank you, but I'm not sure it was courage. It was just one fear overcoming another. When I heard what he planned to do to your mother, I..." he looked up at Gilbert and choked, "I never knew my mother, you see."

Gilbert clapped him on the shoulder. "You did the right thing, and that's what's important. But it will all be for nothing if we can't catch Headmaster Graves and his men. I don't know how we'll overcome their head start."

"We? You're taking me with you this time?" Simon asked with some relief.

"It wouldn't be right to leave you here." Gilbert replied.

"Miss White?"

Alice looked up from her notebook. "Private Archer? I asked you to guard the entrance!"

Archer looked down at the floor. "What happened here?" he asked in wonder.

Alice looked at the muddy footprints and fresh chalk lines on the floor, "This is where Gilbert was revived a few days ago. More sorcery has been done since then, but this mud has obfuscated it."

"I heard gunshots outside," Archer said.

They were in the last chamber of the Mordaunt family tomb. The door to the chamber had been shut and locked when she arrived. The lock she had easily picked; the device was quite old and primitive. Besides this, there was no other protection on the room - no magic, no traps, and no guards.

"Gunshots?" Alice said nervously. "Close? In our direction?"

"No Miss. Near the manor."

"Well, it's unfortunate. I know the captain was hoping we wouldn't have to hurt anyone. I don't think we need to worry, though. This sorcery here is proof enough to justify any level of violence on our part."

"I don't think it was our rifles I heard."

Alice looked up, "How can you be sure?"

"I heard four shots, close together. Then a pause. Then four more. We only have two rifles at the manor."

"The captain has his sidearm," she reminded him. "And you might have miscounted."

"I'm sure I didn't miscount. And I can tell the difference between a rifle and a revolver."

She looked towards the door, then down at the sorcery, then to her notebook. "I must finish making a copy of this circle. I've never seen this before. After that we'll go and investigate things ourselves."

Alice worked as quickly as she could.

"This circle is unlike the one I saw a few nights ago," she said, speaking her thoughts aloud. "The handwriting is much messier. Lots of erasing. The circle is almost egg-shaped. I'm surprised it worked at all."

"Egg shapes are bad?" Archer asked with genuine curiosity. He had stopped in the doorway, but was leaning into the room to get a better look.

Alice waved her hand to shoo him out of the room. "Anything that's not a circle is bad," she replied. "The important thing is that the person who made this circle is not the same person that revived Gilbert. We have at least two sorcerers to catch."

Alice completed her copy and they made their way out of the tomb. She snuffed out her lantern and drew in a deep breath before they stepped outside.

The night air was clammy and cold, filled with the smell of deep autumn. Even though it was early October, the surrounding trees had already turned brown and begun shedding their leaves.

"Also, there's this," Archer said, pointing off into the darkness at the edge of the graveyard. "It looks like a new grave has been dug over there."

Alice crept over to investigate the uneven earth. She crouched and stared intently at the hole. "It's far too wide to be a grave, and too shallow," she whispered. She chewed her lip thoughtfully for a moment. "Unless it's a mass grave. I wonder who they intend to bury here? Oh, but I wish we had just a little more light!"

"We could use the lantern."

Alice looked up towards the house, where dim light escaped the windows. "I don't dare. If someone inside were to look out, they would spot us. Even a candle would be like a beacon in this darkness."

She decided that they should investigate the business at the house. If things proved safe, they could always come back here and investigate this site properly. They moved slowly, walking part way around the house so as to avoid approaching the main entrance. At length they reached the side of the house, and peeked around the corner.

"Looks like two guards prowling around, going through our carts," Archer said.

"Four guards," Alice corrected him. "The two at the carts, and two more guarding the lane."

"So there are! I mistook the other two for statues."

"Then I fear for your eyesight," she said. "They are very animated. I should think they are drunk. But where is our captain? And the others? Surely they wouldn't allow the guards to ransack-"

At that moment, the guards hauled up a body from out of the cart, and threw it down onto the ground with a dreadful thud.

Alice gasped. "No!"

The men continued to rummage through the carts, occasionally showing off spoils and laughing. After a few minutes it became clear that they were not drunk, but simply loud and undisciplined.

"They haven't spotted us," Archer said meekly.

"Are you suggesting we run off?"

"No," he said uneasily. "Well, yes. You should run away, at any rate. Our job was to protect you, and that means not sending you into fights where we're outnumbered like this."

"Your job isn't to protect me only, but the royal family first, Great Britain second, and myself last. And sending me off into the darkness on foot without supplies or provisions while you martyr yourself in a hopeless fight is a dreadful way of protecting me. No, we must at least recover our horses." Alice pulled her hair away from her face and bound it behind her head, "We're going to need to fight these men, and we're more likely to succeed together."

"With respect, Miss. You don't have much in the way of training for warfare."

"If by 'not much' you mean, 'none', then you are right. But these men don't look like they've had much more. We will have to take our chances. They don't know we're here. Let's assail them from different sides, and hope for the best."

Archer gripped his rifle and nodded. "Good luck, Miss."

Alice snuck around to the other side of the carts, staying far away from the lantern light. She was careful to move while the men were talking, which was often. Finally she crouched in the hedges near the two men standing watch. A minute or two passed. She couldn't see what the other men were doing from her vantage point, but she hoped Archer was simply waiting for an opportune moment.

She considered withdrawing to find out what was delaying Archer. Then she realized that they hadn't decided which of them should strike first. They were each waiting for the other.

There came a sound from the house. Someone was screaming for help. It was the voice of a man. It was cut short. Then there was the sound of a great scuffle, and more men were shouting.

The men looting the carts looked worried at this. They stood and took a few nervous steps towards the house. Suddenly Alice heard the crack of a rifle, followed by the sound of cursing.

"I'm shot!" cried one of the men.

The watchmen turned to the origin of the sound, and Alice stood up from her hiding place. She unleashed fire from each hand, turning the men into pillars of flame. The road was illuminated in brilliant orange light, and the night was filled with their screams. She staggered for a moment, disoriented; she had never unleashed two flames at once.

Closer to the house, one of the guards had been wounded. He turned to see the flames, and fired at Alice in a panic. She flinched, but his shot went astray. Archer shot the man a second time, and he fell.

The last guard saw the fight was against him. He began screaming for allies as he ran towards the house. He threw open the front door, and lunged through before Archer could silence him. A moment later he was shoved back out of the house on the tip of Gilbert's sword. The guard's screams became more shrill, and desperate. For a moment Alice forgot the joking and well-mannered Gilbert and saw him as he must appear to their foes: A titan, fearless of blades, wrapped in a shroud of flowing black, his face a horrifying grin of death.

The guard's cries were cut short with another stroke of Gilbert's sword, and the manor fell silent again, save for the crackle of fire from the smoldering men on either side of her. She coughed at the smell of burning wool, and hurried away from her victims.

"Gilbert!" she shouted.

Gilbert rushed down the stairs and set to calming the horses. The fight had agitated them. Alice marveled at the skill he had with horses, and that they had no fear of him as an abomination.

A young man had followed Gilbert out of the house and now stood by his side as he worked on the horse's harness.

"Gilbert?" she said again, more gently this time. "Who is this?"

Gilbert seemed to ignore her. The young man stared at her, wide-eyed and silent. After a few moments Gilbert turned and nudged the boy. "Go on. Introduce yourself."

The boy snatched the hat from his head and stumbled over his words.

Gilbert sighed. “Simon, this is Alice White. Miss White, this is Simon... I don’t know his surname.” Gilbert returned to work.

“I don’t... have,” the boy said with a trembling voice.

“Gilbert, what *are* you doing?” she demanded.

“Freeing the horses from the cart,” he said flatly, without looking up from what he was doing.

“What has come over you?”

“I met Lord Mordaunt. Sort of. His men are on their way to Rothersby, to kill my mother.”

“Your *mother*?” Alice said with incredulity.

“He knew I wouldn’t be afraid of threats to my own body, so he struck where I would be vulnerable,” he replied. The horses were now free of the cart’s harness. Gilbert dug through their scattered supplies and retrieved one of the saddles.

“And I suppose you mean to take this man with you,” she said, nodding at Simon. “And I will assume he’s the young man you spoke of before? The sorcerer in the service of Mordaunt?”

“He’s recently betrayed the viscount, at the risk of his own life,” Gilbert said defensively.

“Admirable, but redemption and forgiveness are not yours to distribute. You hold the life of the princess in your very body, and you are obligated by both word and duty to restore her.”

“And leave my own mother to torment and death? No.”

“You mean to break arrest *and* make off with a known sorcerer? I won’t allow it.”

“You are no less a sorcerer, or.... sorceress,” he argued. “If you mean to stop me, you will need to use force.” His voice was grim and threatening.

“Give the word, Miss White”, said Archer. He had approached Gilbert and Simon from behind, and was holding his rifle at the ready. Simon put up his hands immediately. Gilbert ignored him.

"You know what I can do. You saw it yourself in the library," she said with as much menace as she was able. "We've killed abominations before, and know where to strike."

"You've fought mindless or feral undead, from what you've told me. I doubt you've faced a soldier with all his wits intact," Gilbert stepped forward, leading his horse. His sword was in his hand. "And if you destroy me, you might destroy the vigor, and Sophie will be doomed. If you want the best chance of helping her, then you'll let me go. When I've settled things with Mordaunt's men, I'll be back to help you save the princess."

"Is that a promise? Your word is worth considerably less now than it was an hour ago," she snapped.

"You don't need to accept my word. I'm telling you my intentions. Make of it what you like. Slay me, or stand aside, only stop wasting my time." When it was clear that she didn't mean to assail him immediately, Gilbert turned and set to work saddling the other horse.

"I am at a loss," she said, throwing her arms into the air. "I can't allow you to break arrest, or I do not deserve the office I hold. I can't destroy you, or it will doom Sophie."

"You could always come with us, so we will still be under your arrest," Gilbert suggested.

"I can't abandon our fallen companions and leave their bodies to rot."

"I'll stay," said Archer.

Alice breathed a heavy sigh. "Perhaps that is an option. Actually, I think the important task is to gather up our fallen friends on the remaining cart and carry them back to London. Do you think you can manage that?"

Archer nodded.

"Poor Archer," she said apologetically, "Always left behind. I am sorry this time, but this is the only way I can see to do things."

Gilbert handed the reins of one horse to Simon, and mounted the other himself.

"I don't know how to ride," Simon stammered.

"Then you'll ride with me. There. Now we have a horse for Miss White. Hurry. The men we're chasing were the ones we passed on our way here."

"Then they have half an hour on us. And their horses are fresh, while ours have worked for half a day. And yours is now doubly burdened."

"I still hold out hope of her rescue," Gilbert said. "And if that fails, I will console myself with revenge."

"You'll pay for that," the man screamed.

"So you said the last time I struck you," replied Gilbert. "Either make good on your threats, or stop making them."

The man turned to one side and spat out some blood. "You've got no right hitting another guard, Maypole!"

"Perhaps you should complain to a superior officer," Gilbert shrugged. They both knew there was nobody that would hear his complaint. Headmaster Graves was the closest thing they had to a superior officer, and he was indifferent to the men as long as the posts were filled and the men looked presentable. He had a reputation for punishing the messenger, which encouraged the men to solve disputes among themselves.

"You know there ain't no proper officer here, now or ever. I just want to get to my bunk."

"Then use the door, like a human being," Gilbert said. Gilbert was repairing a hole in the side of the stables. It had been large enough to squeeze through when he arrived at Ravenstead, and had gradually gotten bigger as men used it as a door. Gilbert was now breaking them of that habit through fisticuffs, which was the only thing any of them understood. He was making repairs using supplies and tools he'd purchased with his own money, and hoping that the viscount would notice and approve.

The man - who had been named "Soot" by the Headmaster - spat again. He stood glaring as Gilbert worked on the wall, and Gilbert wondered if he wasn't going to have to halt his project for a proper fight. He didn't want that. He was trying to show himself more disciplined and organized than the other men, and brawling went against that goal. After a few more moments Soot gave up and shuffled inside through the proper door.

The men played cards in their free time. Gilbert adored cards, but the games were ruined by constant cheating, brawling, arguments, and other interruptions. Instead, he saved his coin and spent it on improvements to their quarters. He had been assigned the evening watch, and so spent his free time during the day mending and cleaning.

"Very nice," said a man named Plump when Gilbert had finished. "You sealed up that annoying hole that was letting in all the fresh air."

"You will be glad that the wall is mended in a few months when the winds turn cold," Gilbert said. He gathered up his tools and went inside to check his handiwork.

"But we have to put up with the stench now," Plump replied. Other men in the room muttered their agreement.

"The stench would be less intense if you men kept yourselves cleaner. If the viscount gave us a pig it would refuse to lodge with you. I keep my own bunk and uniform according to military standards. It only takes a few minutes."

"Actually, your bunk is the one making the foul smell," One-eye said with a wheezing laugh.

Gilbert looked, and saw that someone had relieved themselves on his bed. He roared in outrage, and the men erupted into laughter.

"No!" screamed Gilbert.

They had ridden all night, and reached the house in Rothersby sometime before dawn. He had pushed the group relentlessly, only allowing for two brief stops. With each passing hour he hoped for some sign of their prey on the road ahead. He became more anxious as the hours wore on and their own horses began to reach the end of their strength. Both Alice and Simon had begun to falter on the way, their heads nodding in the saddle as he drove them onward.

They arrived to find what he'd feared the most: The house standing open to the night air, and no sign of the men they were chasing. They had already gone. Gilbert drew his sword and stormed up the path, leaving Alice and Simon to wobble after him as they were able.

He rushed through the front door. "Mother!" he cried, "Mother, are you alright?" He heard a stirring in the kitchen, and ran to investigate. The room was dark, but Gilbert caught sight of a large shape moving about in the moonlight. Gilbert lunged and grabbed the figure, throwing him against the wall.

"No! No! You promised to leave me alone! I don't know anything else!" the man cried.

Light filled the room. Alice had arrived, carrying a lantern. Gilbert found himself looking into a familiar face.

"Leland?" he said with surprise. He looked different than Gilbert remembered. He'd put on quite a bit of weight in such a short time, and his face had been recently beaten. One of his eyes had swollen shut, and the other was filled with tears. "What are you doing here?" Gilbert asked at last.

"What?" Leland asked in dismay. "I live here. Who are you? Are you with those other men?"

"You live here?" Gilbert said in confusion. "This house belongs to Victoria Hiltman."

"It did. I bought it from her three years ago. I already explained this to those other men. She moved to America. Jump on a boat to New York if you want to see her so badly. I'm nothing to do with her."

"Three years?" Gilbert said in dismay. He released Leland and turned to face Alice. "What year is it?"

"1885", said Leland and Alice in unison.

Sometime later, Gilbert found himself sitting on the steps in front of the house, staring off into the darkness. A warm light came from inside the house now. Simon and Alice had remained with Leland, and were tending to his wounds. Gilbert felt very alone, and lost.

Alice emerged sat down next to him. They waited together for a while in silence, save for the occasional yawn from Alice.

"Are you all right?" she said at last.

"You mean aside from being dead?"

"You seemed stricken when you learned you'd been dead for three years. The swords you've had in your chest have done you less harm than learning the proper date."

"I don't know how I went for so long without realizing it. Why did I never ask the date?"

"We don't usually ask what year it is when we wake up. If you awakened with the feeling that you had not been asleep long, you probably trusted that notion, however wrong it may have been. You said yourself that your memories were scattered. I assume you have not recovered them?"

"Some. But I still don't recall how I died. A bit more takes shape each day."

"Forgive me if this seems callous, but I don't understand why learning the year has been so upsetting. Certainly you missed the last three years, but that seems a small loss in comparison to the loss of your natural life."

Gilbert drew in a long breath, which produced an unsettling sound. He didn't need breath and he was pretty sure he didn't even have lungs, but his body seemed to magically move air around as if he did. He was in the habit of taking a slow breath when gathering his thoughts, and apparently that habit had followed him beyond the grave. "My father died when I was about seventeen. I expected the funeral would be painful, after which the pain would fade. It would get easier as I got used to his absence. But when you lose someone, you don't just lose them once. You lose them a thousand times. The funeral was the easy part. The hard part was the first meal without him. My first birthday without his blessing. Our first Christmas without him. The day I left for the military and he wasn't there to see me off."

"My father died three years ago," she said quietly. "I'm still discovering moments like those."

"Well, I seem to be going through this again, but for myself. For my lost life. I keep thinking about all the things I'll never do. I'll never get married. Never give Mother the grandchildren she always wanted. Never get to have the career I wanted. Never own my own house. Three years have vanished. Mother moved back to America and I never got to see her off. I wonder if she even knows that I'm dead."

The wind stirred. The trees swayed, dark clouds of shadow against the starry sky. Unlike the trees in Ravenstead, the trees here had not yet decided to give up their leaves, and were noisy in their movement. Alice shivered and rubbed her arms to keep warm.

"Gilbert," she said, looking down at the dark stone at her feet, "I am sorry I was so uncaring towards your mother. Back at Ravenstead, I mean."

Gilbert nodded.

"The danger is not yet passed, I fear. I spoke with Leland about his attackers. Is he a relation of yours?"

"No. He was just a neighbor. I guess he bought our house when Mother returned to America? I wouldn't have expected that."

"Well, Mordaunt's men took him for a member of your family. They treated him badly, as you saw, but they threatened him with far worse. These are horrible men we're chasing. In the end, Leland bought his own life by telling them where to find Mrs. Hiltman."

"I wonder if they're really willing to go all the way across the ocean to inflict their harm on me," Gilbert said, looking down the road as it ran west.

"Leland seemed to think so. They were very interested in how to find her, and the distance didn't seem to concern them."

"Did you say anything to Leland about us, or explain why we had invaded his home?"

"I baked him a story. It was not wholly true, but truth was among the ingredients. I told him we were chasing a group of ruffians, and that we only invaded his home because we expected to find them inside. I'm not sure what he'll make of your confusion over the date, but there's nothing to be done about it."

"Did he recognize me?" Gilbert asked suddenly.

"No. Not that he let on, anyway. He didn't seem to recognize you as someone that he once knew, and I'm sure he didn't recognize that he was speaking with an abomination. In truth, I think his wits are in worse condition than his face."

"Do you think he suffered any permanent damage?" He was surprised to find out how concerned he was for Leland's well-being. He never cared for the boy, and thought him too slow and lazy, but it enraged him to think that an innocent party had been so senselessly harmed on his account.

"I'm sure he'll be fine in a few days. They threatened him with a knife, but struck with their fists only. The damage didn't look nearly as dreadful once Simon had cleaned the wounds. He has some skill in treating injury. He is quite unexpectedly gentle and timid for a sorcerer and a servant of Lord Mordaunt."

"More slave than servant. I don't think he ever had any choice in the matter until tonight."

"I think you should hurry and stop the men who are set on harming you mother," Alice said firmly. Gilbert thought this almost sounded like an order.

"You're not coming with us?" he asked.

"I have to report back. You are mourning the loss of your own life, but I have to report the loss of four men, including our captain. I suppose we will eventually be assigned new personnel, as we have in the past. We've lost men before, of course, although never this many at once. The Ministry is in ruins. The men are all dead, save Archer. Lieutenant Jack is now our adversary. And I am still missing my father. No, I can't go with you. Do you have any money?"

"A little. I found that some of his Lordship's men had coin in their pockets after I pulled them off of the end of my sword."

Alice nodded.

"So I am no longer under arrest?" he asked.

"I would say that you are, but I no longer have the means to restrain you."

"What about Simon?"

"I have not placed him under arrest, and I would not do so now."

"You're letting a necromancer go free?"

"Not if he plans to engage in further necromancy!" she said testily. "I imagine you don't realize it yet, but you will need his help. You can't do business without a face. If you intend to inhabit the civilized world, you will need someone to speak for you. It would not do the princess any good to have you run off alone, where your nature would eventually be discovered. You would soon find yourself fighting the church."

"I'm not afraid of the church," Gilbert said defiantly.

"You should be. What they lack in skill is more than offset by their numbers and their tenacity. They destroyed many abominations before the Ministry was created, and I'm sure you would fall to them once they brought their full strength to bear. And even if you think you have greater cunning than most abominations, just *think* of what such a contest would look like. You would be obliged to slay dozens of zealous young men. Even if they are poorly trained, or misguided, their aim is to defend their homes from the ravages of witchcraft. How many of those men would you cut down to save your mother?"

"You are right," Gilbert relented. "I will need to use my head more than my sword if I want to reach her."

Alice yawned again, "Are you off now? It will be dawn soon."

"I don't think so. Our horses - *your* horses, really - are spent. I will need to see to them. Simon as well. Once we've taken some rest, we'll head for Liverpool. Hopefully I can catch these men before they board the next ship to America."

To Gilbert, the British Isles were inhabited by three brothers: The English, the Irish, and the Scottish. Each was likable, honorable, and made for good company, save for the fact that they unaccountably hated each other for the most inscrutable reasons, and vigorously denied their brotherhood. (There were also the Welsh, who were somewhat unifying. The other three agreed that no matter how much they might dislike each other, the Welsh were worse. Gilbert hadn't encountered many Welsh, and did not have any opinion on them either way.)

In particular, he always felt that the English view of the Scottish was more than a little unfair. The Scots were viewed as belligerent drunkards, having poor singing voices and worse taste in music. Their speech was incomprehensible to the point of comedy. They ate more than they should, as long as it was of no nutritional value. They had no head for education. They spoke louder than was reasonable and with much profanity. Gilbert had known a few Scotsmen during his time in the military, and he found all of these views on the Scottish people to be wildly inaccurate - even slanderous - until the day Ivar arrived at Ravenstead.

It was in the early part of September when Ivar was added to the list of guards in Lord Mordaunt's employ. The scorching August heat had relented and blessed the men with cool air and slight breezes, but Ivar spent every day since his arrival bathing in his own sweat. He was not as tall as Gilbert, but he was broader, barrel-chested, and probably a bit heavier. He seemed to be the origin of every bad stereotype Gilbert had ever heard, and was capable of sustaining them single-handedly. He tended to stare at people without provocation. In idle moments he would set his wild eyes on whoever was closest, clenching his jaw and daring them to meet his gaze.

Ivar had been given special treatment by the headmaster. He was the only one of the men to be called by his proper name. Instead of forcing him to improve his slovenly appearance while on duty, Headmaster Graves assigned him to guard the rear entrance. It was obvious he drank on duty, although he was never in too much of a stupor to stand and watch at his post. This was tolerated without comment, even though the other men knew better than to attempt the same themselves.

Gilbert did not immediately confront Ivar as he'd done with the other men, and Ivar never attempted to shame Gilbert with his angry stare. The two avoided each other. Everyone could see that a conflict was inevitable, but neither man was rushing into it.

Gilbert had beaten the men into shape. Not proper *military* shape, but at least they were less of an embarrassment. Their barracks were looking less like stables by the day, and Gilbert had gone for over a week without having to punch a man for throwing refuse on the floor or drunkenly pissing in the corner. Their pranks were less frequent and less destructive, and they were beginning to accept him. Perhaps not as a superior officer, but at least as a bully they could appease through proper manners.

Ivar changed all of this. The men saw weakness when Gilbert ignored Ivar's offenses. They began to return to their old ways. They acted like Ivar when Ivar was around, using him as their shield. Gilbert couldn't correct them for something when Ivar was committing the same crime just a few steps away. Gilbert saw his project slowly coming undone.

Ivar was used to being the dominant force in the room, and it obviously frustrated him to see the men so often defer to Gilbert. The two men were at a truce, but neither of them was happy with it. They never spoke to each other.

Sooner or later, one would topple the other. When that happened, the rest of the men would make the winner their leader in all but name, and the loser would become the target of their many pranks. Neither man was in a hurry to face that trial, and so this storm was slow in building.

Their first confrontation came late one morning while Gilbert was whitewashing the outside of the barracks. He'd stripped off his shirt and tied a cloth around his waist in order to protect his clothing.

"Well, look at the pretty lady come to fix up our humble cottage!" boomed Ivar from behind. The words were horribly mangled, and it took Gilbert a moment to sort them out and realize they were directed at him. He turned, and saw Ivar was regarding him with a malicious smirk.

Ivar was a man of diabolical ugliness. The top of his head was perfectly hairless, and on his jaw was a great beard of untamed black hair. His face was red with windburn and his skin had the texture of uncured leather. His nose had been broken at some point, and had healed at an unsightly angle.

Gilbert hesitated. Now was not an ideal moment to settle things with Ivar. Gilbert was tired, shoeless, shirtless, and in the middle of important work. His bucket of whitewash was standing open nearby, and it would be a financial loss to him if it was spilled.

A few men stopped bickering over their card game to come outside and see how things turned out. Gilbert cursed his luck. He didn't dare back down with the men watching. He sighed and stepped away from his supplies.

"A nice dress you're wearing," Ivar slurred, pointing at Gilbert's makeshift apron. He was drunk. This was the first time he'd been drunk this early in the morning. He was just now coming off duty.

Gilbert snatched the cloth away and tossed it into Ivar's face, "You can have it, if you're so fond of it."

Ivar pulled the cloth away to see Gilbert was now standing just a few inches from him. The two men locked eyes. Ivar clenched his jaw and breathed out a noxious cloud of alcoholic vapor. The other men were slowly gathering into a circle around them, elbowing and whispering to each other. Money began to change hands.

Suddenly Ivar slapped Gilbert on the shoulder with one of his thick hands. It was like being hit with a steak. "Keep up the good work, soldier!" Ivar laughed uneasily before turning away. He wobbled inside, muttering to himself.

The men could not hide their disappointment. They shuffled off and did not return to their cards.

Once he was alone, Gilbert let out a long, slow breath.

"Why are you sighing?" Simon asked.

"There's only so much amusement a streetlamp has to offer," Gilbert answered. He pulled his hood tighter around his head. Passers-by were staring at them as Simon stood gawking at the light.

"It's a marvel!" he beamed, his glasses glinting in the light. "And so many. They go all the way down the street. So much brighter than gas lamps."

"I can't believe you've never seen one before. They began putting them up around London two years ago. No, five years. I keep forgetting. Dreadful mess. They dug trenches through the streets to lay the cables. It was impossible getting around."

"I've never been to London. I've never even been away from Ravenstead. Most of my life was spent at the academy," Simon paused and flinched slightly with the memory. "After that I spent time both at the academy and the manor."

Gilbert was quiet as a group of men hurried by. He was never sure how safe it was for people to hear his voice. Once they had passed he answered, "I guess that explains why you never saw an electric street light. But haven't you seen them elsewhere?"

"You, know, it's funny," Simon said, finally taking his eyes off the lamp and turning to Gilbert, "His Lordship did have electrical apparatus in the cellar. I saw it only once, and it wasn't in use at the time, but I remember a large thing draped with copper wires. I brought down a load of coal once and placed it in a bin next to the machine. Had no idea what it was at the time. I guess it was for making electricity."

"A strange thing for him to have in his house. I don't remember seeing any electric lights anywhere in the place." Gilbert looked up and down the sidewalk nervously. "Let's keep moving, I think we've made ourselves enough of a spectacle for tonight."

They had arrived in London early the previous morning. They were still chasing Headmaster Graves, and hoped to catch him before he and his men boarded the ship to America. They had spent the night in London, where Simon got a bit of long-overdue food and sleep. They set out again when evening came. Gilbert wanted to start out sooner, but he wasn't willing to push the boy any harder. Simon had spent most of his life being neglected, hungry, and tired, and Gilbert didn't want to add to his sufferings.

The boy had perked up considerably, and was now dashing through the dreary London night, full of joy and wonder. "Where are we headed next?" he asked once they had left the curiosity of the electric light behind.

"The train station. From there we head for Liverpool. You'll be able to sleep a bit more on the train if you need it." Deprived of his mortal needs and desires, Gilbert found the business of eating and sleeping to be mercilessly tedious.

"I couldn't possibly sleep now!" Simon beamed. He was walking along, looking almost straight up to see the tops of the surrounding buildings against the black sky. Gilbert steered him away from trouble as they walked.

The train station was a place of ornate desolation. A relatively new building by London standards, it was clean and well-kept, and decorated with much elaborate ironwork. Yet it felt cold and somehow empty despite the many huddled passengers. The sounds of footsteps echoed in the space as if they were descending into a tomb. A large clock scowled at them overhead. The place smelled of burning coal and engine oil.

Gilbert looked at the schedule and worked out which train and which platform they would need. Then he gave Simon most of their remaining coin and sent him to purchase their tickets.

"We're in luck," Simon said once he returned. "Our train has just arrived."

Gilbert hung his head. “Then we are not in luck. Somewhere ahead of us is the headmaster, and his men. If fortune was on our side, then our train would have arrived hours ago, and our quarry would be waiting for us on board. As it stands, they left on the previous train. Or even the one before that, if they didn’t stop for rest.”

“What makes you think they didn’t-” Simon was cut off as Gilbert yanked him sideways and dragged him to the other side of the platform. A group of Red Sashes was coming towards them and Gilbert wanted to get out of their way.

“I don’t know if they rested or not,” Gilbert explained when they were at a safer distance. “Remember that the Headmaster doesn’t know we’re chasing him. He has no reason to hurry on our account. The last time we saw each other, I was on my way into his master’s trap. Now that I’m thinking of it, it’s possible he went back to Ravenstead to report to your master.”

“He’s not my master anymore,” Simon muttered.

“You’re right. And I’m glad to hear you say it,” Gilbert said warmly.

They boarded and tried to find a cabin where they might be left alone. They sat in silence until the train departed. Simon was enthralled with the experience at first, but after a while he became used to the gentle rolling sensation. The lights of London faded into the distance.

Finally Simon turned from watching the darkness drift by their window, “Gilbert, what do you think will happen to me? When this is over, I mean?”

“I don’t know,” Gilbert said. “You speak well. And you’re literate. You’re young, and you’ve been taught proper manners. You should be able to find work somewhere.”

“I don’t know how to do that. There’s a lot I don’t know. Most of my life has been spent studying things that would get me hanged.” He took his hat from his head and fidgeted it with it in his lap. “I’m always afraid of saying or doing something that will give me away. It’s one of the reasons I went back to the manor after you freed me. I just couldn’t imagine myself walking out into the world and living my own life."

"You're not a slave anymore. You shouldn't be asking what will *happen* to you next. Instead, ask yourself what you want. You should find it easy to figure out what to do once you have a goal."

Simon looked down thoughtfully. "Up until now, my only desire has been to escape the hunger and the beatings. Now that I've achieved it, I'm not sure where to go next. I guess what I want is to stay with you a while longer. I had many boys that I called friends in the academy, but the truth was that any of those boys would have socked me in the eye if it meant an extra handful of bread that evening, and I suppose the same was true for me. We weren't friends, really. We were just people who shared a common misery. I think you're the first person I could ever call friend. I haven't forgotten what you did for me back at the church."

"Don't forget that you've paid me back for that kindness by saving me from your former master. I owe you my life, or whatever this is called. And if we're very lucky, my mother will owe you her life as well."

"Well, if the question is what I want to do with my life, then I seem to be doing it already," Simon said with a smile. "I'm happy to help you with your mother, in exchange for your guidance and protection."

Gilbert laughed, "You might need protection less if you weren't with me, but I accept your offer. You'll be my face, and I'll be your sword."

Simon planted his bowler on his head again. "Agreed!" he said, holding out his hand.

Gilbert shook it. "Agreed."

"Alice, you're a sunrise to behold!" beamed Lord Moxley. "What brings such a beautiful sight to so dreary a place?"

They were in the ministry building on King Charles Street. It was not at all a dreary place, but an elaborate construction of Italianate architecture. It was a place of stratospheric ceilings with intricate red and gold ornament and stencil work. Great arching windows welcomed the cold, colorless morning sun.

"I'm afraid I have bad news," she stammered weakly. She felt so out of place here, and wished she could just return to the library and bury herself in her work.

"I cannot imagine a better way to receive bad news than to have it delivered by a messenger such as yourself," he cooed. "Where did you get that dress? Is it French?"

"Indeed. A gift from my mother, sent to me the last time she was in France," Alice replied.

"Extraordinary beauty in that country. Clothes. Climate. Food. Exquisite, all of it. A shame about the people." Lord Moxley led her up a grand staircase and into one of the many offices upstairs.

It was strange to think that if the Ministry of Ethereal Affairs was a more conventional sort of place, they would be headquartered here instead of Grayhouse. Alice wondered to herself how the royal palace must look, because she couldn't imagine what anyone could do to make a place grander than this, short of making everything out of solid gold.

"I'm very sorry you have bad news for me," he continued, "But I'm afraid I must repay you with bad news of my own. You'd best be sitting down when you hear it." He motioned her into a nearby chair. She took it only reluctantly. The chairs here looked too lavish to be sat upon. He took a seat facing her. There was also a desk in the room, although it was hard for her to imagine that Moxley ever used it.

"Perhaps you should go first," she suggested, "My news is likely the worst."

"I sincerely doubt it, but if that's the case then you should go first. I'd rather get the worst of it over with. And besides, now that I think of it, Captain Turpin should be present for my news. It concerns him and his men as well."

"That's part of why I'm here," Alice said, her voice shaking. "Captain Turpin has... he's dead. He was killed two nights ago, along with all of his men, save for Private Archer."

Moxley placed his hand on his heart in an exaggerated expression. "My dear, twice in one week you have utterly shocked me. This is going to be a terrible bother to sort out. I concede that your news was indeed the worst by far, but it has the unexpected benefit of rendering my ill news of no value." Moxley was using roughly the same tone of voice he used to decry the rain a few days earlier.

Alice was strangely comforted by his reaction. If Lord Moxley had wept or grieved, it would have cut her to the heart and she would have begun crying. King Charles Street was not a place for common tears. Mastering herself, she tried to reply with a similar level of detachment. "So your news concerned the Captain?"

"Yes. Well, all of the men. I'm afraid the arrest of Sir Edward Brooks and his accomplices has had political repercussions."

"Who?"

Moxley sighed. "The Four Horsemen, I believe you called them?"

"Oh! I am so silly. I thought that business was dealt with."

"Not in the slightest. These men - Brooks, in particular - are making the case that Ethereal Affairs is reckless and ill-managed. They are saying that the ministry has been less successful since the loss of your father, and that reform is needed. Specifically, more oversight."

Alice hung her head, "Lord Moxley, a week ago this would have been devastating news, but now the world of political maneuvering seems so tiresome and silly in the face of so many deaths. What's the worst Parliament can do to us?"

"They have done it. Our funding is cut. The men are recalled to the service of Her Majesty. The ministry is to halt all activities until an investigation can be conducted. I called on you two days ago to give you the news, but rumors told that you had recently departed."

"I can't believe they would do that. Close the Ministry, I mean. It is popular and successful."

"But not as successful as it was in the past. And common success can sometimes be mistaken for failure when compared to triumph."

"So people are unhappy that we're catching fewer malefactors?"

"Not unhappy. Simply less impressed. Your organization has risen to the point where it has been taken for granted. Few endeavors attain such honor."

"I suppose it was inevitable that we would falter. I can't hope to fill my father's shoes."

"Nobody suggested that you should take his place alone. Besides, you are undervaluing yourself. The ministry has done well enough in the last few years. And don't forget that the reason you have fewer witches to catch today is because your father caught so many in the past."

"I suppose. But it doesn't matter if we're to be closed."

"Not closed. I did not say closed. Not even our foes, as powerful as they are, can accomplish that. They have taken the wind out of our sails, not sunk our ship. Remember that the Queen's husband is exceptionally fond of us. Albert Prince-Consort has little legal power, but he has a large number of allies as well as the hearts of the people. He hasn't gotten involved yet. I'm curious to see what he will do."

"Couldn't you go to him?" Alice asked.

"Bless you, Alice. Your naïveté is often invigorating. But no, that is the last thing I should do. If I go to see him, it will be known. It would only make him appear weak. Imagine, him making an appearance and defending the Ministry at the request of a distant subordinate! No, the trick with his power is that he is strongest when he appears most aloof. Rest assured that he knows what is happening, and will move when the time is right. It would do no good for me to go and tell him what he already knows."

"Well, he might be in more of a hurry if he knew what we'd found in Ravenstead," Alice said.

"You have proof of witchcraft?" Moxley asked with surprise.

Alice nodded, "We found evidence of ongoing necromancy in the family crypt. The residents cannot possibly hope to feign ignorance this time. Also, we were assaulted." Alice then explained the ambush as she'd been able to unravel it, and the battle in front of the manor.

"Well, that's some comfort," Moxley replied once she'd told her tale. "That should leave more than enough evidence to move against Edward Brooks. Remember that he is the legal owner of the Ravenstead estate. If we can show that Captain Turpin and his men were slaughtered on the grounds, it would unmask Brooks. His allies in Parliament would abandon him, and our ministry would be restored. Now, what of the Princess?"

Alice shrugged, "I can't say. We didn't find her at the estate."

"I see there's something you're not telling me," Moxley said slyly. "You haven't said why you left Private Archer to recover the bodies on his own. You also haven't mentioned what became of the abomination. It has been said that the Witch Watch buried someone in Tyburn. And I read in the papers that you left two days ago with a large man in black, and that he did not return with you. There are a great many pieces missing from your tale."

Alice opened her mouth to speak, but he silenced her with a dismissive a wave of the hand, "I don't care about the messy details." Then he leaned in and lowered his voice to a whisper, "Be careful what secrets you speak here. Our foes would be fools not to attempt some sort of divination in a place like this."

Alice nodded. She understood that she shouldn't speak of Gilbert, but she wasn't sure what other secrets would be dangerous. Hadn't they already divulged a number of dangerous items in their conversation? She sighed. She simply had no head or patience for this business of subterfuge.

Moxley looked her in the eye. His gaze was probing, almost to the point of interrogation. He spoke in a firm, quiet voice, "I just want to know what you're trying to accomplish."

Alice was suddenly offended, "I want to restore the princess, and put her abductors behind bars, of course!"

Moxley nodded and smiled brightly. "Good girl! Most people would want to clear their own name. Or reclaim their job. Or avenge their fallen friends. But you are not thinking about yourself at all. Even when your own life is in turmoil, you are focused on helping and protecting others. You are very much your father's daughter. This is the answer I was looking for."

"You speak as if you have some sort of plan," she said suspiciously.

"A plan? No. But I can offer some help."

"More help would be welcome. Private Archer and I are hardly a match for our foes."

"I am sorry to say that even Private Archer is of no help to you. He will be returned to regular military duty the next time he reports in."

"So I'm alone?" Alice asked mournfully.

"I could put in a request to replace the Captain and his men, if I wanted to have a large number of people laugh at me to my face. But I do not think you are alone. If I am reading things correctly, you have at least one ally left. The one of whom we do not speak. The one you omitted from your tale of two nights ago?"

"Yes. I guess that is an ally of sorts," she said thoughtfully.

"Well here is another ally," Moxley said as he handed her a purse. "But don't open it here!" he scolded as she tried to peek inside. "Virtue, strength. Idealists always have these in excess. But they always forget the third thing you need for victory. Then they march off to ruin and defeat."

"So what is the third thing?" Alice asked with amusement.

"Money, you silly girl!"

Alice weighed the purse in her hand.

Lord Moxley spoke before she could offer gratitude, "The Ministry has never been as thorough about spending all of its funds as it could be, and that purse is the reservoir that has captured the excess. My advice is for you to do whatever you can to save Sophie. Her disappearance is now becoming generally known around Buckingham. Even the daftest of the chambermaids is observant enough to notice a missing princess. Gossip spreads much like a disease, and before long it will spill over to us here at King Charles Street. Once that happens, the story will take to the papers, and the real chaos will begin. If we are very lucky, you will rescue her after this happens. Don't look at me like that. I'll be happy with her rescue whenever it takes place, and I know you would not delay it for personal gain. That's one of the reasons I'm entrusting you with the purse. But our recovery will be much more expedient if we can resolve a public crisis."

Mr. Brooks,

You asked for guidance on where you might learn more about the language of sorcery, which is commonly called Black Latin. I would urge you to be careful in this line of study. Some parties in the church consider the study of the profane language to be itself an act of witchcraft, even if done purely for academic purposes. I do think this study is important, but I do not wish to send you unaware into danger. We are ever starved for educated allies, and practitioners of witchcraft have benefited greatly over the centuries by having their own, secret language with which they might communicate.

You asked if the book by Friedrich Kappel might be a good starting place. I would say that in your case, it is not. The book is primarily linguistic in nature, and can often become quite dense and tedious. Moreover, the subject of Black Latin occupies only a small part of its pages. This is, I'm sure, the only reason the book has escaped the notice of the church. I have a copy of the book myself, but I turn to it only at great need, when all other resources have failed.

Rather than send you after yet another volume, allow me to give you the kernel of knowledge that I obtained when I began my studies. From there, the choice of study materials will become far more obvious.

The language was most likely named by the ignorant (possibly even illiterate) witch-hunters of the 15th or 16th century. To them, Latin was the "mystery" language of the church. It was a tongue they could not understand in either the spoken or the written form. When they encountered a new, unknown language in the manuscripts of captured sorcerers, they concluded it was a language in opposition to the (to them) holy language of Latin. So it was called Black Latin, although at the time nobody could read it.

In the middle of the 17th century, a man named Aleksander Nowicki somehow found himself in possession of a number of books of sorcery. In secret, he undertook the task of unraveling Black Latin, possibly on his own but possibly in connection with Jagiellonian University, where it is believed he was a man of some position. What he discovered was that Black Latin wasn't a new mystery language at all. It was simply Greek, disguised under an alternate alphabet. He managed to translate a number of pages of sorcery notes and a small number of circle diagrams. He shared his findings with his colleagues, was accused of witchcraft, stood trial, and was executed, along with his wife. His name was blotted out of the record at the University and his work was destroyed. The knowledge he gained would have been lost entirely, if not for the fact that he outlined his findings in a letter to a friend in Salzburg, and that letter survived.

While using an alternate alphabet obscures the meaning of the text to outsiders, this was not its original purpose. The alphabet arose sometime during the early days of the Byzantine Empire, when the cultural and legal tolerance of sorcery allowed the practice to flourish. The alphabet was probably invented simply because it was more convenient than the standard Greek alphabet. The minimalistic characters were made from straight lines. This made it easier to carve them into stone, as was common in those days. The regular width of the characters made it easier for the sorcerer to plan the lettering so that each line or stanza formed a complete circle.

This system began as a basic alphabet substitution, but grew in complexity over the years. Most notably, new characters were invented to stand in for common letter groups. For example, the Greek letters "αίμ" are used often in spells involving blood, and so a replacement character was invented that could represent all three letters combined. This character does not appear in all cases, and was most likely only used when the careless writer found himself running out of room in his circle. This system of unpredictable letter substitution had the unintended effect of making it much harder for us to decipher their work, a task which has consumed a great deal of my attention over the last few years. (I would write a book explaining these findings myself, were it not so politically dangerous in my current situation. Hopefully that task will be undertaken by another.)

After a few generations, the proliferation of undead, madness, mind slaves, and destruction throughout the Byzantine Empire led to the outlawing of sorcery, and once again it became taboo. However, the great number of active sorcerers and the overabundance of texts made it difficult to stamp out the practice. It wasn't until centuries later that the church rose up and became the primary protection against sorcery. Once this took place, sorcerers saw Black Latin (which was just an encrypted form of Greek to them) as a way of protecting their secrets.

I have enclosed a small diagram showing the mapping of Black Latin characters to their original Greek counterparts, along with the few group characters I've identified. I hope you will find it useful in your studies, and I urge you to be careful with this knowledge. We are caught between foes who should not be allowed to read these things. On one side are aspiring sorcerers who would use this knowledge to hurt others. On the other side is the church, which would use this knowledge as a justification for hurting us. Seldom does the road to understanding pass through a more narrow or more perilous way.

In friendship,

Sir Donovan White

Director, Ministry of Ethereal Affairs

February 24, 1877

CALLISTO

CALLISTO

V

“The ship leaves in the morning,” Simon reported.

“Blast it,” Gilbert said. “And how much is it to buy passage?”

They were standing along the docks, amongst the shadows. They had spent the day in Liverpool, looking for signs of Headmaster Graves. Their only glimmer of hope came from a woman who owned a boarding house. She claimed to have given a bed to someone matching his description the previous night. He’d had two traveling companions with him. They had arrived late, said little, and departed early. Beyond that, she could tell nothing more.

“The price of a ticket is many times what we have,” Simon replied sadly. “And that’s just for one. In steerage.”

Gilbert cursed and turned to face the sea. It was now night. In the distance they could see warm light shining from the portholes of the SS Callisto, a venerable steam vessel. Against the dark sky they could see skeletons of her four masts. Her sides were painted black. Her superstructure stood several decks above the main one, and was painted white. A great smokestack rose from her center like the trunk of a mighty tree.

“Can we even be sure he’s on the ship?” Simon asked.

“I can’t imagine any other reason to come all the way to Liverpool and board this close to the docks. I suppose it’s possible he’s bound for some other ship on another errand. And I would feel better if he would poke his ragged head out for a moment where we could see him. But I don't doubt that he's on the Callisto."

"But what can we do? A ticket is more than we can afford."

"I might go myself. I hate to end our partnership the day after its forging, but it might be the only way to save Mother. I might swim out to the ship and... I don't know. Maybe I can cling to the bottom? I don't need to breathe. I could just ride the ship along with the barnacles, then swim ashore when we arrive."

"And what would you hold onto?" came a nearby voice. "You'll find nothing on the belly of the ship but smooth iron and rivets. The only places you might grasp are near the propeller, where you would be smashed to pieces."

"Alice!" Gilbert said with alarm. Simon stammered a fragment of a greeting and blushed.

"And what if your grip failed during the journey?" she asked. "What would you do then? You're dry skin and bone, now. You would sink right to the bottom, lost to the hopeless depths."

"How did you find us?" Gilbert asked indignantly.

"Do not distract me, I was making a point." She crossed her arms and looked out to the boat thoughtfully, "*Perhaps* if you sunk you might walk along the bottom of the ocean and arrive in America sometime in the next century. Assuming you knew which way to go in the dark, and you never lost your way. And assuming no marine life took an interest in you as food. And assuming the pounding salt water and crushing pressure didn't ruin your body."

"Maybe we could sneak aboard?" Simon blurted out.

"That plan is twice as deadly as the previous one. The bulk of the cargo is already loaded. Of what remains, nothing looks large enough to conceal you, much less Gilbert. And when you are discovered, Gilbert will be thrown overboard and you will be put to death for owning an abomination."

"We don't actually need to go anywhere on the ship," Gilbert said as he looked longingly towards the Callisto. "We just need some way on board long enough for me to slay the Headmaster. And his followers."

"So he is not alone?" Alice said, raising an eyebrow.

"Rumors suggest he's with two other men."

"I think that committing a murder on a crowded ship would be supremely difficult. Three murders will be more-so. I doubt you could catch them all unaware. And even if you did kill them, getting away from the murders would be more impossible still. You would need more than swift legs to escape that level of justice. And again, getting caught would doom Sophie."

"If you are trying to convince me to abandon my mother to her death then you are wasting everyone's time," Gilbert said with irritation.

Alice was dressed as a proper Englishwoman today. She was wearing a white dress and a wide hat. The only thing that gave her away as an eccentric was the device she wore on her arm and the rather bulky belt around her waist. Gilbert saw she was also carrying a man's cane, which he'd mistaken for an umbrella in the dark. He felt ashamed that she had been able to get close enough to hear their conversation without his noticing. He'd heard the footsteps on the boardwalk, but assumed it was a stranger without bothering to look.

"Don't be silly. Of course I'm not trying to entice you to abandon your mother," she replied. "But throwing yourself to the bottom of the ocean would not help her. Or Sophie."

"Then what are you suggesting?"

"I suggest that Simon take my bag, and the three of us purchase proper, legal passage on this ship."

"We don't-" Simon began to say.

"I have coin," she said firmly.

"Thank you!" Simon said with joy. "I've never been on a ship before. This is going to be grand!"

"I thought you couldn't leave?" Gilbert remarked.

"That has changed, obviously. For now, I'm all that remains of the Ministry of Ethereal Affairs, and my only duty is to save Sophie. If I come with you it will reduce the chances of you winding up in the ocean."

"Now that you're here, couldn't you just go and arrest them?" Simon asked timidly.

"Alas, no. If I were to attempt an arrest, I would be laughed at for my trouble. Would you submit to arrest at the hands of a young woman?"

"It depends on what the charge was, and what she had in mind by way of punishment," Gilbert mused.

"And on you not being dead," Alice reminded him.

"Of course," Gilbert said, remembering himself. "So it's settled. We'll go on the ship. I'll get your bag." He took a step towards the imposing luggage sack lurking behind her.

Alice grabbed his sleeve and stopped him short. "I would not dream of having my ancient grandfather carry my heavy luggage," she said as she pressed her cane into his hand. "He is deaf as a post, and never speaks. Also, he's nearly blind." She pushed his head forward so that he was looking downward. "There. We're going to be in close quarters for the next few days, and the less attention you attract, the better we will fare. Leave the luggage to your grandson."

Simon stood still for a moment until he realized she was talking about him. He hurried over and took up the bag.

"This is a sudden change," Gilbert said as they walked to the ship. "A few days ago you were adamant that you couldn't come with us."

"I'm glad I did, since you were so intent on taking Sophie's vigor with you to the bottom of the ocean. And I'm only doing so on the condition that you keep your word and rescue Sophie once your mother is safe."

Gilbert stopped and turned to her. "Miss," he said with sudden seriousness, "We can't tell what will happen during the course of this endeavor. Maybe Sophie will die before we can save her. Maybe I'll be destroyed. Maybe His Lordship will devise some new way to frustrate our purpose. Rather than make a rash promise and then be obliged to break it when circumstances change, let me replace my earlier defunct promise with a better one..."

Alice cocked her head to one side in curiosity. His tone seemed to have surprised her.

He drew in a deep, hissing breath, "On my honor as an Englishman and a soldier."

"Former," she corrected him.

"Very well. On whatever honor I might have left as a man who was once an Englishman and a loyal soldier, I promise that once my family is safe, I will aid the Witch Watch in setting things right with the time I have left. Whether by rescuing Sophie, or avenging her death, or whatever else needs to be done to protect Queen and country." Gilbert ended with a modest bow.

Alice smiled and gave a curtsy. "You military men and your oaths!"

"How long will the journey take?" Simon asked as he walked behind them.

"It took about three weeks to cross the Atlantic when my family moved here," Gilbert said.

"That must have been some years ago," Alice replied. "These newer ships can make the journey in ten days, weather permitting. It won't be a long journey, but long enough for us to get some proper rest."

"Good!" said Simon, who seemed uncharacteristically subdued. "I'm feeling very tired."

Gilbert yawned. He'd been moved to the afternoon watch again, and his sleep was still sorting itself out. He could have gotten a stretch of sleep this morning, but he preferred to finish whitewashing the barracks. These hours spent standing watch were taking their toll on his legs, reminding him that he was no longer twenty-two.

A visitor came up the path and the men straightened up. Everyone besides Gilbert was prone to slouching and leaning when they thought nobody was looking. Gilbert knew from his military days that behaving well when you incorrectly thought you weren't under supervision was the best way to distinguish yourself. He stifled another yawn and put his eyes forward.

Nothing amused the on-duty men more than surprising visitors. People would walk up the path without noticing the guards. Once they had passed, the guards would deliberately make noise or move in order to see how badly they could startle the newcomer. They had all been startled themselves when they arrived. None of them really questioned it. It didn't matter. This was simply how this path worked.

This fellow looked to be easy prey. He was looking down, very much absorbed in his thoughts. He was a narrow man of perhaps 40 or 50, with a thin mustache and a quick step. He was wearing a grey suit and a matching coachman hat.

The men held their breath. The secret to alarming people was to wait until they were in the middle of the circle of guards before making any sound.

The man stopped and looked up. He furrowed his brow, as if something was bothering him. Then he looked directly at one of the guards. "Ah!" he said suddenly. "How fascinating!"

His cry had startled the guards, and they all flinched with the sudden noise.

The man looked again at the house, and then back down at the guards. He could very plainly see them and did not mistake them for statues as people normally did. He walked into the circle and poked at some of the flagstones with his shoe. He walked around, and examined the guards from different angles.

"How very curious," he muttered to himself as he proceeded up the steps to the manor.

"A state-room! How magnificent!" Simon said.

"Are you sure the two of you are willing to share a room with a corpse?" Gilbert asked as he poked around their new room. "The journey will take us over a week -- a long time in such close quarters."

"I don't see why that should present any difficulty," Alice said. "Only two of us need to sleep and for that we have a bed and a generous couch. There is space enough for privacy when we need it. And besides, my supply of money is not endless. We don't know what other expenses we might encounter on this journey. We don't want to waste coin on comfort when we might need it later for more serious concerns."

The room was lavishly furnished. Wood had been put down to hide the metal deck and bulkheads. Curtains had been put up to create the illusion of additional windows on the inside wall. The furniture was crafted from rich, dark wood and the chairs were finely upholstered. It was as if someone had plucked the drawing room and bedroom from an English manor, and set them on board the ship.

"Feel the wall!" Simon said as he brushed his fingertips over the red and gold wallpaper. "It's bumpy!"

"Perhaps later," Alice said politely. Turning to Gilbert she said, "So now we're on the way to America, as you wished. What will you do if our Headmaster is not headed the same way?"

"I'm sure he's here. Did you see the bald fellow with the open shirt on the way to our room?"

"He was hard to miss," Alice admitted.

"That was Ivar the Scotsman. He and I were guards for Lord Mordaunt together. I'm betting he's one of the Headmaster's traveling companions."

"So our course is correct," Alice said with satisfaction.

"I hired you as a guard, not a governess," Headmaster Graves said, his thin, pale lips pulled into a sneer.

"I signed on with that understanding. But then you saddled me with wayward children." Gilbert said this with the practiced, respectful insolence that he saved for fools of superior rank. He was standing at attention. Headmaster had no rank, but it was easier for Gilbert to understand his place in Ravenstead if he thought of him as an officer.

"You've made quite a mess of the stables," Graves said. "His Lordship won't be pleased."

"If you ignore the men, the place is cleaner now than it has been at any time since it was built."

They were standing in the barracks. Gilbert had finished his renovations. The outside was whitewashed. The roof no longer leaked. The gaps in the walls had been mended. The broken furniture had been repaired or replaced. The stove no longer leaked smoke into the room. The tub now held water, so that the men could, in whatever miraculous circumstances might impart the urge, bathe. Gilbert had spent most of his pay and his off-duty time accomplishing this. The only thing wrong with the room now was the blood on the floor and the bruised men at his feet.

"I never liked you, Maypole. You always thought you were better than everyone else."

"A soldier is never better than his work. Or worse," Gilbert replied calmly. The fight had begun when he found one of the men defacing the wall. He tried to make the man clean it off, the man refused, there was a brawl, and some others joined in. Gilbert suspected Ivar had put them up to it.

"Well now, I've got three men who can't work. It wouldn't do to send them out all beaten up like this," Graves said, kicking one of the men at his feet. A groan came in answer.

"They had me outnumbered. If they lost then the shame is theirs, not mine."

"We'll see what His Lordship thinks of the way you've treated his property."

Gilbert was about to ask if Graves had really intended to call the men "property", when a new voice surprised him. He spun to see that Barrington Oswald Mordaunt, Viscount of Ravenstead, was standing in the doorway of the barracks. This was the first time he'd been in the same room with his employer.

"I have many enemies. I have reason to believe that some of them may come here with the intent of doing me harm," said the viscount.

The men on the floor struggled to their feet. The others in the room jumped up and, for the first time in their careers, stood at attention.

"I expect you to protect me. I expect you to fight. I expect you to not be duped by disguises, lies, or tricks," he continued.

The viscount was not a tall man. Most of his hair was gone. He was clean-shaven. He looked dangerously thin, perhaps even malnourished. His cheekbones stuck out and his dark eyes were set deeply in his head. He walked with an ornamental staff in one hand, as if he was a member of the clergy. He looked very proud and imposing, despite his modest stature.

"You will kill anyone who comes here with intent to harm, or you will die in the attempt," he concluded.

The men agreed eagerly and quickly. Some bowed, or nodded, or saluted (incorrectly) to show their acceptance. Then the viscount turned and left.

"These men need a day to recover from their injuries," Graves said once the master was gone. Then he turned to Gilbert. "You'll take the next four shifts to make up for it."

"Gladly," Gilbert said defiantly, but inside he was crushed. The master didn't seem to care or even notice his efforts. The men were dogs, and the viscount was content to employ dogs, and wanted nothing more. He mistakenly thought that Ravenstead was lacking in discipline, but what it really lacked was honor, and he had no cure for that. He had wasted his time trying to teach shiftless men to live by a standard they couldn't comprehend, for a man who couldn't tell the difference.

He wanted to quit now that his project had failed, but if he left without serving his punishment it would make him look like a hypocrite and a coward. The men would never have discipline, but he was going to show them what it looked like before he left.

It would be time for him to sleep soon, but instead he was going to have to guard the manor for the next thirty-two hours.

Once Graves had left, he began polishing his boots.

"I'm no longer tired. Why don't you take the bed while I work?" Alice suggested.

"I'm not tired either," Simon responded. "I'll help you with your work, and when you're tired you can have the bed."

Gilbert sighed. This had been going on for over an hour. Both of them were tired, but both of them insisted that they would sleep on the couch and the other person should sleep on the bed.

"Simon, would you do me a favor?" Gilbert said suddenly. "Would you see if there's anywhere on this ship where you might acquire shoe polish? My shoes are in ruinous shape."

Simon blinked, "At this hour? Surely everyone else is asleep. Wouldn't it make more sense to wait until morning?"

"Would you be willing to look anyway? I don't have anything to do here but listen to the two of you talk about sorcery."

"I'll do what I can," Simon said agreeably. He donned his hat and strode out of the room with a purpose.

"Stick to the upper deck, don't go below!" Gilbert called after him.

"Thank you!" Alice said once Simon was gone. "He is surprisingly stubborn," she yawned. She put one of the pillows on the couch and began to make it her bed.

"Actually, I asked him to leave so that I could insist that you let him have the couch."

Alice looked at him in surprise. "I couldn't possibly. No, he deserves the bed."

"Why?"

"You know why!" she said in bewilderment. "After all the boy has been through. He deserves the bed."

"So you're saying you want to give him the big, luxurious bed because he's had a hard life? Because you feel sorry for him?"

"Don't you?"

"Of course I do, and that's why you should take the bed yourself. He's young and naive, but he can tell you feel sorry for him. Making him take the bed will shame him."

She shook her head. "I'm not trying to shame him, I just want to take care of him."

"He doesn't want to be taken care of. He wants to help. He wants to be brave. He wants to be strong."

"He wants to be like you," Alice suggested.

"I know. I'll admit he certainly could have chosen a better role model, but the fact is that he doesn't want to be a burden."

'We could share it," she suggested. "The thing is enormous."

"Out of the question," Gilbert said.

Alice raised an eyebrow. "I did not expect you to be so prudish, of all people. I got the impression you were something of a scoundrel with regards to women."

"Among other things. I'm not worried about the two of you having an illicit affair while a walking corpse is sitting in the same room. I'm just concerned for Simon. Do you realize he's probably never spoken with a girl his own age before?"

"I hadn't thought of that," she admitted.

"You've spent most of your life around men. You're comfortable around them. You sleep next to them in the field without a second thought, don't you?"

"It's only practical," she said defensively. "And practicality should come before propriety."

"I agree. But Simon would be scandalized by the very suggestion. When I was in the military-"

"You say that often," she pointed out.

"It comes to mind often. Anyway, *when I was in the military*, I spent about ten months in a bad place. In all that time, I never saw a single woman. No girls. No mothers. No grandmothers. Nothing. Ten months of nothing but men. When I went on leave, I... purchased a bit of company for the night."

"Wouldn't it be more accurate to say the company was *rented*?"

"As you like," Gilbert shrugged. "This woman was not very healthy and did not have a comely face. She was ragged. She stank. She was rude and thick."

"I hope you're not searching for sympathy."

"No. You don't understand. After ten months, that woman was the *sun*. My heart was pounding in my chest just *talking* to her. And that was with a homely woman, after just ten months. Imagine what it must be like for poor Simon, who has been alone for a lifetime, who is faced with a stunningly attractive lady, and who must regard women as a complete mystery."

"On the point of my allegedly being 'stunningly attractive'-" Alice began.

"Do not deny it or I will become cross," Gilbert warned.

"Very well, I will allow the assertion to go unchallenged for the sake of not antagonizing you. I guess your description does explain why he goes red in the face whenever we speak."

"Imagine how much more intense his anxiety would be if he were in the same bed with you. He would never fall asleep."

"I would make sure to wear something-"

"You could fall asleep in the clothes you're wearing now, and it wouldn't make things any less scandalous for him."

She stood up from the couch and began moving her things over to the bed, "Very well. He may have the couch."

"Thank you."

"He is a remarkable boy," she said, stifling another yawn. "To have suffered so much and not become hardened or bitter. He is very gentle and kind, even though not a single person in his life ever taught him so."

"I've seen cases where good, decent people ended up with an unaccountably malicious and villainous son," Gilbert said thoughtfully. "I guess the reverse can sometimes be true as well. Although, I'll wager it's rarer."

"Like finding a rose growing amongst poison ivy."

"A rose? A few days ago you condemned him as a sorcerer," Gilbert said.

"And you rightly pointed out that I was one as well. But our job was never to simply go after sorcerers. My father's belief - and indeed the entire point of the ministry - was to oppose dangerous, harmful sorcerers. But I don't think anyone can look at Simon and conclude he's interested in hurting others. I'm sure he's probably done evil things, but not of his own volition."

"I imagine the Headmaster takes most of the blame for any evil perpetrated by Simon's hands, as well as the evil inflicted on him."

"And yet the boy doesn't seem inclined to revenge."

"I can't say the same. I plan to run the man through as soon as the opportunity presents itself."

"I do find it curious that both you and Simon have had dealings with the man. How is it that you met him?"

"His title is 'headmaster', but he was really just the viscount's right-hand man. He ran whatever staff worked at the academy, and he ran the men who guarded the manor. Twisted fellow."

A few minutes later the door shot open and Simon rushed in. He slammed it shut again and leaned against it. He looked around the room, wide-eyed.

"Are you alright?" Alice asked.

"Headmaster. I saw him. He saw me. It was... I came around the corner and there he was, grinning with those awful teeth of his."

"Blast it," said Gilbert. "I'm sure he's in steerage. I didn't expect him to be prowling around the upper decks."

"I would like to have gone a bit longer without him knowing we were trailing him," Alice lamented.

"I'm so sorry!" Simon said.

"It's not your fault", Alice said gently. "I'd rather blame the one who sent you out on so frivolous an errand in the middle of the night."

"Oh! That reminds me," said Simon. "I found you some shoe polish."

Gilbert felt like the walking dead. He staggered into the barracks, listing like a sinking ship. He'd been awake for, what? Two days? Since the last time he slept he'd finished repairing the barracks, gotten in a fight, and stood watch in front of the manor for thirty-two consecutive hours. His vision had narrowed. The world around him seemed muffled and distant. The only thing he could perceive with any clarity was the relentless pain in his legs and back. His head drooped forward, and it took a great deal of concentration to keep from going face-first into the floor.

Gilbert shuffled across the room and stopped. Ivar was standing between him and his bed.

"The scullery maid looks tired out after all her cleaning. Maybe she wants to go to bed?" Ivar grinned.

Gilbert looked around, wondering what scullery maid Ivar was talking about. The punch in the side of his face woke him up a bit, and he realized what was going on. He lunged forward to repay Ivar for the unsporting opening, and found his arm was caught on something. A blow to the opposite side of his face gave his mind another jolt, and somewhere in the back of his mind he became aware that he was in trouble.

He tried again to strike but his other arm was caught as well. He realized someone had grabbed him from behind. He threw himself backwards into the wall, crushing the man behind him. A yelp sounded, and he recognized the voice as belonging to Soot. Ivar drove his knuckles deep into Gilbert's sternum, which put a stop to his breathing for a few seconds. Gilbert stumbled onto his hands and knees, at which point his attackers switched to kicking.

Gilbert looked up. Before he passed out he saw that the walls of the barracks had been defaced. Ugly, lewd scrawls covered the walls around his bunk.

The Saloon of the SS Callisto was a grand hall that extended the entire width of the vessel. Generous portholes opened to give patrons a view of the sea. The top of the room opened to a great dome, which was crowned with a skylight. Beams of richly colored wood crossed below this, with pots of green plants hanging from them. At the front was a piano that filled the air with gentle music.

"You don't remember your parents?" Alice asked.

Simon shook his head. He opened the corner of his mouth to draw in a noisy draught of air as he chewed the enormous mouthful of meat pie. After some furious work the food was driven home, and his fork immediately delivered another.

"Do you remember anything about your life before you began serving the viscount?"

"Rrphnage," he gulped.

"Orphanage?"

Simon nodded and his fork scooped up another heap of pie.

"My goodness, Simon," Alice said when his appetite showed no signs of diminishing, "Did Gilbert feed you at all while you were with him?"

"Lots," he choked.

"Then why do you eat so ravenously?"

Simon looked down at his food, and then he met Alice's eyes. He gave a slight, apologetic shrug and returned to work.

"I see. He fed you well but didn't bother to teach you any manners. Typical. This won't do! You're making a spectacle of yourself," she warned.

Simon slowed and looked around to the other patrons. The saloon was sparse at this hour, being slightly past midday. Some passengers were travelers, connoisseurs of cultures and exotic sights. Others were industrialists, men of wealth and power conducting their trans-Atlantic business. Simon and Alice were among the youngest of the passengers, and a few people took them for newlyweds. (Since they could apparently imagine no other reason that two people of their age might be sharing a room across the Atlantic.) One man even shook Simon's hand and wished him well, although the man's eyes had been on Alice while he did so.

At the moment, a few people were glaring at Simon. The rest were pretending they didn't see his display, lest they become enraged and so spoil their own meal. The center of the room was brilliantly illuminated by the sun streaming in through the windows, but their table was in one of the dim spots at the edge of the room. It was hardly secretive or even private, but at least it didn't bring them additional attention.

"Sorry," Simon said, once his mouth was properly empty. He sat looking at the food for a few moments. After what seemed like a polite interval, he took a more conventionally proportioned bite, and then began chewing furiously.

Alice winced. "Slowly!" she pleaded.

Simon stopped his chewing and sat for a moment with the food still in his mouth, as if waiting for permission to begin again.

"I didn't say stop. Just... eat tiny bites if you must, but try to slow the rate of your intake. You should not need to gulp for air." She held up her own fork and took her own small bite in demonstration.

Simon nodded and did his best to emulate her.

"Nobody will snatch the plate from you, and I'll be happy to order more if you need it."

"Thank you!" Simon grinned through another bite of food. As his meal drew to an end he looked down at his plate thoughtfully. "I'm sorry again for my manners," he said.

"You already said so," Alice said dismissively. "With practice I'm sure you'll learn the art of eating without drowning in your meal."

"It's just that... at the academy... we never got to eat like this. We were only given a few minutes to eat, and groups of us often shared a common bowl. If you didn't eat quickly, you wouldn't get enough."

"Well take heart," she replied. "Those days are behind you now."

A shadow passed over the table. Alice ignored it, thinking the waiter had returned prematurely and was trying to hurry them along. But then a foul smell reached her nose. She looked up and saw a man in a ragged suit standing over them, leering menacingly.

"What do you want?" she demanded. She assumed he was just there to beg. She was not normally against charity, but this fellow had an unwholesome look. She glanced across the table to see that Simon was paralyzed with fear. His eyes were open wide and he was clutching the tablecloth desperately.

The man took a seat without asking, grinning at Simon. "Having fun, Mouse? Got your belly nice and full?" His accent revealed him to be a man incapable of pronouncing the letter 'H'.

"You must be this 'headmaster' I keep hearing about," Alice said hotly. "Get yourself below decks before I call for help. Steerage passengers aren't permitted in the saloon."

He laughed at this, "Abominations aren't permitted on the ship at all, I'd imagine. Along with a couple of traveling witches. If you give me up, I'll make sure to return the favor. We'll see who comes out worse for it."

"Make your accusations if you like, assuming you can find an ear among the crew willing to hear them."

Graves lowered his voice, "The master is very displeased at what you've done, but he's of a generous disposition right now."

Simon let out a fearful squeak at this, which amused the headmaster.

Alice glared at the boy, but he was transfixed by the headmaster and would not look away. "Is he really?" Alice replied. "And what can a traitorous, dead, cursed, *failure* like Lord Mordaunt offer us in his generosity?"

The headmaster was amused by her anger, "Well, Mouse here can scurry away, free as you like. The master is done with him. And His Lordship will grant a reprieve for Maypole's mother. Just don't go back to England. Stay in America or go where you like, but England belongs to Lord Mordaunt now."

Alice raised an eyebrow, "So your master's generosity consists of offering us what we already have? And in exchange, all he asks for is a continent? Grand dealings for a man who has yet to escape the dirt he was buried in."

"You're a cheeky bird, aren't you?" Graves said. "If that's your thinking then we'll see to Maypole's family. His mum, and whoever else shares his name or blood. We'll cut their throats and find out if a dead man can weep. After that we'll take Mouse here back home with us."

"No!" Simon gasped.

"Your threats are empty. We'll be allowed off the boat long before the steerage passengers. You have no chance at reaching Mrs. Hiltman ahead of us, and you cannot hope to prevail against us in a fight."

Graves rose up as if he were going to make some move, but stopped when a man cleared his throat behind him. Three crew members had gathered around him. They grabbed him and hauled him out before he could speak in his defense. Their waiter came and apologized profusely for the intrusion. He asked if Alice was unharmed so many times that she nearly got angry with him.

Gilbert awoke in confusion. A bell was ringing. Did he hear gunshots a moment ago, or was that a bad dream?

He found himself soaking in the tub. It was a small thing, more suited for a lady than for a soldier, much less a man of his size. He stirred, and was suddenly reminded of the numerous wounds and bruises all over his body, which is what led to the bath in the first place. The water was murky with dirt, and tinged red.

He rubbed his eyes, gently. He drew a deep breath, despite the protest from his ribs. How long had he been asleep? The water had long gone cold. The barracks were inexplicably empty. Even the beds were stripped. The place was deserted. He sadly noted the fresh graffiti on the walls. Also, the wall he'd repaired had been smashed open again.

He lifted himself out of the tub uneasily. Once he was standing on the cold wood floor, he noticed that all of his things were gone. There was nothing that he might use to dry off, much less clothe himself. He sighed. The men had returned to their pranks.

The bell was still ringing. It was the alarm bell, and was most likely part of the prank. Clearly the men stole his clothes and anything else he might possibly use to cover himself, and then rang the bell to oblige him to run outside naked.

His boots were still sitting on a chair beside the tub. He'd intended to clean them while he bathed. He did his best to push the water off of himself using his hands, and then pulled on his boots.

Gunshots rang out. They were distant. Gilbert's heart jumped as he realized they might be coming from the manor. The alarm could very well be real. He remembered what the viscount had said to the men a few days earlier.

Prank or not, his duty was to protect his master. If that meant running afoul of this prank, then it was his duty to run across the grounds naked and endure the scorn. No fit soldier could ignore the alarm and keep his honor. He exited through the broken wall.

It was sunset. The red sun slid beneath the ocean of dark trees like a man drowning. The manor was already in shadow. Not a soul could be seen outside, not even the scurrying kitchen servants, who were usually moving about preparing the evening meal at this time. Gilbert thought he heard screams and sounds of struggle above the sound of the wind.

A gunshot sounded. This one was unmistakable. The alarm bell fell silent.

He charged up the hill and hid beside the bushes near the rear entrance. He crept around to the side of the house to see two men wearing red sashes. They were dragging one of the house guards away from the bell. The man was limp in their arms.

Quickly he returned to the rear entrance. Who was attacking in such numbers? He'd never heard of anyone having the audacity to assault the home of an English nobleman.

His teeth had begun to chatter. The early autumn air was quickly sapping his strength. He needed to get indoors before he froze.

He ducked in through the back door and found himself in the kitchen. A pot was boiling over. A lamp was lit for the cook, but the room was empty. There was shouting elsewhere in the house, the cries of men fighting. The place smelled like potatoes, and Gilbert was suddenly aware of how ravenously hungry he was.

He'd looked through the back door a few times, but he'd never been in the kitchen proper. He had no idea where to go from here. There was no sense in him charging into the battle unarmed and naked. He glanced around the room for something that might be of use as a weapon. There was a paring knife on the counter, a tiny thing made for the hands of a woman. He took it. Hopefully there would be something more substantial nearby.

Gilbert opened up the door to the nearby closet, and found two women huddled inside, blinking at the sudden light. One was the portly cook. The other was a young servant that Gilbert had never met before. They screamed first with surprise, and then wailed in terror when they saw their hiding place was discovered by a naked man brandishing a knife.

"No! Shh!" Gilbert said desperately, but the women were inconsolable. Over their cries he could make out the sound of booted footsteps in the hall.

In a panic, he lunged for the nearby stairs. He strode up the curving staircase and reached the top just as the screams were renewed below. The shouting of men's voices was heard. They did not sound like anyone Gilbert knew. At first he thought he'd abandoned the women to death, but their cries continued. It didn't sound like they were being hurt; only frightened.

Gilbert was at one end of a long hallway that seemed to run all the way to the front of the house. This was his first time inside of the Manor, and he was surprised at how ghastly it was. The place was made of dark wood, covered in dust. Cobwebs clung in the corners. Did the maids not clean here? Claw-shaped fixtures protruded from the walls, holding up small candles against the smothering dark. A rich, yet frayed red carpet ran along the floor.

He almost went through the nearest door, but then stopped himself. If the men gave chase then that would be the first place they would look. Hoping he was being clever, Gilbert ran several doors down and opened a door at random. This brought him into the bedchamber of His Lordship Barrington Oswald Mordaunt.

This was plainly the master bedroom, although it did not look lived-in at all. Heavy curtains blocked out the waning light of the sun. Gilbert pulled these open so that he could see. The room was much like the rest of the upstairs - expensive and in a terrible state of decay. The fireplace was dark and cold. The bed was covered in a generous layer of dust, so that the slightest disturbance would send clouds of it into the air.

He needed to do something about his nakedness. He opened the wardrobe nearby, which was full of shirts that were too small to be put on. He sighed, and pulled one down. Perhaps he could tie the arms around his waist and fashion himself a sort of kilt. It would leave his backside exposed, but it was better than nothing.

Suddenly he noticed the back wall of the wardrobe was split with age, and a dim red light was seeping through the cracks. He pushed on it, and it seemed to give a bit. It rattled like a shut door, although it was too dark to see any hinges or handle. He gave another shove and the door gave way with the sound of splintering wood. He shrugged. There was probably a less destructive way to open it, but he didn't have the patience for that sort of search.

Through the door was another room, one not connected to the main hall. The walls and floor were made of rough, unadorned wood. Unlike the neat, dusty bedroom, this room looked well-used. Books were piled beside a cluttered desk. There was a table nearby with several abandoned plates spread around a single lit candle. As Gilbert entered, a rat grudgingly gave up the plate of crumbs it had been working on and waddled off into the shadows.

Instead of carpet, the floor was covered in smears of white dust. It was chalk. It almost looked as if someone had been writing and erasing.

A white robe was hanging on a hook just inside the door. Gratefully, Gilbert slipped it on. It was light and thin; clearly something designed to be worn over one's regular clothes. Jagged letters were embroidered on the front, although the work was so poorly done that the letters were impossible to recognize.

Beside the robe was a large staff, like the kind carried by a church hierarch. It was nearly as tall as a man. It was made of brass, and had a good bit of heft to it. The top was an elaborate headpiece. These were usually icons or the faces of saints, but in the flickering candlelight this one sort of looked like a skull. Curiously, the tip was a clamp that held a piece of chalk. He pulled this out, and found the tip of the clamp to be moderately sharp. It wasn't a proper weapon, but it was long, heavy, and pointy, which was close enough to a spear for his needs.

He was clothed and armed. Now he just needed to locate the battle and join it. He was worried at how quiet things had become. The shouting had died down a few minutes ago, and the thumping had stopped shortly after that.

There was another door opposite of the one he had come in. It opened quietly with just a gentle push. Gilbert stepped through and found himself at the top of the imperial staircase. Harsh voices came from below. Gilbert drew close and saw that the Lord Mordaunt was standing at the base of the steps, amidst a field of carnage. Many of Gilbert's fellow guards were piled around the door, along with the bodies of a few men in (formerly) white robes. Aside from His Lordship, everyone was wearing red sashes.

The battle was clearly over, and it had been a decisive victory for the opposition, who were obviously members of the church. They had come in overwhelming numbers. Gilbert was baffled. He couldn't imagine what sort of thing would drive them to this level of violence.

A hierarch was standing in front of Lord Mordaunt, reading something to him. (At least, Gilbert assumed the man was a hierarch. His robes seemed to say so, although he bore a sword instead of a scepter and was wearing a good deal of blood.) Gilbert crept closer in order to hear.

"These are your own words," the hierarch said.

"They are," Mordaunt said proudly and defiantly.

The hierarch furrowed his brow and looked around to his men, who replied with shrugs. Scratching his head he said, "In all my years of service to the church I've never heard of such a thing. You admit, openly, to capital witchcraft."

"I never confessed to 'witchcraft'. Witchcraft is the name given by fools. Its proper name is sorcery. The dark art. The *great* art." The men grumbled at this.

"But, you do not renounce it?" the hierarch asked.

"Never!" Mordaunt said. Gilbert could not see his face from where he was, but he thought the viscount sounded almost smug.

"Then why did you send us your confession?"

"Because I defy you. I defy you, your church, and your impotent god!" Some of the young men had to be restrained at this, so fierce was their desire to punish him for this blasphemy.

The hierarch looked even more baffled, "Was it your purpose to have us come here and kill you?"

"My purposes are beyond your understanding. But if you find the courage to raise your blade to me, I will be much amused."

The hierarch looked down at his sword doubtfully, "If you are so eager for my blade, then why did you send your men to throw away their lives in your hopeless defense?"

Mordaunt gave no answer.

"Do you have *nothing* to say in your defense?" the hierarch asked.

When it was clear the man was unwilling to speak, the hierarch pronounced his judgment, "Lord Mordaunt, by the rights given me by God, the saints, and the throne of Her Majesty the Queen of Great Britain, and on the basis of your own confession both written and verbal, I condemn you to death. I would beg God to have mercy on your soul, but I'm sure you would only refuse it." The hierarch ran the viscount through.

"That is the most inexplicable arrest I've ever performed," said the hiearch, shaking his head. "He didn't run, or fight, or deny the charges, or claim bewitchment."

"They always claim bewitchment," one of the men lamented.

"Who is this?" came a voice from behind Gilbert. Suddenly every eye in the room turned from the viscount to the top of the stairs. Gilbert turned around and saw a pair of Red Sashes had come up behind him.

Gilbert wasn't sure if he should hold onto the staff to defend himself, or surrender. In a panic, he tried to do both and raised the staff over his head.

"Spellcraft!" boomed the hierarch. "Arrest him!"

The men tried to lay their hands on Gilbert. He grabbed one by the arm and flung him down the steps. The other he stabbed in the foot with his scepter. It was a clean strike, although the tip snapped off in the man's boot. As the zealot stumbled, Gilbert spun his weapon around and struck the man in the side of the head. He had no desire to fight these men, but he was frightened, confused, and acting on instinct.

The Red Sashes began flowing up the stairs after him. He turned and fled back to where he had come in, only to find the secret door had sealed itself. He couldn't find any latch or seam that might tell where the door had been located. He clawed at the wall, cursing and banging furiously on the wood. He considered simply running down the main hall, but that way was hopeless. He couldn't hope to outrun this many men. He needed to vanish from sight.

He was still beating the wall when the men cornered him. He swung his scepter. One man was struck in the nose, another was tripped, and another doubled over from an elbow in the pills, but then they overwhelmed him. He was pinned and his weapon taken.

"Don't let him speak," commanded the hierarch. "I see his game now."

Many men had put their weight on him. Someone put their hand over his mouth, although it wasn't needed. Gilbert could barely breathe, much less talk.

The hierarch stood over him, "So, your deception is revealed, your Lordship. I don't know why you sent the confession, if indeed you did. But now I see your plan. You hoped your men would drive us off. When that failed, you bewitched one of your own servants to come and claim to be you."

Gilbert looked at the hierarch, wide-eyed.

"Yes. I see I guess right," the hierarch smiled. "Let us put your trickery to an end."

Gilbert felt a sharp pain in his chest as the sword came down. He began to feel very warm, and wet, and eventually drowsy. The voices in the room faded, and darkness overtook him.

VI

“What a horrible way to die,” Alice remarked.

“I don’t know that it was particularly horrible,” Gilbert replied. “I’ve seen men die worse deaths.”

They were walking on the promenade deck. The sun had gone down, and Gilbert had come out for a stroll as soon as the bulk of their fellow passengers had gone to bed. He walked with his head bowed. He leaned on his cane, which made it easier to obscure his face if someone happened by. Alice was carrying a parasol because it amused her. Simon had remained in the room. At last exhausted of new sights to marvel at, he had fallen asleep happy and full.

Alice placed her hand on Gilbert’s shoulder, “I admire your attempt to be brave about your demise, but your own voice unmasks you. You are unsettled by the memory.”

“I suppose,” Gilbert admitted. “I was not expecting... Well, I don’t know that you can ever expect to die in any particular way, but I am surprised by the circumstances of my death.”

“When did this come to you? And are you sure of it? I’d heard that the viscount was executed by the church but I had heard nothing of the battle.”

“The memory came to me earlier today, when you and Simon were dining in the saloon and I was alone. My memories usually come back to me at these times, when I am sitting alone and quiet. They might have returned sooner if the days since my awakening hadn’t been so filled with chaos. And yes, I'm sure the memory is correct. The details are vague, but the parts I've told are the parts in which I have confidence. Since I was awakened I've been struggling to recall how I met my end. Being dead is bad enough, but being dead and not knowing how you died is even worse. I thought it might have been an accident that took me. Or the work of one of my fellow guards. Or chance illness. Or perhaps some treachery on the part of my employer. But the church?"

They listened for a moment to the soft churning of the sea below. The engines of the ship rumbled in the distance, a low sound that was more felt than heard. Overhead, the smokestack did its best to blot out what remained of the night sky, and the half-moon watched them from behind shreds of dark cloud. The lights were going out on the ship. A few suspicious faces appeared in windows as they strolled past at this unnatural hour.

"You died in the line of duty, if that's of any comfort," Alice said at last.

"It is, although it might be overly generous to call my actions 'duty'. I was running about unprepared and confused, and in the end I didn't do anything to save my master."

"Did you want to?" Alice asked curiously.

"I'm not sure. It was very confusing. A soldier is honor-bound to protect his charge. On the other hand, the viscount seemed to be attempting suicide by way of the church. And he was a blasphemer and a sorcerer. To defend him or abandon him? It was dishonor, either way. Which probably explains why I did neither and simply stood there like an imbecile."

"But part of the mystery is untangled," Alice said brightly as she twirled the parasol on her shoulder. "The fact that your master and his men were slaughtered by the church explains how you came to be mistaken for His Lordship. And to their credit, their blundering undid his plans."

"I hadn't thought of it that way," Gilbert said. "If the Witch Watch had performed the arrest, he would have been buried in his proper tomb, and he would have been revived instead of me."

"Not so. If the ministry had taken part in his arrest, we would have taken his head."

"The Witch Watch beheads prisoners?" Gilbert asked in surprise.

"Not as a manner of execution. It's seen as a barbaric and gruesome means of death. It's publicly unpopular, you understand. We usually take the head after death, before burial. We also bury sorcerers and necromancers in our ground at Tyburn, and not on their own property." Alice stopped and looked at Gilbert thoughtfully, "You know, this may explain why the viscount gave himself over to the church. My father had been suspicious of Lord Mordaunt for a long time. Perhaps the man learned that he'd attracted the attention of Ethereal Affairs. Then, fearing our more certain execution, he baited the church into killing him instead."

"That seems like a terrible risk," Gilbert said doubtfully. "I don't know. It doesn't fully explain his behavior. Why not flee? Or feign death?"

"He's working towards becoming a lich. It sounds like death was part of his plan," Alice pointed out.

"Then why not simply take his own life?"

They stopped, and Alice leaned out over the railing, looking down into the dark, noisy ocean below. "I don't know," she said at last.

"You appear to have some admirers," Gilbert said, nodding towards the balcony above them. As she looked, two crewmen turned away abruptly and pretended to be interested in something else.

"Those two again," she said. "I saw them watching us earlier today. I wonder if the headmaster has put some malicious words in their ear."

"It's more likely they're sailors who have taken notice of a pretty girl," Gilbert said.

"I hope you're right," she said doubtfully. "But you have again hijacked my thinking. Whatever his reasons, Mordaunt wanted to be killed by the church. He arranged for it to happen, on purpose. He's working on some plan, even if we don't yet see it."

"He showed a lot of foresight by collecting my family information when I was hired," Gilbert agreed. "And again when he sent his men after my mother. It seems like he planned for many eventualities, both good and bad. Which worries me. So many of his actions seem foolish or random to us, but it's clear he is very wise and calculating. There is a great deal of his plan that we do not see."

"If what Mr. Graves says is true, then we have angered and frustrated His Lordship. Whatever his plans are, we are likely ahead of them."

"I hope you're right. Another thing that Graves said is puzzling me. You said that he threatened to report me to the captain."

"An empty threat, I'm sure," Alice said. "The crew would never trouble a first-class passenger based on an accusation made by someone in steerage."

"I disagree. If several people made the same accusation, they might be able to persuade the crew to action. Remember that seamen are famously hostile towards sorcery."

"But that would be disastrous for them. They need to recover the vigor, which they won't be able to do if you're discovered. It's to the advantage of both sides to avoid taking action during this journey."

They had reached the front of the ship. They were at the tip of the knife as it cut through the ocean. Alice shivered a bit. Out of habit, Gilbert almost put his arm around her. Then he remembered himself. He was grotesque. Moreover, he had no heat to impart. He felt suddenly depressed.

"A question comes to mind," she said suddenly. "Mr. Graves said that His Lordship was displeased with us."

"I imagine he would be," Gilbert said, happy to have something to think about besides being dead.

"Yes, but how does he know what has happened? You explained how they were able to commune with His Lordship using blood. That technique was new to me."

"It was new to me, too," Gilbert said dryly.

"Clearly Mr. Graves came to us at the behest of his master. Which means he spoke with his dead master since coming aboard. They are reporting in and receiving orders."

"You're suggesting they're performing necromancy on the ship?"

"Is it still called necromancy if you commune with the dead and do not revive or animate a body?" She asked idly.

"You are asking the wrong corpse. I have no understanding of such business."

"Of course. I wasn't really asking you. Anyway, yes. They must be performing sorcery here on the ship."

"That sounds like a reasonable assumption," agreed Gilbert.

"A moment ago I said it was to the advantage of both sides to avoid conflict, but perhaps we can move against them indirectly. If they were discovered in the midst of their magic, they would be executed before we reached port. As you pointed out, ship captains are very superstitious and extremely prejudiced against magic."

Gilbert nodded. "If they are discovered by the crew, nobody will listen to what the headmaster has to say about me. We could be rid of them without risking discovery ourselves. All we need to do is find them and point the crew in the right direction. I assume they must go somewhere below to do this thing?"

"I agree. They would be discovered quickly if they attempted to perform their villainy on the shuffleboard court," Alice said.

"This ship is over five thousand tons of floating iron. The area below is vast. You could search for the entire voyage and not find their hiding place."

"We won't need to search," Alice said brightly. "At least, not the whole ship."

They returned to their room to find Simon awake and restless. He was disappointed at missing out on their walk. Alice explained their suspicion that the headmaster was using sorcery on the ship. She retrieved her strange device from her bag and fastened it to her arm.

"My ethergram," she explained. "It can point us towards magical activity."

"A *machine* that detects magic?" Gilbert marveled. "I can't imagine how that's possible. How does it 'know' about the magic?"

"A bit of wisdom from a Dutch physician and sometime-necromancer named Rutger de Bray. About twenty years ago he noticed that his stores of ether would react to the presence of magic. It boiled and expanded, as if attracted to the supernatural activity. He was later discovered and executed by the church, but before that he relayed his findings to a fellow sorcerer here in England. For a while sorcerers were convinced that the liquid itself had magical properties, or that it could be used to augment magic. Ten years ago there was a rash of explosions around London as various sorcerers blew themselves up experimenting with it. It is highly flammable.

"My father learned about this through confessions and confiscated materials, and he constructed a crude device to detect magic. It was just a canister with a bell inside that rang when the ether was agitated by magic. I took his design and improved upon it. It has very small vials of ether, contained under pressure, which will send the needle in the appropriate direction. It's mostly made from watch works. See?" She held up the device, which had the face of a watch set amidst the tubes and wires.

"Based on ether? Now I see why you call it an 'ethergram'," Gilbert said, slightly regretting asking the question.

"My father called it my 'witch watch'. He thought this was very funny."

Simon stood by her and admired the device. "So you just follow the dial on your wrist and it will take us to the source of the sorcery?"

"I'm not sure it will be that easy," she replied. "The device is not terribly accurate, and you must hold very, very still to get anything out of it. And it reacts slightly to Gilbert's presence, which means I have to stand away from him in order to use it properly. The motion of the ship might be enough to render the thing useless. I'm sure I could build a better one if I had smaller parts and finer tools. My tinkering has faltered in the past few years as I've been obliged to study sorcery instead. Even if the device does work on the ship, I don't know how close we will need to be."

"Is there any way we can run a test?" Simon asked.

"How very scientific of you," Alice said with approval. "There is, but it means doing sorcery ourselves."

There was a silent moment, which Gilbert broke. "Commit sorcery? Here on the ship?"

"We already have an abomination in our company. I don't know that this is going to increase our danger of discovery," she replied.

"Can I help somehow?" asked Simon.

"By all means," said Gilbert. "We need to make sure that none of us are innocent."

Alice glared at him, "This entire adventure is full of peril, and has been undertaken for your benefit."

"For my mother," Gilbert corrected her.

"In either case, I should think that after all of the reckless chances you've taken so far, this would seem like a small thing to you."

"It's not the risk," Gilbert said. "It's the hypocrisy. And sorcery... unsettles me."

"We are only fighting fire with fire," Alice argued. "And I'm sure your fear will be tempered by the apprehension of our foes." She drew the curtains and then placed her bag on the bed. From this she drew out a large, heavy block of undergarments. Simon gasped and blushed.

"I was worried that someone might peek inside my bag," she explained. "But even the rudest of busybodies will pause before rummaging through a lady's undergarments." She unwrapped a large book from the frilly package and returned the rest to her bag. Turning to Simon she said, "I brought along your book. Or Lord Mordaunt's book, which you used in reviving Gilbert. I have many questions about it that I hope you can answer."

Simon blinked, and slowly realized she was talking to him. He pulled his eyes away from the mouth of her bag and met her gaze dumbly.

“The book?” she smiled, holding it up.

“Oh, *that* thing,” he said sadly. “I’d hoped I’d seen the last of that book. It was a source of misery. Whenever I see it I can only think of being hungry.”

“Hungry?”

Simon dropped himself onto the couch, “I mentioned before about the Ravenstead Academy for Boys.”

“You have only spoken about the place in hints so far, but the little that I’ve heard has been disturbing enough.”

Simon continued, “There were two groups of boys - the scholars, and the laborers. The strong ones are laborers. They do manual labor and help take care of the other boys. The smart ones become scholars and sit all day and copy books like the one in your hands. The really smart ones - or at least the ones with a good memory - are taught Black Latin and sorcery. I was one of the latter sort. Often we weren’t allowed to eat until we got the spell to work.”

“Sounds like a dreadful place,” Alice said. “Did you have friends?”

“Once. There usually wasn’t room for friendship. Every boy had to look out for himself just to fill his belly. I was a scholar and was given extra food when I did well, but the food was given to me when other boys were around. They usually ganged up on me to take it for themselves. I suppose they were friends with each other. Or at least, they liked one another better than they liked me.

“When I was perhaps fourteen, I met a laborer named Dillon. He was strong. Husky. He was also quiet, and not very bright. But we worked together. He protected me from the other boys, and I shared my extra food with him. We never made an agreement. Not verbally. It just happened. I don’t even remember which one of us acted first, but it seemed very natural. He defended me from bullying and pranks, and I helped keep his belly full. He protected me even when I didn’t have food to share, and I shared even when his duties prevented him from protecting me.

"We rarely spoke. There was nothing to talk about. His work was too dull to discuss, and my work too terrifying. He couldn't read and didn't care about magic. Neither of us had any memories of our parents. We sat and ate in silence, day after day.

"Then one day he was chosen by Headmaster Graves for leech duty."

"Leech duty?" Gilbert asked.

"Headmaster Graves is a wizard, and wizards need someone to leech. There was a stone room in the basement with a metal cage. There was a feeding circle etched into the bottom of the cage, so you couldn't erase it. A boy would go into the cage and then the headmaster could cast magic spells."

"A wizard doesn't need to feed off of another person," Alice corrected him. "They're simply limited to a few spells before they become too weak to cast them."

"Well, the headmaster never did magic under his own power. He always used a leech."

"If the headmaster is drawing energy from the boy, wouldn't that make him the leech, and not the boy?" asked Gilbert.

"Properly, I suppose," Simon admitted. "But the boys didn't know anything about leeches. They figured, if you're on 'leech duty', then you must be the leech. Sometimes we were picked at random. Sometimes it was a punishment. He'd usually gather up a few boys and drag them to the basement for leech duty. He would practice his magic until the boys were spent." Simon took a deep sigh and seemed to be looking far away. "Being in the cage - in the feeding circle - is the worst feeling in the world. Worse than hunger, cold, beatings, or loneliness, because it sort of feels like all of them at once. It's not pain. Not like the other kinds of pain, anyway. It feels empty. Like an ache that begins in your heart and expands out to your fingertips. Like being poured out over cold stones. Like breathing ice into your lungs. I would always press against the bars, as far from the center of the circle. It never helped, but I always clung there until I collapsed."

Alice took him by the shoulders and lifted him up, "Well, I promise you there will be no starvation during the course of this magic. And we won't be using the book right now, just a few notes of my own. If you like, we can probably still get you some food before we start."

Simon declined, and insisted they get started right away.

She handed Simon a bit of chalk. Then she walked into the middle of the room and threw aside the rug that lay between the couch and the bed. She showed him a bit of paper that she'd tucked into the book, "Can you do this circle for me?"

Simon looked at the sorcery depicted. "I've never seen this spell before. It doesn't make a lot of sense. I can't see what it does."

"Nothing," Alice said. "It's a spell that does nothing. It activates and draws power like a normal spell, but it doesn't make anything happen. I found it in my father's notes, and I use it for testing."

Simon handed her back the page. She looked down at it with disappointment, "You won't do it?"

"Of course I will," he said, and went to work. He crouched down and began drawing a broad circle around himself.

"But don't you need to look at the page to..." she began but her words faltered and she stood in wonder and watched him work. He'd drawn a perfect circle without using any sort of guide. After that he drew the inner circle, and the connecting arcs. The arcs were all the same size, evenly spaced. Then he began writing the characters. He turned the chalk in his fingers as he went, so that he wouldn't flatten out one side and end up with lines of differing thickness. Alice looked down and saw his work matched the page in her hand perfectly, except that perhaps his was more accurately proportioned.

"Amazing," she whispered.

"I learned early on to remember what I saw and reproduce it accurately," he said without looking up. "I had a better chance of eating that way. Although, some days even that wasn't enough. Since they were copied by other boys, the books themselves sometimes contained errors."

She shook her head in disbelief. "That circle would have taken me a quarter hour."

"Spending a quarter hour on a drawing that size would have earned me a thrashing," Simon said glumly. He stepped away from the completed circle, brushing the chalk off of himself.

Alice suddenly looked down in shame. "Simon, I'm so sorry that I asked you to do this. It was thoughtless of me to ask you to do something that brings back such painful memories."

"Seems a bit late to arrive at that conclusion," Gilbert said. He was sitting in a corner of the room, looking bored.

"You're right," she said. "I just... this was how my father and I worked on things. He would hand me a bit of chalk, we'd draw a circle, and discuss it."

"I'm not bothered by this," Simon said defensively. "I always liked sorcery. Well, not the magic parts. That was usually frustrating. Or disquieting. Or terrifying. But I enjoy the circles. Making them as large as I can. Making the curves. Drawing the letters just so."

"You must have been two of the creepiest children who ever lived," Gilbert said. "The idea of doing sorcery with youths is perverse."

"And what did your father teach you?" Alice asked.

"Swordfighting," Gilbert nodded with satisfaction. "We'd go out and find a couple of sticks, and he'd teach me fencing. We also practiced the bayonet. And archery. I wanted to learn boxing, but Father said it was barbaric."

"And you think these are more wholesome things to teach children than sorcery?" Alice asked.

Suddenly there was a heavy knock at the door, and the three of them froze. There was an open book of sorcery on the bed, Gilbert was sitting by the door with his face exposed, and there was a large and unmistakable sorcery circle in the middle of the room. They stood looking dumbly at one another for a few moments, and the knock came again.

They all lunged into motion at once. "Who's there?" asked Alice as she stuffed the book under the bed covers.

“Purser, ma’am,” came a man’s voice.

Gilbert dove into bed. Simon threw the rug over the circle on the floor. It was too small to conceal the sorcery, so he yanked the blankets off of the bed to cover up the rest. This exposed both Gilbert and the book, and began an argument of frantic whispers. Alice tried to explain that they should put the blanket over the sorcery and the sheets over Gilbert. Their own arguments and the pounding on the door drowned her out, but they came to the same conclusion and after a bit of tugging and dashing about they had the room situated.

Alice pulled open the door to find an old man with a furrowed brow and a bushy beard of grey hair. He was dressed in a suit like a footman. He had just turned to leave when she opened the door, and now came back and removed his hat.

The man was cordial, “I beg your pardon for the late visit, ma’am, but I saw you strolling on the promenade not long ago, and the light was still on, so I thought...”

“Of course. What can I do for you?” Alice replied quickly, glancing over her shoulder to make sure nothing was missed.

“Well, I wanted to warn you. A couple of fellows from steerage came ‘round this evening. Acted as if they knew you. Made some rather scandalous accusations.”

“Oh?” Alice said uneasily.

“Nonsense, all of it,” the man said. “Not worth repeating. But they seemed to have it in for your... grandfather, is it? The fellow in the cloak?”

“Yes. He’s quite cold, all the time. And deaf as a post,” Alice smiled bravely.

“Ah, I see,” the purser said gently. He seemed to be just as uncomfortable with this exchange as Alice was. “And I understand that earlier today a man from steerage came into the saloon and made trouble for you. Maybe the same one, nobody can recall.”

"That's true," she said guardedly. She had only opened the door part ways, and was trying to cover the aperture with her slender frame. "I don't... Some of the crew took him away. They were very kind. There was no harm done. Was the man punished somehow?"

"Not that I heard. And I'm glad you're none the worse for it. Don't know how he slipped in," the purser rattled on. He seemed to have been working himself up say something, and came to it at last, "Are you in some kind of trouble, miss? Something you need help with?"

"No," Alice said quickly. "Thank you, but no."

"I see," he said with some disappointment. "Well, if you feel unsafe or need us to do something to help you or your grandfather to feel safe, please let us know."

The conversation dragged on like this for another minute, with the purser standing at the door and rattling on. He told her who she might speak to if she was in need of help, when she might speak to them, who she should seek out if those people were not available, and how much all of them were concerned for her well-being. No matter how many times Alice thanked the man for his trouble, he didn't seem to be inclined to stop offering them his help.

Suddenly Alice felt coins being pressed into her hand from behind the door. She thrust the coins to the purser, "Thank you. Here is something for your thoughtfulness."

Things suddenly fell into place. He expressed his gratitude, gave her one final assurance that the crew was ready and eager to help her in a very non-specific way with problems she may have or may encounter in the future, and then he departed.

"I suppose he means well," Alice said once he'd gone. "But did you really have me give him half a crown? I'm not against kindness or even charity, but there was no reason to pay him. He hasn't done anything for us."

"He did. He provided us with information," Gilbert said. "We know that one of the men we're chasing tried to rouse their suspicions against us, and that his efforts failed."

"For half a crown, that gossip was greatly overpriced."

"You did not give him half a crown for the gossip. You gave him half a crown to create gossip. He is now telling his fellow ship-mates about the lovely woman who recklessly hands out coin for news about herself or the three ruffians in steerage. If new information surfaces, however trivial, we can count on them bringing it to our door. We have recruited the sailors as our spies. The money will also make it difficult to believe that we're involved in evil business. Think of it as an investment."

"Hm," Alice said doubtfully.

Simon uncovered the sorcery circle and touched up the parts that had been smudged, "So what do we do now?"

"Now we take another walk," Alice replied.

Gilbert sat in the room and tried to ignore the sorcery circle while Alice and Simon took a stroll around the promenade. She stopped often and stared at the device for nearly a minute before moving on.

"It works," she said once they had returned and warmed themselves a bit. "But not particularly well. The device only responded to our sorcery circle on about a third of the ship."

"Meaning you'd have to be close to the sorcery before your contraption would tell you about it," Gilbert said.

"Yes. Although, this is not very strong magic. More potent magic would show up more readily. I imagine their spell to commune with the dead is stronger than our circle."

Simon got down on the floor and wiped the circle clean with his sleeve, "Why don't we try again with the proper spell?"

"I don't know it, and it's not in your book."

"I drew it once. The book called it 'the Dead Call'. I'm sure I can draw it again."

"You drew the circle to commune with the dead? When?"

Simon thought for a moment. "Four years ago? Maybe three and a half. It was just a little after my master was killed. My former master, I mean."

"And you think you could recreate a circle from four years ago, that you only drew once?" Alice asked incredulously.

Simon had already begun the work. "Yes. I remember it. Although, I'll need to replace the name. The one I drew called Lord Mordaunt. I don't imagine we want to talk to him."

Gilbert stood up. "You're not really thinking of performing actual necromancy in our room, are you?"

"No. And we don't have anyone to call," Alice answered slowly. She was marveling at Simon's work.

"What about your father?" Simon asked.

Alice looked up in shock, "You mean you could...?"

"I'd just need to know his name," Simon said.

"No," Gilbert said to Simon firmly.

"Donovan White," Alice said, almost as if in a dream.

"No," Gilbert said again, this time to Alice.

Simon stopped writing. The two of them looked at each other for a long moment.

"Alice," Gilbert said firmly, "Think about this. You are no longer just 'studying' the Black Arts. You're about to start *using* them. Not to catch the malefactors, but to your own ends."

Alice nodded slowly.

"And then what will you do once you summon him?" Gilbert continued. "How do you think your father would respond to his daughter using sorcery?"

"Of course," she said suddenly. "This is madness. I'm sorry. I was just surprised."

Simon seemed equally eager to drop the business. The sorcery was put away and they did not speak of it again that night.

The SS Callisto was greeted by a cruel and ugly morning of belligerent wind and rain. It wasn't dangerous, but it was uncomfortable, cold, and nauseating. Passengers stayed indoors and shut the curtains. Even the experienced crewmen looked oppressed by the weather. The only other passengers outside were clinging to the railing and looking more than a little green.

"Do we have to do this today?" asked Simon. He squinted at Alice through his rain-splattered spectacles. He was holding his jacket over his head as he walked, although the wind saw to it that the rain found a way through.

"No, we do not have to do this today. We should do this today. And so we will." She was watching her ethergram carefully as they walked.

"It just seems unlikely that we'll find anything with the ship moving about so much."

"It's true," she admitted. "We won't see anything unless we're very close to them while they're in the process of performing sorcery. It's almost hopeless, but not completely hopeless. And we have little else to do on this journey. We don't know what we might learn from this."

"Is this what it's like working for the Witch Watch?" Simon asked.

"Yes. Although we usually have more men and more guns."

Simon was quiet for a few more moments before he asked again, "Are you worried about being attacked? Gilbert seemed to think that was possible."

"It's possible. Our foes are likely not expecting us to be scurrying around below, so I doubt they will ambush us. And if they do, I have some ability to defend myself. Did you know I'm a wizard?"

"Oh?" Simon said. "That's marvelous. I wish I was one."

"So if we're attacked, just stay behind me. I can roast our foes if they're foolish enough to come close."

"The headmaster can do the same," Simon cautioned.

Alice stopped, "That is... alarming. My father faced a few wizards. I never have."

"Should we bring Gilbert with us?"

"We're going to have a very hard time getting below. The doors are generally watched. Gilbert isn't going to be able to go below unseen. If questioned, there isn't any way to explain him going down without giving away his disguise."

"I see," Simon said, disappointed.

"And it will be almost impossible for him to hide his face if he encounters someone in the tight spaces below."

"I understand," he said.

"And don't forget why any of us are on this ship in the first place. This mad journey across the Atlantic is just a distraction from their real goal, which is to take the vigor from Gilbert. If they were to lay another sorcery trap like the one Gilbert encountered in Ravenstead, they could easily claim their prize."

"I am fully persuaded in this matter," Simon said.

"And we need someone to guard the room, given the amount of contraband we have there."

"Mercy!" Simon said at last. "Lead on."

They came to the door that led below. It was watched by a member of the crew, who strenuously urged Alice to turn away. He tried very hard to understand what she thought she was doing going down into steerage without blatantly asking her business. He was polite, but made it clear that this was a very reckless thing for her to be doing. His objections wavered when she told him that she'd heard seasickness could be reduced by riding lower in the ship. She put a coin in his hand and he stepped out of the way.

Gratefully, they ran down the stairs and into the steerage section of the ship.

"You do that often," Simon said.

"What?" Alice asked.

"Lie."

"I didn't lie. I told the man that I'd heard seasickness is lessened in the lower parts of a ship. I have heard that. I have no idea if it's true, but I've heard it said. If you were suffering from seasickness I might run some experiments and find out."

"Hmmm," replied Simon doubtfully.

"Lie or not, the deception is necessary. At least, I can think of no alternative that allows me to do my job. The problem is that a great deal of my job is against the law. We live in strange times. Attitudes towards magic are changing, but there is still much superstition, confusion, and needless oppression. If I declared the truth, we'd all be roasted or hung. If I gave up, many malefactors would run rampant and see their schemes come to fruition. Lives would be lost. So the choices are our deaths, the deaths of innocents, or lying."

Simon nodded and looked thoughtful.

They had entered the accommodations for the steerage passengers. It was a long corridor, wide but crowded. Bunks were packed together on the port and starboard walls. The ceiling was low enough that Gilbert would have needed to stoop if he were here. Lights hung from the ceiling, swinging with the rocking of the ship and casting dizzying shadows onto the walls. Each "room" was an alcove with a bunk on one wall and a bench on the other, situated so that there was just enough room for a single person to stand between the two and bang their shins. The rooms had thin wooden dividers between them, and were open to the main corridor. In some places curtains had been hung to offer some approximation of privacy. There were no portholes.

This first section was for single men. Grim, dirty faces greeted Alice and Simon as they entered. The air here was foul. It stank of sweat, vomit, and a hint of sewage. Alice gagged as she entered. Many men were crowded near the door, preferring the damp icy air of the outside to the pestilent air further in.

"My accommodations at His Lordship's prison-school were more comfortable than this," Simon whispered.

They walked to the end of the section, where a curtain had been drawn across the corridor to divide the single men from the married couples. Alice and Simon proceeded through.

"I did not see our foes amongst the single men," Alice.

"Neither did I," replied Simon.

"I don't expect to find them here, but I'm just being thorough."

"And curious," Simon suggested.

"And curious," she admitted.

They reached the end of the section and another curtain.

"This corridor seems to go on forever," Simon said. "How many people live down here?"

"Eight hundred, or so I've heard. But we are near the end," she peeked through the curtain. "The area beyond is the smallest section, and is for single women only. Wait here." With that, she vanished through the curtain.

She seemed to be gone for a long time. Simon stood awkwardly in the corridor. There was nowhere to sit, unless he was to enter one of the alcoves that were called rooms. A few men were giving him suspicious looks. Or perhaps they were simply curious at seeing a sudden new face. He'd accepted being led into the section for married couples while being escorted by a woman, but now he was alone and felt like an interloper.

"I did not expect to find them within, but I wanted to see where it led, in case there was some space beyond," Alice said when she returned.

She led them back to the men's section, then into the dining saloon for steerage. It was crowded even when uninhabited. The long tables were close together, with just enough space for the benches between them. The ceiling was low, which made the room feel smaller still.

"We did not see them above, and it's doubtful they would linger in the weather without reason," Alice said thoughtfully. "They are not in their assigned section of the ship, or the saloon. They must be below, in the crew area of the ship, as we suspected."

They passed through the galley without anyone stopping them or asking their business. They passed into a small storage area and then into the cargo areas of the ship.

"This is not a very organized search," Simon said after some time. "I doubt we'll find the headmaster like this, and I fear we've lost ourselves."

"I'm not worried about getting lost," Alice said. "We only need to head up if we want to escape. And we are not moving randomly. There is a purpose to our path."

"It escapes me," confessed Simon. "Sometimes we turn left. Other times right. Sometimes we go down and sometimes we don't."

"We're coming from the men's section of steerage, where the headmaster lives with his friends. Imagine we are them, and we are looking for a place to perform dangerous sorcery. Assuming none of them are blessed with your remarkable speed, they will want to find a space where they can be left alone for half an hour or so. They will want a place where there is no traffic. They will want to be far enough away that their voices will not draw attention. They will need room, more room than is available in these passages. They will not pass through doors that are watched. With those goals in mind, I feel we are on the right course."

"But if they are not performing the sorcery at this moment, we won't find them," Simon pointed out.

"True," Alice said, consulting her ethergram. "And I don't think I see any activity now. But they might still leave signs for us to find. Be on the lookout for chalk or charcoal residue on the floor. Or for places where things have been moved to make room for their work."

They continued on. After making many confusing turns and going up and down many ladders they found themselves near the engine room. At this point an older crewman stopped them. Alice confessed to having a fascination for machinery.

"Do you?" he laughed mockingly. "Well there are nice pictures of sailing-ships you can look at in the saloon, and men who will tell you all the sailing stories you care to hear. Now clear out of the engine room or I'll have you sent to the captain. I've no time for tourists."

"Please," Alice pressed. "I've never seen a dual expansion engine in operation."

“Oh?” the man said, raising an eyebrow.

Alice nodded, “When I was young I got to ride on one of the early ships in the Cunard line, a fourteen hundred ton iron-screw. I saw the simple engine in operation. Of course, those ships were not as large and grand as your Callisto so perhaps the comparison is unfair, but I’d like to see for myself.”

“Well!” the man said, suddenly much more friendly, “I didn’t realize I had an *engineer* in my engine room.” He still didn’t seem to be inclined to let them look around, but he seemed pleased to have a visitor with genuine interest in his work.

“I’ve heard gossip that men are designing ships with two screws, and *triple*-expansion engines,” Alice said seriously. “I imagine those will be very impressive once they take to sea. They might reach speeds as great as twenty knots. Almost double that of proud Callisto.”

“Not quite double!” the man said defensively. “Callisto makes better than twelve knots if she isn’t fighting the wind. And I don’t think much of this talk for sticking more screws on a ship. If you want a better engine, you build a better engine. You don’t build two engines and pretend you’ve made something new. Two ships tied together don’t make one big ship. I’ll show you how a proper ship is built.” Then he nearly dragged the two of them through his engine room.

The man introduced himself as Mr. Armstrong, and although he never bothered to say so, it was obvious he was Callisto’s Chief Engineer. (He had almost nothing to say about himself. He was either talking about Callisto, or his mouth was closed.) He showed Alice around the inner workings of the ship. Each and every bit of machinery seemed to have some tale attached to it, and each tale ended with a lesson in the supernatural strength and reliability of Callisto.

At first Simon suspected that Alice was feigning interest in order to flatter Mr. Armstrong, but it soon became clear that her amazement was genuine. She was truly delighted to be so close to the heart of the ship. She was grinning like a child.

The talk of machinery was baffling to Simon, and he heard many new and mysterious words as Alice and Mr. Armstrong discussed boiler design, coal delivery, the benefits of steel over iron, and the dangers of breaking shafts - whatever that meant. When the tour was over it was clear that they had a new friend, and he insisted that Alice come for another tour if she found herself aboard Callisto again. She agreed, and asked for leave to explore the rest of the lower decks. This was granted, and Mr. Armstrong passed the word along to his men.

That night, Simon and Gilbert were standing outside, enduring the cruel rain. Gilbert had grown restless in their room and wanted to move around. Simon had gone with him to perpetuate the notion that Gilbert was a sickly old man in need of help.

"I don't know how much longer I can stay out here," Simon said through chattering teeth. "Aren't you cold?"

"I never feel cold. Or warm," Gilbert said sadly. "I can tell the weather is cold, but it doesn't bother me."

"You're lucky," Simon said.

"No, I'm dead."

"You keep talking about it as if it was a bad thing, but I don't understand you. You don't fear pain. You're strong. You have your senses. You're ageless."

The two of them looked over the railing together and watched the white frothy waves rise and tumble below. Finally Gilbert spoke, "After I was captured by the Witch Watch, they took me back to Grayhouse, their headquarters. I lived there for a few days. Alice lives in one half of the house, and the other half is for general use. The men don't go into her half of the house. I didn't understand this division. Nobody had bothered to explain it to me. They just assumed I would sit in the library all the time. Eventually I got bored and went into her part of the house to ask her if she had a deck of cards. I found her getting ready for a bath."

Simon went wide-eyed and swallowed, "Was she...?"

"She was wearing a very small amount of clothing," Gilbert said. "But the remarkable thing wasn't what I saw, but what I felt."

"I imagine it must have been sad to realize you would never..."

"Nothing. I felt nothing. Just describing the scene has put red in your cheeks and gotten your heart beating. I was there to see it with my own eyes, and it didn't affect me any more than a painting of a sunset. I can tell she is pretty, but I am no longer struck to the heart by the sight of a woman."

Simon drew a deep breath and wiped the raindrops from his spectacles, so that new ones would have room to land.

"I'm *dead,*" Gilbert said sadly. "I'm dead. I'll never enjoy food. Or the company of a woman. Or a cold drink on a hot day. Or a soft bed after a day of toil."

"It seems you're immune to both the joys and sorrows of living," Simon stood shivering for a few moments before continuing. "Now that I think of it, I suppose the two go together. You can't enjoy food until you've felt hunger. You can't appreciate a warm fire unless you're cold. The enjoyment of a bed is expensive indeed if the price is a day of toil. I suppose you can't have joy without suffering. That's a sad thought."

"It's foolish of me to complain to you. Life without joy is a burden, but it's nothing compared to your life of steady misery."

Simon nodded and stomped his feet as he struggled to keep warm, "You can't have joy without suffering, but you can have suffering without joy. You can't enjoy a meal forever, but you can feel hungry all the time."

"That's a terrible thought," Gilbert said.

They walked a bit further, moving away from the superstructure, which tilted and rocked overhead like a building that had gone for a walk. A very small number of crewmen remained on deck, watching the ship and the sea from whatever places they could find that might shield them from the gusting wind.

The wind faded for a few moments and Simon spoke again. "If it's as unsatisfying as you say it is, then I wonder why wizards choose undeath."

“I suppose it’s an attractive possibility for old men who are facing their end. Most of their physical pleasures are lost or faded.”

“Or maybe there’s something they value more than physical pleasures,” Simon suggested.

“I wonder what it is that Lord Mordaunt is after. Does he have some goal beyond attaining lich... ness?”

Simon didn’t answer. His back was to Gilbert. He was looking up at the higher decks of the ship, where the crew lived. Or perhaps at the bridge.

“What’s wrong?” Gilbert asked.

“I don’t want to live like that again. As a slave, I mean. At the time, I was always afraid of being killed. Now I’m always afraid of somehow being dragged back to that old life. I fear that more than I fear death.”

Gilbert clapped him on the shoulder. “You say this like it’s a thing of shame. If you fear slavery more than death, then good! That means you’re discovering courage. The time may come when you will need to fight to keep your freedom, or other things you hold dear.”

Simon nodded, although he seemed shaken by the prospect of fighting.

Seeing Simon’s unease, Gilbert said, “Resolve yourself to it now, so that when the moment comes you won’t falter.”

“Thank you,” Simon said. “I will.”

Simon and Alice spent the next several days exploring the lower decks and searching for signs of sorcery. During the day they moved around the ship, watching Alice’s ethergram for activity. At night Gilbert watched the device while they slept. For days the gauge refused to move, but at last one night it trembled very slightly. Gilbert roused Alice and Simon, but the ethergram fell silent again before they could discover the origin of the magic. The following night they stayed awake, and waited below.

Just after midnight the ethergram showed a frenzy of activity. Simon had dozed off at the bottom of a ladder, and Alice had been pacing to stay awake. Once Alice woke Simon, they ran off into the depths of the ship in search of the origin. They tried to both run and move silently at the same time, which didn't really work. They wanted to find the source quickly, but they didn't want to reveal themselves to the headmaster and his men.

They closed in, but then the ethergram seemed to be leading them in circles. Too late Alice realized the sorcery must be going on above or below them. The sorcery ended before they could discover the proper deck. Eventually they found a storage room that had been recently mopped, but it contained no other clues.

The next day they were gathered in their room. Alice was studying the book she'd brought with her. Gilbert was pacing. Simon was eating. Alice had been ordering extra food for her 'grandfather', and bringing it back to the room so that Simon could enjoy a second meal.

"It seems like our task is hopeless," Simon said between mouthfuls. "Even if we find where they are doing their work, I don't see how we can arrange to have them caught. We can never tell where or when their meetings will take place."

"I would still like to find them if we can," said Alice. "I'm very curious what is so important that they're willing to risk discovery. What is it that they have to tell their master that can't wait until they return to Ravenstead?"

"Perhaps they aren't giving him news, but receiving it," Simon suggested.

Gilbert began imitating the aristocratic accent of the viscount, "Gentlemen! So good of you to summon me. I just wanted to inform you that I am *still* dead."

Simon laughed and almost choked on his meal.

"I'm glad you find it amusing, but our position would be improved if we knew what they were doing," Alice said.

"I don't know that we'll get another chance," Simon said. "We've been at sea for over a week. I thought we would have arrived by now."

"It's been nine days," Alice said. "The weather has delayed us. I've heard that we should expect to arrive in New York sometime near dawn tomorrow."

"New York!" said Simon. "I'd never traveled outside of Ravenstead before. Now I've seen London, Liverpool, and I'm going to see New York."

"Do you have a plan for when we land?" Alice asked.

Gilbert stopped pacing, "We could head directly to where Mother is living, and keep watch over the house. We should be let off the boat long before the headmaster. Furthermore, I know the way we are going, while they might need to ask for directions. We should arrive long ahead of them."

"But, your mother just recently moved to America. How is it that you know the way?" Alice asked.

"My mother is living with my sister Ruby and her husband. I grew up in that house. I don't know what our foes will do if they arrive and find the place watched. I'd rather they not besiege the house. It would be better if we could engage them on the road between the city and the house."

Their last day on the ship passed slowly and uneventfully. Simon spent the day on the bow, looking longingly towards the horizon. Alice explained that they would not see land until morning, but Simon could not pull his eyes away. Gilbert spent the day brooding in their room.

They went to bed early and fell asleep late, anxious for what the morning would bring.

Alice sat up in bed. "What is it?" she muttered. Her eyes were reluctant to open and even less inclined to focus on things. "What time is it?" The lantern had been lit, and gave off a dim glow in the darkened room. The low, soothing rumble of the engines and the gentle rocking of the ship threatened to lull her back to sleep.

"I apologize for waking you, but this might be important," said Gilbert. "The watchmen just changed, so it must be about four, first watch." He handed her the ethergram.

"Oh my," she said once her eyes had settled. "This is very strong. How long has it been like this?"

"I don't know. I admit I haven't been watching it closely. The last time I looked at it was around midnight."

Alice stood and turned the ethergram in her hand. Then she moved around the room, watching the needle carefully. "The sorcery is either very close, or very, very strong."

"Do you want to investigate? We land in a few hours. It might not be worth the trouble."

"I think we should," she yawned. "I don't want to let this run unchecked. At the very least, we should make sure the sorcery isn't being done nearby, with the aim of harming us."

"Perhaps I should come with you," Gilbert suggested.

"No, I'll take Simon. You should continue playing the old man. No sense in endangering our disguise now."

She woke Simon and they hurried aft, following the ethergram. Once they reached mid-ship, the ethergram lost its way again.

"Perhaps we are too late, as before," Simon suggested.

"I think not," said Alice as she turned in place and watched the gauge. "The needle is still moving on its own. It's just indecisive. Let's go below and see if we can make sense of this."

They plunged deep into the ship, and eventually found themselves in the dimly lit and little-traveled passages. They were low enough that the smell of bilge water reached them whenever they were near a ladder.

"Did you hear that?" Alice asked suddenly, bringing their search to a halt.

Simon stood listening for a moment before shaking his head. "What did you hear?"

"Footsteps," she whispered back. She turned her head one way, then another, listening intently. "I no longer hear them, and I can't decide which direction they were coming from."

They listened for a few more moments before moving on. They passed through several passages, heading starboard. Alice watched her ethergram as she walked, and Simon watched the floor.

Eventually they spotted a dark pool, sloshing from one side of the passageway to the other. At first he assumed it was oil, but Alice's light revealed it to be blood.

They were in a short passage that ran fore to aft, with a hatch at either end. There was no light here, save for that of Alice's lantern. The dark metal bulkheads were reluctant to accept illumination. Huge rivets lined the walls, which vibrated with the life of distant machinery.

Simon was alarmed for a few moments, but he mastered himself when he saw how steadfast Alice was. He did his best to show a brave face.

They followed the trail of blood and it led them to a man laying face-down in the corridor.

"Unconscious?" Simon whispered hopefully.

Alice shook her head as she knelt over the body. "Dead. Trauma to the back of the head. Bruising around the throat. Looks like he was strangled."

"I can't imagine the headmaster throttling a man like this. Even if he took him by surprise."

"It might have been one of his friends. Perhaps this crewman discovered them in the midst of some evil business."

Simon looked around, "I don't see any sorcery on the floor. No markings. No sign of cleanup or erasing, either."

"Neither do I."

Simon was shaken. This was not the first time he found himself in the presence of a dead body. He tried to put the fear out of his mind by focusing on their work. "This should be the outer hull, correct?" he said, pointing towards the starboard bulkhead.

"I believe so," Alice said. Their exploration over the last few days had given them a passing familiarity with the lower decks of

Callisto, and the ability to move around without becoming lost.

"So why is the needle pointing starboard?" Simon asked as he looked over her shoulder at the ethergram. "On the other side of this wall should be ocean. We're below the waterline. If there's sorcery being done out there, it's being done by fish."

"It's not really pointing that way. Give it a moment and it will move again. It's been swinging between fore and aft."

"Maybe there's more than one circle," Simon suggested.

"That's a strange thought. Why would they-" Alice stopped as Simon gently put his hand over her mouth. She faced him so that she might more readily glare at him.

"I heard the footsteps," Simon hissed. "I'm confident they're ahead of us."

Alice listened for a moment, "One set, or more?"

Simon closed his eyes, "I'm reasonably sure it was just one set of footsteps."

"Then it might just be a member of the crew, making his rounds."

Simon suddenly cried out in fear and surprise as he opened his eyes again. Alice spun around to see the headmaster standing in the open hatch at the end of the passage. He was just on the edge of the lantern light, his grinning face hovering in the darkness beyond the doorway.

"Hello Mouse," he said to Simon. "Having fun with your new lady-friend? You oughtn't have gone against the master. Now you'll get repaid for that."

There was a loud clang, and the hatch behind them slammed shut. The wheel turned, securing the door.

Alice handed her lantern to Simon and stepped forward, "The rats scurry into the open at last. Is this your trap? To corner us in a passage? Has the great and mighty Mordaunt been reduced to mugging his foes?"

"You'll see it's more than a mugging His Lordship has in mind for you, and you'll lose more than your coin."

Alice hitched up her skirt. Simon was so preoccupied with the sight that he nearly overlooked the small silver pistol that had been holstered to her leg. She aimed it casually at the headmaster, "I think we'll be the ones doing the mugging."

The headmaster reached into the room and grasped the handle on the door. Alice warned him to stop moving by pointing her pistol at him more firmly, but he gave it no heed. Alice fired a shot as he hauled the door closed. The shot went astray. The sharp crack of the gunshot was answered with a thunderous boom as the door slammed closed, leaving Alice and Simon alone in the passage.

They ran forward and stopped as the light fell on the closed door.

"Madness!" Alice cried. "How did they manage this?"

The back of the door had been covered with a broad sorcery circle, which was visible now that the door was closed. A faint mist seemed to be gathering around it. The door in front of them led forward. The door at the opposite end led aft. Both were closed. The passage was completely dark, other than the meager light supplied by their lantern.

Simon squinted at the writing in the flickering light. "Looks like it was written in grease pencil. Some of the circle was written on the door frame, and some on the door itself. The circle wasn't completed until the door was closed. That's a neat trick."

"But why?" Alice asked. "I don't recognize this spell. Let's open the door and break it again before it causes any mischief."

"Wait!" Simon pleaded. He murmured to himself as he read for a moment. "This spell is... the outside is a containing circle. If your spell is volatile or needs time to gather energy, you put a containing spell around it, to keep it from activating while you're still working on it. Once you're ready to use the spell, you erase the outer circle."

"I don't understand."

"This spell isn't doing anything yet. It won't activate until we break the outer circle."

"Which will happen if we open the door."

"Yes."

"Then I guess we should understand what it will do before we unleash it. Oh!" Alice said with alarm, "We should work fast. Look at how quickly it's gathering." The steel had become powerfully cold, and mist was pouring from it.

"So what does the inner circle do?" she asked. "I see 'enérgeias' and 'seismós'. It's gathering a great deal of energy, and... I don't understand. What's this word?"

"Kradasmoús", Simon said quickly. "It means something like 'vibration', I think." He dashed off to the other end of the passage. He was careful to step over the body, as well as the puddle of blood that slid from one side of the passage to the other with the gentle rocking of the ship. His light fell on the far door, "This one is similarly marked. I guess that explains why your device was so confused. It was torn between these two circles."

"Not so," Alice said. "My device can't detect a circle until the spell is active."

"That means there might be other circles like these around the ship!" Simon said with alarm. He turned around to face her and realized he'd left her standing in the dark. "I'm so sorry!" he said as he hurried back.

"Yes. Gilbert noticed the ethergram moving an hour ago, and it may have begun long before that. If there are other spells like this one, then they have been gathering power for a long time."

"And sooner or later someone will stumble on one of them," Simon said. "If it's on a door, like this one..."

"Let's first worry about the one in front of us," she said, struggling to remain calm. "This spell is still growing. Frost has begun to form. Whatever this spell does, it's going to do a great deal of it."

The lantern grew dim as Simon held it close to the door.

"Careful!" Alice scolded. "If that goes out we will be lost."

"If this were on the floor we could set candles around it."

"If we had candles," Alice said.

"Yes."

"And if we wanted to feed this spell, which we don't."

"Of course."

"I am at a loss," Alice said after another minute. "Can't we just erase the inner circle?"

"The energy is gathered," Simon said. "If we erased it, that energy could come out in unpredictable ways."

"Better than the intended way, I should think."

"It might still be enough to kill anyone standing close to the door. But look! The author left a lot of gaps. I suppose this is Headmaster's writing. This is sloppy work, even for him. If I were to insert something in these spaces, then the spell might discharge safely."

"Yes. But as you said, the energy will need to go *somewhere*," she said quickly.

"I think I can turn it back into heat," Simon replied as he stared at the circle intently

"Then I suggest you write while we can still see the lettering," Alice said urgently. Condensation had been gathering on the top edge of the door and flowing downward, and this had now begun to freeze. The door was rapidly becoming sheathed in ice.

Simon put his hand to his pocket and let out a frustrated sigh, "I have nothing for writing!"

"I didn't bring any chalk!" Alice groaned. "I brought a gun, and no chalk!"

Suddenly heavy footsteps were heard on the other side of the door.

"You may yet need the gun," Simon said fearfully.

The wheel on the door began to turn. Alice and Simon threw themselves against it and began pulling it the other way.

"What's going on here?" came a muffled voice. "Why is this hatch secured? And who's put out the lights?"

“Don’t open the door!” Alice pleaded.

“Who is that? What’s a woman doing down here? And why is this shut?” the voice replied. The turning of the wheel had stopped for the moment.

Alice pulled a narrow tool out of the leather folds of her ethergram and handed it to Simon. “Use the blood,” she whispered.

“The *blood*?” Simon asked incredulously.

There was pounding on the door and the crewman spoke again, “Look here, you stop fooling about. I hear you talking to someone else, and I’m sure I know what you’re up to. You’ll open this door right now if you know what’s good for you.”

Simon and Alice traded confused and desperate looks as the man spoke, and finally Simon understood. Timidly, he walked over to the dead body and dipped the tool into the blood.

“That’s it! I’ve been patient enough,” the man boomed. The wheel began turning again. Alice threw herself against it, but she was hopelessly outmatched by the crewman on the other side.

Simon dashed back and added his strength to the effort. He held the wheel with one hand while he struggled to write with the other. He scratched furiously at the door, leaving bloody gouges in the ice. The brutally cold metal was painful to touch, and agonizing to grip. Their hands began to ache after just a few seconds. The ice melted under their hands, making the wheel slippery and further hindering them. As their strength failed, the wheel began to turn against them.

Alice let out a cry as she fought to push it back. Simon gave up trying to write and put both arms into the work. Suddenly his grip failed and his hands slid from the wheel. There was a clank as the mechanism released, leaving the door free to open.

“We’ll see about this!” boomed the outraged voice. The wheel stopped moving, and they heard the man stomping away.

“I’m sure he’ll be back with help,” Alice said. “Hurry up and finish your work.”

Simon had to look around for the tool, which he’d dropped in the struggle. Then he returned to work, loading it with blood and editing the circle on the door. After a few trips between the door and the blood puddle, he stood back to examine his work.

"Is it safe now?" Alice said cautiously.

"I think so. I hope so. I don't know for certain. I don't think there's a way to test it safely. I guess we should count ourselves lucky that the crewman went away."

"I'm sure he'll be back soon. Although, it occurs to me now that perhaps he just took an alternate route to come through the opposite door."

Almost as if he'd been waiting for this cue, the far door groaned with the sound of the wheel being turned. In a panic, Simon yanked open their own door, was briefly shocked that no magic took place, and stumbled through. He turned, expecting Alice to be on his heels, but she hadn't moved. She was still staring into the darkness. There was a metallic creak as the hatch was opened. A light flashed and Simon was nearly blinded for a moment. Then there was a titanic blow, like the hammer of God striking the anvil of the world. Simon was pushed back, and it felt as though the air itself had struck him in the face.

He was nearly deaf from the sound. The world seemed muffled and distant. When his eyes recovered he could see the tortured metal of the hull, bending and twisting like a crumpled note. Simon of course was familiar with the idea of leaking ships, but in his mind he'd imagined that water would simply flow into the ship like water from a leaky bucket. But at this depth the water surged with a great fury. A wave of white foam roared down the passage. Alice had finally shaken off her stupor and was struggling to follow him. Simon watched helplessly as the wave overtook her, and swept her off her feet.

He moved to help her, but the wave struck his lantern and everything went black.

Gilbert was pacing the room. Alice and Simon had only been gone for a little more than half an hour, but the lack of news and the uncertainty made the minutes long.

The door banged open. Gilbert turned, expecting to see his companions. Instead he saw an older man, dirty, with an unkempt beard and a crooked smile. He was holding a lantern.

He was struck with an abrupt flash of recognition, "Soot!"

"Morning, Maypole," the man replied, and then he hurled his lantern into the room. He fled the doorway before it even landed.

The lantern burst and burning oil spilled over the bed. Without hesitating, Gilbert scooped up the blankets and lifted them away. He charged out of the room with the fiery bundle and hurled it overboard. Then he beat out the flames on his chest and head. He was glad that he didn't have a face, since this would have just burned it off.

Soot was running aft. Not to Steerage, as Gilbert expected, but towards the cargo area of the ship. Enraged and still smoking slightly, Gilbert gave chase.

Soot intensified his flight when he saw that Gilbert was in pursuit. He kept better pace than Gilbert would have thought possible for a man his age, but he wasn't fast enough to escape. Gilbert was tireless and had longer strides, and quickly closed the gap. The early morning quiet was broken with the heavy pounding of their footsteps on the deck.

Gilbert saw that the door leading below was curiously unguarded. Their chase led down into the ship, through the twisting corridors, drawing closer to the cargo area. Gilbert was pleased with this. He could corner and kill Soot in the cargo area without worrying that the deed would be discovered. Sadly, he realized he'd have to perform the killing with his bare hands, since there hadn't been time to put on his sword before the chase began.

Gilbert had nearly caught up to the man while they were up on deck, but Soot had begun to pull away again amongst the confusing dark turns below. Gilbert couldn't take advantage of his greater strides in such tight spaces.

"He's coming!" Soot screamed as he ran. He shouted this again and again, his voice faltering near the end from his desperate panting for air. Soot was stumbling as his strength ran out.

At last Soot jumped down a ladder into the hold. It was a long drop, but Gilbert saw there was a net at the bottom to break his fall. Soot was still gasping, "He's coming. He's behind me! He's coming!"

Gilbert followed, and on the way down he saw the net wasn't there to break anyone's fall. It was lying slack on the floor, which was a very strange thing. No self-respecting crew would leave something like that unsecured.

Gilbert landed in the middle of the net and realized too late what a profoundly stupid thing he'd just done. There was a loud bang and the net gathered him up and pulled him into the air. Gilbert found himself suspended from the ceiling of the hold. There were other items up here as well - bits of luggage or cargo that needed to be kept safe from rats or water. He was face-down, with his arms dangling helplessly below him. He tried to turn over, but he had no leverage and he simply wiggled about impotently in the trap.

Soot limped out into view, gasping and holding his side. At first Gilbert thought the man was coughing, but then he realized Soot was simply trying to laugh. A large man, bald and bearded, stood forth holding a lantern, the only source of light in this part of the hold. It was Ivar, and clearly he'd been the one to spring the trap. He pounded Soot on the back and joined him in laughter.

"You must be... the *stupidest...* son of a whore.... I've ever seen," Soot huffed.

"I guess we'll find out if she's a whore or not when we meet her," Ivar grinned. "We'll have a *fine* time with her."

"Scream for help if you like," Soot taunted. "I'm sure the crew would be happy to cut you down." The two men left, leaving Gilbert in darkness.

He pulled on the ropes helplessly. His face was pointed at the floor and his legs were pointed at the ceiling. He couldn't see what he was doing. Eventually he gave up the struggle and began gnawing at the ropes like a rat. Progress was slow and not particularly flavorful.

A few minutes later there was a terrible sound. What was it? They were too far south for icebergs. Did a boiler explode? While he was still pondering this there was another explosion. And another.

Simon pulled his head out of the water and sputtered, "Alice? Alice!" His ears were still ringing from the magical detonation, but he was almost positive he'd heard more explosions in the past few minutes.

The surge of water had pushed him through the ship, and by now he'd lost his bearings. The tumble had sent him flailing, groping for purchase with one hand while holding his glasses to his face with the other. He'd managed to lose his hat in the process. Eventually he'd been washed into a place where the water allowed him to stand. He could see a ladder leading hopefully upward to the light. He clung to it for a few moments, hacking and coughing up the icy seawater he'd swallowed. A body floated past in the surging foam. It was the slain crewmen.

He was dangerously cold. Even the slightest bump against his hands produced intense pain. The water had stolen his strength, and he was afraid he would lose his grip on the ladder.

"Alice!" he called again, more weakly this time. He looked up the ladder. It seemed an impossible climb. Alice was missing, and was most likely drowned. He felt so tired, and everything seemed hopeless. He thought he might just let go of the ladder. He could let the waves take him to a swift and merciful end. He'd stolen a few days of warm food, companionship, and joy. Like a prisoner who has just finished his last meal, it was time for him to meet his end.

Simon remembered the many seeming friends in Ravenstead. Although he could no longer recall their names, he could remember the faces of boys who died of sickness or punishment, and many others who were taken from the group by their masters and never returned. Simon had learned to accept these random cruelties of the world and came to understand that life was a long road of loss and misery. He pushed through his life with his head down, hoping that each day's ration of savagery would fall on someone else.

Then Gilbert and Alice had entered his life. They believed that misery and heartlessness were not the natural way of things, that these things might be resisted or even pushed back. They had kindled a flame of hope in him and seemed to know a world less desperate than the one he inhabited. Now it was plain that the last few weeks were simply a final cruel trick, a twist to give him something to love before taking it all away and sending him to die alone at the bottom of the cold ocean.

The water had been at his knees when he came to the ladder, and now it was at his hips. He looked down into the swirling water, wondering about the best way to get this nasty business over with.

Something floated by, a tangle of bright ribbons and hair. Simon reached out and hauled Alice out of the water. He pulled her to himself and shook her gently while calling her name. She didn't respond, but his thread of hope had not yet been broken. He looked up the ladder. Drawing a deep breath, he slung Alice over his shoulder. She was alarmingly heavy for such a slight woman, mostly due to her waterlogged dress. He looked down at the black water, and then up towards the light. He knew he didn't have the strength to carry himself up the ladder, much less with the additional burden of Miss White. But he thought it would be better to try. He imagined that was what Gilbert would do. He let out a furious (if perhaps slightly hoarse) cry and set himself to the challenge.

The ladder wasn't perfectly vertical, but was sort of like a very steep staircase. That, combined with the alarming list that Callisto had developed, meant it was just barely possible to climb the ladder without plummeting back down with his burden. His arms were both numb from the cold, yet burning from the exertion. His legs were weak and faltered many times on the steps, causing him to strike his shins on the metal. Gritting his teeth, he gave a final cry and heaved himself onto the next deck.

Simon leaned against the wall and pulled Alice to himself. "Please wake up. Please wake up," he whispered.

Alice vomited seawater and opened her eyes for a brief moment. Then she closed them again and began shivering. The two of them huddled together, slumped against the wall and breathing uneasily.

A great commotion came from above them. There was the sound of a multitude of footsteps and the voices of men and women shouting. Above this came the sound of a bell, ringing furiously.

Simon couldn't tell how long they sat there. At one point he looked down and saw Alice's eyes were open. Her breathing had stabilized and her teeth were chattering.

"Are you all right?" Simon asked quietly.

She nodded unconvincingly.

The water raged and surged below them, and each time it seemed to strike a bit higher than the time before.

"We need to move soon," Simon said.

Alice sat up and pawed at her face with numb hands, wiping away water and pulling the wet hair out of her eyes. "Thank you," she said in a barely-audible croak.

"Can you walk?" he asked.

She braced herself against the wall and pulled herself up. She wobbled for a moment and then took an uneasy step away from the wall. "Yes," she said at last.

"I'm glad. A while ago I was very worried you had died."

"I'm fine," she said. "And I'm sure you've gotten the worst of it."

"Me?" Simon laughed. "I have no problems that can't be cured with a warm fire."

"You silly man," she smiled weakly. "Your head is bashed open!"

Simon wiped at his forehead and came away with a handful of blood. He'd assumed the wetness was just water draining out of his hair. "Is it bad?" he asked.

"It looks nasty, but I don't think we should let it hinder our escape.

The water will overtake us in a few more minutes if we don't hurry. How can the ship flood so fast? Surely the ship can survive a single hole in the hull."

"It's more than one hole," Simon explained. "I heard several explosions after the one we saw. Some were close, some were distant."

It was not easy to move around. Callisto was listing gently starboard, and their wet shoes did little to help them on the smooth sloping floor.

"Up," Alice said, pointing along the passage to the next ladder.

They stumbled along, slowly working their way out of Callisto's belly. Crewmen sometimes dashed by them, sent on one desperate quest or another.

Finally, they emerged on deck. Light was slowly gathering in the early morning sky. A brisk wind washed over the ship. The decks were lined with passengers, elbowing and pushing their way to the rails. Lifeboats were being loaded and lowered.

"We need to fetch Gilbert," Alice said.

Their room was in shambles. The door had been left open. Gilbert was gone. The bed had been stripped. The furniture had been ransacked.

"My bag is gone," Alice said, horrified.

"A few of your clothes are still here," Simon said, holding up an item that had been left on the floor.

"The book was in my bag," she scolded him.

"Of course," he said, suddenly feeling very silly. "But Gilbert is gone. Perhaps he's already left the ship?"

"I can't imagine they would load an old man before so many younger passengers, and so many women, but I can't imagine where else he might have gone. And I can't picture him being willing to carry a ladies' bag, even if it were full of gold, or beer, or whatever the man values."

"Maybe he came down after us," Simon said worriedly.

"That would be very foolish, and is therefore very likely. I don't know what we should do if that's the case," she sighed. "Well, we shouldn't stand here waiting for the sea to rise up over our heads. He might be gone, he might appear later, but we need to find our own way off Callisto."

The Callisto held roughly eighty first-class passengers, and the lifeboats had been offered to those people before the other passengers were allowed out of steerage. The crew was directing the passengers to allow women and children on first, followed by couples, followed by single men. The problem was that this was the opposite of the order in which the rooms were arranged. Men were bunked closest to the doors, while women were furthest in. The allowance for married couples before single men was unexpected, and created a sudden new marriage economy where men were offering valuables to shrewd women if they would agree to present themselves as wives. A great many arguments and a great deal of haggling was going on just a few steps from the boat loading. The crewmen noticed the sudden inflation of married folks, but they couldn't afford to stop loading in order to sort things properly.

"We're close to shore," Simon noted hopefully. There was enough light that they could see the coast just a few miles away.

Alice glanced over the side of Callisto. The sea seemed alarmingly close. The ship shook and groaned with unseen damage as water filled her belly and she was pulled inevitably towards the bottom.

"The coast is near, but the ocean is closer still. There are so many people here. I don't know that we'll all find boats before Callisto falls." Her voice was still weak. The cold water and exertion had taken their toll on both of them.

They walked along the tilting deck, watching the boats being loaded. Alice, still dizzy for her ordeal, stumbled for a moment. Simon caught her. As she stood again, she noticed streaks of red in the water rolling aft.

"Was someone hurt?" she asked as she steadied herself.

"Killed," came a voice from behind. They turned, and found Armstrong on the deck. He looked very out of place outside of his engine room. He continued, "Three or four men came out on deck before the evacuation had even begun. Helped themselves to a lifeboat. One of the watchmen tried to stop them, and got a knife in the belly.

"What did they look like?" Alice blurted out.

"It was dark. Witnesses only saw them at a distance. They were men, and not crewmen, but that's all we know. And if they didn't have anything to do with this sabotage, then I'm the queen," Armstrong looked towards the shore. Callisto was now adrift and had turned so that her bow pointed north. Armstrong spoke bitterly, "Their boat will reach shore first, before news of them." He looked like he might weep.

Simon actually found it very frightening to see a strong man reduced to tears. He had no idea how to act. It seemed rude to ignore it, but offering comfort would seem like an insult. He took a step away and averted his eyes.

"But look at me, going on about those villains. We need to get the two of you on a lifeboat."

The crowd was thinning. Most of those remaining were single men who weren't able to bargain for a temporary wife.

"First-class passengers here!" Armstrong boomed to the officer loading the boats. This drew resentful looks from the remaining passengers.

"No," Alice pleaded, "I don't think it would be fair to-"

"Married, first-class passengers here!" he shouted. Alice opened her mouth to protest but he again shouted her down, "Young, married, injured, first-class passengers of exceptional character here!"

The crowd parted more willingly at this, and Alice and Simon were more or less shamed into their seats. They huddled together and tried to warm themselves as the boat was loaded. As the lifeboat was lowered, Simon caught sight of the crewmen working. Their faces were not fearful like those of the passengers, but empty. These were faces without hope. Some of these men were going down with the ship, and they knew it.

It took another half hour for Callisto to succumb to the sea. Her list grew worse near the end, and the few people left on deck were dumped into the Atlantic. The ship groaned as it rolled sideways, and there was a rumble as her contents shifted inside of her doomed belly. Soon there were loud bangs as parts of the ship broke under the unnatural stress. Suddenly there were two muffled explosions, which startled everyone in the lifeboat.

Alice looked at Simon, "The hull is probably twisting under the strain. This might wrench open doors on the lower decks." She dared not say more in front of the other passengers, who didn't know what to make of her remark.

Gilbert heard the cargo sliding around below him. He took this to mean that the ship had begun listing, which he couldn't feel because he was hanging from the ceiling in a net. He could see a tiny bit. The sun was coming up, and a narrow line of daylight slipped through the closed cargo door overhead.

The cargo was comprised mostly of immense burlap sacks and wooden boxes, but there was also a mix of raw building materials and a section of wooden barrels. The goods had been tied down, but as the ship tilted these ropes began to snap. Occasionally the moving cargo would strike the rope that held him up, and his net would be jerked around.

His rope-gnawing project had finally produced some slight progress. He was nearly through the first rope. He chewed more vigorously as he neared the end, and finally his teeth stripped away the last few strands of the rope in front of his face. Since he was still cradled in the net face-first, the net opened slightly as he did this, and his head fell through. The hole was too small to allow his shoulders to pass, and now his mouth was too far from the net to continue gnawing.

After another long stretch of time spent squirming and cursing, he heard the bubbling of water below. The cargo began to move around more freely, and soon there was an avalanche of tumbling goods. His net was yanked violently. A rope snapped, and suddenly he found himself falling.

He landed with a splash in a swamp of debris, seawater, oil, floating papers, and chunks of shattered containers. The ship was rolling quickly now. He wrestled with the net and the tumbling cargo, narrowly managing to escape being crushed by a wall of water-logged sacks. Once he was free, he spent several minutes trying to climb over the cargo faster than it was falling on him. He escaped to the upper side of the room, away from the water.

The screaming and yelling had stopped. Maybe the ship had been evacuated. Maybe people were just holding their breath in anticipation of the coming swim.

The roll continued, and The Callisto went fully sideways. There were more explosions. The immense cargo doors burst open and the Atlantic flowed in. For a moment the space was lit with brilliant daylight, and then the room rapidly grew dark as the ocean swallowed everything.

Once the crushing flow of water relented, Gilbert found himself floating in the middle of the room. Everything was eerily quiet now. To his surprise, rivulets of tiny bubbles were flowing out of the cracks in his skin. They came out of his clothes, and out of his face. The air that had rested beneath his dead skin was now escaping with urgency. He hovered for a moment, watching the sparkling flow and marveling at the sudden end of the furious tumult The Callisto had created in her death throes. The bubbles were a strange and alarming sight, and produced a mild tickling sensation.

Swimming vigorously, Gilbert passed through the yawning doors and escaped the hold, but he found he was not floating as he expected. He swam for the surface, but it grew ever more remote and dark. He was no more buoyant than the iron ship, and he was destined for the same grave.

He fought fiercely against gravity, waving his arms as fast as they could move. He was falling more slowly than The Callisto, but he was still falling.

The sea itself shook when The Callisto struck bottom. There was a roar so loud that it seemed to shove him away. A cloud of silt blossomed. It was pitch black against the deep blue around him. Helplessly, he plunged into the expanding cloud and came to rest at the bottom of the Atlantic.

Mr. Brooks,

Once again I must thank you for your continuing support. I'm afraid I must beg a special favor of you.

Over the past three or four years, we've collected an unusually high number of contraband books and sorcery supplies. Over time, our investigation has revealed a curious pattern. A notable portion of these items were in the hands of people - mostly commoners - who had recently had dealings with Viscount Mordaunt of Ravenstead, or who had been located somewhere near Ravenstead when captured.

Although it is not widely known, I am aware of the special friendship that exists between Lord Mordaunt and Albert Prince-Consort. I am not making any accusations against the viscount, but the fact remains that I simply must speak with the man in order to continue my investigation. I admit that I have ignored this matter longer than I should have, hoping to discover some other thread that would lead us away from Ravenstead. I do not wish to make trouble for a man who is a dear friend of both yourself and the prince.

Would you be willing to speak to His Lordship on my behalf, for the purpose of arranging a meeting? Please let him know that I would meet with him privately, without the usual military escort. I understand that my men can be imposing, and their presence can draw unwanted attention. It's entirely possible that this mischief is the work of someone in his employ, or some other party only loosely connected with Ravenstead.

In friendship,

Sir Donovan White

Director, Ministry of Ethereal Affairs

September 2, 1882

WOODBRIDGE

VII

Alice barked at the passengers to disembark from the boat as she and Simon struggled to haul it onto the beach proper. The boat was filled mostly with women, who seemed absolutely oblivious as to what they should be doing and who were very reluctant to put their feet in the ocean. Perhaps they would have been content to sit in the boat as Alice and Simon pulled it overland all the way to New York. Even when Callisto sank, many of the women sat with their bags in their laps with their eyes transfixed on the shore, waiting for someone to take them there. It took a great deal of cajoling to find enough hands to put all of the oars to use.

Callisto had fallen just beyond the mouth of the Hudson River, some three miles east of the barren coast where Alice and Simon had landed. A small number of the boats seemed to be of a mind to sail upriver to the port, which would be more than double that distance. Alice shielded her eyes with one hand and looked out into the brilliant sunrise. She could see a few boats traversing the cold glittering waves, heading north. The rest of the boats were heading for this spot. The ship had carried thirty or forty lifeboats, with a capacity of about thirty passengers each. Alice cursed herself for not talking a more careful count. She was curious how many had gone down with the ship.

They were on a sandy bit of coast. There were already perhaps a dozen or so boats scattered along the beach, extending for about a mile north and south. Some of the passengers had set out for the city the moment they disembarked. Others paced up and down the beach, hoping to reunite with friends or relatives. Others looked out to the open sea and wept quietly.

"Do we have tools for making a fire?" Simon asked quietly.

"None besides witchcraft," Alice replied in a whisper. "But I desperately need to warm myself. We've been soaking wet for almost three hours. Never a good idea this late in October."

They walked a bit inland. The trees were sparse, but they managed to find a few handfuls of leaves and sticks. They brought these back to the beach and arranged them into a pile.

"Simon, would you shield my fire with your jacket so the wind doesn't put it out?" Alice asked innocently.

Simon understood her meaning and took off his jacket. He held it so that nobody could see how the fire was being created. Alice pantomimed lighting a fire with tools and then set the leaves to burning with a flash of wizard flame. The burst was stronger than she intended, and she set Simon's jacket on fire.

"I'm so sorry!" she cried.

Simon dropped it in a panic, tried to pick it up again, dropped it again, and then came to his senses and kicked sand over it. He lifted it up to see that the garment was ruined. He threw it onto the fire with a sigh.

Alice was even weaker after making the fire, and she lay down on the beach as close to the flames as she dared. Simon rubbed his hands back to life over the flames. The heat was invigorating, and the color began returning to their faces.

The fire began to burn low, much to the disappointment of the people who had gathered to share the warmth. Finally Simon walked down the beach and began pulling on their lifeboat. The weight was too much for him alone, but a few of the other passengers saw his thinking and joined him. They pulled the boat over the fire and let the flames lick at its hull. Eventually it caught, and grew into an immense blaze. Alice was obliged to lift herself and move further back.

The fire quickly became a beacon and a meeting place for new arrivals. People seemed to shake off the terror of the morning as they warmed themselves. Soon they began talking and making plans. For a few hours the normal class divisions were eased slightly, and they related to each other as peers from the common class of people who had not drowned that morning.

The last of the lifeboats rolled in. Groups that were reunited headed north. Those that were still missing members continued standing on the beach, hoping against hope. By late morning news of the sinking had reached the city, and ships had come out to offer help. They sailed around where Callisto had vanished. Although it was impossible to tell at this distance, Alice hoped they were rescuing those who hadn't made it to the lifeboats in time.

"Perhaps we should head inland and try to stop the headmaster ourselves," suggested Simon. "I know we don't have much of a chance against them without Gilbert, but I'd like to try. For his sake."

"I'm not against it," said Alice, "But he never told us how to find his family. I don't even know where to begin looking. We have no money. The purse was in our room, and that was taken."

Afternoon came and the beach was largely cleared. They burned more boats to keep warm. The heavy rains for the last few days had visited here as well, and there was a good bit of fresh water to be found a ways inland.

"We should go and find food," Alice suggested. "We need to keep our strength up."

"I know," said Simon. "But I don't feel like eating."

The sun set and the rescue ships stopped their circling to return north. The last few stragglers left the fire and headed for the city. Alice and Simon had silently agreed that this would be the last boat on the fire, and when it burned down they would follow. They talked about how they might earn money to keep themselves fed. Neither one had many skills that they might market to decent people. Alice spoke of working as a mechanic or perhaps repairing watches, but it seemed more a dream than a plan. Few people would be inclined to hire a young woman with no tools. Again they fell silent.

As the fire ran low they gathered themselves and prepared to head for the city. Simon gave one last look out over the ocean.

"Look!" he shouted.

A small black shape was rising out of the water. Its movements were slow and lurching. As it drew near the fire they could see the shape of a man.

"Gilbert!" Alice shouted.

There was no answer. Instead Gilbert drew close to the fire and gargled at them. His movements were plodding, as if he was carrying a great weight. He seemed to have swelled. He leaned forward and expelled a great deal of seawater. More was flowing from the cracks in his skin. He looked like a sopping wet sponge, suddenly squeezed. After more gurgling and coughing, he seemed to settle down.

"I'm glad the fire belonged to you," he said at last. There was a still a wet, bubbling quality to his voice. "I wasn't sure who I would find when I came out of the water."

"Gilbert!" Alice said again. "We've stood here all day expecting some sign of you, and now that I see you I'm still shocked. I take it you walked along the bottom?"

"I did," he admitted. "The bottom of the ocean is a bewildering place. I was most afraid of losing my bearings and heading out to sea. Where are we?" Gilbert looked anxiously over the water as he said this.

"Richmond County, according to the other passengers," Simon answered.

Gilbert nodded, "Good. We're close to New Jersey, where Mother lives. If the ship had gone down just a bit further north, we would have wound up on the other side of the river in Brooklyn City."

"Gilbert," Alice said gently, "The headmaster was probably one of the first people ashore. He's had all day to..."

"I know," Gilbert said curtly. "I've had nothing to do all day but crawl along the ocean floor and dream of revenge."

Gilbert stormed off to the west. Alice and Simon followed, doing their best not to stumble in the dark. Along the way he explained how he'd been goaded into leaving their room and chasing after Soot.

"That was very foolish of you," said Alice. Her eyes were on the ground in front of her. It was soft and grassy, but also uneven and seasoned with stones. She was weary and would have found keeping pace with Gilbert to be a challenge even on the open road. Here in the dark it was both exhausting and dangerous.

"I don't think so," he said, "I was under the impression that they wouldn't take any action against me. I thought they wanted to take me alive, as it were. For the vigor."

"I'm not talking about our foes. I'm talking about the passengers. What would people think when they saw a supposedly old man sprinting all over the ship and getting into brawls? People were already curious about you in your mysterious hood."

"Yes, that was foolish," he grumbled.

They entered a small village called Grasmere.

"There are a lot of refugees here," Simon observed upon seeing so many faces from Callisto.

"I wonder why more of them didn't head for the city," Alice said.

"We are on an island," Gilbert explained, "I haven't been here since I was a boy, so perhaps things have changed. But at the time there was only one small ferry running between here and Manhattan. It's likely that ferry couldn't handle this many passengers in a single day."

"If the ferry can't handle all of these people, then how will we get where we're going? I don't think I'm up for swimming," Simon said uneasily.

"We're not going to Manhattan, so the Manhattan ferry isn't a problem for us. If we crossed the water to the north, we'd be in

Jersey City. If we crossed the Hudson to the east, we'd either be in Brooklyn City or New York, depending on where we landed. But we are going west, to Woodbridge. My family home is there. I don't expect the Arthur Kill ferry to be very busy if everyone is making for New York."

"Arthur *Kill?*" Simon asked.

Gilbert laughed, "In this case, 'kill' is a Dutch word meaning 'channel'. And the only difficult part of crossing it will be dealing with the ferryman." It sounded like most of the water had worked its way out of his head, although they could still see droplets coming from his clothing in the moonlight.

They had moved beyond the warm light and tired-eyed refugees of Grasmere, and were now on a road heading west. Along the way Alice and Simon took turns explaining the events on the Callisto.

"It's a shame your shot at the headmaster missed," Gilbert said once the tale was over.

"A shame, but not a surprise. It holds only one shot. It has a short barrel, even for a pistol, and it's not rifled,"

"I don't know what that means," Simon admitted.

"It means it's not very useful for targets more than a few paces away. My father told me to think of it as a knife that can reach across the room. I pleaded with him for a more substantial weapon, although I admit I only wanted a more complex firearm because I wanted to take it apart and examine its workings. In the end, Father proved right. Walking about obviously armed would set people on their guard and make them less inclined to answer my questions. At the same time, men never expect women to have weapons, and having one hidden has saved my life more than once."

"Well, it's still a shame you didn't shoot him. Even more so now that he's killed all those people. Imagine sinking an entire ship, just to kill the three of us!"

"That is strange," Alice admitted, "And not at all what I would expect from those three. They are unnaturally bold. They slew a man in the open to escape the ship, after the ship was obviously sabotaged. Even if they slip from our grasp, the official investigation will lead in their direction. I can't imagine how they plan to evade the law for a crime so drastic. Why would they perpetrate something so horrible, just to hurt Gilbert's mother? No, there must be another explanation for what they've done."

The road was dark now.

"Another thing that confuses me," continued Alice, "is why the headmaster suddenly decided to get rid of Gilbert. Their plan was clearly for him to go down with the ship, and stay there."

"I suppose it's too much to hope that they're just giving up on the idea of reviving the Viscount," said Gilbert.

"I don't know what to think. His actions seem irrational and brazen, and yet his men remain unscathed, and several steps ahead of us."

They walked in quiet for perhaps a half hour before Simon responded to the growling of his stomach, "I wish we'd gone looking for food when you suggested, Alice. This exercise is putting me in a mood to eat."

"Eat when you can, regardless of appetite, because you don't know when your next meal will come. Sleep when you're allowed, because you don't know when you'll get permission again." Gilbert said this somewhat reflexively.

"Is that more military advice?" Alice asked.

"It is."

"It's good advice," Simon said. "Especially if I'm going to spend more time with the two of you."

It was perhaps five miles to the ferry at Arthur Kill. At the end of the road they found themselves in a salt marsh. Long grass reached out of the moonlit water, and the air had a damp, slightly stagnant smell to it. The road had been built up with wood beams and bits of stone to keep their feet out of the muck.

"I can't believe it," Gilbert said as they drew near. "Mr. van der Byl is *still* running the ferry. He was running it when I was a boy, and I remember him being old even then."

"What's wrong? Is he troublesome?" Alice asked.

"No," Gilbert said with a sigh. "Only excruciatingly cheerful and talkative. Mother used to bring me across the water to Milliken once a week, and Mr. van der Byl would grin at us and chat our ears off the whole time."

Alice raised an eyebrow, "That is somewhat less dangerous than the other perils we have faced today."

"It might amuse you," Gilbert said to his smirking companions, "But the man drove me to irritation with his relentless chatter and gossip."

"I suggest we chance it in spite of the danger," Alice said.

Van der Byl stood firm and sure on the deck of his ferry. His neck leaned forward under the memory of burdens past. Shaggy white hair framed his dried face. His body was lean, but not withered. He was assisted by a scampering blond-haired youth who tended to the more physical duties.

His ferry was a broad wooden platform with a small shack near the middle. A small smokestack rose from the building, which contained a boiler that drove the paddle. The wooden construction was made of so many planks of varying lengths and thicknesses that the entire craft looked like it might crumble apart at any moment. However, the apparent age of the ferry indicated that it had gone for years without doing so. A bright lantern swung from the side of the shack.

Gilbert paid Van der Byl the last of his coins and stood at the edge of the ferry, looking out into the darkness across the water.

Despite Gilbert's warnings, Van der Byl was not unnaturally cheerful and he did not assault them with overwhelming conversation. He lit the engine. Its operation was not impressive to Alice, and she did her best to hide her frustration at such an ill-kept device.

"Last trip of the night," he said as the boiler began to chug and the paddlewheel lazily pushed them out into the water. "I usually head home at sundown, but I've tarried in hopes of news about the sinking."

“We are survivors of the same,” Alice replied. “But I’m afraid we have little in the way of news.” Alice then told the man a few bits of what had happened on the beach.

“You’re the second group of passengers to ride with me today, although I can’t say the other ones made for as pleasant company.”

“Three men? One in a top hat? Perhaps all looking ill-kempt?”

“You know the gentleman?” Van der Byl said nervously, suddenly embarrassed of speaking ill of them.

“No. But we are following them.”

“Ah! So you’re going to call on Mrs. Hiltman as well?” the old man said with sudden cheerfulness.

“Did the men tell you they were going that way?” Alice asked.

“Me? They said naught to me except a bit of rudeness in greeting and parting. But the news from Milliken is that they spent most of the day in town, asking after Victoria. I guess someone finally told them what they wanted to know and they came this way. I asked them to give my best to her, but I doubt they’ll remember. Rude men. I hope they’re more kind to her than they were to me. Victoria is a fine and handsome lady, and doesn’t deserve that sort of harshness.” His face was lit with a sudden smile as he spoke of Victoria.

“Is she?” Alice said with curiosity.

Van der Byl laughed warmly, “Oh indeed. Lovely woman. Why, if I was half as old and twice as rich... well, I’d probably still lack the courage to say aught to her. Still, she’s a welcome passenger when she comes.”

Gilbert turned to look at the man, and cocked his head to one side in sudden wonder.

“Well, we’re not as interested in Victoria as we are in the men you met earlier,” Alice said with seriousness. “We believe they mean her harm.”

Van der Byl was so upset with this news that he lifted his stooped shoulders in indignation, “I knew those men were up to no good. I didn't feel right about delivering them, but I couldn't very well refuse them passage. If I barred the rude and the ugly from my ferry I'd be out of business by Friday."

"How long ago did they cross?" Alice asked, almost afraid of the answer.

"Perhaps an hour," Van der Byl replied bitterly.

"An hour?" Alice shook her head. "Close enough to give hope, but still far enough to nearly dash it."

Van der Byl landed the ferry with reckless haste and apologies. The three of them disembarked quickly and set themselves to the road.

"Hold!" Van der Byl called.

"If you want us to help Mrs. Hiltman, you should not delay us," Alice warned.

"I only ask that you delay long enough to take our horses. I don't like the thought of walking home in the dark, but I'd rather go without a horse tonight than go without my favorite passenger tomorrow."

Two horses were hitched nearby. Gilbert mounted one without a word and galloped off into the darkness. Alice and Simon scrambled to follow as quickly as they could. Van der Byl called after them, asking that the horses be returned in the morning.

After a few minutes of riding they came to a halt at a nexus where several roads met.

"What's wrong?" asked Alice once they had caught up.

"I don't know which way to go," Gilbert said in a panic.

"I thought you said you once lived here," Simon protested.

"Many years ago. The memories are distant, and the land has changed. Only three roads met here, not five, and the trees I remember are all gone." He turned his horse in a slow circle, looking one way and then another, trying to reconcile his memories with what he was seeing. "There was a small barn on the north side of the main road. It's now gone, and I see a much larger one on the south side. Wait. This road had the deepest ruts, so it must be the oldest."

Gilbert moved forward, but Alice halted him. "Ruts are deep from use, not age. A well-used road may have deeper ruts than an older one with less traffic. Use your head. Panic will not help your mother now."

Gilbert climbed down from his horse and sighed with frustration, "I wish it were daytime. It would be easier to get my bearings if I could see farther." He paced around the intersection, looking from side to side. "I can tell it must be one of these two roads," he said after a few minutes, "But they are so similar in size and heading that I can't decide between them."

"Trees are deceptive landmarks," Alice said. "They feel unchanging, simply because they change so slowly. Try to ignore the trees and look at the shape of the land."

Simon slid down off the horse he was sharing with Alice. He walked over to a gap in the grass and found the grass was hiding a wide rock. Stomping on it he said, "What about this rock? Is this familiar?"

Gilbert rushed over and placed his hand on the rock. It was mostly flat, rising just a bit in the middle. Then he sprang up onto it and posed with his arms folded, "Here! I remember walking with my father. I used to pretend I was the captain of a sailing-ship, and this rock was my vessel. And sometimes I pretended the road was the shore. This road!"

Gilbert sprang onto his horse and tore through the night.

Gilbert arrived home to find the front door open. A lantern hung by the door, casting a warm glow against the endless darkness. More light came from inside, followed by weeping. Alice and Simon arrived just as Gilbert ran into the house.

Gilbert took in the scene in a quick glance. Mother was on the floor in the middle of the room, bound. The headmaster was copying a sorcery circle from a book, drawing it onto the floor around her. Ruby was sitting on the couch, weeping. Her husband was in a heap in the corner. He was badly bloodied. Ivar was standing over him, threatening him with Captain Turpin's sword.

Gilbert exploded into the room, his long dam of vengeance and rage finally breached. His battle-cry was a long, beastly wail.

The smile vanished from the headmaster. He dropped his chalk and bolted for the back door. Ivar dove at Mother, aiming to drive the sword through the helpless woman. Gilbert batted the blade aside with his arm and put his bony knuckles to work on the bridge of Ivar's nose. Simon and Alice dashed in through the front door, saw Gilbert, and decided to chase after the headmaster.

The scuffle smashed a vase, knocked pictures off the wall, and reduced a small table to splinters. Ivar lost the sword when he buried it in the side of the china cabinet. Not wanting to see any more things destroyed, Gilbert grabbed Ivar by the beard and pulled him from the warm light of the sitting room to the icy darkness in front of the house.

Once they were out in the yard they broke apart and began circling each other.

"At least being dead didn't sully your looks," Ivar laughed. Gilbert's hood had been thrown back in the scuffle.

"We'll see how well the grave treats your face in a minute," Gilbert shot back. The two began poking at each other with their fists as they circled.

Ivar spat out a bit of blood, "Ye should worry about your own head, Maypole. I've no fear of ye."

"A lie you tell yourself. You picked a fight with me when I was too weak to fight. And you *still* needed Soot's help to best me."

Ivar began laughing. Gilbert decided to put a stop to it, but he found himself grabbed from behind. Soot held his arms long enough for Ivar to join in, and they wrestled Gilbert to the ground. Ivar locked his hulking arms around Gilbert, pinning his arms to his sides. Soot slipped away for a moment while Gilbert struggled to break free of Ivar's grip.

Soot appeared again, dragging an axe. He held it over Gilbert's throat to prepare his swing, and then drew the weapon back, nearly stumbling in the process.

"Hurry," grunted Ivar, who was losing his grip.

The axe came down. Soot stumbled under the weight of the swing, and the blow landed beside Gilbert's head. Gilbert pulled an arm free and grasped the handle. He pulled it away from Soot and suddenly all three of them were fighting for the axe. There was screaming and punching and profanity. The axe head wound up between the two large men as Soot pounded impotently against Gilbert's frame.

Ivar kicked Gilbert between the legs, which did him no harm. Gilbert returned the favor and enjoyed more success. As Ivar stumbled, Gilbert pulled the axe away and slew him with a single messy stroke.

Alice stopped as she drew near the large barn that loomed over the Hiltman house. She'd lost sight of the headmaster and didn't want to be ambushed in a blind chase. She wished she'd been able to change into more practical clothes before this. Running in a dress was hard work.

"Where did he go?" Simon asked, finally catching up to her. Not wanting to leave a half-finished circle unattended, he'd paused in the sitting room to clean away the sorcery.

"He ran towards this barn," she said. "But I lost sight of him after that," she rasped. It was hard to be short of breath and quiet at the same time.

Simon pointed towards an orchard, where a figure was skulking about. They gave chase.

"Be careful," Simon said as they ran. "Remember that he's a wizard."

"I know," Alice said, after which they were nearly blinded by a spurt of fire. Alice tumbled, hurled fire back in answer, then beat out the flames on her sleeve. They sat for a moment, trying to quiet their panicked breathing and blink their dazzled eyes back to usefulness.

The trees had been stripped by autumn, and only a few daring leaves still clung to the branches. Some of these leaves had begun to burn, and motes of scorched foliage floated in the air around them like a rain of glowing embers. Rather than making their stand in the light, they crawled away and took shelter in the shadows.

"I think you singed him," Simon said.

"Did I?" she asked weakly.

"His hat was on fire. He looked like a lit candle."

They heard running footsteps, but when they turned to look they saw only moving branches. There was another sound behind them. Alice spun and released flames in a panic. Another tree was singed.

"What's wrong?" asked Simon. Alice had fallen to her knees.

She panted for a bit before answering, "I'm tired. Hungry. It's hard to use magic. I'm very dizzy right now." She pawed at her dress and pulled out her pistol, "I don't think I'll be able to cast another one."

Once she'd recovered her balance she ran to another tree for shelter. A burst of flame warmed her on the way. She had to check to make sure her hair wasn't on fire.

"Are you okay?" she said as she turned to one side, but Simon was gone.

There were more footsteps. She couldn't tell if they belonged to the headmaster or to Simon, or even which way they were going. It was becoming obvious that the two sides had ruined their ability to see in the dark, and were now fumbling around in the orchard and setting the wrong things on fire.

Her hands were shaking and her mouth had gone dry. She was still panting with her mouth open. She felt light-headed. Her eyes strained in the darkness. Bracing herself against the tree, she pushed herself upright.

A glint of metal entered her vision on the right side. Reflexively, she threw up an arm and her hand caught the knife blade that had been aimed at her throat. The headmaster was behind her, perhaps to one side. She spun away and fired her pistol in a panic. There was a grunt from the headmaster, who stumbled backwards while clutching his stomach.

Alice stretched out her hand. She thought to finish him with magic, but only a tiny whisper of flame drifted from her fingertips. She was spent. She swooned and tumbled sideways from the effort.

As she lay on the ground with her face pressed into the grass, she could hear laughter coming from the headmaster.

The headmaster's voice taunted her from the darkness. "Has your fire gone out, little bird?" He was wheezing as he spoke. Alice heard his faltering footsteps drawing close. With one hand she pushed against the damp earth and rolled over onto her back. Her eyes burned and flowed with tears. She longed for sleep, to close her eyes and breathe deep. It was beyond her strength to even draw enough breath to cough the smoke from her lungs.

A few steps away, the headmaster was swaying about, cursing and clutching his belly with one hand. He steadied himself and pointed at her with the knife. "Let's open you up and see what we find," he laughed as he took a step towards her. Through her tears she saw him looming closer, his hat still smoldering. His knife glinted in the firelight. She lifted her arm uselessly. She felt like she was moving through sand. The world seemed dim and remote to her eyes. Sounds were muffled as if her head were immersed in water.

Her eyes cleared and she drew a sudden breath. The sounds of the flame around her snapped to sudden clarity. Reaching out with both hands, she summoned a roaring pillar of flame. It didn't strike the headmaster so much as pass through him. The orchard was bathed in light, as if it was daytime. When she stopped the flow, the headmaster was gone. All that remained was a pile of smoking refuse and ashes.

Alice stood. Aside from the slash on her forearm, she was unhurt. But where had the sudden potency come from? Even now, she didn't feel drained from the effort. She rubbed her face and drew another deep breath. Where had she found so much strength?

Then she realized what must have happened. "Simon, you fool!" she cried to herself, and hurried off to find him.

Alice discovered him in the barn. He was curled up in an empty spot on the floor, shivering. He was in the middle of a chalk circle, drawn in his own hand. It was a feeding circle, inscribed with Alice's name.

"You fool!" she said again once she'd reached him. "What have you done?"

Simon's eyes turned slowly to her, "Alice! You won!"

VIII

"Stop!" Soot pleaded at the sight of Gilbert with a ready axe. "I was only following the Master's orders."

"That's why I'm killing you," Gilbert nodded.

Soot continued to back away, heading for the front door, which was still open. It looked like he was trying to hedge his bets. He might dart inside, or he might flee into the night.

"See here," Soot sputtered. "I've done you no harm yet."

"Should we ask inside and see if any harm has been done?"

Finally Soot was backed into the door, and he had to choose which way he would go. He glanced sideways into the house, perhaps hoping to see the headmaster. He didn't, but he spied the lantern hanging by the door.

"It's not right killing an unarmed man like this," Soot protested.

Gilbert could see where this was headed. Soot was a devious man if he got behind you, but he was neither quick-witted nor subtle. Gilbert obligingly tossed the axe away. Soot then grabbed the lantern and flung it at Gilbert.

With little trouble and even less surprise, Gilbert soft-handed the catch, then swung the lantern and smashed it over Soot's head. Soot was showered with burning oil and became a pillar of screaming flame. He began running around in a panic. Worried that the flames might endanger the house, Gilbert grabbed Soot by the belt and gave him a shove in the direction of the road.

Gilbert shook his head as he watched the man run around the yard and collapse. Soot screamed and writhed for a bit, and then stopped moving. Slowly the fire burned itself out.

Mother's voice drifted out of the house, "Gilbert sweetie! Are you all right?"

Gilbert spun around to see his mother standing just inside the door.

"I was so worried about you. Where have you been hiding?" she said as she lifted up a small child. "Don't worry, Grandma has you," she said as she bounced him gently. Then she shut the door, leaving Gilbert in darkness.

The Hiltman homestead was enshrouded in the billowing white fog of the early morning. Alice crept out the back door. She passed the outhouse, the barn, and hopped over the wooden fence to enter the singed orchard.

The dampness and the lack of leaves had saved the orchard from burning down entirely, but the fire had claimed a few of the trees before it burned itself out. Their black trunks stood silent in the fog.

"Gilbert?" she called softly. "Gilbert! Are you here?"

One of the black shapes stirred and walked towards her, "I am."

"I wasn't sure if you would be back so soon. You saw to the bodies?"

"I'd thought to bury them beyond the line of trees," he said, pointing off into the whiteness. "But there's another house over there now. I had to drag them north a bit."

"Still, you hauled away all three and buried them in a very short time."

"Their graves are not deep. And there was very little of the headmaster left to bury, deep or not. They deserved far worse than they got. After what the headmaster did to Simon, and all the other boys, and the men who went down with Callisto, and the terror they inflicted on my family, not to mention my death and all the crimes that are unknown to us..." he let out a heavy sigh, "It seems an injustice for them to be buried at all. I'd have let them rot where they fell, but I didn't want them stinking up our property. Also, I recovered these." Gilbert handed her a shoe, one of the small number of items belonging to the headmaster that had survived her inferno.

Alice took the shoe with obvious distaste. It was covered in ash. Inside were a large number of coins.

"From the headmaster," he explained. "His purse was burned, but the coins survived. I imagine this is the money he stole from our room before Callisto sank."

"That and more. I suppose this is our money, added to his." Alice dropped the coins into one of her many hidden pockets, "At least we'll have funds to return home, although I would have liked to have recovered my coin-purse as well. It was a gift from Lord Moxley, and quite valuable. I guess those villains simply threw it away."

"I imagine so. But I'm done thinking about those wretches. Tell me how Mother is doing. What did you tell her of our business?"

"I told her as little as I could, although she is a smart woman and she knows I've left things unsaid. I told her we were working for the Witch Watch, and that we were chasing these malefactors. Your mother saw your face - or lack of one - when you stormed into the house. I told her that you were a monster drawn here by their evil magic."

"Which is true, in a way," Gilbert observed.

"The danger isn't that she would see that you were an abomination - which is plain enough already - but that she would discover we were traveling together. Circumstances corroborated my story. We arrived shortly after you, instead of beside you. There were two horses outside, and not three."

"Which reminds me, we need to return the horses to Mr. Van der Byl this morning," Gilbert said.

"Your mother knew my story was off. She asked several times what the monster was, why it had attacked the headmaster's men and not the household, and where it had gone when the fight was over. I was evasive as possible without being rude. I'm not sure what she thinks now, but she let the matter drop."

"I'm just glad she wasn't hurt."

"Hurt? You would scarcely know she had been attacked at all. Brave woman. Resilient. Your sister is not nearly as sturdy, and is still shaken."

"I'm disappointed in Ruby, then. I'd always thought she was tough under her feminine appearance. A bit like you, I suppose. No, the opposite of you. You're feminine under your tough appearance."

"Don't be too hard on your sister. The headmaster set out to terrorize them, and he was good at his job. Through her sobs I managed to sort out what his plan had been. He was going to put your mother into a feeding circle, and use her to feed his magic. Then he planned to roast her family in front of her. Including your namesake, your nephew Gilbert. Speaking of which - I didn't know you were *Uncle* Gilbert!"

"The boy wasn't born until after I died. I didn't realize I was an uncle until last night. Is he unharmed?"

"Not a scratch. He was quite cheerful once the commotion had passed. And although you didn't bother to ask about him, his father will recover from his wounds."

Gilbert shrugged.

"How awful!" Alice said angrily, "Walter is your brother-in-law. You should at least care for him for the sake of your sister. And nephew."

"I never liked the man," Gilbert admitted. "Always stood with his head bowed. Shy. Scrawny. That thin little mustache of his. I don't know. I always took him for a coward."

"Well then you will be happy to know that he fought hard, even in the face of hopeless odds. He surely would have died if the headmaster hadn't wanted to save him for roasting. They had to hurt him many times before he stopped getting back up. He didn't cower, not even in the face of that beastly Scotsman."

Gilbert was quiet for a while. "I guess I was wrong about him. I took him for a man who would have fled the house and left his family to the evil men. I'm glad he had the courage when the time came, even if he didn't have the strength. That's what really matters. I wish I was alive so I could go and apologize to him."

Gilbert sat down underneath one of the trees that had been spared the fire. Alice stood nearby, looking up at the sky through the naked branches. She reached up and pulled gently on a limb, as if she was of a mind to climb it. She tilted to one side, swinging from the tree like a schoolchild. They remained like this in silence while the yellow light of the morning sun pierced the clouds and began to burn away the mist.

At last she spoke, "I know it must be hard for you, coming home like this. How are you?"

"Dead," he grunted.

Alice hurried over and kicked him.

"Ouch! What was that for?"

"You needn't bother saying 'ouch'. That kick would barely hurt a living man, and I doubt it hurt you at all. You needed it. Stop feeling sorry for yourself. I realize being dead is unfortunate, but sooner or later you need to accept it. Or at least stop moping about it."

Gilbert grunted a reluctant acknowledgment that she had a point. Then he asked, "Where is Simon?"

"Still sleeping. Your mother practically forced food down our throats once she was free of her bonds. It was all we could do to persuade them to let us sleep on the floor and not in the family beds. We've been running weary for a long time, and the feeding circle robbed what strength he had left. I imagine he won't be awake anytime soon."

Gilbert nodded and went back to staring into the vanishing mist. The morning slowly brightened, and as the veil rolled away they could see more and more of the surrounding countryside. Finally he spoke, "You were right. It is hard, being home like this. I grew up here. I used to climb these trees. There's a little brook just west of us. I used to pretend it was the Delaware River, and I was General Washington, crossing it on Christmas to fight the filthy English."

Gilbert laughed at her disapproving frown, "Then I turned fifteen and Father returned to England, and I became the English."

"Your father was an Englishman who lived in America?"

"Not just an Englishman. A British soldier. He served in Her Majesty's army."

"In New York?" Alice asked slowly, as if he was being very stupid.

"The laws regarding magic are much more lax here. Or at least, much less strictly enforced. The church has almost no power to act directly against witches. Her Majesty sent one of her advisers to New York on some lengthy errand or other. Something to do with trans-Atlantic trade. Very private and serious. So serious that she was worried about mind-control and divination being used on her representative."

Alice smiled, "Because clearly New York is brimming with malefactors."

"Clearly," Gilbert agreed. "But the English are notoriously sensitive about magic."

"Not without reason!" Alice said defensively. "We seem to attract more than our share of magical disasters."

"Granted. But the Queen insisted that some men from her own army be allowed to protect His Lordship the trade advisor, whatever his name was. My father was sent here as part of the retinue of men to protect the Lord. So they were a contingent of British soldiers, living in New York, protecting a British Lord from unseen magical threats that never materialized. While stationed here, my father met my mother. They married, and settled here. Had me. Had my sister. Then the business was concluded and Father was called home. And that's how I came to live in Rothersby. The next thing I knew, I was serving in the army I'd pretended to defeat over and over again as a boy."

"I gather you liked your time in Her Majesty's service?" Alice asked.

"I did. Best time of my life."

"So why did you leave?"

Gilbert stood and looked east. The sun had broken through. He pulled back his hood and let the sun fall on his face. "Another time. I don't want to tell that story now. It's sad. This is the first time the sunlight has touched me since I was awakened. It almost feels warm."

"It's not, I promise," Alice said. Her cheeks were red from the damp, chilly air.

"I feel cold all the time. It doesn't matter what the temperature is around me. I feel it when I stand by a fire. I feel it in the rain. I felt it when I was walking on the bottom of the ocean. That sore, aching chill you get when you've been outside too long and your joints feel bruised. But now, standing in the sun, I almost feel warm again."

"You're not feeling sorry for yourself again, are you?"

"I'm just relating the experiences of the dead, purely for academic purposes," he said slyly.

"Then I will withhold the kick I was about to give you."

Gilbert took up a shovel that had been leaning against a nearby tree and rested it over his shoulder. "Speaking of death, I should return Mother's shovel to the barn before it's missed."

Instead of answering, Alice looked at the shovel thoughtfully.

"Is something wrong?" Gilbert asked.

"I'm now remembering our last visit to Ravenstead. I found a mass grave near the place where you were revived."

"Recently filled?" Gilbert asked.

"No, recently dug. The hole was empty, as far as I could tell. At the time I thought it was curious that our foe had a hole ready for us before we even arrived. Since then I haven't really given it further thought."

"I can see you're doing that now. So what do you think? How did he know to dig a hole before we arrived? Was there a traitor in our midst?"

"No. In fact, I don't think the grave had anything to do with us at all. I think this was not a newly dug grave, but an old one that was recently uncovered. Consider: The church buried you in His Lordship's tomb. But where did they bury his men? You said that many men died defending Mordaunt. The church wouldn't have wanted to haul those bodies away. It would be quite unlike them to attempt to identify the men and notify their families. No, they would have wanted to be rid of the bodies as quickly as possible. I can think of nothing more convenient than digging a pit near the graveyard and throwing the men into it."

"And if they mistook His Lordship for one of his own servants..." Gilbert said with sudden understanding.

"Then Lord Mordaunt was buried in that mass grave," Alice agreed.

"And he has been recently unearthed," Gilbert added.

"Probably in anticipation of recovering your vigor."

"Sophie's vigor," Gilbert corrected her.

"A shame we didn't have more time to explore the manor. If we had found his body we might have taken his head and dashed his hopes forever," she muttered.

"In any case, His Lordship is above ground now. I wonder if they're looking for other means to revive him," Gilbert muttered.

"I have no doubt of it," Alice replied.

In all, they spent three days with Gilbert's family. Alice and Simon stayed in the house, and Gilbert lurked on the edges of the property, walking the woods and remembering. On the second day, Alice and Simon came out to meet him, and he took them for a walk.

"Where are we going?" asked Simon after they had walked some distance to the east.

"Up this hill," Gilbert replied flatly.

Simon was silent, but Alice responded with irritation, "Obviously we're going uphill. I'm sure Simon was wondering if you had a destination in mind, or were just of a mind to wear our legs off."

"Our destination is the top. There's a clearing."

It was late afternoon, and the sun was shining. The late October air was chill, but the sun provided the illusion of warmth. Gilbert had thrown back his hood and let the light fall on his rotting face.

"We shouldn't go too far," Alice cautioned. "If we linger until after sundown, Victoria will worry."

Gilbert stopped and turned back, "Has she mentioned me?"

"She has not spoken your name, yet you seem to occupy her thoughts a great deal," Alice replied.

Simon explained, "Mrs. Hiltman discovered that Alice wasn't married, or even being courted. She started to speak excitedly, saying that she should introduce Alice to someone. But then she stopped herself and dropped the subject."

"It happens often," Alice added. "She is continuously avoiding talking about you. I suppose we are as well."

"Does she know for certain that I'm dead? Or does she think of me as merely 'missing'?" Gilbert wondered.

"It's impossible to say," Alice sighed. "We would have to ask her directly. Which would be foolish, I think."

Gilbert nodded and they resumed their march. At last they came to the crown of the hill and found themselves looking east over the vast expanse of barren trees. Amongst the grey branches were a small number of trees which were slow to release their leafy covering. To the southeast were the taller hills of Richmond County. These largely blocked their view of the Atlantic. The water of Arthur Kill crept along below them. To the northeast, across the Hudson, were the green pastures of Manhattan, which were dotted with clusters of buildings.

"A lot has changed since I left," Gilbert said after they had looked a while.

"It's so strange here," Alice said. "In London you can find buildings which have stood for a thousand years. Even most of our 'young' buildings are older than any of the buildings in front of us. And your streets! How does one decide to build a new street? The streets of London were laid centuries ago. Their origins and authors are lost to history."

"That never occurred to me," Gilbert said. "You certainly have an appetite for aging secrets."

"That reminds me!" Alice said as she set down her bag.

Simon came over, eager and curious to see what she had carried all this way. "Oh," he said with disappointment as she brought out two books. "I was hoping you had brought lunch"

"We had breakfast before we set out," Alice said in surprise. "You managed to eat everything that was set before you, and much of what was set before others. And you still have appetite? I despair of ever filling your belly."

"You brought sorcery with you on a walk?" Gilbert asked with annoyance.

"It seemed much better than leaving the books in the house where they might be discovered. The larger book we already know. It's the one Simon used to revive you. This smaller one belonged to the headmaster. He abandoned it when he fled the house."

Simon kicked a stone away and snorted. "He needed a book to make a feeding circle? It's a simple spell. Just two stanzas in a two-ring circle with very little interconnection. All of it clockwise. I could have done something like that from memory when I was nine. And he would have sent me to bed hungry if I failed." He sat down with a huff.

"Well I have been eager to examine his book since we recovered it, but this is our first real opportunity." Alice set the book in her lap as she said this and began to turn the pages. Gilbert walked away some distance and pretended to be interested in an outcropping of rock.

"Most of these are the same spells that I have in my book," Simon observed after a few minutes of reading over Alice's shoulder.

"Yet there are fewer spells in this one, and the annotations are more detailed," she said. "Also, this is not original research. The pages here were copied from elsewhere."

"How can you tell?" Simon asked.

"See how the writing gets smaller at the bottom of this page? The scribe was attempting to reproduce another work, but he was writing in a larger hand than the original author. So he was running out of space. If he was writing this on his own, he would simply have moved to a new page."

"I know this handwriting. This is the headmaster's. And those egg-shaped circles are clearly his. I always assumed our assignments were sloppily written because he was in a hurry and didn't care if they were easy to follow. But now I suspect he can't draw proper circles."

Alice ran her finger down a page, "The book is small, and each page is unrelated to its neighbors. I suspect this is for carrying about common spells, and not for study. These first few pages are little more than simple tricks. Divination. Feeding circles. Here's one for communing with Lord Mordaunt."

"Look at how worn the page is," Simon said with sudden irritation. "He must have used this constantly. You know, when he was our master I always assumed he was a sorcerer of great knowledge."

"Clearly that was not the case. I would say the man had no head for it at all. He simply had access to a good library."

Simon stormed away, ranting, "I can't believe he was so stupid he couldn't even do these simple spells without needing to copy them from a book. I thought... I thought that, even though he was cruel and his lessons were hard, that his knowledge was deep. I thought I was receiving a rare education for my pains. But now I see he was useless! Why did His Lordship employ him?"

Gilbert looked up, "Are you really complaining about the quality of your profane and grotesque education? Would you really be happier if you'd been taught sorcery *properly?*"

"*Yes!*" Simon said in frustration. "It's the only thing I was ever taught. And now I learn that it was useless. There's no reason I couldn't have learned more with less hardship under a more qualified tutor."

Alice looked up from the book. "I'm sure the headmaster was chosen not for his skill, but for his methods. Or rather, his willingness to do what decent men would not."

Simon had turned away, and was looking out over the sunlit woods beneath them.

"Besides," she added after a few moments, "I think you have undervalued your learning. Whatever his evils, the headmaster gave you knowledge that surpasses that of the expert in Her Majesty's Ministry of Ethereal Affairs."

"I hate him so much," Simon said in a trembling voice. "I never wanted revenge. All I ever wanted was to escape. I just wanted to be free of his mistreatment. And now I *do* want revenge, but he's already dead!" Simon kept his back to them. He sniffed and wiped his nose on his sleeve.

Concerned, Alice looked over to Gilbert. He shrugged.

"What spell is this?" Alice asked as she returned her attention to the book. "I've never seen anything like it."

"I'm sure I've done it a dozen times," Simon said bitterly. "Let me see."

Alice held the book while Simon looked over the page. Finally she spoke, "This is the only circle that appears alone on a page like this. All of the others come with some form of explanation or instruction."

"This is a very strange way of writing a circle," Simon said after examining the diagram.

"It's as if the author wanted to make a circle without lifting his pen."

"It's more than that. The circle has been drawn out of order. See how the line strays from one ring to another?"

Finally Gilbert's curiosity got the best of him, and he came to look over Alice's other shoulder. He found that the mystery circle looked just like all of the other sorcery he'd encountered; it was a mess of incomprehensible symbols, drawn in a series of concentric circles with jagged lines drawn all around. Finally he shrugged, "What makes this one so special?"

Simon explained, "There are two major styles for drawing large, complicated circles. Some sorcery is done by making the outer circle first, and then working inward. This makes it easy to start with a nice, neat circle, but it means you have to plan ahead, as well as write the stanzas in reverse order. Also, if you're writing on the floor it's hard to finish the center without scuffing your work. Usually sorcery is done by starting at the center and working outwards. Some people have trouble keeping their work neat using this method, and they don't like all the moving around you have to do for floor work."

"So which is this?" Gilbert asked.

"Neither," said Alice. "This is... this is the work of a madman. The line starts inside, then does some lettering in the middle, then moves to the outer ring. It's random."

"It's not really random," Simon countered. "It's sort of lazy. The author was just moving to whatever was closest." He pointed to one of the characters on the page, "This symbol ends on an upward stroke. Going clockwise, the sorcerer would have to move his pen back down to the bottom of the line. Rather than do that, he moved the smaller distance to the line above and began working there instead."

"So what was he trying to do? Save ink?" Alice asked rhetorically.

"I don't know," Simon admitted. "The entire circle is done in one line. Trace over it, and eventually you'll end up back where you started."

"I don't know what the magical significance of that might be. Perhaps it's of no significance of all. The Greeks used to etch their circles into stone, which produced a careful, minimalist style that looks odd to us today. Popular spells are sometimes embellished with elaborate penwork, particularly if they're being woven into cloth for use as decoration."

"Do they?" asked Simon with surprise. "I would like to see that. But isn't that dangerous to have an active spell hanging on the wall?"

"It depends on the spell, of course. But often extra decorative strokes are added to spoil the spell. But this spell is probably not decorative, and it would be *more* work to etch this into stone as it is presented here. I don't know." Alice cocked her head to one side, "It's very hard to read like this. What *is* this spell?"

"It's a feeding circle. For Lord Mordaunt," Simon said, pointing to the name nestled amid the swirling characters.

For a while they sat in the cold October sunshine and toyed with theories about what the circle might mean. Eventually they grew bored with the subject. The page was otherwise empty and there was no way to really know its purpose. It could have been nothing more than the work of an idle hand searching for amusement, a profane scribbling of the bored.

When midday came they returned to the house, and Gilbert returned to his lurking among the trees.

During their stay, Victoria took an instant liking to Simon and doted over him. She cut his hair, mended his jacket, and nearly succeeded at the impossible task of keeping his belly satisfied. In the afternoons they would go for a walk and meet with Gilbert, who would pester them for news of life inside the house. He would ask them the most mundane questions about what was said, what food was prepared, and about what amusing things younger Gilbert had done or said. He even asked about Walter. Gilbert was greedy for this news, but it always made him sad. Once they were out of things to tell him he would begin sulking, and they would leave him alone.

"Are you sure we have to leave today? Victoria practically begged us to stay," Simon protested as they slipped away in the early morning of the forth day. He looked back at the house wistfully as they hurried along the road.

"We can't possibly remain another day," Alice replied sharply. "You heard her yourself at dinner last night - she's heading into town today."

"We can wait for her to get back. Or perhaps we could go with her!" Simon said cheerfully.

Alice stopped and turned to him, “Oh? You think we should all go into town together? You know we have to ride the ferry to get there, don’t you?”

Simon looked at her dumbly.

“What do you think the ferryman will say when he sees us?” she continued. “Remember we rode the ferry a few nights ago. Remember he has a special affection for Mrs. Hiltman. We told him she was in danger. And he saw us traveling with Gilbert.”

Simon’s face fell, “I see. I suppose there’s no way to avoid having them talk about Gilbert.”

“He will certainly ask about what happened. As the ferryman, what he learns will spread quickly. Consider: He knows we were traveling with a man in a black cloak. She knows that an abomination came to her house, wearing a black cloak. She was already suspicious of my story. I doubt the truth will elude them for long.” Alice sighed in frustration, “We should have left days ago. He could have visited the house, or sent messengers to check on the Hiltmans, and then there would have been trouble for us.”

They made their way to Jersey City, and then across the harbor to New York. The city was busy and crowded, and Alice felt more at home among the taller buildings and noisy streets.

There they found that the sinking of Callisto was still the subject on everyone’s lips. Numbers varied, but it sounded as though perhaps two dozen men had been lost in the sinking, nearly all of whom were members of the crew. A ship was set to leave that day, but the sinking of Callisto had created an overflow of passengers, and they couldn’t bargain their way on board. Steerage space was available, but none of them thought it would be wise for Gilbert to live in such close quarters with other people.

They secured a room at the hotel closest to the harbor. They kept to themselves as much as they could, and Alice maintained the fiction that she was caring for an aged grandfather. During the day Alice and Simon explored the city, and in the evening they came home and puzzled over the sorcery books. On one of these expeditions, Alice took Simon shopping for hats, to replace the one lost when the ship sank. To her disappointment, he insisted on replacing it with another black bowler. She was taken with many of the American hats, but Simon wouldn't even try them on.

Their stay lasted a week. October ended and November began with a dusting of snow.

As she returned to the hotel, she was greeted by a young voice saying, "I'll tell you a secret for a nickel."

Alice turned to see a boy of perhaps ten years. His nose and cheeks were red from the cold. He didn't have a coat, but Alice thought she could remember seeing him before, and she was pretty sure he'd been wearing a coat at the time. She looked him over. His smile was a bit too broad for one supposedly so destitute. She considered it likely that he would simply run off if she handed him a coin.

"I'm afraid I can only pay in quid," she said at last.

"England?" said the boy. "Some places around here will sell me food for that money, but they charge extra."

The mention of food had been a cunning play. He looked well-fed enough, but she was willing to humor him. "You're not sure if you want my money, but I'm not sure I want your secret. In fact, I'm not sure you have one at all."

The boy had to think this over. Finally he said, "It's an important secret. Someone was looking for you."

This caught her attention, and too late she realized her interest had probably shown on her face, "Very well. I'll pay you the pence and you tell me the secret."

The boy folded his arms, "Pence? I think it's worth a shilling."

"A shilling is worth a good deal more than a nickel," she shot back. In truth, she was glad to see he was clever, since it increased the odds of him having useful news. Only a foolish boy would make a habit of defrauding strangers. A smart boy would realize that business like that would catch up with you.

"Not around here. Not by much," he said firmly. She could see he was standing his ground. His price was a shilling.

She gave him the coin. “Let’s hear it,” she said.

“A fellow came up from Richmond county. Was asking around about a man, a lady, and a big man in a black cloak. Sounds like you. Sounds like your old man.”

“What did he look like?”

The boy held out his hand for another shilling. Alice gave him six pence instead. The boy looked down at the coins, did the math, and answered, “He was an older gentleman. Husky. Had two young fellows with him that might have been his sons.”

Alice thought to ask him more about their clothes and accents, to see if she could work out where they were from and what class they were. Before she could speak, the boy determined that his opportunities for profit had been expended, and ran off.

Alice returned to the room and informed Gilbert and Simon that they were being looked for by someone new. “He came from Richmond county, which is where the lifeboats landed. He might be after us concerning the events on Callisto, or he might be curious about Gilbert. Perhaps he has news from the ferryman. Perhaps he means us harm, or perhaps he means us well, but in either case we would do well to avoid him. I suggest we move to someplace more discrete. There are lodgings on the docks. We should move there today.”

“We’re more likely to stand out on the docks!” Simon complained.

“We’re less likely to be *looked for* on the docks,” she countered.

They rented a room in a drafty wooden building that had been built so poorly they could see daylight between the boards. Their room had a small coal furnace that lost too much heat and retained too much smoke. Their neighbors were sailors, drunks, or some combination of the two. The area around the house always smelled like urine and vomit.

On their third day on the docks, a freight ship arrived. Alice tried to obtain passage, but they sent her away when she explained she was traveling with a boy and an old man. Finally a passenger ship arrived, the Artemis. It was of the same line as Callisto, but older in design. The three of them secured a first-class room and enjoyed an uneventful voyage back to Liverpool.

LONDON

Remedies
mixed
While
You Wait
CLOSED
PATENT
DIGESTIVE
TONIC
FERTILITY
OINTMENT
1
PATENT

IX

The trio stood in front of Grayhouse. The front door was hanging open. Several of the first-floor windows were smashed. Bits of refuse littered the porch.

It was late afternoon. They had just arrived from the train station. Alice and Simon were tired. Alice had described the house to Simon on the voyage home, and invited him to stay until Ethereal Affairs returned to more conventional duty. They were all looking forward to a warm house that didn't roll beneath their feet, and now they had come home to find the house in disarray.

Gilbert tore a notice from the front door and read from it, "Be it here known, the most Holy Church, instrument of the almighty and refuge of the blameless, with regard to the exigencies of acting as a vanguard against all forms of witchcraft on behalf of HER ROYAL HIGHNESS QUEEN VICTORIA, has hereby deemed this premises to be of a dangerous and vulgar nature." Gilbert sighed and read silently for a moment. "It is a writ of seizure, giving the church the authority to invade the premises and take whatever they deem to be magical contraband. Apparently we did something to anger the queen?"

Alice stomped up the steps, boiling with anger. "I'm sure the wording was designed to leave the reader with the impression that this is done with the blessing of the throne, but I have seen these writs before - usually on the door of a house where the church has thwarted our investigation by burning the evidence and executing the suspects. The church issues these writs themselves, *to* themselves. While they claim to be acting on behalf of the Queen, their actions are more *tolerated* than appreciated."

"Still," said Gilbert, "You've always had 'contraband' here, but they didn't give themselves a Writ of Breaking Into Your House until the recent troubles."

"Yes," she sighed. "This is more politics than piety. Let's see what damage has been done." She walked over the sparkling pieces of glass that littered the porch and proceeded inside. Gilbert and Simon followed.

"Weapons!" she cried when she saw that the sitting room had been stripped almost bare. "Why would they take the weapons? And why are the furnishings so tossed about? Look! Someone slashed the sofa! What religious text demands this sort of needless vandalism?" Her hands were clenched into fists and her face was red with fury.

Gilbert looked around the room, "The furniture has been overturned in a search for valuables. If you look at the front door, you'll see it was forced open and no longer shuts properly. I suspect the church forced their way in. The door was left hanging open, an invitation to robbers and vandals."

"Oh! You are right," Alice growled. "Who knows what foul sorts have been here, or what they've taken. I suspect most of our valuables..." she trailed off, her eyes going suddenly wide with fear. "Oh no!" she cried as she dashed upstairs.

Simon stood just inside the doorway, having never been properly invited in or asked to sit. He took his bowler from his head, holding it gently under one arm. He busied himself with cleaning his spectacles on his shirt. Gilbert headed for the back door, intending to see if it was still secure. They both stopped when they heard a shriek from upstairs. Worried the Alice was in danger, they stormed up after her.

They burst into the library. The room was barren. Not a single book was left on a shelf. No shred of paper remained that had any writing on it. The ink and the pens were taken. Not a fragment of chalk remained. The bookshelves had been pulled away from the walls. While the church hadn't found any secret doors, they hadn't bothered to put the shelves back where they found them. But none of this concerned Alice.

They found her sitting at her workbench, weeping. It was bare.

"My tools," she said after a minute of silent tears. "All of my tools. My watch-works. My electrical supplies. My copper parts. Everything."

Simon and Gilbert looked at one another. Gilbert shrugged.

Alice turned to them and sniffed, "My father gave me these things. Some of them were rare and expensive, some of them were less so, but all of them were gifts from him. It was all I had left."

They were silent. Alice looked behind the scattered shelves and under the tables, hoping to see some glint of metal, some small item that might have been overlooked or dropped. She shoved the tables and shelves as she searched. Gilbert followed along behind her, checking where she had already looked. He suspected she was likely to have trouble seeing clearly through her angry tears. Finally she returned to her stool and sat down in a huff, defeated.

"Alice?" Simon asked meekly after a few minutes had passed. He looked very nervous. His hand was inside of his jacket.

Her shoulders fell, "I'm sorry to make such a scene. I would like to have given you a better welcome."

"No, it's not that. It's just that..." he drew out an object from his coat and placed it in front of her on the workbench. It was a fine pocketwatch. On the back was engraved the name 'Donnovan White'.

Alice took it up in trembling hands and examined it closely. "How?" she asked in a quiet voice.

Simon cleared his throat. "I've had it for some time. Years. I realized it belonged to you during our trip to America, but I was too embarrassed to say anything. It was a gift."

Alice looked up from the watch and eyed him suspiciously.

He continued, “It was a gift from my old master. About three years ago, he gave it to me when I ‘graduated’ from the academy.”

Alice went red again. Her eyes flashed. She let out a scream of anger and frustration. Then she stormed out of the room, leaving the watch behind.

Simon sat down on the floor beside the cold fireplace, dumbfounded. “I’d hoped that she would be glad to have an item of her father’s.”

Gilbert shook his head. “You didn’t just give her an item of her father’s. You gave her proof that her father is dead.”

Alice turned down the narrow street; carefully following the directions she’d been given. She counted five doors, turned left into a narrow alley, and found the black iron staircase. She was now behind a tight line of weary houses.

The sun was setting. The smell of a dozen meals floated from the nearby homes. People lived close in this part of the city, and they kept careful track of who belonged. She could feel the eyes on her back as she fumbled through the twisting streets.

Earlier she had visited King Charles Street, hoping to meet with Lord Moxley. As she entered, she saw the place was filled with young and unfamiliar faces. She headed for Moxley’s office, but was headed off before she could reach it. The man pretended to know her and flirted with her. He took her hand as if to lead her away from the office. Alice, already greatly distressed, had nearly lashed out at the unwelcome gesture, but she felt a slip of paper pressed into her palm. The man shooed her away playfully, giving no sign that he’d given her anything at all. Alice thought this subterfuge was absurd. Couldn’t he have simply handed her a message? Certainly most people who worked here would have a passing familiarity with her face. Then again, these new men did not, and this show was most likely for their benefit. She departed, and examined the note. It contained only directions, which were signed simply ‘M’. The journey had taken her to this poor and unfamiliar area of the city.

Alice found the door marked with yellow flowers, as the directions had promised. The buds were quite sad and withered by now, and were more brown than yellow, but this was the address. She knocked, and a man of thirty answered the door. He was a pale and slender dandy, with red lips and thin eyebrows. His head was topped with long dark locks. He regarded her with bemusement. For a moment Alice thought he was going to slam the door in her face without a word, but instead he waved her in.

The apartment was small, even smaller than she might have guessed from the outside. It was little more than a bed, a table, and a stove. A man sat at the table, illuminated by the square of fading red sunlight that reached between the London rooftops and entered the small window. His face was drawn, and bags were under his eyes. His head was covered in short grey hair. Alice scarcely recognized her old friend.

"You are sure you'll be all right with her?" the younger man at the door asked suspiciously.

"Even safer than I am with you," Lord Moxley replied. "Do not underestimate the woman. She is cunning, but trustworthy."

The pale man rolled his eyes, and departed.

"I hope you will forgive dear Byron," said Moxley. "He's been out of sorts lately. Also, he's never been particularly friendly towards the fairer sex. But he's a valuable ally in these troubled times."

"Your hair is white," Alice blurted out. "Of course it's white. I don't know why I thought..."

Moxley blinked in rare surprise. "I am flattered that you mistook my wig for my own hair. You are gullible, but very kind."

"I don't know that I mistook it, I just... I never thought about it until I saw you without it." She was shocked at how old he suddenly looked.

There were only two chairs at the small table. Moxley waved her into the one he was not using. She entered the house only reluctantly. It seemed a strange and unwelcome place.

Moxley ran one of his soft hands over his head. "Well, my ceaseless vanity has worked to my advantage. I am able to wear my proper appearance as a disguise. I thought to grow a beard, but Byron wouldn't hear of it." Moxley stood and walked over towards the stove to add fuel, "Curse that I've been forced into hiding in winter. Still, one cannot reschedule disaster."

"Disaster?" Alice asked. "I originally sought you for advice, but now I see you are in some sort of trouble yourself. What has happened?"

Moxley did not answer right away. Instead, he stood over the stove and warmed himself for a while before returning to his seat at the table. He refilled his wineglass and held up the bottle to offer some to Alice.

"Thank you, no," she replied.

Moxley shrugged and returned to his seat. He began with a deep breath, "About five days after you left for America, I became aware that there was a great number of new faces at King Charles Street. Faces come and go as ministries hire and fire their lower staff, but I had never before seen so many at once. Worse, they seemed to spread themselves throughout the place, poking their noses in where they weren't wanted and listening in on business that did not belong to them. They were young men. Fit men. This alone was alarming enough. Only the highest offices have the financial means to hire in such numbers, but more troubling still was their attitude. They did not respond to threats or demands from the old names. These men had no respect for the order of things, and were beholden to someone higher. Or at least, someone who they thought would *eventually* be higher.

"And the young men were not wrong. There was power at work. Some ministries were closed. Some were suspended. Our ministry was merely the first of many to find itself without support or funding. Others have followed. A few men complained, and were relieved of their positions entirely, without explanation."

"Were you put out? Was Ethereal Affairs closed forever?" Alice asked in alarm.

"No. I'm shrewd enough to lie still and listen when my betters are at odds. I watched and waited, and drew no attention to myself. I heard rumors. Some of the men who were dismissed complained loudly, and I was able to gain intelligence from their downfall. All paths led to Sir Edward James Brooks."

"The Member of Parliament?"

"The Member of Parliament you threw into prison, yes. One of the 'Four Horsemen', I believe you called them? Dangerously charming fellow. I saw that much of the money and influence being exerted was flowing from him."

"And this drove you into hiding?" Alice asked doubtfully.

"Well, if Brooks were a more conventional man I would have done the smart thing and begun polishing his boots, as it were. I would have ingratiated myself to him, or to his supporters.

"That's very unseemly!" Alice said.

Moxley shrugged. "Not particularly. Not in this line of work, at any rate. I've done so before. The power structure has changed many times over the years. The key to survival is to fit oneself into the new order before things settle. It happens every ten or fifteen years, by my reckoning. And I'm sure the cycle itself is older than Buckingham Palace. No, what drove me into hiding was the connection between Brooks and the late Viscount of Ravenstead."

"You think this is some scheme of Mordaunt's?"

"I don't know that His Lordship is *instigating* it from beyond the grave. I will leave that sort of conjecture to your expertise. But we know Brooks is a powerful man with powerful friends, and the large and sudden following tells us this is a stroke long planned."

"I suppose you see the danger more clearly than I do, or you wouldn't have come to this dreary place to hide."

Moxley gasped and placed his hand on his chest in feigned offense. "You wound me, madam!"

Alice folded her arms and looked at him seriously.

Resigned, he abandoned the pretense. "It *is* a baleful hovel, isn't it?

But don't say so if Byron returns. This is his place. Not his *proper* residence, mind you. He keeps this room in London for when he needs a bit of privacy. I am only staying here out of necessity. I could have remained at home, or gone to visit one of my many colleagues, but I wanted to disappear for a time. I wanted to watch from a distance, where I would not myself be watched. I would be looked for in the other places, but my dealings with Byron are secret, even to my peers. Unless I have been very reckless, I will not be found here. Of course, this is all a dreadful bore to Byron, who has no patience for this sort of thing."

"But how can you spy on the dealings at King Charles Street from this place? And why hide? Do you think you are in danger?" Alice asked impatiently.

Moxley drained his glass. Again he proffered the bottle. When she refused again, he shrugged and poured himself the last of the wine. "I did not say my spying was limited to King Charles Street. As for being in danger? I'm not sure." He sat back and rubbed his chin thoughtfully. "A man like myself is usually seen as reliably unreliable. That is, I can be trusted to follow whoever has the most power. We're generally overlooked in power struggles. Each side will see me not as a threat, but as a prize to be won. The players will generally focus their attention on the loyalists. But! I'm the head of Ethereal Affairs. If this new power is aligned with witchcraft, they will have no use for my friendship. As for how I observe from here, I do not intend to reveal all of my secrets to you. Not out of lack of trust, of course. But there is nothing to be gained by telling that long tale. Suffice to say, I have others acting as my eyes and ears."

"Like the gentleman who passed along this note?" Alice said, holding up the paper she'd been given.

"Exactly so," he nodded, "Although you should not have carried the note with you." Quickly, he snatched the paper away and tossed it into the stove. "So, now you know what has occupied me in your absence. Now it is your turn. How fared your journey?"

So Alice told him of their voyage on Callisto, their dealings with the headmaster, the sinking of the ship, the events at the Hiltman home, and recounted a bit of their journey home.

"I had heard about lost Callisto. It wasn't until you arrived at Grayhouse earlier today that I knew you'd survived."

"You saw us this afternoon?" she asked incredulously.

The question clearly pained him, "Of course not. Not *personally*. But I have my spies and my rumor hunters. They are only as loyal as the coin I give them, but I trust them to tell enough of the truth that I may re-create the whole. Grayhouse is watched."

"So you know the house has been emptied?"

"I knew it was invaded by the church. I did not know that it was emptied. Once I saw that the protection of Prince Albert had vanished, I knew that a visit from the church was unavoidable. I had hoped that you were perhaps more cunning than you seem, and had hidden the most scandalous and valuable items out of sight."

"No. Although, if we had used a secret compartment it would not have helped. Their search was very thorough."

"Nonsense! If we get through this with our positions intact, I will instruct you in the art of keeping your treasures secret. It's a delightful endeavor."

"It sounds tedious to me, but I will be glad to hear your instruction if we make it through." Alice stood and walked over to the window. The sun was lost below the rooftops and the room had fallen into darkness. The stove was now the brightest spot in the room. Moxley still didn't seem inclined to light a candle. Alice wondered if he owned any. She looked out over the city, watching the black soot waft into the sky as London struggled to keep warm.

"I suppose your next question will be regarding Archer," Moxley said casually.

"Oh! Archer! I am awful. I had forgotten about him." Alice was glad for the darkness to hide her blushing.

Moxley seemed to take no notice of this. "He reported to me two days after you departed. I gathered you left him to recover the bodies of his fellow soldiers and return to London with them. He had a strange story to tell when I saw him. Apparently, a few hours after your assault on Ravenstead, more soldiers arrived. He ran off before he was discovered, and watched until dawn as the men cleared away the bodies and cleaned away the blood."

"Lord Mordaunt seems to employ an alarming number of men."

"He may," nodded Moxley, "But these were not his men. These were proper British Soldiers."

"But how?" demanded Alice.

"As I said, Brooks has more supporters than any of us had guessed. They cleared away the bodies, and did not return them to us. The bodies vanished. They made off with the carts, the horses, everything. Archer was obliged to return to me on foot. Poor lad was half-starved by the time he found me. It wounded me to tell him that after all his hardship, he was simply being folded back into regular service. I gave him a few coins and my thanks. I hope he didn't take offense, but I had nothing else to offer."

She left the window and stormed back across the room. "This is worse than I would have thought possible! Our own soldiers, working for a cult. My father never allowed a crisis to get this bad."

"He never had to face one this broad," Moxley countered. "Now please don't stomp your feet so. Byron rents this room from the neighbors downstairs. They are old, temperamental, and very particular about noise."

Alice sat down at the table, and wished she'd taken the wine when it was offered. Exasperated, she said, "Now I know what has happened while we were absent, but I'm no closer to knowing what to do next. Our enemies are suddenly and inexplicably legion, Grayhouse is plundered, our forces are slain, and our ministry is without support."

"I don't know," admitted Moxley. "But we need to move soon. Our foes grow in power. In service of Mordaunt or not, Brooks controls a great deal more of the government than I had guessed. Possibly more than the Queen understands. I might go to Prince Albert, but my instincts are telling me that is an unwise move. Albert is a card we can only play once, and I fear that my rumors and guesses - as all of this will sound to his ears - will not be enough to rouse him into action. He has other business on his mind."

Alice slumped in her chair, defeated. "You have no advice at all? Is there nowhere we might look for allies? Is there perhaps someone we might watch, or question?"

"Well, there is one thing," Moxley said, digging through his pockets and producing an envelope. "This invitation was delivered to my office, and another one to my normal residence. I don't know who it's from, but I'm told it was delivered by one of the new faces on King Charles Street. The invitation asks me to visit an address near London. Tomorrow night. Likely as not our foes are hoping I'll appear and save them the trouble of hunting me down."

"Do you plan to go?" Alice asked in surprise.

Moxley laughed in response.

"What does the invitation say?"

"It's a dinner party, hosted by Brooks himself, if the invitation is to be believed. According to the papers, many people from King Charles Street have been invited. None of those invited are people I count among Brook's loyalists."

"So this is an invitation to a dinner-party for all of Brooks' foes, hosted by Brooks himself?" Alice asked.

"I wouldn't say foes. Independents. Holdouts. Rivals."

Alice nodded. "Well, perhaps I might go in your stead."

"Don't do that!" he scolded. "I was only offering it as a lead, something to investigate. If you walk in the front door, they will be able to stab your back as easily as mine."

"Not as easily, I think, unless you've developed a talent for fireballs while I was gone."

"Don't go *alone*, at least. I wish Archer was still available to us."

Alice laughed. "I do not think he would be able to offer me much in the way of assistance."

"What do you mean? Was he unsatisfactory as a soldier?"

“Sometimes,” Alice said reluctantly. She had often been exasperated by his shortcomings, but he was a decent fellow and she didn’t enjoy giving an ill report of him. “Perhaps not as attentive as he should have been. He was given to complaining. The captain always said he ‘lacked backbone’. He did seem to linger behind the other men when it was time for manual labor.”

Moxley looked at the ceiling and gave an exasperated sigh. “Well, if Captain Turpin had wanted brawn he should have said so, and I would have sent him a mule. But on many occasions he expressed his frustrations with getting his men to hit their targets. As he explained, you often needed the men to be able to shoot with precision. Previously, I had selected men based on bravery, as I assumed it would take a good deal of courage to face all of the unnatural things you find. When Turpin expressed a need for marksmanship, I spared no effort in obtaining him the best possible man.”

“Private Archer is the best marksman in the British army?” Alice asked skeptically.

“I did not say that. But he was the best I was able to find. The army is always testing new rifle designs, and he was apparently an important part of that process. Apparently, he was one of a small handful of men who had both the skill and knowledge to really compare the various rifles being produced and… I don’t know, to be honest. Whatever it was they needed to know about new rifles, he was able to tell them after just a few shots. He was the son of a gunsmith of some renown, as I understand. In any event, the army was slow to release him to me, and I had to bully them a bit to secure Private Archer for you.”

“But, if he was such a remarkable marksman, why didn’t you say so when you sent him to us?”

Moxley shrugged, “I assumed the captain would know what to do with him. I must admit to feeling rather unappreciated when he never expressed any gratitude for Archer.”

“No. The captain had no idea. Archer had said something about being good with a rifle, but the captain assumed he was boasting as soldiers do. Or simply trying to avoid strenuous work. I suppose, looking back, it's clear that 'boasting' was never one of his faults. Oh, foolishness. I can't believe we made such a blunder. My father would never have made that mistake."

"No, he wouldn't," Moxley admitted quietly.

There was a long silence. Finally Alice took up the invitation, which Moxley had left on the table between them. She couldn't read it in the dim light, so she tucked it away for later. "You said that Prince Albert has other business on his mind. What could be more important than this plot?"

Moxley sighed. "Leopold, his son, has been missing for a fortnight."

X

When Alice returned to Grayhouse, she found Simon and Gilbert sweeping away the debris and putting the house in order. They had found an enormous ash pile in the garden where the church had burned their books. It had since rained, and much of the ground was now black mud. They did not speak of anything, aside from the affairs of the house.

Alice gave Simon the sitting room for the night, and retired to bed. Simon found some old coats that he could use as blankets, and slept on the couch. Gilbert spent the night prowling about in the shadows, and was disappointed when the looters failed to return.

The next day was cold, overcast, and quiet. London itself seemed to be subdued. The people were apprehensive and ill at ease. The faces on the streets were grim and reluctant to meet the gaze of strangers. Alice spent the day running errands. First she had to buy food. What little was left at Grayhouse had spoiled during their trip. After that she visited the glaziers and arranged to have the windows replaced. Finally she traveled the streets near Grayhouse, learning what she could about the visit from the church. People were slow to talk, but she eventually learned what she already suspected: An aging Hierarch, leading six young men in red sashes, had invaded the house in late October. They had kicked in the door, and sometime later the smoke of a bonfire rose over the place. The only curious detail was that the fire had been set in the garden, and not in the street as was their custom.

Gilbert and Simon spent the day working on the house. Many of the storage rooms had been ransacked by robbers. Most of the contents were either of little value, or too large to be easily carried, and so the floors were awash in unwanted possessions. The two of them set to righting these rooms and clearing out enough space that Simon could have a room of his own.

"Do you think I should say something to her?" Simon said abruptly as he was carrying an armload of clothing out of his future room.

"You mean about the pocketwatch?" Gilbert asked, following behind. He was carrying a chair that was too uncomfortable to sit on, too ugly to use as decoration, too large to leave in a room that anyone planned to use, and too expensive to throw away.

"Yes."

"No. She is angry. Not at you, not really. But if you get in the way of her anger you may feel the brunt of it."

Alice returned home and began cooking the evening meal without a word. The silence that seemed to infect the city had come to Grayhouse as well. She prepared enough for three, and even set three places at the table. She realized her mistake when Gilbert took his seat and casually asked what was for dinner. She looked suddenly stunned at the question. She had lived with him for almost a month now, and had no explanation for why she had made such a blunder.

"What is it that has you so preoccupied?" Gilbert asked once the other two had begun eating.

Alice shook her head. They ate in silence, save for Simon's frantic chewing and gulping. His plate was clean before Alice had made any serious progress on her own. He was grateful that she had prepared extra. After cleaning off Gilbert's plate, he hurried off to the kitchen to get more.

"How did you get it?" Alice asked suddenly as Simon returned to the table.

Simon looked down at his plate in confusion.

"The watch!" she said impatiently. "How did you come to own the watch?"

Simon blinked, "As I said, it was a gift from Lord Mordaunt."

Alice fixed him with an expectant gaze.

“I was... I was brought to a large house, just outside of London.” he continued. “The Four Horsemen took me from the academy and brought me to the house, where His Lordship was waiting for me. He said I’d done well in my studies and that I wouldn’t need to study under the headmaster any longer. That’s when he gave me the watch.”

“Did he say anything else? Did he mention my father, or what happened to him?” her voice was tense.

Simon shook his head. He stopped eating, and looked very frightened, as if he expected Alice to strike him at any moment.

“What did he say about the watch? Why did he give it to you?”

Simon shrugged, “He said it was a gift, on ‘the occasion of your graduation’. Those were his words. After that I was returned to the academy, but allowed my own room, away from the other boys. I was fed more regularly. Not a lot, but at least I didn’t need to fight the other boys for every mouthful.”

“What was the date?” she asked after a long pause.

Simon was looking down at his plate and moving his food around with his fork. “I don’t know. I never had a calendar. We rarely kept track of dates at the academy, because all of the days were the same. Sometime in late summer, I think. I know that Lord Mordaunt died on October first, although I didn’t hear news of it until the end of the year.”

“Father disappeared in late August of 1882. He didn’t say where he was going. I hadn’t even heard the name Mordaunt by that point.”

“He didn’t tell anyone else in the Witch Watch where he was going?” Gilbert asked.

“No. At the time, I wasn’t a part of the ministry. He would never discuss the particulars of his work with me. We studied the books he confiscated, but he never discussed his field work. He worked alone most of the time, and only took the soldiers with him when he needed to make an arrest. He found it was far easier to gather information when he was alone. He said that having a large group of men with him would only cause people to scatter. When he vanished, I was given his investigative duties, and it was decided that I would always have an escort."

"So what are we going to do next?" Simon asked with a full mouth.

Alice looked out the window. "I called on Lord Moxley last night, and he gave me an interesting lead."

Their carriage rolled through the gates and left them in front of a large manor, walled by towering hedges. They had passed through a broad iron gate. It was flanked not by private guardsmen, but by proper British soldiers. They waved Alice and her companions through.

Alice had instructed the carriage driver to stop well short of the doors, and allow them to approach the house on foot. Out of habit, Gilbert exited first, and helped Alice down. This irritated her, since it betrayed the notion that he was an old man. Simon climbed out reluctantly, holding his coat closed with his arms. It was evening, and the November wind worked diligently to punish them for daring to go outside at this late hour.

Alice had deliberated on what to wear. If this was to be a meeting with someone from the ministry, then she would want to be dressed like a proper lady. If this was a trap set for Lord Moxley, then she would want to be wearing something more suitable and less flammable. In the end, she decided to wear a dress. Her father's watch now hung from a chain around her neck.

"There aren't any streetlights here," Simon said with disappointment. He was still captivated by the sight of electric lights and had spent the entire trip looking out of the windows, watching the lights dance by.

"What do you say now?" Gilbert asked. "Earlier you said you didn't know if this was a trap or a party. Now that we're here, what do you think?"

"This is not a trap," Alice said definitively. "At least, I don't expect anyone to attempt to murder us on the spot. Look at how many servants are about, and how many carriages are here. The house is brightly lit…"

"Those are electric lights!" Simon said with excitement.

"Yes," Alice replied patiently. "But more important is the fact that the house is prepared for a party, and other guests have arrived. I doubt Brooks is the sort of man to butcher his foes over dinner. Whatever is in store for us tonight, I doubt our lives will be threatened."

The house would no doubt have some space near the kitchen where carriage-drivers could go to keep warm while their charges were entertained. Alice gave their driver firm instructions to not do this. He was to stay with his coach, in the street, in the cold. He did not take kindly to this suggestion, but she placated him with enough coin that he vowed to wait until dawn, if need be.

"It looks very spooky and ominous," Simon said as they approached the house.

"It looks ominous because you're not used to seeing a house glow like this. This house is probably very similar to its neighbors, aside from the lights," Gilbert said.

"No, I think Simon is right," Alice said. "This place has an unwholesome look about it."

"And smell," Simon added. "It smells like something rotten." He sniffed the air as the wind blew, holding his hat onto his head with one hand.

Gilbert clapped his hand on the boy's shoulder, "Bad smells and spooky lighting can't hurt you. If anything more dangerous comes along, I have my sword."

"The invitation was extended to Lord Moxley," Alice said to Gilbert suddenly. "We are no doubt going to meet one of his political rivals. It would be unwise to introduce such a person to an abomination. I think it would be best for you to wait outside."

"But if these people mean us harm, we will want to stand together," Gilbert countered. "There is no sense in bringing along a bodyguard if you plan to leave him behind when you go into danger."

"I could call to you if there is trouble."

"And if I am very lucky and you scream very loud, I may hear you above the sound of the wind. Then I can assault the house alone and run around frantically looking for you. Perhaps I will even arrive in time to avenge your death."

"I am hardly defenseless!" she retorted.

"I would never suggest otherwise. Yet you may find yourself in a position where setting everything on fire is not the best strategy."

"I also have my pistol."

"An excellent option for situations where you only plan to face a single foe," Gilbert said, nodding towards the cluster of guards gathered around the main gate.

Alice relented and they approached the house together.

"I've been here before," Simon said suddenly.

"What?" Alice asked in surprise.

"The day I graduated. This is where they brought me. I wasn't sure when we arrived. On my last visit it was daytime, and summer. This place looks very different now. But this is the same place. I was led around the left side of the house. There's a garden there, and an entrance that leads to a room full of sorcery books."

They reached the front door, which was flanked by a pair of British soldiers. Alice had concocted an elaborate story to explain why she was attending in Lord Moxley's stead. She also had reasoning to explain who her companions were and why she had brought them. Her tale was so thorough and so detailed that she was genuinely disappointed when the doormen failed to question her.

"You've missed the meal," said one of the guards. "The guests will have gathered in the ballroom by now."

He began to give her directions to the ballroom, but Alice dismissed him with a wave of her hand. “Oh, I always come through the garden entrance when I visit,” she insisted.

A row of dim electric lights lit the path around the house. It was a lane of red brick, winding its way through the grass and around the house. The grim silhouettes of bare trees hid just off to the side, at the edge of the light.

They followed the path, with Gilbert walking out in front, gripping the hilt of his sword.

“Did you meet Lord Mordaunt when you visited?” Alice asked.

“I did. Our meeting was brief, but he shook my hand and gave me the watch.”

Alice nodded, but said nothing. She fingered her watch nervously.

The path ended at a large circle of brick paving, ringed with bright electric lamps. Beyond those was a circle of low hedges, and beyond that were gnarled, sickly trees. There was a set of grand double doors here.

Gilbert pulled them open and led everyone inside. Another pair of guards greeted them with surprise. “‘Evening!” said one cheerfully, giving Gilbert and Simon a strange look. “I’m afraid you’ve missed the meal. The other guests will be in the ballroom now. Just down that hallway and turn left.”

Alice thanked him and they moved on.

“I remember this,” Simon whispered once they were out of earshot. “This is where I met His Lordship,” Simon pointed to a closed door.

Alice opened the door and peeked in. It was a very curious room. On the far wall was another door. There was also a fireplace, some chairs, and a bookshelf. The near side of the room was bare. Between these two halves were strong iron bars that ran from floor to ceiling, with a prison door affording access. The room was dark, but they could clearly see chalk dust had been worked into the floorboards on this side.

Simon stepped a few paces into the room, “I stood here and performed sorcery, while the master and his men sat on the other side of the bars and watched."

"What are the bars for?" Gilbert asked.

"To protect the observers, obviously," Alice explained. "It's common for sorcerers to lock themselves in rooms or other places where their work won't be a threat to others. If a man dabbles in necromancy, he doesn't want his creation to escape and menace his family or colleagues."

They had stepped into the darkened room, while Gilbert stood in the door and held one hand on his sword. "We shouldn't be in here." he said.

"Are you frightened?" Alice teased. "You can wait in the hall if this is taxing your nerves."

"Certainly. If a guard comes by I will strike up a conversation to distract him from your trespassing. Perhaps we can have a chat about what it's like being dead."

"I wish I could reach that bookshelf," Alice said, pointing to the opposite side of the room. She held herself against the bars and squinted into the dark. "Someday I will build an electric lantern that can be carried around. I can't see the spines, and I want to know what they are."

Simon gripped the door and tugged lightly, "Locked. I don't imagine they would keep the key close at hand."

"It *would* render the gate pointless," Alice admitted, nudging Simon out of the way. She produced a pair of small tools from the folds of her dress, and went to work on the lock. After a few seconds of clicking and scraping, the lock gave way and she slid the door open.

"Careful!" Simon whispered as she stepped through to the other side of the room. He looked around nervously.

Alice put her hand on her chin and examined the books. Occasionally she would pull one out and leaf through it.

Finally Gilbert grew impatient, "Have you learned anything?"

"Indeed yes," she replied, putting back another book. "Our host appears to be a great admirer of Lord Tennyson."

“A sorcerer?” asked Simon.

“A playwright, I think,” Gilbert said.

“Poet,” Alice corrected him.

“I suppose you’re looking for books of witchcraft. Have you found anything useful to our investigation?” Gilbert asked warily.

“Not a one”, she said with disappointment.

Simon rubbed his finger on the floor, “This is more dust than chalk. It’s been some weeks since the last attempt at sorcery was performed here. I wonder what they were doing.”

Alice rejoined the men on the other side of the room and knelt down to examine the chalk marks, “A shame they erased so thoroughly. I would like to know what they were doing as well.”

“This is truly captivating,” Gilbert said. “I imagine if we apply ourselves for the next several hours we might discover many secrets about how our foes clean their house.” He stepped into the room and let go of the door, which began to swing shut behind him.

Alice lunged and caught the door before it latched, “I’ll thank you not to shut the three of us in a dark room.” She pulled the door open and the light flowed in again. “Look! There is no latch on our side. If the door had shut, we could have been trapped in here.”

Everyone was suddenly anxious to leave the room. She held the door open and motioned them out.

They proceeded down the hall and went left as directed. As they approached the ballroom they could hear the echo of someone addressing a crowd.

The ballroom was cavernous. The ceiling was laden with piercing electric lamps that stung the eyes, yet the light seemed ineffectual against the dark wood of the walls. There was a pale green tinge to the room, and a pervasive haze of tobacco smoke sat at eye level. There were perhaps two dozen men gathered near the center of the room, huddling together and sustaining the tobacco cloud. A small number were accompanied by women, but for the most part this affair was attended by men in tuxedos. Most of the heads were white, or gray, or bald.

Sir Edward James Brooks was standing and speaking to the men in a proud, strong voice. Three old fellows stood at his side.

"The four horsemen!" Gilbert whispered, his hand returning to his sword-hilt.

"Steady!" Alice commanded. "We are here to learn what we can. We are *no*t here to assassinate the gentry of London."

"They're here. They're working for Lord Mordaunt. Why not be done with them?" he asked reasonably.

"We caught them in the act of necromancy a few weeks ago. Or at least, *supervisin*g necromancy. If that was not enough to put them up at Tyburn, then I imagine we have even less grounds to walk into their house and assassinate them in front of the most powerful men in Great Britain. You might be immune to hanging, but Simon and I are not, and I would like to keep our necks out of the noose if it's all the same to you."

"You're right," Gilbert grumbled.

The crowd was laughing. Brooks had charmed them with wine and wit, and they were nodding and laughing as he spoke. "Now, I want to introduce a few friends of mine," he said brightly. "I'm sure you saw them at dinner, but they're much too humble to announce themselves. Humility is not one of my vices, so that duty falls to me."

Brooks was standing in front of the crowd. The other three horsemen stood at his side, looking slightly self-conscious. All of them wore dark suits. Brooks pointed to the oldest, "Perhaps some of you recognized this gentleman? This is General Bornholdt. Despite his reputation, he's a fine fellow."

"As long as you're not Russian!" one man joked before returning his pipe to his mouth.

"Quite right!" Brooks smiled.

The other guests nodded appreciatively, except for a young man in uniform, who began a sudden and incongruous clap. There was a look of awe on his face.

"The serious looking fellow next to the general is Benedict Butler, the man who brought electric light to London." There was polite applause at this. "And finally Judge Brown. Do not mistake his silence for rudeness. Since his sentences end mostly in death and transportation, his silence is actually the gentlest of compliments." This earned another laugh from everyone except for Brown himself, who did not look like a man who knew how to smile. He nodded politely.

Brooks continued, "But as excellent and as noteworthy as my colleagues are, I did not call you here tonight to meet them. No, I invited you here because I have something important to tell you." Here the laughing and whispering in the room stopped. A man stopped himself from re-lighting his pipe, lest he make unwanted noise. The crowd hung on Brooks, who gazed out at them with a cunning gleam in his eye. Brooks was a skilled orator, which no doubt explained his endless success as a politician, and tonight he was playing the crowd like an instrument.

There was a significant pause as the anticipation in the audience built. Finally Brooks continued, "I want to talk to you about our beloved Great Britain. She is not as strong or as dominant as she was a century ago. Our forefathers left us the greatest nation in the history of civilization, but if we are not very careful we stand the risk of giving our children much less. The American colonies rebelled and we allowed them to slip away. Now they are expanding, thriving, discovering gold. That fortune and prosperity is ours by right. Their riches should be flowing to our shores. We sowed the crop. We cultivated it. And now harvest time is come and we have no share in it. Instead of prosperity, we have a rival."

Brooks paused and met the eyes of many in the crowd. They nodded as his gaze fell on them.

He continued, "Thirty years ago we fought the Russian War, and paid too high a price for our gains, and shared too much of it with the undeserving French." The general nodded firmly at this, and a look of bitterness overcame his face. "Now the Transvaal Colony has rejected our rule. I wonder if any nation will be inclined to yield to us. And indeed, I can hardly blame them. They look to us for guidance, enlightenment, and leadership. If we cease to provide those things, then is it any surprise that they would seek to rule themselves? If we cannot lift the colonies out of their savagery, then we do not deserve our place as the leaders of the world. Perhaps the French will do a better job? Or the Italians? The Germans? India has rejected our rule once, or tried to. Was it their fault that they turned from us? Did they reject our greatness, or have we simply failed to be great?"

The audience was quiet for a moment as Brooks allowed them to consider the question. Finally he continued, "Each colony that kicks away from us dooms itself, to be sure. But worse than that, every failure to keep control only encourages the others to rebel. The world is a great scale, you see. On one side is civilization, and on the other is savagery. We are gathering all we can onto our side, the side of civilization. Bad enough that our losses take away from our side, but they are then added to the other, multiplying our failures!"

Brooks took up a glass of wine. A few others lifted their glasses, thinking he had been working up to a toast. But he drained the glass and set it back down again without a word. His mood was serious. "Much of this is a problem of leadership. Who can lead a nation? Those of you who know me well can recall my tales from the floor of Parliament. It is an orchestra of madness. Fools, elected by the ignorant and educated by the idealistic, are sent to accomplish contradictory goals. For my part, I strive to soften the blows of madness that Parliament inflicts, but that is only slowing the poison. No, the healing our nation needs cannot be provided by men in my position. Forgive me, for I am not trying to bore you with politics."

The audience was hardly bored, but appreciated his humility. They were nearly holding their breath, waiting to see where the man was going with such scandalous talk. Brooks paced a bit and gestured to one of the servants to refill his glass. After another drink, he continued, "Where was I? Ah yes. Leadership. Who can lead a nation? And if that nation is Great Britain, then who can lead the world? Kings? Sometimes. But kings are flesh and blood, and prey to the frailties of men. In their youth, they are brash and short-sighted. In their age they are addled and absorbed with their impending demise. Only a few years in the middle give us a hale man of character and leadership. That is, assuming he is a man and nobody has done anything so foolish as to put us under a queen."

The older men laughed readily at this, while the younger men smiled nervously and looked to the women at their side, who were stony-faced.

"It's an endless cycle", Brooks continued. "A young prince is frustrated with his father's neglect towards the kingdom, and fantasizes about all of the grand changes he will make when the power rests on his shoulders. Then at last! He takes the throne and behaves with exceeding foolishness. After some time he learns from his failures and spends his middle years correcting his old mistakes and fending off challengers to the throne. Finally, age overcomes him and he drifts away, while his son dreams of the grand changes he will someday make. The pattern repeats for decades. Centuries. Millennia. A king has too few good years to push us forward. How many good years? It depends on the man, I suppose. Truly, we are a doomed species.

"How many lives have been lost to pointless wars of succession? Two bloodthirsty men fight, neither of which is bright enough or honest enough to lead the nation. All the people can do is choose which fool they will follow to their ruin. It's no wonder it's taken us thousands of years to come as far as we have. But what is to be done?"

Brooks halted and looked again at the audience. *Yes, what is to be done*? This was the question in their minds, because he had placed it there, and they were now hoping he had some sort of answer. "What if... what if we had a king who could remain, ageless, in those years of energy and wisdom? A firm hand, a wise hand. A man not afraid of mortality. A man not tempted by the sins of flesh. A man who would not need to occupy his time with securing a proper heir."

Several people blinked. They thought he was about to propose some sort of reform, but this new line of thought caught them by surprise.

Confused, they listened on in eager silence.

"I'm sure many of you remember Oswald Mordaunt? He was a dear friend who was lost in strange circumstances a few years ago."

Many people nodded at this.

"I owed him a dear favor," one man said suddenly and solemnly. "Never got a chance to pay him back before he passed."

Another man raised his glass, "I had a similar debt. More than I can speak in public. He was a good man."

"He was," Brooks conceded, as if surprised by the response. "Many of us owe him such favors. And let's be honest. The man is passed so we no longer need to protect him from the consequences of his own mercy. He was a healer, was he not?"

People looked around nervously at this. None wanted to be the first to respond, but eventually slight nods gave way to greater nods, which led to emphatic agreement.

"I'm willing to wager that all of you have known someone, or heard rumors of someone who was made whole or spared great suffering by the work of Oswald's hands. We do not speak of it because magics - even benign, beneficial magics - are outlawed. Under pain of death. It was, in fact, this very work that led to Oswald's demise. For those of you who have not heard the tale: The Church discovered The Viscount's work. They came to his home, slew his personal guard, and murdered the man on his own doorstep. He died, because of what he did for all of you." Brooks suddenly picked a face out of the crowd, "David, your wife. Where would she be today if not for Lord Mordaunt?"

The man looked around the room, red-faced. Finally he stammered, "Dead."

Brooks pointed to another man, "Phillip? What about your daughter Anna?"

Phillip swallowed, "She... she would be bedridden. Her legs were lame."

"He was a good man, would you agree? Despite the magics. Yes, I said the word. Despite the merciful, kind, and entirely free *magic* he performed on behalf of our loved ones, he was a good man, was he not?"

The room agreed silently. Glasses were raised. Some heads bowed.

"He was a good man, killed by superstitious fools," Brooks said, agreeing with their agreeing with him. He watched their heads nodding. Brooks looked them in the eye and drew a deep breath, as if he was marshaling his courage. "I have good news. Shocking news, but good. As of three nights ago, Oswald is no longer dead."

The room was stunned. A woman gasped.

"Yes. His powers are not only in healing, although I'm sure he would have preferred to remain a healer. He is no longer dead, and he is on his way to London. Barrington Oswald Mordaunt - Viscount of Ravenstead - will be king."

This was outrageous. People took offense. The wine and speech had softened them, but not enough for them to embrace the idea of a new king. They did not run off and cry treason. They merely scowled and shook their heads.

Surprisingly, Brooks seemed to be smiling, like a card player about to reveal a winning hand, "Yes. He will be king. I have seen the man, and I can tell you he wields the power of a nation. An army of ten thousand could not overcome him. He will arrive in London the evening after next, and before morning he will rule this wayward nation. I see many of you are offended. Do not for a moment imagine that I am asking you to pledge to his cause. Heavens no. I do not expect you to take my word for his abilities, or to swear fealty to his throne before it is even established. While he is eager for your support, he fully expects to earn it.

"No, the only thing I ask is that you not throw your life away opposing him. He does not love bloodshed and bears no ill will towards any of you, which I hope he demonstrated when he helped you in the past. He longs for the same things we do: A powerful, prosperous, and secure nation, under the leadership of a sensible king. He wants to make the realization of that dream as bloodless as possible. So please, for your own sake and for the sake of our nation, only stand aside and allow the contest to proceed. His majesty will need talented and experienced advisers and ministers in his kingdom. Yes! You will all keep your positions. I invited you here tonight because you represent the finest this nation has to offer. You are all people of skill and dignity, and it would be disastrous for your posts to fall to lesser men. Indeed, his majesty hopes to increase your responsibilities, and so your loss would impoverish the kingdom."

Against this they could say nothing. The people blinked and looked at one another, wondering what had just happened. They had just been offered their own positions - or perhaps a promotion - and all they had to do was not oppose a tremendously powerful man who seemed, by all accounts, to be a reasonable fellow. If his bid for the throne failed, they would not be implicated. If it was a success, then it was to their advantage.

Heads had begun to nod again. Some people shrugged their shoulders. Certainly this royal politicking was over their heads. Surely it was better to sit and see how things turned out?

Brooks was looking quite pleased with himself. He called for more wine. Their glasses were refilled, and he opened his mouth to propose a toast. Then he stopped. A woman had pushed through the crowd and now stood before him. Her white dress seemed all the brighter against the backdrop of dark suits.

"Miss White!" Brooks said with sudden recognition. "I'm sure I would have remembered inviting you to my home."

"You didn't," she said coldly.

"Of course! I'm sure Moxley gave you his invitation. The old fox. He should have come himself, but perhaps he feared for his safety. He's been exceedingly cautious as of late. Nevertheless, the offer is open to him as well."

"Offer?" she said warily.

Brooks had been slightly shaken when she appeared, and for a moment his mask of charm had slipped and given way to irritation. But he had recovered now, and gave every indication that he was simply *delighted* to have her as a guest in his home. He took a friendly step towards her and smiled, "The same offer I gave to everyone else in this room. If he will direct his ministry to stand aside, then he will retain his position in the new regime." Brooks looked sideways at the other ministers. This was the bargain he'd offered, although perhaps it sounded unseemly when stated explicitly.

"So you're buying supporters by offering them the jobs they already have? Perhaps you could entice me to join your cause by offering to give me the dress I'm already wearing?"

"My dear, you have both your father's intellect and idealism. And like your father, they seem to always be at odds with each other."

"Do not pretend to know my father!" she scoffed.

"Miss White, I tell you with all sincerity that he was a dear friend. Closer than I count most of the men in this room. We exchanged many letters over the years. Ask these people if I was not one of the most vocal supporters of Ethereal Affairs."

Alice looked around, and the faces seemed to assent to this position. "Then how do you reconcile your support for Mordaunt with your support for Ethereal Affairs?" she asked accusingly.

"Reconcile them? They are both parts of a greater whole – a plan to bring about a reinvigorated Great Britain. Do not imagine that the King plans to allow all forms of magic. Practitioners of magic will be limited to the art of healing, just as His Majesty was. There will still be a place for witch-hunters like yourself in the coming days. If you like, you can continue to do your work and protect our nation from supernatural threats."

"Provided I turn a blind eye to the fact that an abomination sits on the throne?"

There was murmuring at this, and guests exchanged surprised glances. Brooks faltered for the slightest moment. Alice had intended to simply confront Brooks, but now she realized that the two of them were now contending for the hearts of the audience.

"You neglected to mention that, didn't you?" she pressed. "If you have your way, Britain will have an undead king."

"Miss White, you stand among the finest and most intelligent men in Britain. I'm sure everyone understood what I meant when I said that Oswald was no longer dead. How else do you propose we attain an ageless, incorruptible king?" The crowd was soothed by his flattery, but it was obvious that Brooks was wrong. Most of them hadn't grasped what their new king would be until Alice had explained it. While Alice had not won them over, she had shaken his grip on their hearts.

"Tell them about the Academy!" Simon shouted as he pushed himself to the front. "Tell them about the boys who die there!"

"Mouse?" Brooks asked with surprise. "Simon," he corrected himself a moment later. "I take it you are accompanying Miss White? It's to her credit that she's looking after you, although this isn't a good place for one so young."

"I've been in worse under your care," Simon said, his voice trembling.

"So what charges do you make against the home that nurtured you? That food was scarce? That it was cold? That the work was hard? That the keepers were cruel?"

"Yes, I suppose so," Simon replied. He was caught off guard by the apparent confession, and didn't know how to respond.

"Well, Lord Mordaunt is guilty, I suppose," Brooks said with a sad shrug. "Guilty, of attempting to help more children than his means and facilities could accommodate. I'm sure you imagine that you were somehow persecuted, but if you visit any of the orphanages in the city you'll see they fare no better. Some of them are no doubt worse. There are more hungry children than the nation can house, clothe, feed, and educate. Oswald financed the Academy himself. He was trying to lead by example. Yes, some died. But some were saved, and that was worth the sacrifice in his mind. I'm sorry you disagree."

Simon suddenly became aware of the eyes on him, and his face turned red. He had neither the skill nor nerve to face a man like

Brooks in front of so many people. He bowed his head and fell silent, wishing very much that he had held his tongue.

Alice took up the cause again. "What of the sinking of the Callisto less than a month ago? That was carried out by one of your own agents."

"I had heard of the tragedy, but I was not aware that the blame should fall to us. I know nothing of the matter beyond what is publicly known. However, I can say that the idea sounds ludicrous to me. His Majesty plans to unite our nation and bring about greater prosperity. Sinking passenger ships runs very much counter to that goal. I see no reason why the man would harm his own kingdom so."

Alice took another step forward. Her voice became quiet and deadly serious, "Earlier you spoke well of my father. Do you dispute that he was an honest and worthwhile man who labored to protect Britain?"

"I do not pretend I loved the man as a daughter might love her own father, but yes. I would tend to agree with your assessment."

"Then why did your supposedly wise and altruistic master have him killed?" she demanded.

"He didn't, "Brooks said calmly and firmly.

"He did!" she spat. She brought out her father's watch. "This was given to Simon by His Lordship. It was my father's. This watch was last seen in the possession of my father, right before he vanished."

"True," Brooks agreed. "I was present when the gift was bestowed. But then-Lord Mordaunt neither killed your father nor took his watch."

"Then how-"

"I did."

Alice looked back in stunned silence for several seconds. She blinked slowly, as if in a dream. Finally she spoke so quietly that the people had to strain to hear, "You said he was a dear friend."

"He was. And so was Oswald. Your father was investigating Oswald under suspicion of witchcraft. His actions threatened to expose this effort to establish a new king, which would have undone a project that all of us have worked on for most of our adult lives. Moreover, it may have exposed all of these people to scandal," Brooks gestured around the room. "It was a bitter deed to kill a man I so admired, but the lives of others were on the other side of the scale, and your father could not be dissuaded. It was an ugly deed, and I accept the consequences of it, but I do not-"

Brooks stopped talking at this point, because his diaphragm had tightened on account of the bullet that had just passed through his guts. Also, the sharp crack of the pistol had startled him. He let out a cough.

Alice stood holding her pistol in her shaking hand. Her jaw was clenched tightly. Tears were in her eyes. For a moment nobody knew what to do. Some people in the back had pressed forward to see what had happened, while the ones who had been nearby were overcome with a desire to step back. The crowd was in murmuring confusion. There was simply no protocol for what to do when a host was shot in front of his own dinner-party.

Gilbert burst through the crowd; his hand on his sword-hilt. He looked around at the scene, trying to make sense of what had happened. Finally he turned to Alice, "I seem to remember you saying that we were not here to assassinate anyone."

"Quiet!" she snapped.

"The memory is very vivid," he added. "You said we weren't going to assassinate them in front of the most powerful men in Britain. Which you have just done."

"So the abomination returns!" Brooks said in genuine surprise. He motioned for someone to bring him a chair. He winced was he sat. A great deal of blood had spoiled his suit, but he was a master at maintaining his composure. "I see you have bewitched him into your own service. That strikes me as being rather shockingly hypocritical."

"I didn't... Gilbert is here of his own volition!" she protested. "He is working to restore Princess Sophie."

"Very well," Brooks said with an alarming smile. He coughed a few more times and pressed his hand into his side. He was playing the part of a perfect British gentleman – stoic and resolute in the face of personal hardship. His sheer willingness to continue to engage his assailant in dialog made him a hero in the eyes of his guests. He raised an eyebrow at Gilbert's sword-arm, until Gilbert released it and assumed a more neutral posture.

Several soldiers filed into the room. Brooks held up his hand to signal them to stand back. "I will accept your request, abomination. If you are truly earnest that your only wish is to return Sophie to her parents, then accompany these men. They will see to it. I will make other arrangements with Alice and young Simon. I would like to spare them the noose, if I can."

"This is absurd!" she cried in anger. "That would only aid your cause. You would be able to present Sophie to her parents as if you had rescued her yourself."

"My dear, I was only taking you at your word when you said that your abomination wanted to restore her. If you object for political reasons, then I can't be blamed for calling your motives into question."

"We need to go," Gilbert muttered. The three of them were standing together, surrounded by stunned guests. The soldiers had gradually encircled the group, and were now only waiting for the word from their master.

Alice looked around the room to see the crowd was against them. She was the villain, and Brooks was the wounded hero. She quickly tucked her pistol away. "Agreed," she said reluctantly. "Although I don't see how…"

Gilbert threw back his hood and let out a roar in the direction of the nearby guests. His otherworldly scream echoed off the walls. They saw his terrible face and the strange light in his eyes and were instantly terrified. They scattered, trampling the soldiers in the process. Gilbert brought out his sword and charged towards the door, holding the blade in front of him. The guests scrambled out of the way, leaving them a clear path to the exit.

As they passed the doors, Alice threw them shut. She pulled Gilbert's sword away from him and threaded it through the looping handles.

“We might need that!” he protested as she dragged him away from the doors, which were now thundering with blows from the other side.

“We might,” she agreed, “But we're less likely to need it now that we have cut off our pursuers.”

Even as she said this, they heard footsteps and shouting ahead. News was spreading around the house. Someone was ringing a bell, and others were beating on the doors of the ballroom, calling to be let out. Gilbert looked back at the sword, but Alice grabbed his arm and led them back into the caged room.

“Where are you taking us?” Gilbert demanded.

“Going out the way we came in would be impossible now,” she replied. “Let's see where this goes.”

They passed through the cell door that Alice had opened earlier and out the doorway on the other side.

“I don’t think we’ll find an exit in the cellar,” Gilbert said.

“No, we won’t,” she agreed. “I’d hoped this would lead outside, or to another part of the manor. You're welcome to charge the front doors, if this way is not to your liking.”

Simon pushed past her on the stairs and made his way down. There was light at the bottom of the steps, and he didn't like standing in the dark while the other two argued.

“They won't all be guarding the front door,” Gilbert pointed out. “There were only four at the entrance when we came in.”

“Yes. Many will be moving around the house. I expect you'll not be outnumbered by more than ten to one. Those are bad odds, even for you. Off you go.”

“My odds would be better if you hadn't used my weapon as a door-stop!” he growled as he followed Simon down the stairs.

The cellar was a maze of old stone. Naked electric lamps hung from the ceiling. Gilbert struck one of these with his head as he arrived, and the swinging shadows made Simon even more nervous. The air was dry and cold. The stone walls and floor reflected the slightest sound, and carried it far away to unseen corridors. At the bottom of the stairs was a coat-rack, were a heavy coat had been hung. A dirty pair of boots sat nearby. They were standing in a passage running perpendicular to the stairs. To the right the way was lit with evenly-spaced electric lamps. To the left was darkness.

"We shouldn't be here!" Simon whispered as he eyed the items uneasily. "Obviously people come down here. Probably Brooks himself. We're hiding in *his* hiding place!"

"He may come down here, but his men may not. They might not even know about it. In any case, they're unlikely to look for us here, which is what matters," Alice replied.

Simon flinched as a terrible thundering sound shook the wooden ceiling. Groups of men were running around the house conducting their search, and their heavy footfalls shook long-held dust from the beams above them.

"But what about the coat?" Simon protested once the sound had passed.

"The coat and the boots are obviously for wearing when one is working down here. Since they are put away, odds are favorable that we are alone."

Simon relaxed slightly at this, but he still stood slightly bent with his eyes darting about, like a trapped animal. He struggled to control his breath. His eyes slammed shut as another storm of stomping boots rolled over them from above.

"Do you hear that?" he asked suddenly once the sound had passed.

"I'm not deaf," Alice said flatly.

"Not them! The… sound. It's like a vibration."

Alice listened more closely. After a few moments she caught it. It was a low, steady murmur. She couldn't really hear it so much as feel it in her feet.

"It's a machine," she said.

Gilbert returned. He had scouted ahead down the lit end of the passage. He was crouching low, to avoid running into any more of the lights.

"This place is likely not as secret as we thought," he reported. "Just down there and around the corner are rooms where wine and fruit are being kept. There's also a set of stairs, and I'd bet my sword on it leading to the kitchen, if I still had it."

Alice sighed. "We should hurry. If the servants know about this place, then his guards know about it, which means they will look here before long."

"I don't want to leave through the kitchen," Gilbert said with uncharacteristic timidity.

"You're willing to fight a dozen men, but you're afraid of the cook?" Alice asked.

Gilbert shook his head, "I don't know. I don't like this. Running around, soldiers everywhere, going through the kitchen. I guess it reminds me of the day I was killed."

"Well, there is wisdom in avoiding the kitchen," Alice said. "The staff likely congregates there. If we were to suddenly emerge from the basement, their screams would bring our foes." Gilbert nodded vigorously at this.

"Do you mean we're going to go charging off into the dark?" Simon asked, looking into the black passage and swallowing hard.

"No," Alice said calmly. She took the coat-rack by the base and shook the coat onto the floor. "Stand back," she said. Then she held up the coat rack and lit the crown with a handful of fire before they could do so. She held the fire out, and led them into the darkness.

Aside from being dark, this passage was rougher and dirtier than the other. The walls became crooked and the ceiling gradually lower. At last it abandoned all pretense of being a passage and was simply a tunnel in the dirt. The vibration became stronger as they went, until they could plainly hear the churning of some great engine. Gilbert tripped over something as they walked.

“Electrical cable,” Alice explained without looking back. She lowered her makeshift torch to illuminate the floor, giving them a better look at the thick black snake beneath their feet. It had been hastily buried, and parts of it were still exposed.

They came to a junction in the tunnel. She waved her light around, peering into the darkness. “Do we go right, or straight?” she asked herself.

“Straight,” Gilbert suggested.

Alice nodded, and turned right. At last they reached the end of the tunnel. The walls straightened up once again, and they found themselves looking at an iron door. Alice set the coat rack down. It was now standing just as she had found it, aside from the fire, which had grown quite vigorous.

“Is it locked?” Gilbert asked, peering over her shoulder.

“Poorly,” she said a moment later as the lock gave way.

The sound of machinery became a roar as the door swung open. They found themselves once again in something approximating a proper cellar with stone walls and a low wood ceiling. This room was large enough that the distant walls were lost in the darkness. Alice seemed to think that they were under the ballroom, and that this space was roughly the same size, although it wasn’t clear to the others how she came to that conclusion. The cable that had followed them down the passage emerged from the floor here and joined with several others, where they ran off towards the sound of the machine in the distance.

Alice’s light was not a proper torch. It was not wrapped in cloth or soaked in pitch, which meant there was nothing to discourage the fire from consuming the entire coat-rack, which it was now doing. Over the past several minutes it had transformed from a handy light source into a large bit of dangerously hot flaming wood, and Alice was now obliged to drop it.

Simon waved the smoke away from his face, “This noise is terrible. The furnace in the academy wasn’t nearly so loud.”

"That's not a furnace," she replied, raising her voice slightly in order to be heard. "It's a generator. Did you notice that the other houses on this street are dark, or lit with candles? Brooks is making his own electricity. I would love to know where he's sending the exhaust. I looked for signs of this machine when we were outside, but never saw any. I suppose he might send it up a chimney, although he would have to do it in an unpopular part of the house. The racket would be unpleasant. Or perhaps he uses underground pipes? But then he would need to guard against blockage."

Alice poked around the room, muttering to herself in this way for a few more minutes. She discovered the coal chute and the tools used to feed the generator, but without a portable light she couldn't venture far enough to inspect the machine itself. She considered making another torch from some of the wooden tools in the room, but was wary of starting a fire with so much coal dust coating everything and infusing the air itself.

Gilbert and Simon were not curious about the machine at all, and urged her several times to move on. Finally the coat rack began to burn low, and they were forced to hurry away before it died and left them in darkness.

On the far wall they could see a dim light, and Alice led them towards it. Gilbert twice struck his head on some tools or other mechanical objects hanging from the ceiling, and once caught his cloak on something sharp.

"Digging tools, I'm sure," she explained in response to nobody in particular. "There's dirt all over the floor here. I imagine some of these tunnels are new. Perhaps they plan to dig more."

They reached the door and found themselves in a smaller room. Several electric lights had been hung together, and the combined light stung their eyes after spending so much time in the dark. Work clothes were hung just inside the doorway, along with a few tools. Footprints of dried mud meandered around the room before ascending the nearby staircase.

"So do we venture up these stairs, or go through the far door?" Alice asked.

"The stairs," Gilbert said definitively. "The longer we run around down here, the more likely we are to get caught. This might lead outside."

"And it might not," she replied thoughtfully. "Those stairs go south, which should lead back to the heart of the manor."

"How can you tell which way the stairs point?" Gilbert demanded. His tone was almost accusatory.

"We entered through a door facing west. It's a simple matter of keeping track when you turn a corner."

"But how…" Gilbert stopped, not even sure which of his half dozen incredulous questions was the most important. "I don't understand how you could tell. It was night when we arrived!"

"Unlike the sun, the moon, and the stars, the buildings of London do not wander around on the horizon with the passing of seasons. Navigators would not need their sextons if they had so dependable a collection of landmarks."

"If you say so.", he said doubtfully, "but I still think it's time we found our way out of here."

"Alice!" Simon practically shouted. He had been trying to get their attention while they argued, and in exasperation he finally raised his voice. The other two turned at the sudden noise. "Look!" he said excitedly. He had crept forward to see what was in the next room.

It was clean and bright here. On the far side of the room was yet another door. The room was filled with fine furnishings. There was a desk as well as a table for work, and many paintings and curtains had been hung to hide the rough stone and make the space feel comfortable. These things escaped their attention; they were focused on the tables in the middle of the room.

Each table had a body on it. One body was positioned with its head facing north. The other lay with its head facing south. (Assuming Alice was correct about their direction.) Around each body was a sorcery circle, which had been etched into the fine wood. One was a man, the other a young girl.

"Leopold!" Gilbert said with surprise.

"So now we see where Brooks obtained the vigor to revive Mordaunt. Moxley said he was missing, and I feared he had fallen into their hands."

"Who is he?" Simon asked.

"Fourth son of Queen Victoria," Gilbert explained. "Also a formidable fencer. I wonder how he came to be captured."

"Probably the same way my father came to be killed. By mistaking Mr. Brooks for a friend."

"That means the girl must be Princes Sophie!" Simon said in awe.

Gilbert had walked around the tables and could now see her face right-side-up. "Wait. I know her. She's the girl from my dream!"

"She's what?" Alice asked.

Gilbert began to speak, but was cut short by the rumble of footsteps on the stairs in the previous room. The three of them froze for a moment, suddenly remembering their situation. There was another staircase in this room. It was very narrow and dark. Not having any other option, they fled this way.

The stairs wound around as they ascended, and Gilbert lost his bearings again. Behind him was Simon, followed by Alice. At the top of the stairs was a door. Gilbert tried to open it and felt resistance. "Locked. Or perhaps blocked. I can't tell. It's plainly a door, but there's no doorknob," he said angrily.

"Let me!" Alice said sharply. She tried to squirm past Simon, but the way was narrow. They were huddled together at the top of the steps and had only enough light to tell their feet from the stairs.

Gilbert didn't wait for her to push to the front. Instead he braced one leg against the exposed framework of the wall, and his shoulder against the door. There was the sound of splintering wood as he pushed.

"Stop!" Alice said. "I'm sure it will open right up if you can find…" She was cut off by the sudden shouts and activity from the soldiers below. Far off, they could hear someone frantically ringing a bell.

Gilbert gave a deep grunt and the door gave way, blinding them all with sudden light. He fell forward onto the door, which was now on top of a grandfather clock. The clock had been blocking the door, or perhaps it was part of the door. In any case, it was exceedingly loud as the various chimes shifted inside, and Gilbert landed on top of it. Simon and Alice climbed over him.

They were in a broad hallway. To their left was a magnificent set of double doors. To their right was a smaller door. In front of them were high windows to the darkness outside.

There were footsteps on the steps behind them. Gilbert leaped off of the wreckage of the clock and sent it down the stairs with a mighty shove. There were curses and cries of confusion as it tumbled downward.

"Go right!" Alice cried, but Gilbert had already started for the doors to their left. He opened them with a needlessly loud and destructive kick.

He rushed through, and they found themselves in a cavernous space of dark wood and bright electric lights. On the far side of the room was a collection of guests, who had gathered in a circle around the wounded and bleeding Brooks, who was now on the floor.

"We're back in the ballroom!" exclaimed Gilbert.

"I *tried* to tell you," Alice said.

The two groups regarded each other, mutually dumbfounded. The guests were so confused by the abomination entering the room on the opposite side from where it had exited, that they forgot their terror. Only two soldiers had remained here with the guests, and they were visibly less interested in violence with so few of them on hand. They stood nervously between the guests and the abomination, exchanging uneasy glances. Gilbert stood for a moment in quiet irritation, going over the secret tunnels in his head and trying to figure out where he had gone so wrong. Simon was struggling to master his fear. He looked to Gilbert for guidance, but Gilbert didn't seem to be doing anything at all. Alice sighed in exasperation.

One of the soldiers came to his senses and lifted a whistle to his lips.

The shrill note broke the spell and the room was set in motion once again. The sound of heavy footfalls returned as the men around the house abandoned their careful searching and converged on the whistle blower. Gilbert spun and made for the closest exit, which was a nearby set of stairs.

"We need to be on the ground floor," Alice said as she chased him up the steps. "Or do you suggest we leap out a window?"

"Maybe," Gilbert replied.

He led them on a mad rush through the upstairs, and it wasn't entirely clear that he knew where he was going. He made more right turns than seemed reasonable for someone who might know where they were headed. The pursuing footsteps grew louder. The men from around the house were converging on them, and it seemed likely as not that they would find themselves at a dead end with a dozen men on their heels.

Gilbert made one final turn and smashed open a set of double doors, shattering the glass in a single blow. They found themselves outside.

"No stairs!" Gilbert cried with dismay.

"No," agreed Alice. "This is a terrace. You thought to find steps here?"

"I did," he admitted. "I saw this in the distance on our way in, and thought..." His voice tailed off. Their pursuers had overtaken them. The route behind them was crowded with armed men. They were struggling to arrange themselves into a proper formation for a fight, and couldn't decide where the swords and rifles should go in such a tight space.

The terrace was made of stone, and brightly lit. Below them was a floor of hard stone, surrounded by a meticulously trimmed lawn.

"There!" Gilbert said, pointing to the side of the house. A bright electric lamp hung from the stonework. From it hung a thick cable that spilled down the side of the house and disappeared into the ground.

"There?" asked Simon in confusion.

Gilbert lifted the boy and almost threw him at the wall. Instinctively he grabbed on to the cable and began sliding down. A moment later the soldiers stormed through the doors and violence ensued. Alice managed to leap onto the cable before any of the men could grab her. She found it was tricky to slide down without either burning her hands or dashing herself on the pavement below. She split the difference and did a little of each, landing with a thud at the bottom.

"I did it! Did you see?" Simon said once she had stood. Suddenly he remembered himself, "Are you all right?"

"I'm whole," she said, looking up.

Above them, Gilbert was engaged with perhaps four or five men. There wasn't enough room on the terrace for more. For whatever reason, the men with rifles had held their fire, and so this became a battle of strength. The soldiers hacked at him ineffectually with their weapons while he beat them with his bony fists. A man was tossed over the railing and dashed against the ground. Alice jumped back just in time to avoid his fall.

Gilbert was an enthusiastic combatant, but not an exceptional one. He slowly overcame his foes not with cunning, but by being strong and durable. The number of upright men dwindled. Gilbert had one man by the shoulders, and repeatedly rammed him face-first into the broken doors. This made a loud, hollow sound. Fragments of glass were shaken loose from the frames by the blows.

"Gilbert!" Alice called up to him. Gilbert seemed caught in the moment, and continued fighting even after his foes had lost interest. "Gilbert!" she said again, more scolding this time.

Several gunshots rang, almost in unison. Gilbert was knocked over by the force of bullets entering his body. They had held their fire while he grappled with the other soldiers, but once he was the only one standing they were intent on shredding him with flying lead.

Gilbert recovered and leaped for the electrical wire. It snapped the moment his weight caught it, dropping him to the ground in a shower of sparks. He very nearly flattened Simon on the way down.

They scrambled to their feet and ran to the front of the house, chased by gunshots. An alarm bell continued to ring. Despite this noise, the men were still shouting to one another, trying to explain what had happened and which way the fugitives were headed.

In front of the house, they found that the driver was not waiting with his coach as he had promised. Gilbert leapt up and drove it himself. He charged the gate, scattering the guards that tried to block their exit. More gunfire rang, but their shots went astray. The coach rolled off into the darkness, leaving the house of Sir Edward James Brooks behind.

Alice stirred and slowly opened her eyes. The pre-dawn light crept over the London rooftops and into the alley where she had dozed fitfully for the last few hours. There was a faint smell of coal in the air as the early risers lit their stoves to ward off the morning cold. She had intended to let Simon use her as a pillow when she nodded off, but somehow this had been reversed as she slept. She slid out from under their blanket (Gilbert's cloak) and stretched. The cold stone had not been kind to her joints.

Gilbert hadn't moved from his spot at the end of the alley since she last saw him. He was a silhouette against the dimly lit streets. Uncloaked and upright, he was strikingly tall and imposing. Alice briefly envied his immunity to the cold, until she recalled all the joys he lost in the exchange.

"Simon insisted he's been subjected to worse beds," she whispered to Gilbert as she joined him. "I can't imagine a bed worse than cold stone. If there is such I thing, I would rather forgo sleep."

Gilbert replied without turning to face her. "I found myself sleeping in some nasty places when I served Her Majesty. It's been said that if you go hungry long enough, your mouth will water at the sight of insects. The same idea applies to sleeping arrangements."

Alice looked back to Simon, who had slumped to the ground and tightened the cloak around him. "Poor boy," she said. "It was foolish to bring him, but he refused to stay at Grayhouse."

"He wants to be brave," Gilbert said. "And anyway, it's good that we had him with us. If he was still at the house…"

"Yes," Alice agreed quietly. Last night they had decided it was too risky to return home. The authorities would be looking for them. Aside from whatever scheming Mordaunt's followers might be engaged in, Gilbert was an abomination, and Alice had blatantly attempted to murder a powerful man in a crowded room. These were not the sorts of things that could be overlooked.

"What is this place?" asked Gilbert.

"I told you last night, this is Witching Street. Or Witching Way, depending on who you ask."

"I've never seen it on a map."

"Oh, that's not the proper name for the street. Actually, I can't even remember that proper name. And it's actually two streets. A few blocks down, the street changes name."

"So witches live here? Wouldn't that make your job easy if all the witches moved to the same neighborhood, and announced it by renaming the street?"

"The name of the street is maintained as a joke by the locals. They like the sense of mystery it gives the place. Most of the shops and homes here dabble in unmagic: herbal medicine, fortune telling, contacting dead relatives through absurd playing cards. Most are harmless enough. A few are simply very enterprising cheats and mountebanks. The church has trouble telling the difference between these people and those who practice authentic magic, and so they show up here now and again to harass people and burn some books of benign nonsense."

"You seem to know this place very well. You knew this alley before we arrived, and this was the first place that came to your mind when we decided we couldn't go back to your house."

"It's not my house, but you're right. I wanted to come here because I knew we would not be looked for here. If we are spotted by the locals, they won't trouble us. Father had a good rapport with many of these people, and they think well of me on his account."

"You say that as if they wouldn't respect you if not for your father. It's far more likely that they admire you for your quality than your ancestry."

"It's kind of you to say so," she replied. "Anyway, Father brought me here now and again. Sometimes real witches come to Witching Way to hide. They never do anything so foolish and obvious as to set up a shop and announce themselves, of course. But if you know the right people and know how to ask, you can find them. Captain Turpin and I hid in this very alley two years ago. At the time, there was a rash of attacks by unliving dogs around the city. Dogs were being killed, preserved, then re-animated and set loose. We killed a lot of them, but had trouble finding the source."

Alice spoke while pointing to the narrow, crooked house on the other side of the street, "That place belongs to a man named Wilfred. More than half crazy, but he's kind and earnest and most of his medicine and poultices are harmless. Some might even be effective. He told the captain and myself about a young man who showed up frequently and at inconvenient hours, looking to buy embalming agents. Wilfred could barely keep the stuff on hand."

"A medicine shop that sells embalming fluid?" Gilbert asked.

"I'm sure Wilfred has stranger things than that on his shelves. His place only qualifies as a medicine shop under the broadest and most generous use of the term. At any rate, the Captain and I spent several nights lurking in this very alley, waiting for our necromancer of canines to appear. It was January at the time, and bitter cold. The captain and I kept warm by standing against that wall where Simon and I were just sleeping. There's a fireplace on the other side, and it loses a lot of heat to the outside. A shame it wasn't lit last night."

"But what about the necromancer?" Gilbert said impatiently. "Did you find him?"

"Yes, although the necromancer turned out to be a woman. Eventually the young man appeared and we followed him home, where we found his wife at work killing and reviving dogs. The husband was nothing more than an assistant. Vicious shrew, she was. She wound up hanging from a rope at Tyburn. I'm not sure what became of her husband, although I think he was spared the noose. He's probably still in prison, although I imagine that's a better fate than being married to that woman. All those dead dogs of hers. Her stench was incredible."

Gilbert sighed and paced back and forth for a few minutes. Finally his thoughts came to the surface. "Grayhouse is closed to us. We're all fugitives in one way or another. Your tools and reference books are gone. We are in a very tight spot. I don't know how we're going to rescue Sophie now."

"Rescue Sophie?" Alice exclaimed incredulously. "I should think not. The idea is absurd."

"I didn't like leaving her behind last night," Gilbert said. "It would have been better to put things right and give her back her vigor. Assuming you know how."

"Foolishness," Alice insisted. "Yes, I know how to restore her when the time comes. The Headmaster's book gave us that secret. But last night was not the time. We would never have escaped without your help. Remember that reviving her means un-reviving you. It's very likely she could be sick, or weak, or disoriented when she wakes. What if she couldn't walk on her own? Imagine how short our escape would have been if Simon and I had been carrying the girl."

"Well, we know where she is. Now we can prepare and mount a proper rescue."

Alice shook her head. "You were at the party last night. You heard the speech as well as I did. While I would be glad for the opportunity to restore Sophie, our main focus should be on unraveling this plot. It's no good saving Sophie if the rest of the royal family dies in the meantime. As for finding allies, that may be harder than you imagine. You saw that our foes control some portion of the military. This will be beyond the understanding or expertise of the constables. Who else could we approach for help?"

Gilbert was quiet and paced fitfully. His voice was full of doubt, "I don't know. But I don't like leaving her now that we know where she's being held. If we're not going to rescue Sophie, then what are we planning to do?"

"An insightful question, for which I have no answer. I think I should pay Lord Moxley another visit. We can leave as soon as Simon is awake."

"I'm awake," said a muffled voice from the alley. "I just didn't want to surrender my blanket."

"There is a bakery not far from here. If you give Gilbert back his cloak, I can offer you warm bread in return."

Simon jumped to his feet and hurled the cloak at Gilbert, "In that case, good morning!"

Crossing the city to visit Lord Moxley was an interesting challenge. He had briefly instructed Alice on how to move around in such a way to avoid or discourage people from following her. She tried to follow this advice, but they also decided to cross the city separately. The authorities would no doubt be looking for a woman, a young man, and a very large man in a black cloak. There was nothing they could do to disguise Gilbert, but it did seem reasonable to split up. Gilbert walked a hundred paces behind Simon, who walked a hundred paces behind Alice, who was deliberately making odd turns and stops intended to expose anyone following her secretly. They all felt ridiculous and conspicuous and it wasn't at all clear if they were being clever or making fools of themselves. Nevertheless, they crossed London without being accosted.

Lord Moxley opened the door and peered out through the crack. When he saw Alice he motioned her into the apartment and quickly shut it again. He returned to the table without a word, and made a vague gesture in the direction of the teapot, in case she was in the mood for a cup. There was a small pile of mismatched papers in front of him. Some were brief scrawls on scraps of paper, while others were proper letters. Some were bits of newspaper with notes written in the margins. Some were crisply folded and others had been crumpled up and smoothed out again. The notes were written by many different hands.

Lord Moxley held two of them, one in each hand. He examined them front and back, holding them up to the light and finally holding one over the other in front of the window. When he was satisfied that he had gleaned the fullness of their contents, he slipped them into the stove.

Alice was put off by this behavior. He was normally so careless, gossipy, or aloof that it was hard to imagine the man sitting down to conduct any sort of serious business.

Alice helped herself to some tea and sat opposite him. "What are you doing?" she said at last.

"I'm reading the papers, silly girl," he replied. "I know I don't normally allow you to see me working. It's unseemly. But these are desperate times. Besides, you seem to feature prominently in these stories and you might be able to cull rumor from fact."

"It looks like you've been at it all morning," she said, looking at his ink-stained hands.

"All night, actually. I haven't yet been to bed," he said flatly. "The papers have been busy for hours, and I have a good deal to do before I can allow myself to sleep. Most of this is due to the actions of our adversaries, although, some of it is your doing."

"Yes," Alice said nervously.

"Did you really shoot Brooks in his own home?" he snapped.

She had never seen him angry before. It was shocking. Given his dandy demeanor, she had always imagined his anger – assuming he was capable of it – would be pouty and given to overly dramatic weeping. Instead, he was another man altogether. He seemed suddenly dangerous.

"I did," she said guardedly. She wasn't sure why she was suddenly so frightened of him.

He leaned back in his chair and regarded her with a blank expression. Soon she began to squirm under his gaze. At last he spoke, "Did you give no thought to what the repercussions might be, even if you hadn't botched the attempt and left the man alive? Do you have any idea how much weaker our position is now? Did you really think you could stop this obviously vast and well-orchestrated plot by assassinating one man?"

"No sir," she replied. "I gave no thought to any of those things."

"Then what did you-"

"He admitted to killing my father."

A flash of understanding came over his face, and Moxley seemed to soften. He glanced down at the notes in front of him. "I see. That detail was not reported to me. Well, that does give me a measure of comfort. Assuming no more men step forward and confess to the crime, I can hope you are cured of your bloodlust for the time being?"

"If Brooks were standing here now, I would not attempt to kill him again. It was a reckless act, and I do not intend to repeat it."

"That is a relief. I was worried you had gone mad. Still, we are in a difficult position. You are now a fugitive, and many people will want to question me about the incident. My list of allies was reduced overnight because of this, and I should probably move soon."

"Allies?"

Moxley shuffled through his papers as he spoke, "More than one of my correspondents suddenly announced that they had news so shocking that they would only tell it to me in person. This of course, means that they want nothing more than to lure me out into the open where I can be captured."

"You are sure?" Alice said doubtfully. "They might simply have news for you."

"I have already read about the plot to dethrone Her Majesty, which was revealed at the party last night. I doubt anything could be more shocking than that. Remember that these people are not members of our ministry. They are friends, schemers, acquaintances, and gossips. They are only as reliable as the coin I give them, and Brooks has many, many more coins than I do."

"You have already heard about the plot?" Alice asked in surprise.

"I have. I may know more of it than you. Brooks spoke more of it after your escape. And now I'm sure you will ask me how I know that, and the answer is of course that you weren't my only agent in attendance."

Alice opened her mouth to speak, but Moxley interrupted her. "And your next question is why I would send more than one. The answer is that two people will give very different reports. I can then use these reports to verify or refute one another, to avoid being misled by liars or back-stabbers. And your final question is to ask why I didn't tell you. Because it's safer for both of you if you are ignorant of each other. Have I properly anticipated and answered your questions?"

Alice shut her mouth and gave a single nod.

"Good. After you left the party, Brooks explained that King Mordaunt plans to seize the throne tonight. He made no secret of this and even encouraged people to spread the word. Most of my correspondence this morning is that single item of news, repeated again and again, as it traveled up the chain of command, and passed along to me by concerned parties. The note at the bottom of the pile is the end of the chain so far, and it comes from a member of Prince Albert's staff. There is no doubt in my mind that the Queen and her husband know of this plot. They are most likely meeting with their advisors right this minute, and taking this very seriously."

"Why would Brooks show his hand like this?" Alice asked.

"Why indeed! He delivered the news knowing it would reach his adversaries. He gave them warning of Mordaunt's coming, but not enough time to plan for it. The Queen has less than a day to devise her response, and she doesn't know how or when he will arrive. Brooks hasn't exposed himself overmuch, but it's still not clear why he exposed himself at all. Why not remain silent and take everyone by surprise?"

"In his speech, Brooks petitioned his guests to stay out of the fight. He wanted them to remain neutral, so that they could live to serve the new regime," Alice explained.

Moxley frowned, "There is perhaps truth in that, but he didn't need to give them a firm date. He could have remained secret on when the struggle would begin. Now that I'm considering it, I'm wondering if I'm looking at this wrong. Perhaps he didn't aim his announcement at the Queen, but at the city itself. This news is spreading quickly. It's known to a few of us now, but scandal of this magnitude won't be contained. By sundown half the city will have heard about it, which is perhaps his aim. What benefit is a coronation if there are no witnesses? Perhaps he wants the Queen to respond, and perhaps he wants to make sure the contest is public. There's an alarming thought. It would mean he was extraordinarily confident of his position."

"Has the Queen sent for you?" Alice asked. "It seems like she ought to solicit our advice when faced with the prospect of an insurrection led by a lich."

He shook his head and stifled a yawn. "Possibly she has, and word hasn't yet reached me. I'm very far from my office on King Charles Street, and messages make their way here through secret routes, not swift ones. Possibly she doubts my loyalty. She might even reach out to the church. They might be a better ally against a large, organized foe. Our ministry is designed to investigate, not fight battles." At this thought, Moxley slumped down into his chair and his face fell.

"You look very tired," Alice said softly. "Are you sure you can't dare an hour or two of sleep? I'd be happy to help, or keep watch, or whatever else you need."

"I would love to sleep, but I must correspond with my helpers, or I will find myself blind and dumb. They write me short, obfuscated notes, and I reply in kind. It's a time consuming process, and it must be done properly to protect both them and myself. Speaking of which, if you are going to continue to call on me like this, I will have to teach you how to do the same. It's much too risky to have you traveling here every day."

"Understood. Although, we were careful to follow your directions on the way here. We might have been noticed on the way, but I'm confident we weren't followed."

"We?" he replied with sudden alarm. "You did not come alone?"

"No. Both Simon and Gilbert came with me."

His eyes went wide with alarm, "Here? Please don't tell me you left them loitering outside!"

"I didn't know what else to do. I didn't think you'd want all of us in this tiny place, and I didn't think you'd want to meet Gilbert."

"You left them standing outside! The neighbors here are spies, gossips, and busybodies. All of that instruction I gave you yesterday on how to move without being followed," his voice trailed off for a moment in frustration, "It does you no good if you simply stand in the open by my door! I thought it would go without saying that you should disappear from sight as quickly as possible once you arrived."

"So I should invite them in?"

"Or flee. Whichever will more quickly remove them from public view."

"Then I think I should flee. I don't think it would help your work to have all three of us crammed into this room."

Alice was about to leave when she stopped suddenly and turned back to Moxley. She gave him a kiss on the head. "Good luck Sir!" she said earnestly.

Moxley rolled his eyes and waved her off, but for a fleeting moment his mask cracked and he expressed something perilously close to affection.

Outside, she found that Gilbert and Simon were indeed standing right in the street. Gilbert was holding out his arm, and Simon was trying to use it to perform a chin-up.

They hurried away.

The rest of the day was spent ducking the growing number of soldiers milling about in London. As they walked, they took turns proposing increasingly large and complex theories on what Mordaunt might be planning.

"Three! That's three streets in a row," Simon said abruptly and somewhat randomly.

"Three streets? What are you talking about?" Gilbert asked with mild irritation.

"The last three streets we've passed have been lined with gas lanterns instead of electric lights."

"Not this again," Alice sighed.

"Before that was one street with electric lights, and of course this street has electric lights."

It was nearing sundown. The lamps were currently dark. Simon had asked many times about when they were normally lit. The group had been walking for most of the afternoon, looking for signs of trouble or activity from Alice's ethergram.

"I don't understand your fixation with them. I would have expected their novelty to have worn off by now," Gilbert said.

Simon stopped at the street corner and turned slowly around, noting the types of lights used on all of the adjacent streets. "I just find it interesting. Why are some streets lit with gas, while others are electric, and others left dark? Doesn't it seem odd?"

"I expect it's mostly to do with the affluence of the neighborhood," Alice shrugged.

"I thought so, too," Simon nodded. "And that theory seems to hold in some places. But there are many exceptions, and I can't figure out what reasoning led to this arrangement."

"I see your problem now," Gilbert replied. "You are looking for reason in a project undertaken by a bureaucracy. The two are mutually exclusive."

Simon grunted, slightly dissatisfied with this answer but content to keep it to himself for the time being. He continued to crane his neck as they walked, counting streets and lights to himself.

"Interesting!" Alice exclaimed, looking at her ethergram.

"That would be a welcome change," Gilbert said dryly.

"The needle has swung around and is pointing north. Which suggests there is strong activity in that direction. Strong enough to overcome your proximity."

"I hope you were talking to Simon. Or to yourself. Because I have no idea what that means."

"It means we're headed north," she said, and led them that way at the next intersection.

"Drat," said Simon. "This is taking us away from the electric lights."

After several blocks Alice stopped and turned around in place. Then she turned around in the opposite direction. "This can't be right," she said with frustration. "We should have arrived at the source by now, unless the magic is moving away from us. We've come far, but the needle is still pointing straight north."

"So now your device is nothing more than an ugly compass?" Gilbert suggested.

"I think the dials have an elegant beauty to them, thank you very much. Let's head west and see if the needle moves."

She led them west, then east again, and then north, stopping often to flick the dial or spin in place to make sure it was still working properly. "This is absurd!" she exclaimed.

"Couldn't it just mean the magic is really far away?" Simon asked.

"Yes. But distance is affected by power, and even exceptionally strong magic isn't detectable until I'm within a few hundred paces of it. Remember how close we needed to be on Callisto?"

"Where is everyone?" Gilbert said suddenly.

They stopped and Alice looked up from her device. He was right. The streets were now empty. Soldiers had been running back and forth all day, and there should certainly have been numerous Londoners hurrying from place to place. It was late enough now that candles should have begun appearing in windows, but the houses were all dark.

"You're right, this is very odd," Alice said slowly.

"Perhaps this area has been evacuated?" Simon suggested.

"Then we should have passed the evacuees," Alice replied.

"Ravenstead is north of London, and I doubt anyone would flee towards danger. No. Even the soldiers seemed to have withdrawn."

"Now that you mention it, doesn't it seem strange that we've seen so many groups of soldiers in the past hour, yet none of them have marched past us?" Gilbert asked. "They always turn away or move to a side street as we approach."

"I doubt the troop movements have anything to do with us," Alice said without conviction.

They slowed as they reached the mid-point of the current block. The houses were built shoulder-to-shoulder here, and the way suddenly seemed very claustrophobic. They felt hemmed in. The streets were silent and watchful.

"I saw a curtain move in that house," Gilbert said, indicating the house with a nod. "There are people about. They're simply hiding. Perhaps they've been driven into their homes by a danger we have yet to see?"

"Let's turn back and head south," Simon said, stopping in his tracks.

Alice turned. "The magic is still north of us. We need to spy it out before we run away. Who else remains to protect the city, if not us?"

A whistle blew, echoing over the rooftops. Another whistle answered. There was a thunder of boots ahead, and a large number of soldiers ran out and blocked the way in front of them. They turned south, but found that way was similarly blocked. The doors of the surrounding houses were thrown open, and soldiers emerged from those as well.

"I really wish you hadn't left my sword behind," Gilbert said.

"Fighting would be pointless," Alice replied. "Would you really attempt to cut your way through all of these men?"

They were quickly hedged in with bayonets. The soldiers called Alice by name and commanded the group to stand still. Some of the men knocked Gilbert down and began kicking him. He lay still. The scene might have been comical in less dire circumstances. Men kicked him until they were red-faced and out of breath, at which point he rose up and stood beside Alice without comment.

The prisoners were taken north. The soldiers walked close behind them with bayonets at the ready, so that if any of them slowed they would quickly feel the point on their back, encouraging them to keep up.

By the time they arrived at the northern edge of the city, the street lights had begun to come on. Simon was obviously frustrated that he couldn't examine them closely.

The company halted, and a man rode out to meet them. He dismounted quickly, barking orders to the massed soldiers. They ran off to fortify in diverse places in his commend, leaving a much smaller group to stand over the prisoners. When the men had been put in order, the officer turned to Alice.

"Lieutenant Stanway!" Alice said in surprise.

"It's Major now, Miss White," he corrected her firmly.

"Of course," she said, nodding at his new uniform. "You seem to be ascending the ranks at an unprecedented rate," she marveled.

The Major drew in a slow breath. "This recent business has been hard on our officer corps. Apparently many were loyal, or perhaps sympathetic, or simply frightened of this Mordaunt fellow." Then he raised his voice, "But the men, the men are loyal to the queen!"

The men cheered at this. Major Jack seemed like a changed man. He was less proud, yet surer of himself. He was less angry, yet more aggressive.

"It would seem we are after the same foe," Alice said. "So I must wonder why you've gone to so much trouble to arrest us."

"You dare feign ignorance? Has the possession of abominations been legitimized since I left the ministry?"

Alice sighed, "Major, surely you can see the value-"

"Witches, sorcerers, and abominations," he pointed at each of them in turn as he said this, "Isn't that what the ministry is to fight against? Why then is that the entirety of your roster?"

"Your job is to protect us from foreign armies, is it not?" she shot back. "Why then do you seem to be leading an army yourself?"

The Major shook his head. "I've always been fond of you, Miss White. Professionally, I mean," he said this with a sideways glance at his men. "But I think your dalliances with the dark arts have clouded your judgment."

"And I think your hatred of the arts has clouded yours. Do you plan to oppose Mordaunt with nothing more than swords and guns?"

"The ministry never had even ten guns, and now we have no less than two hundred at the ready. Back at Buckingham, there are thousands more. Yes, I think swords and guns will suffice."

"His own servants claim he will command the might of a nation," she countered. "That sounds like more than a match for a few hundred men."

"Then you know more than I've been told," the Major replied skeptically. "And perhaps more than is true."

"Are you really suggesting that I'm in alliance with him?" she asked with such abrupt fury that Major Jack flinched. "I shot one of his men last night. In public."

"Yes, yes," he said hastily, "I'm not suggesting you're in league with the Dark Lord, as it were. But his servant may have misled you."

"He was good enough to announce the attack and thus bring us here to challenge him, rather than taking us by surprise. Would he have done so if he doubted his ability to win in an open battle against a prepared enemy? That would have been foolish and reckless of him, and therefore out of character."

Jack considered this for a moment before replying, "You say he will command the might of a nation. What do you suppose that means? He's stolen the loyalty of many, but mostly the wealthy and powerful. There is power in that, but you don't win battles with bankers and barristers."

"Historically, the truly great challenges have come from necromancers who command armies of the undead. The knowledge of powers so broad always dies with their master, but evil men rise, and sooner or later the old secrets are again unraveled. I expect that is what we are facing."

"It would take many graveyards to fill out such a force. We have no reports of empty graves, anywhere in the realm. I can't believe he could marshal a force to challenge our army without creating at least the rumor of necromancy. And you said yourself in the past that it requires vigor to animate them. We should also have reports of slain animals."

"True," Alice conceded. "It would be hard to conceal the building of an army, even if it were done gradually over time. But not impossible. So either our foes are cunning enough to conceal the raising of a great number of undead, or they are foolish enough to warn us of their assault ahead of time and then show up with insufficient numbers to win. Which outcome seems most likely to you?"

Jack conceded the point with silence. Finally he spoke, "Well, if he has nothing more than marching undead, then he's chosen a poor battleground. I'd rather face undead in these narrow streets than have them coming at us out of the dark, out in the wilderness."

The men nodded at this with approval. To the Major's annoyance, Gilbert was nodding as well.

Jack's anger was kindled again. "As for your companions: The abomination will be destroyed, as he should have been weeks ago. The boy – I'm assuming this is the boy who created the abomination - will stand trial for his crime."

"No! I need them both if we're to save the princess!"

"That excuse has kept this abomination whole for a long while, and yet the princess remains absent."

"But now I know where she is!" Alice pleaded.

Jack opened his mouth to speak, but at that moment a horse came galloping to them and the rider called to him, "Major! We've spotted a group of abominations. They're on Shoreditch High Street, heading towards us."

"How many?" the Major shouted back.

"Less than thirty."

The men seemed to breathe a collective sigh of relief.

Jack scoffed, "That's not enough to enter the city, much less breach the palace. Is that the only group? Are you certain?"

The rider nodded, "All roads north have been scouted, and that was the only force we found."

Jack shouted to his men, "We'll make our stand here. Ride to the palace and tell the general. I don't expect he'll see the need to send any of his forces away to help us here. We have two hundred men, which is more than adequate."

The scout nodded and rode off. Jack mounted his own horse and addressed the men in his booming voice, "Hold this street! Rifles first. When you've expended your rifle, throw it down and use your truncheon. Remember these are the unliving, not men. They feel no pain. They fear no foe. They will beg no quarter, and neither will they offer one. They have no blood to spill. But shatter their bones and they will fall."

He paused and judged the faces of his men. Not liking what he saw he continued, "Do not fear them! There are ten of you for every corpse our foe commands. We are the fortunate ones! Thousands of our countrymen stand ready at the gates of Buckingham Palace! Let us be greedy with the glory, and leave them with nothing but bone dust!"

The men cheered at this. Jack lifted his head in pride and held his sword over his head. "God save the Queen!" he cried.

The men shouted this back at him, and began marching forward at his command.

"He's a good officer," Gilbert said quietly.

The Major gave orders to the men guarding Alice and her companions, "Remain here. If any of them try to escape, kill all alike."

"I still don't like him, though," Gilbert added quickly.

The remaining men grumbled at their assigned task. They were disappointed that they would be unable to acquire any glory when it seemed to be available so cheaply.

Alice held up her ethergram for the other two to see. The needle was moving. It had been pointing due north, but was now creeping towards the northwest, where Jack and his men were heading.

The sun had now faded and - much to Simon's delight – the streets were left to the warm glow of electric lights.

Their captors grew restless. Having been denied participation in the battle, they at least wanted to see it play out. At first they simply edged forward to the bend in the road so that they could see the army. As it grew more distant they began to follow, until soon they were openly marching behind, leading the prisoners towards the battle.

The army halted and drew a firm line across the street. In the distance, slow shapes crept out from the darkness. The streets beyond were unlit.

Alice ascended the steps of a nearby building to get a better view of the proceedings. Her captors tried to prevent her, then thought better of it, and followed her up.

"Our foe has chosen his position well after all," Gilbert said. His sudden voice startled a few of their guards, who had been growing increasingly nervous. "The narrow way favors the smaller force."

Despite the advantage offered by the street, it looked like the odds were overwhelmingly on the side of the Queen. The British soldiers stretched all the way across the street, their lines several men deep. Their foes were just a handful of bodies, shuffling implacably southward. Bits of armor rested on their bones. In their hands they held simple weapons, most likely clubs and swords. In the center of this procession was a small robed figure, the late Lord Mordaunt. He appeared very small, and unthreatening.

The two forces stopped some thirty paces distant from one another. Then a low, echoing voice flowed over the crowd. The voice was calm. It did not shout, yet the words traveled far, even to Alice and her companions far in the rear.

“I am your Sovereign, the King Mordaunt. I have come to set my kingdom in order. It is not my wish to harm any of my own subjects. Stand aside and you will all be spared.”

“Surely he doesn’t mean to bluff his way to Buckingham?” Alice wondered.

“His voice is even more terrible in death!” Simon cried. The men guarding them seemed to share this sentiment.

“How does he make his voice travel so?” asked Gilbert in annoyance. “Mine doesn’t do that.”

“FIRE!” boomed the defiant voice of Major Stanway at the front of the formation.

The British rifles rang out, coughing a burst of smoke into the air. The shots seemed to strike the undead closest to Mordaunt. Many of his skeletal servants jerked at the impact. One collapsed, and one was deprived of an arm. The rest were unperturbed.

More shots rang out, and the skeletons gathered in around their master, shielding him.

“This might be a short battle,” chucked one of the guards in feigned disappointment.

“It may,” said Alice, “But our foe still has the use of his own magic. We may lose a few men while he expends himself.”

As the volley of gunfire ended, the soldiers prepared their truncheons. As they stepped forward, Mordaunt rose up above the battlefield, hovering over his own forces. He lifted a gnarled hand over his head and cast it down again, bringing with it a handful of fire. The flame landed in the midst of the men, lighting the British lines on fire and tossing men into the air like leaves caught by the wind.

“Oh!” Alice exclaimed, “Or perhaps he will expend all of his power in a single strike.”

Mordaunt did it again, despite her prediction. Then a third and a forth ball of fire struck the men. There was confusion and screaming now, and smoke was quickly shrouding the battlefield.

“Surely that’s the last of them!” she exclaimed.

More fire came in answer. Once the British lines had broken, Mordaunt began to hurl bolts of lightning to slay the scattered men.

“This is impossible!” cried Alice. “How can he continue to expend so much power? Even the great liches of old had limits.”

The fleeing solders were now running past their small group, weeping and beating at the flames. “To the palace!” they screamed.

Mordaunt continued, despite her earlier incredulity. The battlefield was now behind an opaque curtain of smoke. Like a storm cloud, it flashed with brilliant white veins of lightning and roared with energy. The air was filled with flying debris.

Then from out of the tempest, Mordaunt unleashed his forces. Corpses rushed out of the cloud, cutting men down as they ran.

The guards looked at each other nervously and then at Alice. Then they looked out at the rampaging dead in the streets.

“If you run now you might make it to the castle where you can help defend the Queen,” Gilbert suggested.

The courage of the men had been crumbling in the face of such a sudden defeat. Once Gilbert offered them a way think of fleeing as honorable, they set to it with all their strength.

Gilbert looked north to the looming cloud. “Do we have a plan?” he asked quickly.

“No,” Alice replied.

“Right,” said Simon, who took off running with the other two at his heels.

“We need to get out of this alley of death,” Gilbert suggested.

They plunged down a side street, which was devoid of streetlights. They hurried into the curtain of darkness and then stopped, reluctant to run further for fear of finding a wall with their noses. Alice took up a wooden pole that had been dropped by the fleeing soldiers. She reached up and lit it with her own fire, and held it out in front of them.

“You seem to have set our flag on fire,” said Gilbert.

“Oh! I do feel bad about that,” Alice said, looking up at the burning Union Jack.

The screams of the soldiers had faded. They were all routed or slain. Skeletons were running through the street behind them, oblivious to their own burning.

“One of them saw your torch!” Simon said nervously.

A flaming skeleton had broken away from the group and was drawn towards Alice. Gilbert intercepted it and struck it with his fists. The two bony gladiators then stood face to face and traded blows.

“This isn’t really getting us anywhere,” Alice said after the contest had gone on for some time.

“I don't have a weapon,” Gilbert explained. “I don’t know what else to do with this beast.”

“Snap its neck,” Alice suggested.

“Or crush the skull,” Simon added.

Gilbert grappled with it, but found it difficult to make any progress. His foe was wearing metal armor about his head and shoulders that seemed to have been designed to prevent exactly what they had suggested. Finally he gave up, tackled it, and began slamming its head into the ground.

The skeleton had stopped burning by this time, as everything flammable on its body had already been consumed. It was now blackened and smoking.

“This isn’t working either,” Gilbert said after the pounding had become tiresome. After some additional struggle, he managed to pull its helmet off.

“Hold it still!” Simon said, drawing a bit of chalk out of his pocket.

Gilbert wrapped his great arms and legs around his foe, pinning it in place. Then Simon drew near and timidly scratched a pair of symbols into the ash on the forehead. It took a few tries, as the creature's struggles foiled his attempts at writing. Finally he completed the marks, and the entire thing fell apart into an arrangement of inert bones.

"That's quite a trick!" Alice exclaimed.

"Binding symbols. Or rather, *un*binding symbols in this case. We used them to destroy reanimated dogs and pigs after an experiment was done. I don't think they work on revived beings like Gilbert, but they're useful for enslaved dead."

Alice breathed a sigh of relief. "If I ever get the chance to rebuild my library, I'm going to start with your knowledge!"

"I think the new 'king' has passed. Are we after him towards the palace?" said Gilbert as he brushed himself off

"Not yet," Alice said. "There's no sense in confronting him until we have some idea how to survive the encounter. Let's look over the battlefield and see what we can find."

They retraced their steps, following the trail of bodies and burned wreckage northward. They found a small number of wounded among the dead, most of whom had escaped the flames by hiding beneath their compatriots. The group stopped to help these men and give them what small comfort they could.

They found Major Jack near the start of the battle. His horse had bolted away from the flames and into the enemy, where it had been slain by Mordaunt's servants. Jack had been pinned under the beast when it fell, and was struggling to free himself.

Gilbert managed to lift the horse well enough that Jack could squeeze out. He made some sort of grunt to convey grudging thanks, and then propped himself up against a nearby wall. He gasped and coughed for a few minutes. He tended the wounds on one shoulder where the dead had hacked at him after he fell.

"Did you know?" he asked Alice once he'd regained some strength.

"Know?"

"About the fire. All his power. In all my time with the ministry I never heard of such a thing," he said gravely.

"Of course I didn't know! I'd never heard of such a thing either. Not from my father, not from any of the books in our library. This is something new."

"What if he was using a feeding circle?" Simon suggested.

"I thought of that as well," Alice said. "If he'd drawn a circle nearby and put some people into it, then he could have fed his magic from them. But the power he unleashed… that would have taken many, many people. He continued using the power, even when moving. The street would have needed to be lined with feeding circles, which would have needed to be filled with people."

"What about inside the houses?" Gilbert suggested.

Alice looked down the street doubtfully. "A wizard must be close to a feeding circle to benefit from it. Do you imagine that Mordaunt could have hidden a feeding circle in every house from here to the palace? And then filled them all with victims? And then assigned people to keep the victims contained? Without being noticed?"

"I don't know how it works," Gilbert said with a shrug. "I was only guessing."

"What do you plan to do next?" asked the Major.

"I don't know," Alice admitted. "I am exhausted and can barely summon the strength to produce worthwhile thoughts. Look at how my hands are shaking. And I am so hungry and thirsty."

"Why?" asked Gilbert.

"What do you mean?"

"We barely took part in the fight. We ran a short distance and walked back here. That's hardly strenuous exertion by your standards."

Alice considered this. "I don't know. Perhaps the lack of sleep over the last few days?"

"It just seemed sudden to me," said Gilbert. "Perhaps I'm simply forgetting what it's like to be alive."

"No," said Simon slowly. "I think you are right. This fatigue is rather sudden. I feel it as well, even though I was hale before the battle."

Jack coughed. "I'm wounded, so I'm not at all surprised to find myself spent. But you are the picture of health, Alice. The same is true of your friend." Jack then struggled to his feet with Alice's help. He found the leg that had been pinned under the horse could not bear any weight. He began picking among the debris in search of something that might be used as a crutch.

"Now that I think of it," Simon said thoughtfully, "This feels a bit like being inside a feeding circle myself. All those days in the dungeons, trapped in a cage. It was much more intense then, but this feels similar."

"What do you make of it?" asked Jack.

Simon shrugged. Alice shook her head. Gilbert was busy re-arming himself and gathering supplies from among the fallen.

At length the Major began hobbling around the battlefield, gathering the remaining men and getting them on their feet. "So you're off to the palace?" he asked as Alice and her friends began to leave.

"I don't know," she said.

"Perhaps you should see to the Princess Sophie, if you still know her whereabouts."

"She and Prince Leopold are held at the home of Brooks. The place is guarded by many men. Too many for our small group." Alice then briefly explained the events of the previous evening.

Jack relented at this and let them go on their way.

BUCKINGHAM

THE
LONDON JOURNAL
Press
Weekly
Sunday, November 8, 1885
CORONATION
special edition
Buckingham Palace
Rear
Palace Garden
Coronation
Platform
Audience
coronation to be held in the
garden due to damage to

XI

“I don’t know!” Alice cried with exasperation. This was the fifth time Gilbert had asked what she planned to do when they reached Buckingham Palace.

They reached the palace at the end of a long road of destruction. Apparently the battle they witnessed was the first of many. They examined the dead as they moved, but it was rare for them to find any enemy casualties. At one point they found a skeleton that had been broken in half but not destroyed, and it had continued to crawl along the ground using its arms. Gilbert sat on it while Simon destroyed it with sorcery. They had to route around one area where firefighters were struggling to contain a blaze, and another street that had been thoroughly barricaded.

“It’s surprising we haven’t seen more fires,” Gilbert remarked.

“I think His Deceased Lordship was serious about wanting to spare the city. He could have burned half of it by now,” Alice replied.

When they arrived, they found a great sea of indecipherable chaos. There were cannons, soldiers, heaps of burning wreckage, and men running in all directions. The battle took place in the open fields directly east of the palace, although it frequently spilled over into the surrounding neighborhoods.

Northeast of the fighting they found a tall building that had been hastily abandoned. They slipped inside and made their way up onto the broad roof to get a better view of the proceedings. They found a safe vantage point among the blackened chimneys and observed in silence.

From above, the battle made much more sense. They could see a great harvest of dead strewn about the field. To the west were rows of Her Majesty's forces, arrayed to deny access to the palace. These wore uniforms of red and blue, depending on rank and purpose. To the east were Mordaunt and his forces. The size of his retinue of undead soldiers seemed unchanged since they last saw it. To these were added a significant number of living forces. His living soldiers were dressed in grey. Both were greatly outnumbered by the Queen's forces. In the firelight, it was very difficult to tell the two sides apart, except by how they behaved as they drew near one another.

"Our commanders keep falling for the same tricks again and again," Gilbert muttered after watching quietly for half an hour. "See how Mordaunt sends in a group to challenge our lines? The men act like they're bracing for a cavalry charge and form up tightly. As soon as they become a tight cluster, Mordant hurls fire at them. Then Mordaunt's men… or skeletons… whatever his forces are, they feign to rout. Our men foolishly give chase. The enemy quickly turns to fight, and again our soldiers bunch up and are roasted en masse. These would be foolish tactics, even if we were facing a conventional army." Gilbert growled bitterly.

Alice rested her chin in her hand, "The Major mentioned that some number of our officers defected. Perhaps this is the fruit of that betrayal. Our forces are left with inexperienced leaders."

They watched helplessly as the battle dragged on towards morning.

"I feel so exhausted," Simon said.

"As do I," Alice agreed. "It's the same tiredness we felt earlier. It's unnatural."

"I'll bet our soldiers feel it as well," Gilbert nodded. "That would explain why their movements are so sluggish."

"And I'm sure this is all connected to our foe and his seemingly limitless supply of magical energy," Alice said. "He's found a way to take the might of our bodies and use it to fuel his own wizardry."

The complexities of warfare were lost on Simon, who had wandered away from the others and was staring into the quiet streets north of the palace. He had said little since they left Major Stanway, and had spent a good bit of his time looking out over the city and muttering to himself.

Over the next hour Gilbert watched as their numerical superiority was eroded. Mordaunt was a patient general. He used wind, fire, and lightning sparingly, but to great effect.

"He's trying to spare them," Alice said tiredly. "Given his power, he could certainly rush in and set our forces ablaze in a few moments, just as he did to Jack's men."

"Maybe he's simply trying to spare the palace," Gilbert suggested.

"Perhaps," Alice allowed.

Dawn approached, and the dark sky began to relent. A faint glimmer of light appeared in the east. Suddenly Mordaunt's forces withdrew and gathered around him. The forces at his side and the forces defending the palace were now roughly the same size. Mordaunt strode out from his army, standing alone in the open field.

Some of the Queen's men saw this opportunity and set to aiming one of their few remaining cannons.

"Don't be foolish!" Gilbert said aloud.

A bolt of lightning struck the device. The men around it fell dead, and the wooden parts were set ablaze.

"Now my subjects," Mordaunt spoke. The men shrank away at the sound of his voice, which was strong enough to reach even to Alice and her companions on the roof. "You have fought bravely. You have fought admirably and honorably. But the day is mine. Stand down, and you will be spared. Drop your weapons. Go to your homes. As your new king, I give you my solemn word that your former queen and her family will not be harmed."

"He's broken them," Gilbert observed, even before the men began dropping their weapons. A few fought among themselves and some small skirmishes took place between the deserters and the steadfast, but these were over quickly.

"I wouldn't have thought our own soldiers would surrender so quickly!" Alice said in disbelief.

"All of the brave men died outside the walls, along with the officers," Gilbert said sadly. "It's to their credit they fought as long as they did."

"I didn't expect you to be so forgiving," Alice said.

"Being zealous and obstinate is what got me killed," he said sadly.

He turned from the battle to see that Simon had shimmied up one of the chimney stacks and was looking out over the city.

"What are you doing?" Gilbert demanded.

Simon ignored him and slid back down to the roof. He walked over to a diagram that he'd been drawing on the cement.

"Three two three one-one" he repeated quietly as he drew three lines, left a gap for two more, drew three more lines, left another gap, and finished it off with another line. This process went on for several minutes.

Gilbert and Alice stood on either side of the diagram and examined it. The lines formed regular patterns. Some were parallel, some were at right angles, and others twisted about.

"Now, I'm not completely sure of these ones, Simon said, pointing to the far side of the map. I had to draw those from memory based on what we saw last night, and it was kind of hard to keep it straight in the confusion."

"I take it these are streets?" Alice asked after some examination.

Simon seemed pleased by this. "Almost. This is all of the places where there are streetlights. You can see they're not just in poor neighborhoods, or old neighborhoods, or near residences, or any other pattern that might make some kind of sense. Look what they form instead!"

"It's just a bunch of lines," Gilbert said flatly. "If Alice hadn't said they were streets I would have guessed it was just random nonsense."

"I don't see a pattern either, I'm afraid," she admitted.

"Come over to this side and look at it right-side up. You're looking at it from the north," Simon suggested.

"No. Still nonsense," Gilbert said, slightly annoyed that he seemed to be missing the joke.

Alice shook her head.

"Maybe this will help," Simon grinned, and he began to draw faint dashed lines to connect groups of streets. Eventually Gilbert became bored with the exercise and began to pace.

"A feeding circle!" Alice shouted. "I see it now!"

Gilbert returned and looked at the diagram, which had begun to look like one of those creepy summoning circles. "So they built a sorcery thing with streetlights?" He asked impatiently.

"Not the streetlights. It's made of copper cables. The streetlights were just an excuse to bury the cables," Alice whispered in amazement.

"So Mordaunt will lose his powers when you turn the lights off?" Gilbert asked hopefully.

Alice sighed. "No. The lights and electricity are irrelevant. This circle is like any other, except it's written in copper."

"And the size of a city," Gilbert said.

"And that," she agreed.

"So there's a circle around the whole city, and all of us are in it?"

Simon nodded.

"So why haven't we all shriveled up? Or why haven't you, since I seem to be immune?"

Alice made a grand gesture over the city, "Because there are over three million people in the city. He's only taking a little bit from each of us."

"I guess that explains why he would want to avoid casualties. The more people there are, the stronger he is," Simon exclaimed.

"So then we need to find a pickaxe?" suggested Gilbert.

Alice and Simon looked at each other and thought for a moment. "That would take a lot of digging, wouldn't it?" said Simon.

"Yes," agreed Alice. Then she explained to Gilbert, "Once a circle is established – once it's doing whatever it was designed to do – the magic is fairly stable. You can't stop it by just erasing a couple of corners from a letter."

"You would need to remove *several* letters," Simon said firmly. "We did experiments specifically to test just how much of a circle you must erase before it's nullified. I suppose those experiments were part of this plan, even all those years ago."

"I'm sure this plan goes back longer than that. This plot is probably older than any of us."

Gilbert looked at Simon's map. "So to break this thing we would need to dig up a mile or so of London streets?"

"Without being discovered by anyone loyal to the new king," added Alice.

"What if we removed them by tunneling?" Gilbert asked in a voice that indicated that he thought he was being clever.

"Tunneling that distance, at such a shallow depth? Without giving yourself away to anyone on the surface? That endeavor would take ages, and I'm sure someone would notice that the lights were out before you made much headway."

Gilbert let out a slow breath, the kind that always gave Simon the shivers. "This is absurd! The most dangerous wizard in history is held in power by a length of copper cable?"

"A copper cable that was installed by hundreds of men over the course of several years," Alice reminded him.

"This means Mordaunt will be powerless outside the city!" Simon exclaimed.

“That’s a good point,” Alice said. “Although I doubt he was planning on leaving the city to begin with. He has London. What would we do? Evacuate three million people and move them to another city?”

They fell quiet at this, each of them trying to imagine various scenarios and how their enemy might respond.

XII

"Lord Moxley?" Alice said nervously. The door to the apartment was hanging open, and some of his papers had blown out into the street.

A man was kneeling in the middle of the floor, amidst a mess of strewn papers and overthrown furniture.

"Mr. Byron," Alice said.

"This is your fault!" the man sobbed. "They took him! Because of you! You people and your notes and papers and messages!"

Alice did her best to unravel what had happened, but Byron was irrational, emotional, and not terribly sharp. All she was able to tell was that Lord Moxley had been arrested at some point during the night.

Alice held up her newspaper. "The coronation is tonight," she said. She showed the headline to Gilbert and Simon. WIZARD CLAIMS THRONE, it declared boldly.

It was now morning. They had spent the previous twenty-four hours in a doss-house near the Thames. The proprietor had at first refused Alice entry on account of her womanhood, but he relented when it was pointed out that he didn't have much in the way of boarders to begin with, and that Alice was willing to pay him double.

"Amazing that the papers know about it, and are willing to report it,"

Simon said curiously.

"The report makes no mention of the new king being a lich. Either that is unknown, or Mordaunt has control of the papers," Alice said.

"I can't believe how everyone seems to be going on as if this was nothing unusual," Gilbert said while gesturing at all of the Londoners who were going about their business. "The citizens aren't banding together. They're not fighting. They're not fleeing the city. They're just ignoring it."

Alice lowered the newspaper. "There is very little the common man can do. Fight? Our foe has already defeated the entire city garrison in a single night, with only minimal losses to himself. Flee? Where would the shoemaker go? The blacksmith? The tailor? Uproot their family and flee into the wilderness and wait to starve?"

"Don't we have more soldiers?" Simon asked. "Surely the British Empire has more than a few thousand men?"

Gilbert nodded, "Yes!"

"And what will they do?" Alice chided. "Invade the city? Mordaunt was cunning to keep the royal family alive. It makes him appear merciful, while at the same time gives him a selection of very valuable hostages. Nobody could lay siege to the palace without the risk of killing the Royal Family. The army may converge here on the city, but their leadership is divided. It will be easier for most people to accept this new king as legitimate than to undertake a large, destructive, and possibly hopeless fight that would only result in the death of Her Majesty."

Gilbert sat down on the street corner beside Alice. "This has depressed me."

"So we must stop him ourselves," Simon said nervously.

The other two regarded him with surprise.

"Or are we giving up?" he asked in response to their silence.

"No. You are right. I was only surprised to hear you so eager for danger," Alice said with raised eyebrows.

"I am not afflicted with *eagerness* for danger, I assure you!" Simon said. “Willingness, perhaps.”

Alice closed the newspaper and began rubbing her hands together to warm them. “Well, we must do what we can. It’s the purpose of the ministry, which you two seemed to have inadvertently joined. We are the only ones able to oppose him with magic of our own, which is probably the only thing capable of defeating him.”

Gilbert turned to Simon. “I was considering this when the two of you were sleeping. What about that spell you used on me, at Ravenstead? I remember I collapsed the moment I stepped into the circle. That would give us the victory without a fight, assuming it would work on him.”

Simon scratched his head thoughtfully, “The circle used to retrieve vigor from the reanimated? It’s complex.”

“Do you need a book?” Alice asked.

“That’s not what I mean,” Simon replied. “I remember it well enough, but it takes time to draw. Gilbert blundered into it because he didn’t know anything about magic.”

“I didn’t *blunder*,” Gilbert protested.

“However you came to enter the circle, we won’t have that advantage against my old master. Even if we did manage to draw one where he might enter it, he would know to step back out.”

“I lost control of my body the moment I entered the circle,” Gilbert countered. “Even if I had understood, I was helpless to escape it.”

“That’s one part of the puzzle,” said Alice said hopefully. “Now we just need a way to make an incredibly elaborate sorcery circle and arrange for him to enter it unaware.” She handed the newspaper to Gilbert and rubbed her temples.

“The coronation seems like it would be the time to attempt it,” Gilbert said, looking at the paper. “He will be in public, commoners will be allowed near, and we know where he will be. Much easier than trying to enter the Palace ourselves.”

“I’m still hungry,” Simon muttered.

“Take it,” Alice said, handing him the last of the bread she’d purchased. "And savor it. That bread was bought with the last of the funds given to me by Lord Moxley. We are now homeless, penniless, and without support."

Simon chewed the bread slowly and looked downcast.

"I might be able to raise some money if I were to sell some of my weapons," Gilbert suggested. "This rifle should fetch money enough to keep the two of you fed for a bit longer."

"I'm unsure about the legality of taking and selling gear recovered from our own soldiers. In either case, don't sell it yet. We may need it tonight."

Simon spoke around a mouthful of bread, "I suppose we shouldn't worry about money just yet. I mean, anything could happen tonight. One of us might die."

"One of us already has," Gilbert replied. Alice answered him with a gentle kick.

The coronation was being held in the garden just west of Buckingham Palace, and was open to the public. According to the papers, there would also be a speech given by the newly-crowned king. The area east of the palace was more traditionally used for official gatherings and interactions with the public, but this was still scorched and the dead were still being carried away.

The three of them stood on the edge of the grassy clearing, which was quickly being decorated for the coming event. Colorful flags were being hung and gas lamps were being set in place. Several men were completing the construction of a wooden stage roughly the same dimensions as a railway boarding platform.

"Now we know where the man will stand, but how do we get a sorcery circle there? And then how do we conceal it?" Alice wondered.

"What if we made it very small?" Gilbert suggested.

Simon pushed his glasses up and considered this. "If the circle were very small, then he might tumble back out of it when the magic took hold. Besides, this is a detailed circle and I'm going to have to do this in chalk. I don't think I could manage to make it as small as a dinner plate. And even that would be obvious."

"Perhaps you could draw it, and then we could put a bit of carpet over it?" Alice said, thinking out loud.

"That's a possibility. Although, I can't imagine how I could draw the circle without someone noticing. There are so many people around, and it is very hard to conceal oneself on an empty public stage."

"Just as well," she said. "We have no carpet, and no money to buy one."

"I know!" Simon shouted so loud that a few bystanders looked their way. Lowering his voice, he continued, "What if I could write it on the underside of the platform?"

Alice blinked, "It will still work?"

"I will have to mirror everything, but yes. The ceiling will be very low. I suppose I'll have to draw the circle while on my back, with the wood just a handbreadth from my nose."

"Those are not ideal conditions for sorcery," Alice managed.

"Yet still far better than I'm used to. I think I can manage it."

They had Gilbert move away, lest his large frame attract attention. Then Alice approached the workmen and began asking them about their project. The men were glad for the distraction. While their eyes were on her, Simon slipped around to the back of the stage and crawled under it.

Alice pretended to tour the area, shooting occasional nervous glances over to the stage. It was dark underneath, and the supports mostly concealed him, but occasionally she could see his movements.

"Who are you? Come out of there!" shouted one of the men.

Alice turned to look, and saw Simon's head poke into view. He was quickly hauled into the open and the men gathered around him.

"Look, this one thinks he's Guy Fawkes. What were you up to under there?"

"Just writing, sir," Simon said sheepishly.

“Writing?” the man shouted incredulously. “Here, have a look under there and see what he’s been up to,” the man said to the others.

They got down on their hands and knees and inspected under the stage, but none of them discovered anything suspicious. After slapping him around and searching his pockets, they sent Simon away with a warning not to come back.

Simon left the clearing, straightening his suit and beating his hat back into shape. “I’m glad they didn’t manage to break my spectacles,” he said when he reached Gilbert and Alice.

“Did you complete the circle?” Alice asked.

“Yes. It was a little challenging, but I managed.”

“I don’t think I’ve ever heard of anyone who would call drawing a large spell from memory, inverted, in a dark and confined space, as a ‘little challenging’.”

“I made it as large as I could manage, in the center of the platform and towards the front. I can’t imagine he’ll fail to step into it,” Simon said with rare confidence.

They began making their way back to the doss-house. They didn’t have any particular reason to go back there. It was too dark and smelly to spend time inside, but it was the closest thing they had to a home.

“So we wait for him to enter the thing, and then what?” Gilbert asked on the way.

“Once the circle breaks the connection between the body and the vigor, it must be gathered by holding this crystal over the body.” Simon pulled out the crystal that he always wore around his neck hand showed it to his companions. “This contained Sophie’s vigor before it was used to revive Gilbert, and can just as easily hold the vigor that Mordaunt is using.”

“Leopold’s vigor,” Alice said.

“So you said,” replied Simon.

"Even once the Dead King is down, he will still be guarded. His supporters will likely rush to his aid. I suppose I should gather the vigor," Gilbert held out his hand to receive the crystal.

Alice laughed, "If you tried, you would just collapse on top of him, remember? But you're right, there may be fighting on the stage. We don't know which way the crowd will go, or if they will get involved at all."

"Miss White?"

Alice turned, and saw a group of dirty, tired British soldiers standing beside a stable. One of them stepped forward and gave a nervous smile.

"Private Archer!" she exclaimed.

"Ma'am. Glad to see you're still whole, given the recent troubles," he glanced nervously at Gilbert as he said this.

"And I'm glad you're still standing. We lost a great number of men when we lost Buckingham."

"When I was dumped back into regular service, they assigned me to take care of the horses. I tried to tell them I'm a specialist, but nobody seemed interested."

"I see. And what of your commanders… are they?" her voice trailed off, and she looked sideways at the other soldiers.

Archer nodded knowingly as he replied, "I take your meaning, Miss White. Not to worry. All of us here are loyal to the Queen." The other men nodded in assent, and Archer lowered his voice. "See, I don't know about any of our commanders. Nobody knows what side anyone else is on. We've had three different officers show up in the last day or so, all of them giving us different orders about who should and shouldn't be getting horses. We make excuses or tell them the horses are reserved by people of higher rank, but that's not going to last forever. Sooner or later people are going to start siding with the winners, and we're going to have to fall in line or desert."

Alice smiled. "Well, we're doing our best to turn the tables. We're probably going to get killed in the process. Are you willing to help?"

"Miss White, I know you'd never side with this newcomer," Archer said, clearly for the benefit of his fellows, who gave their approval when they heard this. “So I’m sure we’ll be glad to help any way we can. I suppose you’ll be wanting horses?”

“No,” Alice said. She turned to Gilbert and took the rifle that was slung over his shoulder, ignoring his protests. “I want you to take this rifle, and come with us to Buckingham Palace.”

Archer’s eyes widened at the sight of the firearm. He stopped to ask if the others would be willing to cover for him if he abandoned his post, but they practically shoved him in the direction of the Palace when they heard his assignment. A few others tried to join, and Alice had to discourage them.

Archer wanted to inspect the clearing before the crowd assembled, so the party toured the grounds discreetly while Alice recounted their recent adventures.

The palace garden was filled with a great number of trees and poles which provided little in the way of cover for a marksman but many opportunities to spoil his shots. To the east were the formidable palace walls. To the north was a great stretch of forest. To the west was a manmade lake. To the south were the foot-paths that led to the street. This was where the attendees would enter. The garden was reportedly beautiful in the summer, but in November it was cold, pale, and joyless.

“The coronation will take place at sundown,” Alice said once they had completed the circuit.

“An odd time for a coronation,” Archer remarked. “So your plan is to attack the usurper as he comes to address the people? Who am I going to be shooting?”

“You will be shooting anyone who tries to kill Simon or myself,” Alice said.

“But not Gilbert?”

“Correct. If he’s discovered, our foes are free to attempt his demise for as long as it pleases them. The longer they do so, the better our chances will be at escaping the scene with the vigor. It’s possible that the moment Mordaunt falls, his followers might scatter or surrender. It’s also possible they might try to avenge him. The crowd might rally to our aid. They might flee. Your job, I think, is to shoot whoever might be trying to kill me. Gilbert will also defend me. I'll gather the vigor, and Simon need only keep out of sight. If all goes well, we can escape with the vigor and plan our next move. I expect Mordaunt's followers will unravel quickly with his passing."

They separated and waited for nightfall. Alice and Simon lost themselves in the growing crowd. Archer stood among the other soldiers in the garden, but avoided speaking with them, not knowing which side they might be on. Gilbert lurked in the sparse woods north of the clearing, some distance behind the stage.

The crowd grew. The lanterns were lit, shining on the gay flags and grim faces. The decorations told that this should be a celebration, but the citizenry were attending a funeral. They looked shocked and confused. They seemed to be here just to see that what they'd been hearing was really true. There was no revelry, no singing. A band had been hired, and played incongruously upbeat music, which nobody cared to dance to.

Alice moved as close to the stage as she dared and gripped the crystal in her trembling hand. She looked for her friends among the crowd, but couldn't see any of them.

Archer knelt down among a group of fellow soldiers and set to work checking his firearm. Alice had given him the standard Martini-Henry rifle, a venerable device carried by nearly all common soldiers. He longed for any one of the hundreds of Lee-Metfords he'd tested at the workshop in the days before his assignment to the Witch Watch. Someday that design would be perfected, and British Soldiers would find out what it was to hold the firearm of the future.

This Martini-Henry was in respectable condition. The action was clean, suggesting that either the abomination had meticulously cleaned it or (more likely, he thought) the weapon hadn't been fired at all. The lever was in good condition and didn't show any signs of dangerous wear, which could lead to the jamming for which the rifle had received a (undeserved, in his opinion) bad reputation. The stock had been mildly scorched, but not in a way that would impact the performance of the weapon.

Someone bumped him with their boot. It was one of his fellow soldiers. "What about you?" the man said. "Are you still following your mum?"

Archer recognized this as some gentle hazing. These men had recognized him as a newcomer, and were going to push him a bit to see if he had any spine.

"I am my own man," he said with as much bravado as he could. He expected the men to challenge him in some way. Perhaps they would begin an exchange of insults, or arm-wrestling, or pose some dare. Instead they cheered his answer and went back to ignoring him. He returned to his task.

While his rifle was in acceptable condition, he was not so lucky with regards to ammunition. The rounds he'd been given were the old rolled brass type that was still unfortunately in circulation, and not the newer drawn brass. However, this was really only a serious problem when it was hot. It was now November and he was a long way from Africa, so he didn't suspect that heat would be an issue. The rounds had been poorly kept. They had been touched by greasy hands, and the surface was smeared with grit and ash. Who had handled these? A mechanic? Archer took out each round and cleaned them on his shirt-tail.

As he worked, Archer listened to the men. They were speaking ill of the soldiers that had been assigned to guard the other side of the field, calling them, "mother's children" and likening them to newly weaned babies.

Suddenly it became clear to him. The 'mother' they were talking about was the Queen Mother. The other soldier hadn't been questioning his manhood, he'd been asking Archer where his loyalties were. The soldiers had divided themselves according to which monarch they followed, and Archer was standing among the men loyal to the lich.

He considered crossing over to the others, but they might refuse him now that he'd been embraced by Mordaunt's men. And if they did refuse him, he wouldn't be able to return to these men either.

The two sides were at peace now, but it was clear that they were simply waiting for the opportunity to begin shooting at one another.

He was slightly comforted to see that the numbers were on the side of Queen Victoria. Her soldiers outnumbered those favoring Mordaunt by at least 2 to 1. Or at least, this would be comfort if he wasn't standing with the weaker side, and if the civilian crowd didn't occupy a great deal of the space between the two.

While scheduled for sundown, the Dead King didn't appear until the sky was almost fully dark. First came his entourage, which consisted of three grim-faced men in dark robes. These would no doubt be the rest of the Four Horsemen. When Alice saw these she briefly wondered if Brooks had succumbed to his wounds. Then came the crown bearer, flanked by many guards. Alice swallowed hard. These men would certainly be fiercely loyal, and could easily prove too many for their small group. The crown was placed on a dais on stage, and the Crown Guards stood between the crowd and the stage. After the crown bearer came many important men and dignitaries. She recognized many of the faces from Brooks' party, and burned at their ready betrayal of the Queen.

The crowd had fallen quiet. There was no jeering, but neither was there any applause. They were silent witnesses.

Mordaunt appeared. He was not a tall man. He walked alone, and not even his loyal servants came within six paces of him. He wore a porcelain mask, most likely in the image of his original face. It wore a disturbingly beatific expression.

Mordaunt walked into the open beneath the lamplight, and Alice held her breath.

The crowd had begun to shove. A great many people seemed to be elbowing their way to the front, and Alice was jostled again and again. Finally a pair of young men shoved her to one side and took spots in front of her.

"Excuse me!" she hissed with rage, but they ignored her. She tried to push her way past them and was shoved back by a strong elbow. She was about to speak again when she looked down and saw the men were wearing red sashes.

"Oh no," she muttered. She looked to one side, and saw many more red sashes.

As Mordaunt approached the stage the Red Sashes ran forward with a great cry, drawing out knives and swords.

"No!" she screamed.

The Crown Guards drew their weapons and a fight ensued. The Red Sashes were poor swordsmen, but the numbers were on their side. The crowd was now a boiling kettle of confusion. The people near the front wanted to escape, and the people in the back wanted to move forward to see what was happening. Some British Soldiers tried to contain the people to prevent a stampede.

Finally the Red Sashes broke through and stormed the stage. As the last of the Crown Guards were slain, a ball of fire fell on the wooden platform. Half of the red sashes perished in a single brilliant flash of light. Flames engulfed the stage, and the Red Sashes who survived the blast ran towards the lake, screaming and in flames.

A woman was screaming. She had been pushed too close to the stage by the rioting crowd, and had been caught in Mordaunt's fire. Alice made a gesture and drenched the woman in water.

Mordaunt levitated above his entourage and began striking the fleeing Red Sashes with bolts of lightning.

A single gunshot rang out, and the porcelain mask was shattered, revealing the corrupted face beneath. Unlike Gilbert, the Viscount had not been carefully preserved, and his face was little more than a skull.

More gunshots came in answer. Behind her, two groups seemed to be inexplicably shooting at one another.

Gilbert had watched the battle unfold in complete bafflement. He saw Alice shove her way free of the throng just in time for the stage to explode, drawing a curtain of flame between himself and her.

He watched in frustration as Mordaunt dispatched the Red Sashes and Simon's fine work was reduced to ash. Their plan was ruined. Should he withdraw?

He didn't dare cross near the fire to leave, so he planned to go north and circle around the castle to rejoin the others at the agreed meeting place. As he turned to go, he saw that Simon had been discovered. The grey-robed men had grabbed him and dragged him into the light.

He was terrified for Simon's safety, but he was also just a little relieved. He had dreaded returning home again without striking some small blow against their foes. He drew out his sword and gave a battle cry that turned the faces of Mordaunt's entourage to him.

"I apologize that this is nearly two months late!" he laughed cheerfully as he ran the first of them through.

"Master!" screamed the other two, using voices usually reserved for small girls and not aged men. Gilbert's sword flashed, and one of these fell silent.

"Gilbert!" screamed Simon in warning. He was looking at something behind and above Gilbert.

Rather than turning to look for himself, Gilbert simply grabbed the remaining man by the robes and spun around, holding the man out like a shield. There was a flash of white light and a stunning boom, after which Gilbert found himself to be holding a flaming corpse.

"Run!" Gilbert screamed to Simon. Then he advanced into the group of cowering officials that had come ahead of Mordaunt in the procession. Gilbert didn't see how he could hope to extricate himself from this battle, so instead he decided to secure Simon's escape and make a worthy end for himself.

Another bolt of lightning struck the body in his hand, after which he decided there was not enough of it left to continue using it as a shield. He dashed behind a small tent that had been set up, which was instantly set aflame. From there he ran to a wooden gazebo, which was promptly obliterated in an explosion of fire. The officials had chosen these places to hide when the fighting began, and so this sowed a great deal of chaos into what was already an incomprehensible mess. Gilbert would dash behind some cover, which would prompt all of the officials hiding there to flee, after which the structure would explode.

Gilbert had no plan, although he felt strongly that he should try to form one. He didn't want to simply perish (or whatever one calls it when an abomination is destroyed) but to accomplish something memorable before that happened.

There were more gunshots, and Mordaunt waved his arms as if tormented by stinging flies. Apparently some portion of tumultuous gunfire was directed at him. He hurled another handful of fire at his attackers. There were screams and bodies flew into the air. More gunshots came, and Mordaunt gave out a cry of pure frustration and rage.

"I have held out my hand to you, Britain, and you have spat in my face," his voice rolled over the crowd like thunder.

The shooting slowed, as did the activity of the crowd.

"I have offered you the chance to become the greatest nation in the history of this world. An everlasting, glorious, indestructible empire. But you have struck my face in payment."

He rose higher in the air, and shouted, "I WILL rule you. If you will not be a nation of generals and noblemen, then you will be an island of slaves." At this he summoned a great storm of fire, large enough to engulf a sailing ship. He hurled this into the air, and it burst like a great firework. The ground shook as if by an earthquake. A great column of smoke and burning embers swirled about them, and it began to rain fire.

Alice stepped back from the burning stage. The heat was so intense she was afraid her hair might catch fire. She blinked quickly as she pulled her eyes away from the blaze and tried to focus on the dark crowd around her.

Steel glinted in the firelight. She held up an arm reflexively, and it was slashed open. Some men were closing in around her. She had drawn attention to herself when she extinguished the burning woman, and was now exposed.

She tossed a handful of fire at her attacker and fought to regain her sight. A closed fist struck her face, and someone grabbed her from behind. "Witch!" someone screamed. She was surrounded by Red Sashes.

"Be reasonable!" she screamed. "Let's focus on Mordaunt before trying to kill each other!"

The men were singed, bruised, frustrated, and had just seen a number of their friends die at the hands of an apparently indomitable foe. Alice could see that they were not thinking strategy, or indeed thinking at all. They were angry, and she was to bear the brunt of it.

"Fools!" she said in frustration, and lit one of them on fire as he drew close enough to stab her. Already tired, this exertion stole more of her strength than she'd planned, and she swooned.

There was a gunshot, and one of the Red Sashes fell. More gunshots came in steady rhythm, each one striking the head or heart of a Red Sash. At the fourth shot, the remaining men finally understood and turned to face their attacker. Private Archer was twenty paces away. In the space of a single breath he worked the lever, inserted a round, took aim, and killed a man.

It was clear that if the remaining three men all rushed him at once, he wouldn't be able to kill more than two of them. However, one of the men concluded that this meant they should run, and the other two that they should attack. Archer killed the brave ones, and then shot the fleeing one.

The only remaining man was the one holding Alice from behind, and he was now using her as a shield against the gunman. Alice reached up, grabbed the man by the hair, and lit it on fire. He released her, and she pulled away from him. A final gunshot silenced his terrified screaming.

"I feel rather sorry for shooting that one in the back," Archer said as he helped her up.

"Don't," she said firmly. She wobbled slightly. The magic had robbed her of her strength.

"Stay low," he instructed. "Supporters of the Queen and Mordaunt Loyalists are shooting at each other to the south, heedless of the crowd."

Alice began to ask a question, but was cut short when Mordaunt began addressing the masses. Instead she gestured for Archer to follow her.

It was easier to move about now that the crowd had stopped to listen. The two of them stayed low and moved around to the other side of the burning stage.

They had moved away from the crowd just as it began to rain burning ash from the sky. They crawled on their bellies to stay below the heat and gunfire. On the other side, they found Lord Mordaunt in a battle with Gilbert. The lich was using lightning to avoid roasting his own servants with fire. Gilbert was shielding himself with what looked like a burning official.

"Should I shoot at him again?" Archer offered.

"I wouldn't advise it," she said weakly.

"Can you manage any more magic?"

"I don't know."

There was another flash of lightning and Gilbert found himself on his back, much farther from Mordaunt than he'd been just a second earlier. His grisly shield was missing. On further inspection, so was his arm.

Gilbert ran forward, brandishing his sword. Mordaunt had drifted a little closer to the ground. Gilbert was going to do his best to hack one of Mordaunt's arms off. He didn't know if he could jump high enough or if he could strike hard enough, but his only other option was to wait until one of these bolts hit their mark.

There was another flash of light, and his sword vanished in a shower of molten steel. As he stumbled, he saw Alice and Private Archer drawing near. Gilbert growled in frustration. *Why weren't they trying to escape?* The clearing was filled with the dead. Behind that grim scene, London was burning.

Gilbert scrambled behind some debris, narrowly avoiding another bolt. He was now one-armed and weaponless, and had no way to hurt or even impede the lich. There was another blast, and his shelter was obliterated.

There was nowhere left to hide. Gilbert stood.

Mordaunt hovered over him. For a moment it looked like Mordaunt was going to say something. Then he seemed to think better of it. Before the blow fell, Gilbert heard Simon screaming.

"Gilbert! The circle! The circle!" he was saying. At his feet was a small chalk circle, drawn onto the concrete footpath.

In a hopeless gesture, Gilbert ran towards the lich, holding his remaining fist up in defiance. Mordaunt made a grand gesture, preparing a vindictive final strike for the scurrying rat that had taunted him for so long. As the motion fell, he tumbled slightly to one side and was engulfed in flames.

Gilbert looked to the side, and saw that Alice had expended her strength in this final gesture. She collapsed, striking the ground before her fire had even reached the target. The blow sent Mordaunt's strike awry. Gilbert jumped into the air and grabbed at him, pulling him to earth. They rolled along the ground, and both were wrapped in flame. Gilbert quickly overpowered the smaller man and dragged him into the circle that Simon had prepared.

Gilbert had expected everything to go dark when he entered the circle, but nothing seemed to happen. Mordaunt continued to struggle and curse as the two of them roasted.

Gilbert looked up, and Alice was standing. No, not standing. Hovering. She was floating above the ground, her ragged dress billowing around her feet. She reached up, as if to grab the clouds, and pulled them down in a single motion. Rain fell. Not icy

November rain, but warm rain, as if it were springtime. She held out her arms as the water came down in a great deluge. Soon even the most aggressive fires were overcome, and the inferno ended. Alice bowed her head, and the rain relented.

She spoke, and her calm voice carried over the entire field, and perhaps even into the city, "Put your weapons down. Your master has fallen. Enough bloodshed."

The last few guns now went silent. There was a chorus of plops as people dropped their swords into the mud. A cloud of mist drifted over the field, mixing with the last rivulets of smoke.

"What is happening?" Gilbert demanded.

"Almost done!" shouted Simon eagerly. He was scribbling away on the sidewalk beside Gilbert. He was pushing water out of the way with one hand and writing furiously with the other.

Alice drifted downward and landed gently beside Gilbert. She held out her hand, from which hung the small crystal. "Ready?" she smiled to Simon.

"Ready!" he replied.

Alice nodded to Gilbert. "Careful to keep yourself out of it!" she warned.

Gilbert shrugged and heaved Mordaunt into the other circle. None of this made any sense to him.

Mordaunt landed in the circle with a clatter, and tiny specks of light began to escape from his form. It began with just a few at first, but soon a great stream of them flowed. His body shook and convulsed, and finally his bones fell apart, lifeless.

Alice cradled the brilliant crystal in her hand for a moment before hiding it away. Whatever power had come over her was clearly gone.

"It's over?" asked Archer in disbelief.

Alice looked over the battlefield, "Aside from healing the injured, arresting the guilty, burying the dead, cleaning the debris, and repairing the damage? Yes, it's all over."

“I hope we don’t have to accomplish all of that tonight!” said Simon in a daze.

“No indeed. We should leave quickly,” she said. “We’re all drenched. We’ll freeze in the cold air if we don’t find a fire soon, and I don’t think there’s anything left in this field that’s capable of burning.” She patted the pocket where she had placed the crystal, “This is the life of Prince Leopold, and we need to get it to safety. I don’t know how many of Mordaunt’s servants are left or if they’re of a mind to make further mischief for us, but I’m not inclined to give them the opportunity.”

“What about him?” Simon asked, nodding towards the pile of bones.

“You’re right, we can’t leave his remains there or they might slip away with them and try again,” Alice said thoughtfully. Finally she decided, “Bring the skull. His bones will be useless without that.”

They dried off at the stables and the soldiers took care of them until a carriage could be arranged. They were tired and sore, covered in soot and small burns. They rode to Grayhouse in silence.

The fire had reduced Gilbert to a naked skeleton. He carried his left arm with him, wanting it to be buried with the rest of his bones when the time came. He went upstairs to find some clothing while the others staggered into the sitting room and threw themselves down on the couches.

“Are we safe here?” Simon asked after a few minutes of rest. Their ears were still ringing from the thunder, gunfire, and screaming. “If there are still loyalists about…”

Alice shrugged, “It’s possible, although I doubt any of them will be eager to face me after the performance we put on. I imagine that will leave quite an impression on them. No, I’m willing to wager they are more concerned with saving their own necks at this point. I suppose I might still be a fugitive on account of shooting Brooks, although I don’t think anyone is going to stop rounding up the conspirators to arrest me for that. Certainly not tonight.”

Gilbert entered the room, wearing a shirt and trousers. "I will be happy to guard you while you sleep," he offered, "Provided you explain to me what happened!"

Simon leaned his head back and took a deep breath. "I made a feeding circle, for Alice. It was the best I could do in such short time. Anyone inside of that circle would feed Alice, instead of Mordaunt."

Gilbert considered this for a few moments before he replied, "So when I put Mordaunt himself into her circle…"

"Then all of the energy that was going into him was passed on to me," Alice nodded. She smiled at Simon. "It was very clever of you."

Simon replied by blushing deeply.

Major Stanway called early the next morning. They invited him in, thinking he had come to celebrate or at least hear their tale. Instead he was grim, and gave news of his own.

"The day after the Battle of Shoreditch High Street, I was assigned another company of men," he explained. "Rather than take part in the assault on the palace, I petitioned my superiors for leave to attempt the rescue of Leopold and Sophie. They were slow to give it, but last night we attacked Brooks' estate. He apparently already had news of the defeat of his master when we arrived. He was very drunk. The man should have been in bed, given the wound he was nursing, but instead he came outside to rant at us. We humored him, thinking he was simply giving a confession and was going to surrender his hostages."

Alice winced. "I should have warned you that he is a cunning man, and capable of great deceit."

"I don't think there was anything cunning or deceitful in his designs. He was simply mad drunk. Here, perhaps I'd best show you."

He led them outside. Stanway's leg was still in ruinous condition, but he refused all attempts at aid. He hobbled around on a crutch, directing his men and making light of his injuries. He'd arrived in a cart with a small group of soldiers. Archer, Simon, Alice and Gilbert gathered around as he showed them its contents.

"I stopped his raving when I smelled the smoke and saw the light coming from the house. He tried to flee back inside, and the men cut him down. I think they did him a kindness. It's clear to me he aimed to throw himself into the flames."

The Major nodded to the cart, which contained two caskets. One was open, and the other closed. "I sent men in after them. It was hard with the smoke and fire about, but your directions were accurate. We were able to bring young Sophie out, but the ceiling collapsed on the men bearing Leopold. The closed casket holds his remains, or as much as we could find of them once the blaze abated."

Sophie was carried upstairs and placed on one of the tables in the library. The Major departed, leaving them to revive the princess.

"She's very pretty," Simon blurted out. Then he blushed and fell silent.

"So what do we need to do?" Gilbert asked.

"It's rather simple, I'm afraid," Alice said with some embarrassment. "Apparently all you need to do is touch her."

"That's all?" he asked incredulously. "After all that digging through books, it turns out that we can revive her with a firm poke?"

"Provided it's your finger doing the poking, yes. The vigor is naturally attracted to its rightful owner. That's what the crystal is for. It was a way to extract the vigor and take it to the recipient without it jumping back to where it belongs."

"Do I look presentable?" Gilbert asked. He was wearing a dark, somber suit. "I found this in your hoard of clothes, and it seems like a good suit to be buried in. Don't forget to include my arm," he said, nodding at the adjacent table where he'd placed the detached limb.

"Of course," Alice said quietly, patting him on the arm.

Simon blinked as he suddenly realized what was about to happen, "But… do we have to do this now? Can't we wait a day? Or just a few hours?"

"That wouldn't be right," Gilbert said. "This is Sophie's time, not mine, and her parents miss her no less than we will miss each other."

There were a few minutes of tears and hugging. Alice shook his hand goodbye and he wished each of them well in their future lives. Then he turned to the slumbering Sophie, and grabbed her hand.

Gilbert walked down the line of trees and through the orchard. The grass was a deep, vibrant green, and the world seemed to glow in the light of the sun. He helped himself to an apple from one of the trees. It had been so long, he'd almost forgotten how they tasted. The wind washed over him as the sun warmed his face. He headed past the barn, towards the house. The trip had been an unwelcome distraction, and it was good to be Home again.

The girl was there, again. Her mouth moved, and he knew that she was upset with him. He tried to argue, but she wouldn't listen. He tried to walk around her, but no matter where he went, she stood between him and Home. Finally he grew impatient and tried to force her out of the way, but she was much too strong. He couldn't move her. Not here.

He couldn't taste the apple anymore. Home was suddenly very far in the distance. This place was hers now, and she wasn't willing to let him in.

Her mouth moved again. She told him what to do.

Gilbert sat up, which startled Simon and Alice, who were fussing over Sophie and listening for sounds of breathing.

"What are you doing back?" Alice asked accusingly.

"Why am I on the floor?" he shot back.

"You fell there when you took Sophie's hand. Why are you up again?"

Gilbert tried to answer, and stopped. He felt like a man who had just walked into a room in a great hurry, stopped, and forgot why he'd come here. What was he just doing a moment ago? He had no idea. All he could remember was the girl.

"She said to use the other vigor," Gilbert said.

"She? Who?" Alice asked.

"I don't know. I thought she was Sophie."

"The other vigor?" asked Simon. "Do you mean Leopold's?"

"I don't mean anything. I'm just repeating what I was told," Gilbert said defensively.

"Is that possible?" asked Alice.

"I don't know!" Gilbert replied, slightly annoyed.

Alice shrugged and took out the crystal. She placed it on the princess and stood back. After several minutes, nothing magical had happened at all. They concluded that this wasn't going to work, and a discussion ensued between Simon and Alice. Simon suggested that he simply repeat the spell he originally used to revive Gilbert. Alice responded that the spell was designed to create an abomination, and that if they used it on Sophie they might reanimate her as a walking corpse. Simon countered by saying that no, the spell in question was designed to put a vigor into a body, and did not affect whether they were alive or dead. A philosophical discussion ensued, which Gilbert fled by going downstairs and discussing firearms with Archer.

An hour later the argument had been settled, the circle had been drawn, and the deed had been done. All four of them had gathered in the library to see the result. Sophie sat up, coughed, and asked for some water. She did not scream in terror when she saw Gilbert's grinning skull of a face, which was a relief to the rest of them because they had forgotten to conceal it. Instead she looked at him suspiciously.

Sophie did not, for her part, remember anything about being dead, except for having a dream about a nice man that came to visit her now and again.

The next few days were extremely chaotic. Mordaunt's supporters were rounded up, although once the battle was over it became very hard to tell the people who truly supported him from the people who claimed that they were only pretending to serve him and were really planning to betray him at the first opportunity. A number of obviously and publicly guilty people were rounded up and taken to Tyburn, where the cells were all unaccountably full. On further inspection, the cells were full of people who had no business being locked up, Lord Moxley chief among them. These were released. When the jailer could give no explanation for how the innocent parties came to be in his jail, who had arrested them, how they all came to be entered into his ledger under the crime of "treason", or why they had not been subsequently released, he was put into one of his own cells, along with a few of his lieutenants who were also afflicted with the inability to explain themselves.

The church was bold in announcing its part in the defeat of the Dead King, as Mordaunt had come to be known in the papers. The Red Sashes who died in the battle were given a long and glorious funeral procession through the streets of London.

The sun was streaming into the wide white room. The walls were gilded, and even the gilding was gilded, to the point where it almost seemed a waste to hang such grand paintings over any of it. The furniture was designed to look as ornate and expensive as possible. This required that certain tradeoffs be made in the area of comfort, so everyone had chosen to stand.

It was early December, more than two weeks after the Battle of Buckingham. The papers were still talking about it. Various conspirators were still being rounded up and sent to Tyburn. This morning the Witch Watch had been summoned to the palace to have an audience with Her Majesty, where their efforts would be recognized in an official capacity.

The tall doors swung open and Lord Moxley drifted in, looking very much like his old self: Aloof, preoccupied, bemused, and expensively dressed.

"Are you ready?" he asked them.

Simon looked alarmed and stood up straight. "She's coming now?" he asked nervously.

"No my dear boy. The Queen will not come to you. *You* will go to *her*. This is a waiting room, not a room for entertaining guests. And take your hat off!"

Simon snatched the hat from his head sheepishly.

Gilbert turned from the window, "*This* is a waiting room?" he marveled.

"It's not called that, but yes, that's what it is. It's not even the nicest one," Moxley replied. Then he caught sight of Alice. "My dear, you are radiant! That dress is so remarkable that most people will only be very mildly offended by the childish ribbons in your hair."

Alice spun slowly, showing off the dress. "Another gift from Mother, of course. This one is from Italy, I believe."

"And I see you have elected to scandalize Her Majesty with bare shoulders," he replied with a deep sigh.

"Please don't tell me you expect me to change."

"I think Her Majesty will survive the sight of your shoulders. Her sons may slay one another for your hand, I'm afraid, so do be careful."

"I will try," Alice promised.

"Now, Private Archer. No, I'm sorry, it's simply 'Mister Archer', effective now."

Looking alarmed, Archer protested, "What? I'm no longer a member of Her Majesty's Service?"

Moxley shrugged, as if the question were a trifling detail. "Well, you are still in her service, if you take my meaning, but no longer a member of our armed forces. This is all part of the effort to move our ministry away from its military roots and make it an organization of specialists. No more marching around with a group of men in uniforms now. The Witch Watch will consist of you four."

"I was going to make Lance Corporal soon," Archer pleaded.

"Fine. Return to the military if you like. I'm not in charge of your career. But if you stay with the ministry you'll be making more than a Second Lieutenant."

Archer looked momentarily stunned, "I see. Well, that's all right then."

Moxley turned back to Alice and lowered his voice somewhat. "Now, there's a delicate item that I need to go over with you. For some years Mordaunt was considered the unofficial physician of the Royal Family, and of Prince Albert in particular. This must have been a very well-kept secret, because I never heard even a hint of it. This morning Prince Albert confided in me that Lord Mordaunt had saved his life on more than one occasion. Using magic, of course."

Alice looked troubled. "Is he looking to us to continue the practice?"

"I don't think so. He merely asked if we had any understanding of this healing business, or if any knowledge had survived."

Alice looked slightly pained, "I accompanied the army when they stormed the Ravenstead estate a few days ago, and we were able to recover the balance of Lord Mordaunt's library. It was very large and wide-ranging, and was nearly enough to replace what we had lost to the church. Simon and I have been studying the books as time has allowed."

"You're going to tell me that the secrets of miraculous healing have been lost, aren't you?" Moxley said accusingly.

"Sadly, no. We recovered them in full, and the truth is going to make a great number of people very uncomfortable. All of the healing performed by Mordaunt involved the use of vigor."

"And I take it obtaining vigor is an unsavory process?"

"It involves killing people. The younger the better."

Moxley gasped, "So all of the nobles who were healed by Lord Mordaunt…"

Alice nodded, "All of those healings involved the death of at least one person. Often it involved more. The magic is not terribly efficient."

"If this gets out, it could lead to scandal unending," Moxley said, holding one hand to his brow.

"I don't see how," Alice protested. "I'm sure none of them knew about the origins of their healing."

"True, but 'scandal' and 'justice' are not related and should not be confused. Scandals are very often unreasonable and unfair. At any rate, don't mention any of this during your audience. In fact, don't mention anything supernatural at all!" Moxley addressed this last comment to the rest of the group as well.

Moxley then waved for all of them to join him near the door. "I suppose I should prepare all of you for this meeting. Most importantly, Her Majesty is going to present you with gifts. Alice, you will be given a large set of various watch-making tools and fine machinery parts. Nobody really understood what you might need or use, and so they erred on the side of overabundance. You will not be able to carry them alone."

Alice beamed, but resisted the urge to cry out.

Moxley continued, "Archer, you will be given a rifle. You may open the case to admire it but do not brandish it in the presence of Her Majesty. That would be considered rude."

"What model?" Archer asked eagerly.

Moxley shrugged. "I'm sure I have no idea, and neither does the Queen. The instructions were to obtain for you something grand and ornate, not something advanced. I doubt you'll find it professionally useful. It will probably be a hunting rifle of some variety. The only thing I can tell you is that it is silver-plated, which is probably not the sort of information you're looking for."

Archer looked slightly crestfallen, then caught himself and gave a polite nod.

Next Moxley turned to Simon, "Now as for you… The Queen is giving you property."

Simon engaged in a heroic attempt to hide his disappointment, which failed.

Moxley seemed to have anticipated this reaction. "I imagine you have no idea what you'll do with property here in London. It may sound strange at your age, but in time you'll realize that yours is the grandest and most expensive gift of them all. You will also choose a surname for yourself, and she has arranged for you to be educated, provided it does not interfere with your duties. I'm afraid the Queen was quite taken with your story, and this is how she has chosen to express concern for your plight."

Moxley took a step back and looked over the group one last time. "I have spoiled your surprises for a reason: I do not want you to express an inappropriate level of gratitude. Don't be giddy," he gave Alice a sideways glance as he said this. "Don't be too cold," he said in Simon's direction. "When in doubt, speak quietly and bow."

"What about Gilbert?" Alice said indignantly. "Why is there no gift for him? He's lost more than any of us in this adventure, including Simon!"

"I'm not going to meet the Queen," Gilbert said. Moxley nodded.

"Why not? This is outrageous!" she fumed.

Moxley replied gently, "My dear, we have made great strides in breaking down taboos and opening the minds of the people to our work. We have even come so far that the Queen will officially permit an abomination to live within the city, as property of the Witch Watch. But we are *nowhere* near the point where a monarch would willingly meet with, or speak to, an abomination. It is beyond imagination."

"I prefer it this way," Gilbert reassured her. "Besides, I already have the gift I want." He waved the arm she had bolted back onto his body.

Once Alice had regained her composure, the three of them left to see the Queen. Gilbert and Lord Moxley were alone.

"She was right, you know," Moxley said. They were standing side-by-side, looking out over London. The city had been dusted with snow, which covered over the scars and scorch marks of the earlier battles. "Your sacrifice, however unintentional, saved many lives. Perhaps the Empire as we know it. If you hadn't died, this plot may have succeeded."

Gilbert nodded slowly. "In death, I managed to achieve what I'd always wanted in life. To protect people."

Moxley held out his hand towards the city. "Well then! There's your gift. A whole city full of people, ripe for the protecting! Watch them. Keep them safe. Keep all of us safe, if you can."

"I will," Gilbert replied.

THE END

About the Author

Shamus Young is a programmer specializing in old-school graphics techniques. He's the author of the blog Twenty Sided. He's the creator of the web-comics DM of the Rings and Stolen Pixels. He's one of the hosts of the video-game commentary series Spoiler Warning. He's tired of writing about himself in the third person.

Connect with Shamus online:

Twitter: http://twitter.com/shamusyoung

Facebook: http://facebook.com/youngshamus

Smashwords:
http://www.smashwords.com/profile/view/ShamusYoung

Website: http://shamusyoung.com

Blog: http://shamusyoung.com/twentysidedtale

Author page: http://shamusyoung.com/author

About the Illustrator

Heather Young has been drawing and painting for as long as she can remember. She has done cover and interior illustration for several books, illustrated the game "Sherwood Showdown", and has done numerous commissioned portraits and watercolor painting.

Connect with Heather online:

Twitter: http://twitter.com/HMarieYoung

Google+: https://plus.google.com/u/0/103957402175604659608

Facebook: http://facebook.com/ElasahArt

Website: http://Elasah.com

Blog: http://untraditionalhoome.com

Other Books by Shamus Young

Free Radical

How I Learned

Made in the USA
San Bernardino, CA
11 December 2012